Steamway

By Skeet Dennis

PublishAmerica

Baltimore

First printing

At the specific preference of the author, PublishAmerica allowed this work to remain exactly as the author intended, verbatim, without editorial input.

ISBN: 1-4241-5143-0
PUBLISHED BY PUBLISHAMERICA, LLLP
www.publishamerica.com
Baltimore

Printed in the United States of America

Dedication

I would like to dedicate this book to my loving mother, Margaret J. Suter, who never stopped believing in me.

Born February 7,1938
Died January 27, 2004

Acknowledgements

To my loving wife, Stacy Dennis, without her this book would not be possible.

To my friend and brother-at-heart Steven Potter for making the hardest twelve months of my life tolerable.

To my oldest children Brandon and Crystal for having to sit through four or five readings of the book before I got it right.

And to Zero, my three-year-old, for having to sit down and be quiet during that time.

Chapter 1

It was early spring, cold outside but the sun was shining and the sky held not a single cloud. The wind was blowing stiffly out of the north. The sky was crystal blue, but the wind would chill you to the bone! At the time this all started Skipper was still living at home with his parents, even though he'd recently turned twenty-three. He lived in his parents' basement apartment when he was home, but he was currently attending college at University of Alabama taking a course in chemical engineering so he wasn't home often. Both his parents worked at a local company called Steamway Glass. His father, Stephen Doster, was also a chemical engineer and had been with Steamway Glass for almost twenty years. His mother was the receptionist and had been with the company for seventeen years. They'd just celebrated their 25th wedding anniversary and Skipper, being their only child, had bought them a nice plaque for the wall that said "Stephen & Cindy Doster 25 down 50 to go." His father had always told him that when they'd been married for seventy-five years he was going to trade her in on a newer model. Stephen Doster was a big man, six foot four & 260 lbs. but his mother was just the opposite. Cindy was only about five foot four. They were very good parents to Skipper as a young man, even though he was well disciplined. They were very supportive of many of his activities when he was in high school and that contributed to him winning a partial scholarship to play football for the college. His parents had pushed him to take all the right classes so when he got to college much of what he needed to take for chemical engineering would already be behind him. Having done this he'd advanced very fast and was top of his class.

Skipper had taken after his father in more that just a career. He was six foot three and 240 lbs. College was great for Skipper but his classes absorbed most of his time. Between his classes and football he'd had very little time for socializing.

Skipper led what he considered to be a great life. That is until April 13, 2001. He'd left Tuscaloosa, where the University was, headed home for spring break. He'd tried to call his mother and let her know when he'd arrive home so she could have supper waiting. She always loved to cook Skipper a big home cooked meal to welcome him home, but he'd gotten no answer. He knew his parents seldom went anywhere after work but he didn't think much of not having either of them to answer.

It took Skipper about three hours to drive home from Tuscaloosa to Millbrook. So he just decided to surprise them. When he arrived home, it was around 7:30 p.m. He discovered that neither of them had made it home yet. Skipper, being the worrying kind, called Steamway Glass and the gate guard told him that his parents had left work on time. Just as he was hanging up the phone, the doorbell rang. Skipper yelled, "come in" but the response he received startled him. A deep voice answered and said, "This is the Alabama State Highway Patrol, we're looking for Skipper Doster." Skipper went to the door and opened it to find two Alabama State Troopers. One was a fairly large man, about six feet tall, with dark black hair touched with a bit of gray on each side. He looked to be around thirty-five to thirty-eight years old and approximately 180 lbs. standing beside him was a younger woman about five feet seven and 145 lbs. She was also a state trooper, Skipper assumed she was his partner. The first trooper introduced himself as Sargent Johnson and introduced his partner as Officer Ashley.

Johnson asked, "Are you Skipper Doster?"

Being scared to death, he answered, "Yes sir, I am. Is there some kinda problem?"

Sergeant Johnson asked, "May we come in and have a word with you?"

Skipper said, "Sure come on in."

As the officers started through the door, he asked them again what the problem was. The whole time he was wondering what in the heck he'd done.

Skipper asked them both to sit and offered them something to drink. Both officers declined the refreshment but took a seat opposite Skipper in the living room. Sergeant Johnson started by saying, "Skipper, I've got some bad news for you."

Right then and there he knew both of his parents were dead. His hands started shaking uncontrollably and his heart was beating so hard he thought it would break his ribs.

Sergeant Johnson said, "I'm sorry to inform you that around 4:30 P.M. this afternoon there was a bad accident involving a large tanker truck and both your parents were killed. Apparently the truck's brakes had failed and he ran a red light hitting your parent's car directly in the driver's door killing them both on impact."

Skipper couldn't believe what he was hearing. The officer asked if she could call anyone to come and comfort him, but Skipper told them that he had no relatives and that he'd be fine. Making sure Skipper was ok, both officers offered their condolences and left him a card. Sergeant Johnson said if they could do anything or if he had any questions just to give them a call. When they were gone, Skipper sat around the living room trying to grasp what he'd just been told. Most of his friends had gone home for spring break as well but he knew he could call Smitty.

Smitty had been his best friend throughout high school. They'd done everything together as teenagers and still kept in touch at least a couple times a week. Not long after Skipper had left for college, Smitty met his wife Lisa. She was almost ten years older than Smitty and already had a son, who was five-years-old. For them it was love at first sight. She'd been a waitress at a local waffle house and one night Smitty and Skipper had stopped in to eat after spending a night out on the town. From that night on they were always together. Now after being married for five years they had three kids. The oldest, Smitty's stepson, was ten, they had another boy who was three and a new born baby girl that Skipper had yet to see.

Smitty was born for fatherhood. He was wonderful with the kids. He never looked at Brandon as his stepson. He'd taken to him just as much as he was taken by Lisa. Lisa had married young to an abusive man and after eight months she divorced him. She found out soon after that she was pregnant. To Smitty she was a dream come true. Smitty only lived a few miles away, so after the initial shock of finding out his parents had been killed wore off, Skipper gave him a call. In less than ten minutes Smitty was at his house. When Skipper opened the front door, he could clearly see the hurt in Smitty's eyes. When they were kids, Smitty was at their house almost constantly. He came from a very poor background and had considered Skipper's family his family. He was like the brother Skipper had never had. Smitty was like part of their family and he'd loved Skipper's parents very much.

As he came through the door it was like a tidal wave hit both of them. They burst into tears and hugged each other like they never had before.

Smitty and Lisa decided to stay the night. Lisa had arrived soon after Smitty. She'd taken the children to her parents' house and then rushed over because she knew both would need some comforting.

The next morning, knowing arrangements had to be made for his parents' funeral, Skipper was up early but he didn't have a clue where to start. As they sat at his parents' breakfast table, Lisa, having just gone through this with her older brother six months earlier, helped Skipper make all the necessary calls.

After they'd finished making all the preparations, Skipper felt as if he needed some time to himself. Smitty and Lisa both understood, he had many decisions to make and he really wanted to be alone. Skipper had been alone for about three hours when he received a call from his father's boss, Mr. Morgan. He'd met him only once when he was sixteen and the only thing he could remember about him was that he was a very pleasant man. He'd told Skipper who he was, and asked Skipper if there was anyway he could stop by and speak with him. Skipper told him they could talk after his parents' service.

8

Mr. Morgan said, "That's part of what I need to speak to you about. It's very important that I speak to you this afternoon. I also have most of your parent's personal possessions and I need to drop them off."

Skipper asked, "Would around 3:00 p.m. be all right?"

Mr. Morgan said, "That will be fine and it shouldn't take too much time."

That's when things in Skipper's life started getting really weird. Feeling sorry for himself and really missing his parents' Skipper went upstairs to their room and started going through some old photos. He knew that soon he'd have to start going through their stuff and deciding what to keep or get rid of. Skipper felt strange, almost like he was invading their privacy. As he started going through their room, many things reminded him of them and Skipper couldn't hold back the tears no matter how hard he tried. He was going through their closet when the doorbell rang. Skipper jumped as if he'd been caught doing something wrong. The bell rang again and Skipper slid the mirrored doors shut. As he started down the stairs, Skipper had the strangest feeling he was being watched. The feeling was so strong that he stopped in the hall and looked behind him but no one was there. When Skipper got to the front door and looked through the peephole he saw a man with his back to him. He was facing the street where a champagne-colored Rolls Royce was parked.

With the door still closed, Skipper asked, "Who is it?"

The man turned to face him and said, "It's Mr. Morgan from Steamway Glass."

Skipper opened the door and Mr. Morgan said, "Well Skipper, it's been a long time. May I come in?"

"Please do. I'm sorry I'm not exactly myself today," Skipper said, as he stepped to one side to allow Mr. Morgan to pass.

He was a medium built man, sixty to sixty-five years old and balding on top. The cologne he wore smelled the same as Skipper's father used to use. He was wearing a suit that you could tell was tailor-made for him. He was slightly heavy for his height and what hair he had was gray. Skipper also noticed that he had blue eyes, but not just your run of the mill blue. His eyes were the eyes of a man many years younger than he could be, and when he looked at you it was almost like he was looking through you. Skipper almost felt spooked by them. Once they were inside, Skipper asked him to have a seat and motioned to the couch in the living room where the two police officers had sat and changed his life forever only yesterday.

Mr. Morgan spoke first, "I knew your parents really well, and I can't tell you how sorry I am for your loss. They were both good friends as well as cherished employees. If there's anything I can do to help you through this terrible time, don't hesitate to ask."

Mr. Morgan spoke with a voice so gravelly that it was hard to make out what he was saying, but Skipper understood him just fine.

Skipper said, "Thank you, sir. My parents enjoyed working for you. I'm sure they would appreciate your offer. Would you care for anything to drink?"

"No, No thank you, I just wanted to stop by and drop off some of your parent's personal belongings. This is not all of them but I'll get the rest of them to you in a couple of days."

As Skipper looked through the box of stuff that Mr. Morgan had set just inside the door, he said curiously, "What else was it you wanted to talk about?"

"Yes well of course I'll get to the point. First I understand you've made some preparations for your parent's funeral."

"That's right. I finished all of that this morning."

"Well," Mr. Morgan said, "this may come as a shock to you, but your parents had a burial plan with the company."

"I had no idea," Skipper said.

"The policy gives Steamway Glass full responsibility for all the arrangements. Your parents also picked out their own plots in the company cemetery. This is something we, at Steamway Glass, like to offer to our employees so they will have the peace of mind knowing that their loved ones don't have to worry with arrangements during a sorrowful time."

"They never said anything to me about it."

"Well I had my Personnel Department to cancel the arrangements you made. I hope you don't mind."

"No sir, I don't. This is all such a very big surprise to me, but you seem to have all the bases covered."

"Yes, my Personnel Department is very thorough. Someone will call you in the morning with all the information for friends and relatives."

"Thank you, sir. I wish I'd talked to you yesterday. It would've saved me a lot of time."

"Yes I'm sorry for the inconvenience. I tried to call but got no answer."

"That's quite all right," Skipper replied.

"Skipper, this may not be the right time for this but there's a couple of other things that we need to discuss."

"All right sir," Skipper said. "This'll probably be the only time I have free for the next few days so go ahead."

"Well son, I want to offer you a job with our company."

"A job!" Skipper exclaimed, as he looked at the man as if he'd lost his mind. "Mr. Morgan, I'm in my final year of school and I fully intend to finish, then perhaps I'd consider going to work for your company. I think my parents would've wanted that."

"Ok," Mr. Morgan said, "we'll get back to that. I was hoping you could help me with a little problem that I have. You see many years ago your father brought home a small triangle-shaped piece of glass that we make at Steamway. I was wondering if maybe you might know where it is now. It's not much larger than a quarter so it could be in any number of places like a jewelry box or small safe. It also has some unusual properties for its size and even though it's glass, you can't see thru it, have you seen it?"

Skipper looked puzzled as he asked, "Why would you want a small piece of glass back if you've got a company that makes it by the ton?"

"Well Skipper, you have to understand the glass that we make is very special, any number of our competitors would love to get their hands on even a small piece so they could try to duplicate its construction. It was the project your father had been working on since he came to work for us. Have you seen it?"

"No, no sir, I can't say I have but I still got a lot of their stuff to go thru, maybe it will turn up."

"I sure hope so," Mr. Morgan said, as he looked right at Skipper as if he was looking for some sign that he might know where it was. "It's very important that we recover it."

"I'll keep a special watch out for it," Skipper said.

"I'm sure you will, thank you. Now about that job…"

"I've already told you Mr. Morgan, I still have a year of school left then we can discuss a job."

"At least hear me out Skipper, before you decide. You see your father was a very special person with our company. He was very smart and someone we could trust with our deepest secrets. He also wanted you to follow in his shoes. That's why all your life he's been getting you to take classes that would help you when you went to college and took chemical engineering. I don't know if your parents ever told you or not but Steamway Glass had a lot to do with you getting a partial scholarship. We financed the rest of your education, everything from your apartment and food to the special tutor you used last year. As you know your parents didn't have any money problems, but we had planned for you to work for us from a very early age, so that's why we took care of all your educational needs. Your father was one of our best-paid employees and I'm sure you'll advance to his level very quickly."

This did ignite a spark of interest in Skipper. He'd never known how much money his parents made but he knew that it was a substantial amount. Over the years he'd also over heard bits and pieces of conversation between his parents about Steamway Glass having something to do with his education.

"After your parent's services, why don't you take a week off from school. Call me and I'll give you a tour of Steamway. Then you can make up your mind."

"Well I don't know," Skipper answered, "but I'm already out for spring break."

"Son, I can show you statistics on what an advanced chemical engineer earns in this country and I can assure you, your starting salary will be close to double those figures."

"Double!" Skipper said, with disbelief in his voice. He knew a good chemical engineer made around $70,000.00 per year. This was almost too good to be true.

Skipper said, "Ok, I'll come and take a tour and we can discuss it further then."

"Fine, fine," Mr. Morgan said, "here's my private phone number. Just call when you feel ready and I'll show you around personally."

"Thank you sir," Skipper said, as both men stood and shook hands.

As Mr. Morgan was going out the door he turned to Skipper and said, "Think about this offer very seriously. We really take care of our own and I know you'd become a very valuable part of our company. I just hope you can fill your father's shoes."

"I hope so too. I'll do my best," Skipper replied.

After both saying goodbye Skipper closed the door and leaned back against it going over all that had just happened to him.

When he'd turned sixteen-years-old, his father had given him a good luck charm on a gold chain and made him swear he'd never take it off. His father told him on the day he'd given it to him that one day this charm might save his life. Skipper pulled the chain out of his shirt and hanging on it was a small triangle-shaped piece of glass. He wondered as he rubbed it between his fingers what could be so important about a piece of glass.

Chapter 2

"Take me back to the plant," Colonel Morgan said to his chauffeur, smiling widely. "I've got to let our people know that I think the kid will work out fine and make sure that they're ready for his visit. He's young but according to all our reports he's highly intelligent."

The chauffeur just nodded his head as he pulled away from the Doster's house.

By the time they arrived back at the plant all the security lights were slowly coming to life. They used a light sensor and since it was cloudy outside the halogen bulbs were just starting to glow. Colonel Morgan's car was stopped at the first gate then after checking who was in the car, the guard waved them on through. There were several people still at the plant although they were all security personnel. The plant complex couldn't be seen from the first gate or from the perimeter fence anywhere around the plant. The security staff consisted of twenty-one men, seven on duty on all times. All the guards were heavily armed with M-16 rifles and all types of night-vision glasses and listening equipment. Even though they'd had only one incident when the generators did not kick in as soon as power was lost, the Colonel still insisted that all his security carry night-vision glasses.

The complex was completely surrounded by a sixteen-foot high fence with razor wire on top. If someone managed to get past the fence, there were motion detectors that crisscrossed the 50 acres on which the labs stood.

They arrived at the employee parking lot and the Colonel told his chauffeur he could go on home for the night but to be back by 0700 to pick him back up.

The chauffeur drove off as the Colonel walked the twenty or thirty feet to the building. At first look no door was visible. The building appeared to be solid concrete, with no doors or windows but as the Colonel stepped up to the edge of the building a small glass window appeared. The Colonel placed his right hand on the small window, which in fact was a scanner, and almost instantly a piece of the concrete wall slid to the side. The Colonel went straight to his apartment, where he often stayed even though he had an elaborate house back in town.

He went to his refrigerator, got out a beer, and opened it on his way to the living room where his favorite recliner awaited.

"Well Stephen," the Colonel thought, as he took a large swallow of the beer, and sat down in his chair, "let's see if this son of yours is all everyone says he is."

Two days later at the Doster's funeral Skipper noticed that Mr. Morgan was the only person from Steamway Glass to show up, which he found strange. After all, his parents had been with the company many years and even though they never spoke of any friends that they worked with he was sure they had plenty. Once the services were over Mr. Morgan waited until everyone had left then he walked over to Skipper.

"I'm so sorry about your parent's Skipper. We'll miss them very much."

"Thank you sir. I know I will. They were wonderful people and loved by many but life must go on."

"Yes it must," Mr. Morgan said sadly. "When would you like to come and see the plant?"

Skipper said, "Why don't I give you a call after I've had some time to get my parents affairs in order."

"That'll be fine," Mr. Morgan said, as he patted Skipper on the back. "I'll be looking forward to your call."

That night at the Doster's house, Skipper, Smitty and Lisa sat around and talked, laughed, and cried over all the good and bad times that they'd shared with his parents.

After a few drinks, Smitty, being forward as he always was, said, "I heard a few things today at the funeral that I wanted to ask you about."

If looks could kill, the look Lisa gave Smitty would've been a spear in the heart. Smitty said, in defense, "I know I told you I'd wait to ask him but he's my best friend and now is probably as good a time as any."

Looking back and forth between the two of them, Skipper said, "Well, spit it out and let's hear what's on your mind."

Looking at Lisa as if asking for permission, Smitty said, "Today at the funeral I overheard that guy from your father's company asking you about a visit to the plant. Your father had always told us that no visitors were allowed."

"Yeah I know," Skipper, said, "but he owns the place or at least runs the whole show plus it's not just a visit it's also a job interview."

"A job interview," Smitty scolded, "you can't be serious! You only have a year of school left. You can't be considering quitting school now, not till you get your degree."

"Smitty you haven't heard everything yet so don't jump to conclusions. He just wants me to come to the plant and see the project dad was working on, and who knows I might take the job."

"I can't believe you're actually thinking about quitting school. This all sounds crazy to me."

"It might sound crazy but the money he's offering is incredible."

"That's exactly what I mean. Why would he want you to step in? Surely there are more qualified people available. Besides your father never would tell us what he was working on. He always beat around the bush when we'd ask him. You won't even know what kind of job you're taking or what you'll be doing."

"Hey," Skipper said, "lay off some. It's just an interview. Then I'll know a lot more about what I'll be doing."

Smitty said, "And what's this Colonel stuff. You called him Mr. Morgan but his chauffeur called him Colonel? I thought your dad just worked for a glass company not something military."

"It is just a glass company but you also know they're working on

16

some kind of special glass. I don't know if it's for the government or not. He might be a retired Colonel and just run the place or maybe he still works for them and oversees everything, who knows. I guess we'll find out after the interview."

Lisa broke in and said, "Smitty at least let him go have a look around We've always wanted to know what his dad done anyway. It's not like they ain't gonna let him come back."

Smitty said, "I don't know. Something don't seem right about this, I mean he don't even know you at all."

"I know but he was telling me just after the accident that Steamway Glass had put me through school and paid all the bills. Also, he asked me a few questions about school and other things."

"What other things?" Smitty snapped back.

"Not much, just about my good luck charm and if I knew where it was. He described it to a tee. I don't guess dad ever told him that he'd given it to me and I wasn't about to tell him."

"Why not? It's just a piece of glass," Smitty said.

"I don't know, I guess it was the way he was looking around and just something in his voice. He wanted it back and I'm not about to turn loose of it for nothing."

"Man, you've had that thing since we were kids," Smitty said, in a little calmer voice than he'd been using.

"Yeah I know," Skipper said, "and I ain't gonna part with it now."

"What did he say he wanted it back for?"

"He just said he didn't want it to fall into the wrong hands, you know competition or at least that's what he told me."

"Wrong hands," Smitty said sharply, "it's just a dang piece of glass."

"It's special glass. Dad told me that it might save my life on day and to never take it off. To this day I haven't."

"Well, when are you gonna check out this job of yours?"

"I don't know yet," Skipper said. "I just told him I'd call, maybe day after tomorrow."

The evening went on without much more discussion about the

interview but just as Lisa and Smitty was leaving, Smitty said, "Just promise me one thing."

"What's that Smitty?" Skipper asked.

"Promise me you'll be careful when you go for this interview. Something stinks about all of this and I don't need to lose another close friend."

Skipper laughed and said, "You act like I'm going to war or something, it's just an interview."

"I knew your dad a long time and he never said a word about what he did or what he worked on except it was special glass, never nothing else," Smitty said harshly."Be careful and call us as soon as you get home."

"I will I will, " Skipper said, as he walked Lisa and Smitty to their car.

"Promise," Smitty said.

"I promise I'll be careful ok!"

"Ok that's all I'm asking."

Skipper was walking back toward the house when he got the same strange feeling that he'd felt earlier in the week that he was being watched. Maybe I should be careful Skipper thought as he went inside and closed the door behind him.

Monday morning finally rolled around and Skipper was up early. He loved to have breakfast in the Florida room on the east side of the house. The room was almost completely made of glass and on clear mornings, like this one promised to be, the sun rose over the hills and gave off its golden rays. Skipper stood for a minute in those rays with his eyes closed enjoying their warmth. He remembered how his mother had loved to do the same thing and a small tear came in his eyes. Thinking that he'd never see the two of them again was unreal, never see their smile or hear them laugh.

Skipper had decided to just have a bowl of cereal and a glass of juice for breakfast. He was in no mood to cook. As he sat at the table and ate he could smell all the hanging plants that his mother had kept in here because they needed the sunlight that this room provided. What

Skipper loved was that they gave off a smell that made the room into a fresh spring morning no matter what time of year it was.

Just as he was finishing his cereal, Skipper heard a noise that came from the front of the house. It sounded like the front door closing. All he could think of was Smitty had dropped by and had let himself in with the key that his parents had given him years ago. Skipper called out, "I'm in the Florida Room Smitty, come on in." He sat and waited for a minute or so then when no one came he called out again, "Smitty?" no answer.

He stood and walked to the front of the house but saw no one. Skipper checked the front door, still locked but the dead bolt was open. He knew he'd locked it the night before. When he was seven, the house had been broken into and his parents had added dead bolts and a security system. They were never left undone. First he thought Smitty was goofing around but as he thought about it he knew it just wasn't like Smitty to do so. He began to check around to see if anything was missing and checking all the rooms. Nothing. Yet when he went into his parents' room though nothing seemed out of order, he got the feeling someone had been in there. Skipper went back down stairs and got himself another glass of orange juice. Going to sit in the living room, he began to have doubts whether he'd truly heard the door closing or not. No, Skipper thought it was the door. The dead bolt was open too. As he set his juice down, he saw the card that Mr. Morgan or Colonel Morgan, whichever one he was, had left the day his parents had died. On it was his private number. Skipper decided to go ahead and give him a call.

It was around 9:00 A.M. when Colonel Morgan's phone rang.

"Hello," he said.

"Mr. Morgan, this is Skipper Doster. I was just calling you to set up a time to come by and check out the plant."

"Yes Skipper, good to hear from you. I was beginning to wonder if you were going to call or if you'd given up on us completely."

"No sir, I've been considering your job offer and just wanted to see first hand what I would be getting myself into."

"Well Skipper, how would tomorrow morning be? I'll send my chauffeur by to pick you up."

"That's all right sir. I'll be glad to drive myself, that is if you'll give me directions."

"Your father has been very quiet about what he did for a living if you don't even know where our plant is," Mr. Morgan laughed. "But son, you couldn't get past security if they didn't know you even if I ok'd it. So let me send the car say around 01000."

"All right that should be fine and thank you for this opportunity. I hope I can do as well as you expect."

"I'm sure you'll do fine," Mr. Morgan said, as he turned in his chair to write down the time Skipper was supposed to arrive. "Skipper, there are a few things you need to know before you come. First anything you see or hear…"

"Don't worry sir," Skipper said, as he cut the Colonel off, "I know everything has to be kept secret."

"Yes it does and I'll finish telling you what all we expect from you when you arrive tomorrow. I'll see you around 01030 in the morning," he said to Skipper, as he hung up the phone.

Colonel Morgan sat at his desk, chewing on the end of his pen, thinking about how he'd handle his new visitor tomorrow. He picked up the phone and called down stairs to his head-of- securities, Mark Smith's office, "Mark."

"Yes Colonel, what can I do for you."

"You know the kid that we've been watching?"

"Yes sir, of course."

"Well, he's coming to the plant in the morning. Why don't you take one of your men and finish checking out the house while we know he'll be here?"

"Yes sir, no problem."

"And Smith."

"Yes sir."

"Let's do this as quiet and unseen as possible."

"Yes sir Colonel."

"Thank you Smith. You're a good man."

The Colonel hung up his phone and looked across his desk at the small office just outside his door where Mrs. Doster once sat every day. I should have both spaces filled by week's end he thought. Maybe if everything works out as planned, things should be back to normal in a month or so. The Colonel leaned back in his chair and propped his feet up on his desk. He'd already had someone in mind to fill Mrs. Doster's job. However, he wasn't exactly sure how to approach her with the offer. He'd met her at a dinner at one of his oldest friend's house. George Watson had been with the Colonel since Steamway was first opened and now was retired and living quite comfortably on his retirement. George had three children, the oldest of which was his daughter Crystal.

Crystal was a bright young lady and had just finished her second year at Auburn University talking courses in Business Management. She was quite beautiful, with bright green eyes, dark brown hair and a body to kill for. She'd made the jeans that she'd worn the night of the dinner a memory that the Colonel would never forget, but he wasn't interested in her for her looks, he was strictly business. He knew she was top of her class at school and already had several job offers to choose from. The Colonel decided the best way to approach her was through her father so he gave George a call.

George answered the phone on the third ring.

"Hello my old friend," the Colonel said, with great admiration in his voice, "how the heck have you been?"

"Well it's about time you took the time to call me you old goat! How long's it been, six—eight months now?" George said.

"Oh you still tell the biggest lies. It's only been a couple of months but you always could stretch the truth. Why don't we get together tonight for dinner? I've a favor to ask of you."

"I've already got plans tonight, Colonel. My daughter is in town and I was going to take her out for dinner. We haven't spent much time together since her mother passed away."

"That would make things even better. She's what I needed to talk to you about anyway and dinner would be on me at any place you'd like," the Colonel said, "if I wouldn't be imposing."

"No, not at all that would probably be fine with Crystal. She's off for spring break and will be home for at least a couple of weeks. Why would you need to talk to me about her?"

"Well George, as you know, we lost the Doster's last week and I have a spot to fill."

"And don't tell me," George said, "you'd like for me to talk to her for you right?"

"George, you know me like a book. Do you think she might be interested?"

"Very possible but it would be her decision."

"Of course," the Colonel said, "but you know I'm a hard man to turn down."

"That's the understatement of the year!" George said, laughing a little and rubbing his bald head. "How is 1900 hours for you Colonel?"

"It'd be fine. I'll pick the two of you up then."

"Great I'll see you tonight," George said, as he hung up the phone.

The Colonel once again leaned back in his chair and laced his fingers behind his head and thought, "yes, she should do fine. I'll just have to set up a time to meet with her that won't let her and Skipper cross paths. I doubt it but they might know each other and that might create a problem."

Chapter 3

Skipper hung up with the Colonel. He sat back in his chair and thought about his good luck charm. Should he tell the Colonel about it or just keep it a secret for a while longer? Then as he got up and started to the kitchen, someone knocked on the door. It startled Skipper because he wasn't expecting any company.

"Come in," Skipper yelled.

Smitty came in with a bounce in his step that was unusual for him this time of the morning. "What's up man?" Smitty said, as he followed Skipper into the kitchen.

"Not much, I just got off the phone with Mr. Morgan. I'm going to the plant at 10:00 in the morning for my interview."

"Not this again," Smitty said. "I'd hoped you'd given up on all that by now and had came to your senses."

"Don't start on me Smitty! This is something I've got to do. It's too good to pass up and besides I think my father would've wanted me to at least consider it. He loved his work and I figure I'll love it too."

"You don't even know what it is yet," Smitty said.

"Well I will tomorrow morning. They're picking me up at 10:00 a.m. and don't worry I'll give you a call as soon as I get back."

"10:00 a.m. huh?"

"Yeah, why?" Skipper asked, suspiciously.

"Oh no reason. I just wondered what time to expect you back."

"I don't have any idea so don't worry if I don't call until at least around 5:00 p.m. or so."

Smitty poured himself a glass of orange juice and leaned back against the sink while Skipper started making himself a sandwich.

"So," Skipper asked, trying to change the subject, "how is this wonder kid of yours doing?"

"He's costing me a fortune in equipment," Smitty said. "Most of it I don't even know what it's for. But he loves it. At ten-years-old he's already been offered a full scholarship at Harvard."

"Man, that's something," Skipper said.

"Even though he's my stepson, I love him with all my heart and I know he'll do well for himself. Things you and I had to study hours for he doesn't even have to look at twice. His real father has been giving us hassles, trying to take him away but there ain't no way the courts will let him. All he's after is the money that the kid is gonna make. He's smarter than both of us put together. You'll have to come over and see all the equipment he's got now. We've got a basement full."

"What's it all for?" Skipper asked.

"Heck if I know. Some kind of analysis stuff. He can take just about anything, break it down, and tell you exactly what makes it up. I gave him a piece of steel and he told me every kind of alloy that it was made up of in an hour or so. He can do the same with any kind of drug or just about anything else. Sometimes he's so smart that he scares me."

"Yeah, I bet. I've been going to school forever and I can't do half of what you say he can do now. Hey, maybe Steamway will have a place for him," Skipper said, with a smile.

"Don't even joke about that!" Smitty snapped. "No way I'd let him work for some place like that."

"Who do you think he's going to work for, Smitty? Kmart? With all his skills he's government bound."

Smitty looked at him sourly and, said, "Yeah I guess you're right. I just don't want him designing bombs or weird viruses, you know? Well I got to go, Lisa's waiting on me. We're gonna take the kids to the zoo and spend the rest of the day at the park by the lake."

"Ok," Skipper said, "I'll see you sometime tomorrow."

"No, you won't," Smitty thought, "but I'll see you."

Smitty left and went straight home where Lisa and the kids were waiting anxiously. They loaded up the whole crew and headed for Montgomery where the nearest zoo was. On the way Smitty was so quiet that Lisa asked, "Whatcha thinking about hon.?"

"Not much," Smitty said smiling.

"Oh no, I've seen that sneaky grin before. What're you up to?"

"Skipper told me he was going to that job interview in the morning around 10:00 and I'm gonna follow him to check this place out."

"Oh no you're not! You don't know what you might be getting into."

"Listen honey, Skipper may need me and besides I'm just gonna find out where the plant is, I'm not gonna try to get in."

"I don't know Smitty," Lisa said. "This sounds like a bad idea to me."

"It'll be fine, besides you told me to lay off Skipper and let him go so I'm gonna follow them and wait till they come back out to make sure he's ok."

"How are you gonna follow them? Skipper knows both of our cars. He'll spot you in a second."

"No, he won't because I'm gonna borrow Billy's old pickup. The one he uses to haul firewood," Smitty said, with a grin on his face that told Lisa he was feeling proud of himself for thinking of this.

"Have you asked Billy about this yet?"

"No but he's my cousin and he told me before if I ever needed it just to ask besides it's just sitting there right now. Winter is over so no one needs any wood."

After they left the zoo, the kids were being rowdy, all except Brandon who was reading as usual. They knew Brandon was a special child even when he was very young. He started talking and walking before most children. By the age of four he could read almost anything. They'd entered him in a school for gifted children and he'd excelled to the top of the class in no time. At six-years-old he'd already started showing a strong interest in chemistry so his parents had really shown him a lot of support. For his age, his IQ was off the charts. He'd already received several government grants to help him with his education and the equipment he needed to study. As a result, Brandon became smarter by the day.

As they headed to the park, Brandon asked Smitty, "What kind of job is Uncle Skipper taking that's so dangerous?"

Smitty and Lisa just looked at each other. They weren't aware that he'd been listening to their conversation. Even though they usually underestimated him, they'd thought he was deep in his book. But he had, in fact, been reading and listening at the same time.

Smitty answered, "We really don't know if it's dangerous or not son. I'm just going to follow him to make sure he's ok."

Brandon, never looking up from his book he just smiled and nodded his head as if to say, "Sure you don't."

The Colonel arrived at 7:00 p.m. Right on schedule, George, and Crystal were ready to go. He shook George's hand and turned to Crystal and said, "My you've grown up and became a beautiful young lady"

"Thank you Colonel," Crystal said, blushing slightly.

"Has your father told you anything about why I wanted to join you two for dinner tonight?"

"Yes sir, a little but he also said that we'd go in more detail at supper."

"Yes, of course," the Colonel said. "So George, where would you like to go and spend some of my hard earned money tonight?"

"Oh I don't know I thought we'd leave it up to Crystal."

They both look at Crystal and smiled. She said, "How about Red Lobster? My father and I both love seafood."

"Red Lobster it is then," the Colonel said, and patted his chauffeur's shoulder and told him to drive.

It was only about twenty minutes to the mall where the restaurant was located and George and the Colonel talked over old times. George asked the Colonel how Skipper was handling the loss of his parents and the Colonel looked at him as if it was taboo to discuss it and just said, "He's doing fine." George knew company policy but had no idea that the Colonel had plans to hire Skipper as well.

Crystal just looked at them both with a puzzled look on her face and said, "Who's Skipper and what happened to his parents?"

The Colonel just replied, "His parents were employees of the company and they were killed in an accident a couple weeks ago."

"Was it an accident at the plant?"

"No of course not, it was an auto accident. They were on their way home from work."

"Oh, I see," Crystal said.

They arrived at Red Lobster around 7:25 p.m. The night air was cool but not really cold. They all went inside and as usual there was a waiting list to be seated so The Colonel suggested that they sit at the bar in the lounge till they'd a table available. Crystal agreed and ordered a Strawberry daiquiri. Her father had scotch on the rocks and the Colonel had a beer. He never drank anything stronger.

The atmosphere in the lounge was smokey, crowed and noisy but they managed to get three seats side by side at the bar. At first, the conversation was carried on only by George and Colonel Morgan and Crystal just sat and listened to the two old friends reminisce. Finally the maitre'd came in the lounge and told them the table was ready.

"Well it's about time," the Colonel said, as they started into the dining area.

After they'd all ordered and were waiting on their dinner to arrive the Colonel turned to Crystal and, asked, "So what do you think about coming to work for me at Steamway?"

"Well sir," Crystal said, "I haven't really given it much thought. Mainly I was waiting to talk to you and see what kind of position I'd be taking and what kind of salary we'd be talking about."

"Gets right to the point don't she George," the Colonel said, "just like her old man. Here's what I like to try to do with all of my new employees. First I would like you to come by the plant and see where you'd be working and then I could show you what you'd be doing. Mainly you'd be my private secretary."

Crystal spoke up and said, "Colonel Morgan, I haven't gone to school all these years to be a secretary."

"Oh don't get me wrong Crystal. Your job will be to manage the company. I'm getting too old to do too much work and I need someone I can count on 24 hours a day. Steamway has been in business almost twenty years and we've had the same employees from day one except for eight. Four have died, your father and the other three retired. We treat our people very well and I don't think the salary will disappoint you at all."

"Colonel Morgan, this all sounds fine. When would be a good time for me to stop by?"

"How does the day after tomorrow sound? I would have you come by in the morning but I already have another appointment and it will probably take all day."

Smiling Crystal said, "then day after tomorrow it will be. Just tell me what time."

"I'll have my driver pick you up around 01000."

"That'll be fine. I would ask you about driving my own car but my father has already explained all the security to me and how everything has to be kept hush, hush."

Crystal excused herself to go to the ladies room and finally gave George and the Colonel time to talk.

"How much does she know about us George?" the Colonel asked.

"Nothing, just what all the children were told and I'm sorry about letting that thing about Skipper and his parents slip."

"Yes I'm having Skipper come by tomorrow to check out everything"

"I'd no idea you were already going to move him into his father's place."

"Well," the Colonel said, "I see no reason to wait any longer."

After supper Colonel Morgan took George and Crystal back home where they invited him in for another beer but the Colonel declined saying, "I've already had my limit and I need my beauty rest. As you can tell, I haven't had much of that lately." They all laughed.

"Well thank you for supper and I look forward to seeing you the day after tomorrow," Crystal said, shaking Colonel Morgan's hand.

"So do I Crystal, I think we'll work wonderfully together."

Crystal turned to go into the house and, George said, "I'll be there in a minute honey. I need to talk to the Colonel."

"Ok daddy," Crystal said, as she made her way to the side door nearest the garage. This was the door that they usually used to come and go from the house and they kept the outside light on in case they returned after dark.

After Crystal was in the house George turned to the Colonel and asked, "Well sir, how're things coming along?"

"As we planned George. We should be able to leave in about three more years. It seems like we've been here forever. We were so young when we first arrived. Are you still planning on staying here George or are you coming with us?" the Colonel asked.

"My life is here now Colonel. My wife died here and I'll always stay with her but I want Crystal to know about—well you know."

"Yes I do," the Colonel said. "I wish everyone was going back just like we came but I respect the fact that you want to stay."

"Have you had any more outside interference?" George asked.

"You mean the government? No, they haven't bothered us in quite a while now. We're pretty well out of sight out of mind here."

"Well Colonel, don't let your guard down. They were all over us once and they would be again if they could find us."

"Yes George, I know but we're a long way from there now and with all the systems coming back on line. They can't even see us."

"I know but you still have to be careful, now more than ever. You'll have my little girl in there with you."

"How do you think the kids will take the news?" the Colonel asked George, as he was putting a new toothpick in his mouth.

"It'll shock the hell out of them. But it's not like we're space aliens or something." Looking at each other, they burst out laughing.

Chapter 4
Tuesday, April 29, 2001

Skipper's alarm clock went off right at 7:00 A.M. with a loud beep, beep. But no one was in the room for it to wake up. He'd been up for a while and already had himself a hot shower. He was down stairs in the kitchen starting a pot of coffee. Skipper was excited about the interview today but at the same time he was very nervous. Smitty had gotten him to thinking all kinds of crazy thoughts. Just paranoid, Skipper thought to himself. He could hear his alarm clock going off but wasn't in any hurry it to shut if off. There was no one else in the house for it to disturb and he could hardly hear it.

Skipper had already decided to wear just blue jeans and his favorite light-blue dress shirt.

Mr. Morgan had told him to keep it casual that they'd to change in a 'clean room' anyway. This made Skipper think, "I wonder if I'll have to remove my shirt. If I do and Mr. Morgan is there he'll see my good luck charm." This created a small problem for Skipper. He wondered how clean this 'clean room' was going to be and how it was going to work. He'd decided to put his charm in his pants pocket so he'd still have it with him. He'd the strangest feeling the time was growing near when he might need it. "For what?" he said out loud, as he headed up the stairs to cut the clock off.

Mr. Morgan's car arrived about five minutes after ten and Skipper was waiting in the Florida room when the door bell rang. He headed through the house at a fast pace and grabbed his blue denim jacket off the coat rack behind the front door.

"Are you ready sir?" the chauffeur asked, as Skipper opened the door.

"Yep, ready as I'll ever be. But we need to stop this sir stuff. I'm just Skipper."

"Ok, Skipper it is then and I'm Amos."

"Glad to meet you, Amos," Skipper said, as he offered his hand.

The two shook hands then walked to the car where Amos opened the back door. Skipper just kind of shook his head as he climbed into the car.

The inside was incredible. It had plush upholstery, carpet at least an inch thick and a small bar. Amos got in and started out of the driveway when Skipper said, "How long will it take to get to the plant?"

"Only about twenty minutes."

"That's about what I'd gathered from my father."

"Yes," Amos said, "I'm sorry for your loss."

"Thank you," Skipper said. "I really miss them."

They were both quiet for a little while then, Amos asked, "What all has the Colonel told you about the plant?"

"Not much," Skipper replied, "very little at all. Why do you call him Colonel?"

"He was once my commanding officer," Amos said, as he turned onto the main highway through town.

"Oh really, what branch of the military were you in?"

"I'm sorry Skipper but those are questions you'll have to ask the Colonel."

"I see well how long have you been with him?"

"A very long time," Amos answered, "but again those are questions you'll have to ask him."

"Ok," Skipper said, as he wondered to himself what could be so secret about how long a chauffeur had worked for Mr. Morgan.

"Well," Skipper asked, "is he still a Colonel or what?"

"To me he'll always be Colonel," Amos said, without really answering the question.

"Man is this whole place going to be this secretive?"

"More than you could possibly know," Amos answered, with a smile.

They drove for about ten minutes and Amos said, "Are you planning on living at the plant or are you going to keep your parent's house?"

"Live at the plant?" Skipper said. "What're you talking about?"

"Well some of our employees live in the compound We've several apartments there."

"I've never heard of such," Skipper said.

"Maybe I've overstepped my boundaries by even asking," Amos said. "I don't guess the Colonel has mentioned any of this to you yet. You're in for quite a surprise."

"What?" Skipper asked, almost laughing

"We've had a place for you for quite a while now," Amos explained. "We've just been waiting on the two of you to come of age."

"The two of us? What're you talking about?"

"Nothing Skipper, You'll find out soon enough but times are fixing to get better for all of us now that you two are finally here. But I've said too much so I'll just hush and drive. Once I get to talking it's hard for me to stop," Amos said, with a smile. "Ah, here we are this is the first turn you've to make to go into the plant. We've to go through two check points then you can see the Colonel."

It was a long straight black top road. Well lit on both sides even though none of the lights were on now. At the first check point there were two guards and they asked Skipper to step out of the car so they could get a visual clearance through the closed circuit camera that was being watched by the Colonel.

"That's him Sargent, let'em through," the Colonel's voice came over the radio that the guard wore on his belt.

"Sir," the youngest guard said, "I'll need you to place your right hand on this scanner so we'll have a print to use at all the other check points."

Skipper shook his head but placed his hand flat on the scanner.

"Thank you sir," the guard said. "Your print will be in the system now and you've a class C security rating which'll let you have access to most of the plant. You'll see scanners like this one all through the plant. Your security access will be on the wall above the scanner. Your access won't let you in a class A or B but from C on down you can enter."

"Thank you," Skipper said, as he sat back down in the car. He noticed both guards had on side arms but that was the only weapon he saw. As they approached the second checkpoint and the perimeter fence the first thing he noticed was they were carrying M-16 rifles. When they pulled up to the gate, the guard approached the back of the car as Amos let the window down. He was carrying a portable scanner and asked Skipper to place his right hand on it. Skipper did as he was asked then the gate slid to the right and Amos drove on the employee parking lot.

Skipper said to Amos, "Man, this is wild."

Amos said, "It gets a lot wilder!"

Smitty waited at the entrance of the black top road that lead to the plant until Mr. Morgan's car was out of sight. Then he continued to follow them in his cousin's old truck. He'd never been down this road before but he'd passed it several times on the way to Lake Martin. Within the first quarter of a mile he passed several signs that said, "authorized personnel only everyone else must use this turn around" which was simply a small parking lot on the right side of the road. Smitty didn't know whether to continue or not. Then he thought, "Well what're they gonna do shoot me?" So he kept on going. It wasn't far until he came to another set of signs that said "all vehicles must stop at guard house." That was about the time he saw the cross bars that blocked the road at the first check point. Smitty pulled over to the side of the road and sat there looking at the guards standing outside the building. They were both looking in his direction. He decided to go back to the turn around and wait for the Colonel's car to come back by. As he was pulling away, Sergeant Bryant was watching him through a pair of binoculars and managed to get his tag number which was simply policy for any strange vehicles that got close to the plant.

Skipper got out of the car at the employee parking lot where he was met by yet another security guard who showed him the way to the door at the side of the plant, which led into the waiting area for the 'clean room'.

"Thanks for the ride, Amos," Skipper said, as Amos drove away.

As they walked Skipper tried to make small talk to the guard, whose name tag read 'Cleveland' but like everyone else he just said he was here to show Skipper the way to the 'clean room' where the Colonel was waiting. As they approached the building, a small panel slid open to reveal a scanner. The guard stood by the door and looked at Skipper. Skipper placed his right hand on the scanner and out of the solid wall a door opened. Skipper waited for the guard to say something but he just stood there as if he was a zombie. Skipper shrugged his shoulders and walked inside. The door closed behind him with a swooshing sound and he found himself in a room with just two bench type seats and several lockers. The Colonel was no where to be seen. Skipper walked over to a glass door which led into what he guessed was the 'clean room'. From a door to his left Mr. Morgan walked in with his usual smile and hand extended to be shook.

"Good to see you, Skipper," the Colonel said. "I hope your ride was ok?"

"Yes it was quite pleasant but you were right, all the security here did catch me a little by surprise."

"Yes, well it's necessary. You'll understand why soon. So, shall we suit up to enter the 'clean room' then I can show you around?"

"What kind of suits do we have to wear?"

"They look kind of like radiation suits but it's only to enter the room. Once inside the room will fill with a type of smoke that takes all exterior dust and germs off your body. Then we'll change into standard plant issue clothes. After we put the clothes on, we can enter the plant."

Skipper watched the Colonel as he began to undress and put his clothes into a locker with his name on it. Skipper began to strip too and then noticed that the Colonel had retrieved a radiation suit from his locker. It looked simple enough. Yellow, really baggy with a large hood and a clear face plate that wrapped almost all the way around the hood so you could turn your head and be able to see out both sides.

As the Colonel was showing Skipper how to put the suit on properly Skipper said, "This seems like a great deal of trouble for a glass plant sir."

The Colonel stopped what he was doing and looked at Skipper through the glass face plate. He said, "Skipper, you're going to see things and experience other things that no other person on the earth besides the employees of Steamway have ever seen. Just be patient with me and after we get into the plant, we'll go straight to my office and most of your questions will be answered. All will be answered in time but only after you've been with us for a while."

Skipper said nothing more as they finished dressing and started toward the 'clean room', then he remembered his good luck charm in the pocket of his jeans. Oh well he thought I hope my life don't need saving today. Once inside the 'clean room' the door automatically closed behind them and a very bright orange light almost blinded him. It seemed to come from everywhere. A few seconds later, once his eyes had adjusted to the strange glow, Skipper heard a hissing sound then the room began to fill with a greenish colored gas. The Colonel held his arms away from his side and slowly turned in a circle. After he'd finished, he nodded to Skipper to do the same. As soon as he'd completed his circle. Skipper could see the gas being sucked out of the room through several vents in the floor, walls, and ceiling. Once no more gas was visible, an automated voice said "please stand still for contamination scan." Skipper had no idea what was going to happen. He was just about to ask the Colonel when the same voice said "contamination scan complete. Please remove your suits and put on your plant uniform." The Colonel removed his suit and placed it into a hamper like you'd have for dirty clothes and went to the lockers and retrieved two uniforms.

Handing Skipper one and putting one on himself, the Colonel said, "I wasn't sure about your size. I just had to guess."

Even though the uniform was big on Skipper, he said, "This'll do just fine sir."

Once they were dressed, the automated voice said, "Prepare for decontamination" and once again the room filled with a gas but this time it was almost clear.

"The reason we wear the radiation suits first is the green gas would be poisonous to us but this gas only cleans what might be left on your body and is completely harmless," the Colonel explained.

"Prepare for contamination scan," the voice said again and almost immediately said, "scan complete" and the door to the plant came open with another swoosh.

Skipper was amazed at how big the inside of the plant appeared to be. He saw only a few work stations but no workers were seen. Skipper started to ask about other employees but figured it could wait until they got to the Colonel's office.

"Where will I be working?" Skipper asked.

The Colonel said, "First things first. Let's get to my office where we can be more comfortable."

As they walked down a short hall Skipper could hear only a light whine of machinery the Colonel turned left and Skipper could see a set of elevators.

"This place has more than one level?" Skipper asked excitedly.

The Colonel just looked at him and smiled. They entered the elevator and Skipper asked again, "How many levels are there?"

"Three below and one above," the Colonel said.

"One above," Skipper said, "but this is only a one story building."

"No it's five stories including the floor we just left. My office is on the top floor."

"Where? On the roof?" Skipper said, rather sarcastically. Again the Colonel just smiled.

After Skipper had entered the first checkpoint Sergeant Bryant called Mark Smith and let him know that Skipper was at the plant and he was clear to go to the Doster's house. On his way out of the plant Mark Smith saw an old truck parked in the turn around area at the entrance of the plant road. As he passed by, he noticed a middle-aged man sitting in the cab. After he'd turned onto the main highway, he radioed Sergeant Bryant to tell him about the truck.

"Yea," Bryant said, "he came all the way down here just after the Colonel's car did and turned around. I got a tag number on him. Do you want me to check it out?"

Mark said, "No I'll check it myself when I get back. Just keep an eye out for him to come back."

Mark knew he'd be gone for at least three or four hours. It would take that long to go over the house with a fine tooth comb and, not leave a trace anyone had been there, to see if he could find the key. He'd been watching the Doster's house on a couple of other occasions and had already been inside twice but Skipper had been home and that was dangerous. He thought that Skipper had sensed that someone was in the house both times and so he'd informed the Colonel that he thought it wouldn't be wise to go back until Skipper wasn't at home.

Now was the perfect opportunity. They wouldn't have to use the suits to not be seen so the search would go much faster.

As they arrived at the house there was a garbage truck picking up the trash so they waited until he was out of sight before they started up the steps. Mark already had a key to the house. Stephen had given it to him just as a security measure. This was just procedure for anyone living off plant property. Now the key was useful. After Mark had unlocked the door, he went in first followed by on of his best men. They had a lot of work to do but Mark knew they'd have plenty of time and Sergeant Bryant would radio them when Skipper left the plant.

When the elevator stopped the Colonel pushed the hold button on the panel. He turned to Skipper and said, "You're going to see things from this point on that are hard for you to believe and even comprehend."

"So I understand," Skipper said.

"Well," the Colonel said, "now things get difficult. You won't be able to tell anyone about what you're going to see."

"Yes sir, I already know that"

"No son, you don't know!" the Colonel snapped back. "Let me

finish what I have to say before you interrupt me and then you can decide whether or not I open this elevator door or we go back down stairs."

"Yes sir, I'm sorry."

"That's quite all right Skipper, I just need to make a point of how important it's that it remains completely unknown what we do hear. First, we do work for our government. I suppose you've gathered that much already but I'm not part of the government. Even though you have heard and will continue to hear me be called Colonel. The reason why is most of the employees here used to serve under me. That was a long time ago but it's also why they're trusted with Steamway's secrets. We make a product here that the government uses or should I say will use on things like their stealth fighters and bombers. Do you think you want me to go on Skipper? Because if you do, you must understand that you're signing your life over to Steamway. What I mean is you'll constantly be monitored and watched for security reasons."

"Were my parents watched Colonel?"

"Everyone is Skipper, but not by the government, by us. You'll have no private life that we don't know about but in exchange you'll be rewarded with a salary incomparable anywhere."

"I don't know Colonel, I'm just not sure I'm ready to make that kind of decision yet. This has all caught me by surprise. You're saying I'll never be able to lead a normal life again and I don't know if there's enough money in the world to make up for that."

"I appreciate your honesty, Skipper. Most people would've just agreed so they could see what was behind these doors. Here are a couple of things to think about before you decide. First, were your parents happy here? Was their life difficult in anyway? Didn't they both love their jobs?"

Skipper thought for a few seconds, then asked, "Did my parents know they were monitored 24 hours seven days a week?"

"Yes they did. It's the price you pay for living off grounds, which is something else we've to discuss but first I need your reassurance that nothing you're about to see will ever leave this room. If you can promise me that, I know you're true to your word. We can go inside my office and I'll explain in detail a lot more of what will be expected of you."

"I don't know, Colonel. I mean I've got so many questions I need to ask before I decide and to be honest I get the feeling if I say no to this job I'll still be monitored anyway."

"Just promise me you won't speak to anyone about what you've seen and what you're about to learn, then we can have a seat and I'll answer all your questions that I can. Can you do that, Skipper?"

"Well," Skipper said, "let's see what's behind door number one."

"I guess that's a promise," the Colonel said, with a smile. He placed his hand on the scanner and the elevator doors slid open.

They stepped out into a long hall that was dimly lit by overhead florescent bulbs. The Colonel said, "My office is the last one on the right. I think you'll be pleasantly surprised by the view I have from there."

"Colonel," Skipper said, amazed, "I'm not the smartest person in the world but I'm not the dumbest either. We did go up in that elevator and there was no second floor to this building but yet here we are."

"Yes it's amazing isn't it, Skipper. This is a lot of your father's doings."

As they arrived at the door there was yet another scanner on the wall, which the Colonel placed his hand. The door opened into a very large room with one wall that faced the entrance to the plant and one that overlooked the lawn to the left of the building. Both walls were entirely made of glass.

Skipper said, "How can this be?"

The Colonel crossed the room to where his desk sat and said, with a slight chuckle in his voice, "Skipper, don't just stand there. Come on in and sit down."

As Skipper crossed the office, he could see an adjoining office to his left. It appeared to be where a secretary might normally be.

"That's where your mother used to work, Skipper. She was more than my right hand. She was my whole arm."

The Colonel's office had plush carpet and looked to have been decorated by a professional. He sat down behind one of the biggest mahogany desk Skipper had ever seen. Then he spun in his chair and waved his arm as if to say to Skipper, look what a view. Skipper, still speechless, slowly walked toward the Colonels' desk.

"Have a seat, Skipper, and I'll try to explain how all of this works."

"Sir, this isn't visible from outside. I mean you can't see this floor at all."

"Yes I know Skipper, that's part of what we do here at Steamway."

It was nearing lunch and Smitty's stomach wouldn't let him forget it, so he decided to go back to town and get a burger and check in with Lisa so she wouldn't worry. Smitty, from where he'd turned around, never saw the plant. H e had already decided when he got back that he was going to go for a little walk. He'd figured he could leave the turn around and stay in the woods for a mile or so and he should be past the guard shack where he'd turned around earlier. Driving back to town he decided to buy some bottled water to carry along with him because he'd no idea how far past the guard shack the plant would be. The old pickup spit and sputtered as he turned out onto highway 231 and headed to town. He pulled into the first gas station he came to and went inside to get his water and a few snacks when he came back out he saw the pay phone at the corner of the lot and started walking toward it as he reached into his pocket to see if he had the necessary change. Smitty thought after he called Lisa he'd continue north on 231 to McDonalds. It was only about another mile and a half. After eating he'd return to the turn around where he could park the truck before he started on his little adventure. When he called home all he got, was the answering machine and he left Lisa a small message letting her know he was fine but might be al little late getting home. Then he started toward McDonalds. Turning into the parking lot he'd pumped himself up so much about what he was going to do that he pulled into the drive through to get his order to go and headed for the turn around as fast as the old truck would carry him. He couldn't wait to get back so he could start his hike to the plant. He knew if he stayed deep enough in the woods the guards wouldn't be able to see him. Once he parked the truck he took the plastic bag with the water and snacks in it and started toward the guard shack trying to be as careful as possible. There was very little traffic on the blacktop that led to the plant. Smitty had only seen one other car besides Mr. Morgan's and it was coming from the direction of the plant. The two men in the car looked at Smitty as they went by but Smitty just kept reading his magazine.

Every so often, as he made his way through the woods Smitty would slip out to the edge of the road to see if he could see the guard shack, being careful not to be seen himself. Mostly the woods were made up of tall pine trees with very little underbrush. Dead pine needles covered the forest floor so his approach was very quite other than an occasional "snap" of a twig. Before long Smitty spotted the guard shack so he went deeper into the woods than he'd been traveling before so as to be sure not to alert them of his presence. Several minutes after he'd passed the guards. Smitty sat down on a fallen tree and got out a bottle of water and took a long, cool drink. He was happy with himself for making it around the guards but that was just about the time he spotted it.

Chapter 5

"Sit down Skipper, so we can talk," the Colonel said, as he pointed to the chair in front of his desk.

"I can't believe what I'm seeing or rather not seeing. I mean I see a solid wall except where the windows are, but from the outside nothing."

"Yes, I know," the Colonel explained."It's called bending or fractured light. It's quite simple actually."

"Yes sir, I mean I know what the theory on bending light is but we're years from that technology. I mean you're talking about the power of invisibility right?"

"Please Skipper, have a seat and I'll explain all I can. Of course I won't have time to tell you everything but as the days go on you'll learn more and more."

"I can't believe our government has this technology and no one has found out about it."

"You don't understand, Skipper. This is not what we sell to our government. They know nothing about this."

"You mean to tell me there's more?"

"Yes much more. I'm sure you've got lots of questions so why don't we get started."

"How does 'the bending light' you've developed work?"

"Like I said, I could talk for days and not cover everything. But to make it as simple as I can. It's like taking a camera and placing it on the back of this building. Taking a moving picture of what is directly behind it and transmitting it to a screen like a TV on the front of the building in exactly the same spot. So when you look at the picture, you're actually looking through it. Imagine a billion cameras all over this top floor and a billion receivers opposite them all working at one time. The building would seem to disappear. You see Skipper, we have a central computer that controls all of this."

"But what about different angles?" Skipper asked.

"Well it gets complicated there. The computer, having a billion or so sensors on those cameras, read the retina in your eye and knows which angle to broadcast from. It can do this a billion times over in just a second so as you're walking or running past, the building is still invisible. It also scans for any photo's that might be taken from as far away as orbiting satellites so all they get back is a picture of a singe story building. Does all of this make sense to you?"

"Yeah, kind of, but there's so much that still can't be possible. I mean you surely don't have a billion cameras all over this building right."

"Yes that's true, that's why the glass we make here's so special. We can use one central computer and it transmits and receives the images using only the glass we make here and the program that your father helped design."

"Ok I'll go along with that for now but what about dirt and rain, you now natural things that we've no control over," Skipper said inquisitively.

"Good question Skipper," the Colonel said. "That was one of our hardest obstacles to overcome. That's where your father came in. He was like you, a chemical engineer. So it was his job to make a coating that nothing and I mean nothing would stick to."

"Teflon," Skipper said, with a small giggle in his voice.

"Well you're not really too far off. So that gives you some idea of what you'll be doing for us."

Skipper thought, "This is just great. I'm a dang window washer."

Smitty had not seen the chain link fence from where he'd turned around at earlier but there it was, plain as day, looming over him with razor wire wrapped all around the top. Smitty couldn't see the plant from this part of the fence and there was no way to climb over it so he decided to start walking around it to see if he could find a spot he could see the plant from. At first Smitty didn't see the camera on the corner post of the fence. But he was lucky. It was facing the other way. As it started to rotate toward him Smitty made a dash for the trees. He slid down like a baseball player would slide into home and he believed he hadn't been seen. He sat there for a few minutes trying to catch his breath and taking another drink of water. After about ten minutes he'd rested enough to continue so he peered around the tree he was hiding behind to see where the camera was pointing. He once again was lucky it was facing the opposite direction. Smitty moved from tree to tree as the camera rotated back past him. As soon as it had passed his position he made a run for it. Smitty could almost feel the camera turning back in his direction. So he dove into a pile of brush just inside the tree line. As he laid there, he wondered if there might have been other cameras that he hadn't seen. "Naw," he thought, "they would've been looking for me by now if I'd been spotted." He glanced back to where the camera was and saw it rotate away from him so he once again started moving away till he was out of its sight.

Smitty continued along the fence looking for the plant but now using much more caution than before. He didn't want to be spotted though he thought, "I'm still outside of the fence so I shouldn't be on their property." But Smitty was taking no chances. As he made the second corner of the fence he'd already spotted the camera and knew how to avoid it but he still hadn't been able to see the plant. He picked up his pace a little, it was already starting to get later than he'd planned to be gone but just as he made it past the third corner and was safely away from the sight of the camera he heard a dog barking and it sounded like it was heading his way. He decided to retreat deeper into the woods and just watch to see where the dog came from. Within a minute or two Smitty saw a German Shepard inside the fence headed his way. He was leading a guard who was carrying some type of assault rifle. As soon as he could make out the guard Smitty dashed deeper into the woods even though he knew they couldn't get to him through the fence but he also knew the rifle could. Smitty wasn't sure if the guard had spotted him or not but the dog was barking like crazy and he could see the guard using some kind of radio. Smitty figured it would be best if he stayed deep in the woods until he made it back to the truck. "Glass plant my ass," Smitty thought. "I've never seen any glass plant that needed soldiers to guard it." He moved as quickly as his legs would let him. They were tired and burning like they were on fire. He was in pretty good shape but he'd done more running and walking in this one afternoon than he'd done since high school. Finally he saw the black top road and knew he was getting close to the truck.

The Colonel's phone rang and he asked Skipper to excuse him just a minute while he took the call. Skipper stepped into his mother's old office and closed the door.

"Yes Mark," the Colonel said, as he took the call.

"Colonel, we've been over the house every inch of it and the key is no where to be found sir."

"I see, well why don't you start back this way. Let me know once you're back in your office."

"Yes sir, I'll call you then."

Mark decided to start checking for safety deposit boxes and things along that line. When they turned onto plant road, they hadn't gone far when Mark saw the old truck sitting in the turn around.

"Turn in here. I want to check this out," he said to his assistant.

They pulled up beside the truck and could see it was some type of farm truck. McDonald's paper and cups littered the floor and the ash tray was running over. The seat was torn in several places and the floor board had rusted all the way through by the passenger's door. They looked into the back but there was only bark off of some type of trees there and a can of gas. Mark figured that he must have broken down and felt that the man driving was no threat and was probably walking back to town for help. They turned back out onto plant road and hadn't gone far when he got a call on his radio that one of the perimeter guards had spotted someone running away from the fence. He told Mark that one of the security dogs had led him right to the trespasser.

"Was he inside the fence?" he asked, excitedly.

"No sir, he wasn't but when we went out to see if we could track him down all we found was two empty water bottles and a half-eaten bag of chips. The dogs trailed him for a short distance then they lost the scent."

"That's ok, I think I know where he was going," Mark said. "Turn around let's go have another look at that truck."

"Yes sir." And they spun the car around and headed back away from the plant.

"Something's up with this," Mark explained. "Why would someone stake us out just to watch the fence? He couldn't have seen anything else from there."

As they approached the turn around Mark said, "man, it's gone." The old truck had already left.

The Colonel noticed Skipper walking around his mother's old desk and still trying to make heads or tails of what he'd learned. As the Colonel opened the door and walked over to the desk he asked Skipper, "Are you all right?"

"I guess so. It's just a lot to absorb," Skipper said, as he wandered around the room. While Skipper's attention was on a picture of his mother on the wall the Colonel eased over to the desk and placed the photo that he'd forgotten about face down so Skipper wouldn't notice it.

"She was a beautiful woman," the Colonel said, as he turned the photo over.

"Yes she was," Skipper said, as a tear came to his eyes. "I can tell she was the one who furnished this room. It reminded me of her the second I walked in. I can still smell her perfume in here."

"Yes, well she'll never be forgotten that's for sure."

As the Colonel was speaking, one of the radios on a service counter in the corner of the room crackled to life. The Colonel could hear Mark and one of the guards talking about some kind of intruder. The Colonel reached for the radio as he heard Mark talking to Sergeant Bryant asking him did he still have the tag number for the truck that had turned around in front of the plant earlier.

Then the Colonel said, "Skipper why don't I show you where you'll be working?"

"That sounds great, Colonel. Is that your security that's speaking on those radios?"

"Yes it is but I'm sure it's nothing to worry about."

The Colonel clipped the radio on his side so he could keep up with these unusual things that were happenings. He seldom heard of Mark needing someone's tag number so his curiosity was aroused. As the Colonel and Skipper made their way back to the elevator Skipper wondered what else was in store for him. They stepped into the elevator but before the door shut, the Colonel could hear his phone ringing so he asked Skipper to wait here and told him he'd be right back. Skipper pushed the hold button intending to wait on the Colonel in the elevator but as he did the doors closed anyway. Skipper placed his hand on the scanner and the automated voice said, "Access denied." Skipper was shocked so he pushed the button to open the door but again nothing happened. Skipper stood there with his arms crossed and just waited for the Colonel to return.

"Yes," the Colonel said, rather snappily as he answered the phone.

"Sir, we might have a problem."

"Yes I know. I've been listening on the radio. What's going on?"

As Mark explained the situation, the Colonel decided to cut Skipper's visit short and also decided to call George and have him explain to Crystal what she was getting into. Once he'd hung up with Mark, the Colonel dialed George's phone.

"George, this is Colonel Morgan."

"Yes Colonel, what can I do for you."

"Once again I need a favor."

"Anything sir," George said, "I'm at your service."

"Well I need you to take Crystal through a level-C clearance and explain everything that her classification allows her to know."

"Colonel, I don't know…"

"George," the Colonel interrupted, "we might have a situation here and I'm not going to be able to see her tomorrow as planned. I'm even going to cut Skipper Doster's visit short."

"What's going on, Colonel? Anything I can help with?"

"No, not really. I don't even know if it's important or not. Can you handle the debriefing with Crystal?"

"Oh yea, I've been wanting to do that for years anyway."

"Just remember George, level-C classification only ok?"

"Yes sir. I still remember the routine. I'm old, not senile," George said with a laugh, as he hung up the phone.

As the Colonel made his way back to the elevator, he'd forgotten about Skipper not being able to access it. As soon as he got there, he placed his hand on the scanner and the door slid open.

Skipper stood there with his arms crossed and said, "I don't know if I'll like this clearance stuff or not. I can't even work the dang elevator."

The Colonel just laughed as he stepped back in and they headed down.

Skipper asked, "Did the phone call have anything to do with the guards looking for that truck?"

"As a matter of a fact it did, Skipper. I'm afraid I'm gonna have to cut our visit short until we can sort this out."

"That's too bad," Skipper said. "I was really looking forward to seeing where I was gonna be working."

"We can pick it back up tomorrow if you'd like," the Colonel explained, as they exited the elevator onto the first floor. "Just remember Skipper, don't talk to anyone about what you've seen here today."

"I won't say a word, sir," Skipper reassured him, as they entered a room off to the left of the clean room. "Does this lead outside?"

"No it's kind of like a reverse clean room. You walk in the door closes, then the outside door opens into the locker room. It's the door I came out earlier. Then as you step into the locker room the door closes behind you and the room you just left gets decontaminated. I'm afraid you'll have to wait in the locker room for twenty minutes or so until my chauffeur gets here to pick you up. I hope that's ok."

"Yes sir, of course. I understand," Skipper said, as they entered the locker room.

They both started changing back into their street clothes and Skipper remembered his charm in his pocket. Once they were dressed, the young guard Cleveland picked the Colonel up at the door on a golf cart then as they drove away the door slid closed. Skipper placed his hand on the scanner and the door re-opened. "Well at least I can get out," Skipper said to himself.

As Skipper sat on the bench waiting on Amos to return, he got to thinking about his clearance. "I wonder how far a class-C clearance will get me," he thought. He opened the locker where the suits were and stared at them for a minute then decided what the heck, I got a C-clearance. Once he'd gone back through the clean room and reentered the plant Skipper started toward one of the work stations. Skipper noticed what looked like melted drops of glass on the table. He picked up a few pieces and studied them to see if they were the same glass as the upper floor was made of. He couldn't tell just by looking at them but he knew someone who could. Skipper started back to the locker room when he heard someone knocking on the clean room wall. He could see it was Amos and he let of a sigh of relief. He didn't think he'd get in trouble for reentering the plant but he was glad it was just Amos who'd seen him. He placed the droplets of glass in his pocket and made his way back out to where Amos was waiting.

"I can't wait to give Brandon a shot at figuring out what this stuff really is," Skipper thought.

Chapter 6

Pentagon, Washington, D.C.
War Department
Secretary of Defense 0800

"Mrs. Evans, could you step into my office please?"

"Yes Mr. Secretary. Right away."

As the door to his office opened a young blond woman about 24 years old entered his office. She was wearing a blue skirt and white blouse with a blue and white hat. He noticed how particularly attractive she looked today.

"Mrs. Evans, when did this message from Steamway Glass come in?"

"Yesterday afternoon sir," she responded promptly.

"Why wasn't I notified of this? You know everything that comes in from Steamway comes directly to me no matter the time. Especially if it's coded."

"Sir, you'd already left for the afternoon and it's only a class-C message."

"It's a breach in their security and I should've been notified even at home. Understand?"

"Yes sir."

"Get in touch with our people in Alabama. Let me know when you've got them on the line."

"Right away, sir," she said, as she turned to leave his office.

Ten minutes later Mrs. Evans said over his intercom, "Sir, I have security on the line."

"Thank you, Mrs. Evans," he said, as he picked up the receiver.

"Clark, this is John, how are you doing today?"

"Fine sir, what seems to be the problem?"

"We've got a security breach at Steamway. I received a coded message from our man there. It seems someone was watching the plant from the outside perimeter fence. Do we have anyone on assignment there right now?"

"No, Mr. Secretary, we don't"

"I didn't think so. Listen I have a tag number from an old truck that was seen out front by our man. Why don't you check it out for me and let me know who our visitor is?"

"Begging you pardon sir, but Steamway has their own security and if no one got in why would you want to involve us in something this small?"

"It seems Steamway lost a couple of employees a few weeks ago and has already replaced them. I don't need any interference with this project. They're usually quite resourceful but with all that has happened there lately I don't want to take any chances with someone finding out what we really use them for or rather what they do for us."

"Who's our contact at Steamway sir?"

"Clark, who we have inside is not important. I've got all the information you need. Just use caution when you check this out. We don't know who we're really dealing with here."

"Yes sir. I'll be careful. How do you want us to handle it when we find out who it is?"

"Just keep me informed every step of the way, understand?"

"Yes sir. I'll be in touch."

As the Secretary hung up his phone he thought, "I don't need this to go bad now. We're getting too close to the truth."

"Mrs. Evans," the Secretary said, over the intercom, "bring me all the files on Steamway Glass and get me Mr. Morgan on the phone ASAP."

"Yes sir," she said, as she started toward the file room.

"Oh and Mrs. Evans, for the next few weeks anything from our inside man at Steamway comes in you notify me immediately."

In about twenty minutes Mrs. Evans said, "Sir, Mr. Morgan at Steamway on line one for you."

The Secretary hesitated as he reached for the phone, "Mr. Morgan this is John Stearn, how're you doing today?"

"I'm fine Mr. Secretary, is there something I can do for you?"

"No, I was just checking on the progress of our last project."

"Everything's still on schedule sir. We've lost very little time with the loss of our chemical engineer, as a matter fact we've already replaced him."

"That's wonderful, who did you get to replace him?"

"Believe it or not it's his son!"

"His son?" the Secretary said.

"Yes, he seems to be a very qualified young man."

"Well, you seem to have it all under control down there, when should we expect to receive the next shipment?"

"I'm not exactly sure sir. We've got a small problem here that we need to check out before we get everything kicked back off."

"Oh?" the Secretary asked, as if he was shocked to hear this. "What kind of problem?"

"Well sir, nothing major, we had an unauthorized visitor at the perimeter fence yesterday and I want to make sure there was nothing to it."

"Did he see anything important?" the Secretary asked, with a slight bit of worry in his voice.

"Not from the fence sir, but we're going to check him out just the same. Our front gate guard got a tag number. We should be able to track him down soon."

"All right keep me informed. We don't need any more delays. If you need any people to help…"

"That won't be necessary sir, we can handle it from here," the Colonel interrupted.

"Ok, well let's stay in touch."

Mr. Morgan sat at his desk with his fingers laced together thinking of the unusual phone call he'd just received. He seldom ever heard from the Secretary of Defense and it was usually only when there was trouble, but how did he know they were having trouble? He'd been informed of the deaths of Cindy and Stephen Doster but it was strange that he'd call the day after there had been a security break. How could he have known?

Colonel Morgan placed a call to Sergeant Bryant at the front gate to see if anyone else knew about the visitor they'd had yesterday.

"Yes sir, I called Mark and let him know. Mark told me he'd check it out himself and for me not to worry about it so I just let it go!"

"That's fine, has Mark found out anything yet?"

"I don't know sir. I haven't heard from him today."

"When he checks in, have him to get in touch with me right away," Mr. Morgan said sternly.

"Yes sir," the Sergeant replied.

"Skipper, are you home?" Smitty yelled, as he came through the front door.

"Yea, I'm upstairs. Come on up."

Smitty started up the stairs hitting only every other step as he went. He found Skipper in his father's study sitting at the desk looking over some paperwork.

"So what's all this?" Smitty asked, as he stood looking over Skipper's shoulder.

"I'm just going over my father's notes from work trying to make sense of what he actually did."

"How did things go at the plant yesterday?" Smitty said, smiling.

"It went ok but my interview got cut short. It seems someone tried to break in or something."

"Whatcha mean by break in?"

"Well, a guard radioed that he'd seen someone running away from the back fence and the Colonel was worried about security."

"You didn't find out what your father did there?" Smitty asked, in a disappointed voice.

"I found out a lot more than I could have ever imagined."

"What does that mean?"

"I can't say," Skipper said, as he turned to look at Smitty.

"Why not? I thought that is why you were going. So we'd know what all goes on in there?"

"No," Skipper said, "I went for a job interview. But I found out that everything there's just like my father had said one big secret"

"Yeah that's what I gathered," Smitty said

Skipper started to look away then stopped as what Smitty said hit him, "What do you mean by that Smitty?"

"By what?" he asked, with a smile that reminded you of the cat that just ate the canary.

"It was you, wasn't it?" Skipper scolded."You were the one at the fence. The one that was seen running away."

"Why would you think it was me?"

"I know you, Smitty. Why did you follow me?"

"Hey, I was just watching your back old buddy. And besides they don't know it was me."

"How did you get past the gates?"

"That place ain't no glass plant is it, Skipper?" Smitty said boldly. "It's some kind of military operation right?"

"No, it's a glass plant."

"Yeah right. Then why do the guards carry M-16 rifles and why do they use cameras to watch the fence? Did you know they also have dogs that they use? That's no glass plant Skipper!" Smitty snapped back.

"Yes it is and I'll prove it to you but you've got to promise me that whatever we find out stays with us. I mean these people are for real. I think if they knew I took some of the glass out of there they would have a cow. We could both be in a lot of trouble."

"You mean you got some of the stuff that they make there?" Smitty asked sarcastically. "I mean you've had a piece of it around your neck since we were kids. Why would they care if you picked up some scrap glass?"

Skipper just kind of looked at him then, said, "Do you think we could get Brandon to analyze it for me?"

"I don't see why not. He'd love any new challenge but if you're telling me the truth then it's just glass."

Skipper started to speak then stopped and thought about what the Colonel had told him about someone else finding out.

Then he said, "It's not just glass plus it's not all they do there. They have some kind of government contract that I would've found out more about if you wouldn't have pulled your stunt yesterday."

"Hey don't blame me. I was just looking out for you. Besides no harm done. I got away smooth."

"Well?" Skipper asked, "What did you see?"

"Nothing," Smitty said, "but I got plenty of exercise."

"I have the address you asked for, sir. The tag is registered to a William (Billy) Smith at 120 Bradley Drive in Coosada, Alabama. We can be there in about twenty minutes."

"Ok," Clark Johnson said, as he checked his Beretta.40 caliber to make sure it was loaded, "let's see who this guy is."

They were in a black Ford headed west on highway 14 out of Wetumpka. Clark knew the Secretary of Defense, John Stearn, wanted this to be a clean sweep but he needed to find out what this Billy wanted at Steamway and what he knew about the place.

"Listen to me, Andy," Clark said, "this don't need to get too messy too fast. We need to question this guy understand?"

"Perfectly," Andy said.

Clark Johnson and Andy Tillman had been on clean sweeps together before and Clark knew Andy was quick to resolve the problem before a witness or suspect could be questioned.

"I want you to use plenty of patience when we get there. Do I make myself clear?" Clark said.

"Yes sir, I understand."

As they traveled west they passed a small airport and knew that they weren't very far from the address that they'd received earlier. "It should be just up ahead, sir. It's in some kinda trailer-park so there will probably be other people around."

"Does he have a family?" Clark asked. Not because he cared about kids, he just wanted to make sure no one surprised him once they arrived.

"Only a brother and a cousin. The brother lives in Texas and the cousin in Millbrook about six miles away."

"Ok, we shouldn't have any problems. Let's get this over with."

As they arrived at the address, they spotted the old truck right away. It was parked to the right of a mobile home that must have been ten years old. They parked in the driveway and Clark said, "Are you ready?"

"I'm always ready for this kinda stuff, sir," Andy replied, with a grin from cheek to cheek.

"Mark, this is Colonel Morgan. Have you found out anything about our unauthorized visitor yesterday?"

"Very little sir. But I do have a name and address. I thought I would pay him a visit this morning."

"Who is he?" the Colonel asked.

"According to central records his name is Billy Smith. He lives over by the airport in Elmore. All we know about him is that he's on disability and sells firewood through the winter."

"Any connections with us in any way?" the Colonel asked.

"None I can find yet, sir, but we're not through checking."

"Ok, well keep me informed. Oh and by the way Mark, who all knows about this? I had a call this morning that makes me wonder if we don't have someone here reporting to the Secretary of Defense. He seemed to already know about our visitor."

"Only the security staff, sir. I can find out exactly who but almost all I'm sure. They all carry radios," Mark explained.

"See me once you've checked out this Billy Smith. Let's get this all taken care of today."

"Yes sir. I'll be back in touch this afternoon."

As the Colonel hung up, he wondered who could be the informant and how he could find out for sure.

Skipper and Smitty took the '69 Mustang back over to Smitty's house. This was by far Skipper's favorite car. He and his father had taken a whole summer to restore the old car. It had a 289 bored out to a 302 with a holly 4-barrel carburetor. They'd done all the bodywork and painted the car themselves. They'd thought about trying to do the interior work but decided against it. They painted the car metallic blue and used black pin striping. It would out run most cars like it and was the best looking car in town. Skipper and Smitty had put many miles on it since they'd finished the work but now it mostly stayed in the garage.

They arrived at Smitty's to find Lisa out in the yard working in the flowerbeds. She loved to work the dirt and watch the flowers grow. She stood up as Skipper and Smitty turned into the driveway and she waved to them.

"I see you two are still friends," Lisa said, with a laugh. "I figured you'd be mad after Smitty told you he followed you yesterday."

Skipper looked at Smitty as if Smitty hadn't told him and Lisa thought she'd told her husband's secret before he'd had a chance to. They both looked back at her and started laughing.

She said, "You two drive me crazy sometimes," and she turned to go inside.

Smitty said, "Hey babe, where's Brandon? "

"Where do you think? He's down in the basement messing with all that junk. Why, what have you two got up your sleeves?"

"Skipper's got some glass for him to look at. He took it from the plant yesterday."

"Oh yeah what happened there yesterday?"

"Let's go see Brandon first then we can talk."

"Daddy, I can't believe what you're telling me!" Crystal said excitedly. "You mean that you've known about this all these years and you never told me or mom."

"You have to understand Crystal, you can never say anything to anyone about the things you'll hear and see in Steamway. I was one of the original employees there and after you've been there for a while you'll understand much more than I could ever tell you."

"You mean there's more?" Crystal asked, as she walked to the window that over looked the backyard.

"Yes baby, there's much more but you'll only be given a class-C security clearance and right now this is all I can tell you."

"So what if I don't take the job now dad. Then what?"

"I suspect you'll take it but even if you don't the things we've discussed will have to stay between us."

"I don't know dad, you're telling me I'll be part of a group that has the ability to watch me 24 hours a day plus they manufacture some stuff for the government."

"Yes but like I told you, what Steamway does for the government is just simply for the funding. They know little about what and why we do what we do."

"What exactly is it that 'we' do?"

"I've told you I can't tell you that yet. You'll learn as you go," George answered, choosing to ignore the emphasis she'd placed on "we."

"When do I get to go to see this 'magical world of Steamway' dad?"

"Tomorrow morning the Colonel will send his car for you."

"Dad, I can drive myself."

"No, you can't. You've got too much security to go through and the best way is to use the Colonel's car."

"What're they going to do, pick me up every morning?" Crystal said, with a sneer in her voice.

"No after the first time you go in, they will have you in the system and you can just use the scanners to enter the plant."

"What scanners?" Crystal asked.

"You'll see tomorrow, baby. Just trust your old man. You'll love Steamway. It'll be like coming home."

Billy looked out his front window and saw the government Ford pull up in his yard. He had no idea what they wanted there. He thought, "They must be at the wrong place," as he went to the door to meet them. Clark Johnson was the first to reach the house with Andy Tillman close behind. As they approached, the front door came open and a short balding man about 180 lbs. stepped onto the front porch.

"Are you William Smith?" Clark asked, with his badge in his hand.

"Yeah I am. What seems to be the problem?"

"Maybe nothing, sir. May we come in and speak with you for a minute?"

Not thinking anything about Smitty borrowing his truck the day before, he said, "Sure come on in."

Both agents went inside the trailer behind Billy. The trailer, you could tell was a bachelor's pad. Nothing was in its place. Empty beer bottles sat on the coffee table and books and magazines were strewed from one end of the living room to the other. The kitchen sink was piled full of dishes that needed washing and the house smelled of old wine and beer.

"You fellows have a seat," Billy said, as he shuffled books and newspaper off the couch. Both agents sat down and Billy sat across from them in his recliner.

"What can I do for you boys?" Billy asked, smiling

"We've got a few questions we need to ask you."

"What kind of questions?"

"Well we need to know where you were at yesterday from about 10:00 a.m. until 6:00 p.m."

"Why?" Billy asked.

"Mr. Smith, we'll ask you the questions. You just answer."

Billy didn't like the attitude that the agents took with him so he asked, "Just who are you people?"

"We're with national security sir. Please answer the questions."

"I ain't answering nothing until you tell me what this is all about!"

Clark looked at Andy and then he said, "Well your truck was seen at a secured plant of ours yesterday and we want to know what you were doing there."

Billy said, "I wasn't there. I was here all day yesterday."

"Well sir, your truck was there so who was driving it?"

"That's for me to know and you to find out," Billy said, sarcastically.

When the agents saw he wasn't going to cooperate Andy stood up and said, "Sir, you can tell us what we want to know or we have ways of finding out."

"Andy, calm down," Clark said.

"You two can't play good-cop, bad-cop with me. You don't scare me at all," Billy said, as he stood up.

When he did Andy Tillman pulled his gun and said, "I don't want you to be scared. A scared man runs and a moving target is harder to hit!"

Smitty and Skipper found Brandon down in the basement as usual working on something that only he could have possibly understood.

"Hi dad," he said, as they came through the basement door. "What's up?"

"I have a project for you that I think you'll enjoy," Smitty said.

"I'm kind of busy right now dad. Can it wait until next week?"

"Oh I don't think you'll want to wait," Skipper added.

This drew Brandon's curiosity. "What is it?" he asked, excitedly

"I need you to find out what this glass is made of," Skipper said, as he handed the small droplets to Brandon.

"Sand. Most glass is," he said, as he laughed.

"I don't think this is your run of the mill glass," Skipper told him, as Brandon took the sample from him.

"Ok I'll check for you. Is that all?"

"Well you can check out my charm too. It's probably the same thing but I just want to make sure."

"Where did these come from?" Brandon asked, as he placed the small bits in a dish.

"They make it at the place I'm going to start to work. How long will it take?" Skipper asked.

"Not long. I'll let you know something in an hour or so."

"That's great. Why don't we get Lisa to fix us some lunch while we wait?" Smitty said. "Brandon, do you want anything?"

"No, I just had a sandwich."

"Ok, call us when you know something."

"Ok dad," Brandon said, as Smitty and Skipper started back up the stairs.

Brandon sat down behind his desk where he usually worked and studied the bits of glass that Skipper had given him

"You guys want a beer?" Lisa asked, as they walked into the kitchen where she was working on lunch.

"I would," Smitty said.

"Yea me too," Skipper added.

Sitting at the table, Smitty said, "So what's this place like on the inside?"

"Quiet," Skipper said, "I mean no noise at all and I didn't see a single person."

"On Tuesday," Smitty said, "they weren't working, that don't make any sense at all."

"Yea I know but we got 'interrupted' before I could ask about it."

"Ok, rub it in, I know I screwed up but you'll get another chance!"

Skipper didn't want to say anything about the upper floor of the building or the fact that it was three stories under ground and two above. Smitty was his best friend but he just talked too much.

He was worried that Steamway would find out about Smitty being the one there and that could be trouble.

They sat and ate their BLT's that Lisa had fixed and had a couple of beers but Skipper wouldn't talk much about what he'd seen. After they finished lunch, Lisa said she was going to go back outside to finish her work in the flower beds. As she started out the door, Brandon came running up the basement stairs calling Smitty and Skipper very excitedly.

"Hey guys, check this out!"

They both stood and started to follow him back downstairs. Brandon said, "You ain't gonna believe this."

"Why?" Smitty asked. "What kind of glass is it?"

"That's just it, dad. It ain't glass at all, its metal!"

Mark told his second-in-command, Twan Golson, to get the suits so they could go check out Billy Smith's place and see what he was doing at the plant. By the time they left Steamway it was already around 2pm and Mark knew that Billy should be at home. They only had about a 30 minute drive to the address he'd gotten from Sargent Bryant. Once they arrived, Mark told Twan to stay with the car and he'd question Billy himself, but to keep his radio on and while he was inside to put his suit on. He'd let Twan know if he needed him to come in but he didn't see any need for it right now. They would both come back later when Billy wasn't home and use the suits to check out the house better.

Mark said, "This place don't look like a place somebody would live who would be snooping around the plant to me!"

"Me neither," Twan said, as Mark closed the door and started toward the house.

He made his way up to the porch which creaked as he stepped on the first step. Mark knocked about three quick times but no one came to the door. He could hear a dog barking at one of the neighbor's house but he didn't pay it much attention. After the third knock, Mark tried the doorknob and found it to be unlocked. He didn't open the door but instead returned to the car where Twan was waiting. He already had the suit on and was watching the street for anyone who might notice them parked there.

Mark said, "I'll stay with the car. You go have a quick look inside, the door is unlocked. Just keep your radio on and I'll let you know if he comes back home."

Twan exited the car and crossed the yard to the trailer. As he opened the front door, he knew something wasn't right. The first thing he saw was an empty 40-caliber round lying on the floor just inside the door. Twan took his radio and told Mark what he'd found and Mark told him to be careful but to still check it out. He stepped on into the living room and there he saw Billy's body lying on the floor next to the entrance to the kitchen.

Twan said, "Boss, we got a problem, you better get in here!"

Mark got out of the car and dropped his keys on the ground. As he bent down to pick them up, he spotted what appeared to be blood on the ground. He ran into the house to find Twan coming out of his suit and pointing to Billy's body lying next to a 12-gauge shotgun on the floor.

"What the heck happened here boss?" Twan asked.

"I don't know, but it looks like he put up one hell of a fight. There's blood outside on the ground and that shotgun has been fired. There's an empty shell over there by the table."

As they looked closer at the body, Mark noticed that two of Billy's fingers had been cut off!

"Someone beat us here," Mark said, "but it looks like Billy got a piece of them!"

Chapter 7

"Mr. Secretary, this is Clark Johnson."

"Yes Clark, how did things go?"

"Not so well sir, we've got a small problem."

"How small?" the Secretary asked, with a bit of roughness in his voice.

"Well sir, I had a man injured."

"To hell with your man, what does this Smith know?"

"Nothing we could find out sir. We went in to question him and he became very uncooperative. We started to lean on him and he grabbed for a gun and we were forced to shoot him."

"Dang it, what did you find out?" the Secretary asked.

"After some pressure he did tell us that he'd lent his truck to his cousin yesterday but we couldn't get a name. I mean this guy was tough but he didn't look like anyone we'd need to worry about."

"How did your guy get injured?" the Secretary asked, with a little more calmness in his voice.

"After we finished questioning him, we had full intentions of taking him with us, since he'd already lost a couple of fingers but we got distracted by a dog barking next door. Smith dove for a gun that we hadn't seen by the bar in the kitchen. He was hit three times before he reached it but still managed to get a shot off. He hit my partner in the upper part of the shoulder and part of his face."

"I hope you had the mess cleaned up, Mr. Johnson," the Secretary said.

"Well sir, we sent a clean-up team in right away, but when they arrived, two men from Steamway were already there. That's why I'm calling you, to see what you would have us do next? The men from Steamway have already left but I know they saw the body!"

"How is your man doing? Is he ok?"

"Yes sir, he'll be fine but in the hospital for a while."

"That's good, listen to me carefully, Clark. I want you to go ahead with the cleanup and I'll handle Steamway's people. Do you understand?"

"Yes sir. I'll take care of it right away."

"Good. Make sure no one in the area saw or heard anything. Do a routine investigation after you're done with the cleanup."

"No problem Mr. Secretary, but no one around seemed to be home so I don't think we've a problem with that. I'll send the cleanup in right after dark."

"Thank you, Mr. Johnson. Stay in touch."

Colonel Morgan was asleep in his office when he got the call from Mark.

"Sir, it seems someone else was interested in Mr. Smith more than us."

"Why, what do you mean Mark?"

"When we arrived sir, the front door was unlocked so I sent Twan in and he found Mr. Smith's body on the floor next to the kitchen. He'd been shot several times and two of his fingers had been cut off."

"I see, well that could only mean two things. Either he didn't get the information he was supposed to or someone wanted the information he'd gotten."

"Sir, neither him nor his place seemed like someone who would need any information about us. I don't think he was there to spy on us."

"Then what was he here for Mark?"

"I don't know sir, but we're still not finished with his background check, and sir."

"Yes Mark."

"This job was government all the way."

"You think the government killed Billy Smith?"

"No doubt about it sir. Too dirty for anyone else. They didn't care who saw or heard anything."

"I don't know Mark, if it was the government there wouldn't have been nothing left for you to find."

"Yes sir, that's the only part that I don't understand."

"Head back here Mark. We can sort through all of this when you get back."

"On my way sir. Oh and Colonel."

"Yes Mark."

"It looks like he put up one heck of a fight. There was blood in the front yard and he'd fired a shotgun at somebody. I think he got a pretty good piece of one of them. So we should be checking out the local hospital to see…"

"No just come on back. If it was government, they won't be at a civilian hospital."

"Yes sir, on my way."

"What do you mean metal Brandon? You can see through it."

"Yea I know and that's not all. You see it has been changed on a molecular level. This is metal but you can see through it just like glass."

"How is that possible?" Skipper asked.

"It's not, at least not yet but that is not why I called you down here. You see theoretically this is possible but it's never been done. At least not until now, but what is so amazing is that all these pieces, droplets as you called them have a specific design to them. Kind of like a jigsaw puzzle."

"You mean each of those tiny pieces can be put together?"

"Not just put together, but put together to form something strong."

"Strong, how so son? We don't understand."

"Well dad, it's like this. Kevlar, bullet-proof vests."

"Yes I know what Kevlar is."

"Well they're about a half an inch thick right?"

"I guess so."

"This stuff is only 1/100 of an inch thick and has twice the strength of Kevlar."

"So you think it's used in bullet-proof vests?" Skipper asked.

"No more like tank armor. Plus by being metal it has electrical properties."

"Meaning exactly what?" Smitty said.

"Meaning it's like being full of wires. They could use this for, well there are thousands of possibilities…"

"Like projecting a picture," Skipper said, as he turned away.

"Yea like that," Brandon said. Brandon and his father both noticed Skipper's sudden concern in what they'd learned.

"You see," Brandon said, "I think that being 'bullet-proof' is the least of what it could be used for. This stuff is light enough that you could coat your clothing in it and all your clothes would be 'bullet-proof' but you'd need an oxygen tank with you because it's also airtight when it's placed together right and very flexible."

"At least that would be the theory."

Smitty looked at Skipper and Skipper kind of just turned away.

"What about my charm, Brandon. Is it the same?" Skipper asked.

"I don't know yet. I was so excited about all of this that I'd forgotten all about it but I'll start to work on it now."

Brandon went right to work on the necklace and Smitty and Skipper started back upstairs. Once they got back to the kitchen table Smitty looked at Skipper and said, "You already knew about it didn't you?"

Skipper just picked up his warm beer and took a long swallow, "No, I didn't know. I thought it was glass."

"That's not what I mean, Skipper," Smitty snapped. "I mean about the strength of this stuff and how it's being used."

"Being used?" Skipper said."Who said it was being used. He said it was possible but not probable."

"You saw something yesterday Skipper, maybe you ain't supposed to tell me but you know something. I mean metal that you can see through. What kind of company is this?"

Brandon was down in the basement for the rest of the afternoon without coming out. They'd checked on him a couple of times but he'd just told them, "No results yet."

At about 7:30 p.m. Brandon came upstairs and sat down at the table with his father and Skipper. He said, "Well, this gets better by the minute."

Lisa came in and was cleaning up in the kitchen when the phone rang. She answered it and stood listening for a second then both her eyes filled with tears. Smitty stood up and walked over to her as she hung up the phone. She said, "That was Ted, Billy's neighbor. Billy's trailer burnt tonight. He died in the fire."

Smitty couldn't believe what he'd just heard. Skipper stood and walked over to them. Smitty just dropped his head as Brandon came to him and wrapped his arms around him.

It was after midnight before they left Billy's place. The fire marshal had told Smitty, being the next of kin, that there were some suspicious circumstances and he'd be in touch.

The next morning Skipper had to be at Steamway so he told Smitty he was going home but if he needed him just to call. They said goodbye and as Skipper turned to leave.

"Heh Skipper," Smitty said, as he was looking at Billy's truck, "you don't think Steamway could have had anything to do with this do you?"

"How could they? They don't know who you are."

"Yeah but yesterday when I came to the plant. I used Billy's truck."

The next morning Skipper got ready for work but as he dressed he couldn't help but think that he was forgetting something. He went to the Florida room to have breakfast like he did most mornings and thought about the events of the day before. It was hard for him to imagine that Colonel Morgan would've anything to do with Billy's death. As he sat in deep thought he couldn't believe his parents would work for someone who would murder people just because they tried to get a look at the plant.

Once he'd finished his orange juice, he looked at the clock and decided to give the Colonel a call before he started to the plant. The

Colonel hadn't told him when to come back to work but he was ready to get started.

The Colonel's phone rang but he got no answer so he decided to use his private phone number that the Colonel had given him when they first met. He dialed the number and the phone rang.

Amos had already picked Crystal up for her job interview and was headed to the plant when the phone in the car rang. Amos answered it and said, "Yes sir, I have her in the car with me now."

He raised the privacy window between the front and rear seat where Crystal couldn't hear the conversation. Just as the window closed the phone in the back seat rang and Crystal looked at Amos as he continued to talk on the phone in the front. Crystal kind of just shrugged her shoulders and picked up the phone, "Hello," she said.

"Who's speaking please?" Skipper asked.

"This is Crystal. Colonel Morgan's not here right now. Can I take a message for him?" she replied.

"Yes, this is Skipper Doster and I was wondering if he wanted me to come in to work today or not."

"Ok Skipper, as soon as I see him I'll ask him. Does he have your number?"

"Yeah he does. Are you his secretary?" Skipper asked.

"Well maybe, I'm going for my interview today."

"You sound like me. I just started as well and if I know the Colonel you're in his car with a nice man named Amos. Am I right?"

"I guess so. I'm in his car anyway but the chauffeur hasn't introduced his self yet."

Skipper laughed, "Well he will."

Amos looked in the rear view and saw Crystal on the phone as he hung up the front phone. He let the window down and asked who she was speaking with.

"Hold on please," Crystal told Skipper, as she looked at Amos. "He said his name is Skipper Doster and wants to know if he should come in to work today or not."

"Crystal, please ask Skipper to try the Colonel back at his office. He can answer him."

Crystal told Skipper to call the Colonel at the office and he told her thanks and hung up.

Amos said, "Crystal, please don't answer the Colonel's personal line. He'd be very angry."

"Well you were on the phone and I couldn't get your attention. I meant no harm."

"Oh I think everything will be fine. Just please let me answer if it rings again."

"Ok," Crystal said, "who is Skipper Doster? He sounded cute."

"All I can say is that he's a new employee at the plant, same as you."

"I'm not an employee yet," Crystal said.

Amos just smiled and said, "Yeah I know but I'm sure you'll soon be."

As she sat alone in the back of the car, she thought. 'Skipper Doster' I can't wait to meet him.

As Skipper hung up the phone, he wondered what the girl with the angel's voice looked like. He'd never had a serious relationship with anyone but just this girl's voice excited him. What was so different about her? He couldn't wait to meet Crystal.

Around 11:30 a.m. Smitty received a call from the sheriff's office. It was from an investigator named Carpenter.

"Mr. Smith, could you come down to the station, I've got a few questions that I need you to answer."

"Sure," Smitty said, "I can be there in about twenty minutes or so."

"That'll be fine, Mr. Smith"

As Smitty left for the station he wondered what all kind of questions he'd have to answer. He didn't know if he'd say anything to them about borrowing Billy's truck and going to Steamway or not, so he called Skipper on his cell phone to ask his opinion. When Skipper answered the phone, he seemed to have a light jingle to his voice.

"Hey buddy, what's going on?"Skipper asked.

"I'm headed to the police station to answer some questions about Billy,"

"Why do they want to question you?"

"I don't know, do you think I should mention anything about using Billy's truck?"

"Only if they ask, don't offer them any information."

"I'm not, what about you, have you got to work today?"

"I don't know yet. I just called the Colonel's car and got the finest sounding girl I've ever heard."

"Who was she?" Smitty asked.

"She said her name was Crystal. She's starting to work with the plant today, so I hope to get to meet her soon!"

"Well I'll call you when I leave the station."

"Ok man, if I'm at work leave me a message."

"Yea all right, see ya," Smitty said.

Smitty pulled up into the police station parking lot and saw a man in plain clothes waiting on him.

"Are you Mr. Smith?"

"Yes sir, I am."

"Come with me please, we can go into my office and talk."

As they entered the building there was a buzz about the place like bees on honey. Smitty knew that this small town station shouldn't be this busy. Once they got into Mr. Carpenter's office he pointed to a chair on the opposite side of his desk and said, "Have a seat. This shouldn't take long."

Smitty sat down and Carpenter offered him some coffee.

"No thanks, "Smitty said. "What's going on."

"Mr. Smith, do you know of anyone who might want your cousin Billy dead?"

"No of course not. Why? I thought he died in a fire."

"Well sir. The fire wasn't the cause of death."

"What?" Smitty asked.

Ignoring his question Mr. Carpenter asked, "Did your cousin owe anyone any large amounts of money?"

"No, Not that I know of. Why don't you tell me what's going on here? And I could answer your questions better."

"Did he ever have dealings with drugs?"

Smitty just crossed his arms and looked across the desk at Mr. Carpenter without saying a word. Carpenter nodded his head and stood up. He got a file out of his drawer and threw it on the desk in front of Smitty. Then he began, "Your cousin was murdered."

"Murdered!" Smitty exclaimed. "How?"

"He was shot at least four times and we found traces of some kind of fuel used to start the fire that burned his trailer."

As Smitty looked through the folder. He couldn't believe the things he was being told, "Shot," he said.

"According to all we've found out it looks like he got a shot or two off himself. Now if there's anything you can tell me that might lead me to catching his killer…"

"I can't tell you anything," Smitty said, as he interrupted. "Billy was a great guy and I can't think of anyone who wanted to hurt him for any reason."

"Well sir, we don't think it was robbery."

"Why not?" asked Smitty.

"Because they cut two of his fingers off before they killed him. Now are you sure you can't think of anyone who might be out to get him."

"Only Steamway Glass," Smitty thought, to himself.

Crystal couldn't believe the security that she had to go through just to get into the plant but once inside she found herself in a locker room where the Colonel was waiting.

"Ah Crystal, good to see you," the Colonel said. "We just have a few things to go over and we can go to my office."

"What things?" she asked.

"Well, I have to show you how to go through the 'clean room' but don't worry we've got a privacy screen you'll be able to use as we go through."

She was glad. She didn't like the idea of getting naked in front of a total stranger.

After they exited the 'clean room' he led her to what would be her office.

"This is where you'll be working. I hope everything suits you."

"This is a lovely office sir. I'm sure it will do fine."

"Crystal," the Colonel said.

"Yes Colonel."

"You haven't said anything about us being on the second floor yet. Haven't you noticed anything strange about that?"

She kind of laughed and said, "You mean like there isn't a second floor on this building?"

"Yeah I guess you've noticed."

"My father told me what to expect," she said, as she sat down at Cindy Doster's old desk. "What all will I be doing, Colonel?" She raised a picture that was laying face down on the desk and studied it.

"You'll handle everything pretty much. All the paperwork for the government and such. I thought your father had already explained…"

"He did, is this him by you in this picture?"

"Yes we were very close then."

"Man, you guys were so much younger then and what kind of plane is that all of you are standing in front of?"

"Just a plane I used to command years ago and those people in that picture were my crew."

"My father never told me about his military career."

"Well Crystal, what we did was kind of like Steamway 'Top secret'."

"Where was this taken?" Crystal asked.

The Colonel just looked at her and smiled.

"You mean I can know that you can make a building invisible but you can't tell me where a picture was taken?" Crystal said.

"You'll know soon enough, Crystal."

Her next question caught the Colonel by surprise, "Who is Skipper Doster and where does he work?"

"How do you know about Skipper?" the Colonel asked.

"He called when I was in your car and you were on the phone with Amos. He wanted to know if you wanted him to come in today or not."

"I'll give him a call. You'll meet him soon but not today."

As the Colonel showed Crystal what all was expected of her she wondered why her father hadn't told her about being in the military.

Chapter 8

Smitty dialed Skipper's phone number and the answering machine picked up, "Skipper it's me pick up if your home," Smitty said, as he drove away from the station. Nothing.

Then, "Hey man," Skipper said, as he answered the phone.

"He was murdered Skipper. Somebody shot him."

"What?" Skipper said, as he sat up on the couch where he'd been taking a nap.

"Yeah, the cops told me he was shot at least four times then the trailer was burnt down around him."

"Did they ask you about using his truck?"

"No they think he either owed somebody lots of money or he was involved in drugs."

"Not Billy," Skipper said. "He worked too hard for what little he had."

"Yeah I know. It had to be Steamway Skipper!"

"That's just hard for me to believe, I mean I know their security is tight but murder just don't seem to fit in. My parents loved their jobs and they would never have been involved in something like that. Why don't you come by and pick me up? We can talk then, like they told me, they could be listening now. Besides I want to see Brandon. He still has my harm."

"Ok I 'll be by in about ten minutes."

When Smitty arrived Skipper was ready to go. He jumped in Smitty's car and they drove back out the drive toward Smitty's house.

Skipper said, "I'm sorry Smitty. I know how close you two were."

"I can't help but think it was my fault. If I wouldn't have borrowed his truck then he'd probably still is alive."

"You still think Steamway had something to do with it?" Skipper asked.

"Who else?" Smitty said, as he looked harshly at Skipper.

"You don't know that…"

"I knew something was wrong from the start of all this," Smitty interrupted, "Now my stupidity has gotten Billy killed and Lord knows who else. My whole family could be in danger if they got Billy to talk."

"To talk? What're you saying Smitty? You think they questioned him?"

"No! They tortured him. He had two of his fingers cut off."

"It couldn't have anything to do with Steamway but I'll find out. Next time I'm in the plant I'll do some snooping around."

"You just be careful Skipper. You could be next."

They turned into Smitty's driveway and parked the car. As they started toward the house Brandon, coming out met them.

"Hey dad, I've been waiting on you two to get here! I've got more you should see!"

"I don't know how much more I can take," Skipper said, as Smitty led him into the house.

"What's up now, Brandon?" Smitty asked, as they headed down into the basement.

"You know Uncle Skipper's good luck charm? Well it ain't glass either."

"I know," Smitty said, "it's metal right."

"Kind of," Brandon said, "but that's not all."

"Well," Skipper said, "what is it?"

"I'm not positive Uncle Skipper but I think it's some kind of key!"

"A key to what, Brandon?"

"I don't have a clue but I'll bet you one thing, there ain't no more like it, not yet anyway."

Crystal expected the Colonel's phone to ring through her office first for her to patch calls through to him but she noticed right away that it didn't happen that way. The Colonel was sitting at his desk when the phone rang right into his office. Crystal was sitting at her desk going over some files for shipments that went to the war department for a chemical that could simply be painted on and would form a safety barrier against many different things from water to bullets to heat. She could see the Colonel talking on the phone to someone but didn't really pay any attention to what it was even though she could hear some of the conversation. As she looked through the documents, she found out that the chemical was called 'liquid steel' and was used on the heat shields of the space shuttles and in many types of armor. She couldn't find any documents on any glass or other products that Steamway might make other than a project called 'sound wave' which was supposed to be completed in about a year. There were many invoices where shipments had been made to the Department of Defense but all were small quantities of 'liquid steel'. There had been many payment advances made for the project 'sound wave' but nothing had ever been shipped or as best she could tell, never been demonstrated except one time when the project first began. It was only a video when Steamway showed the Department of Defense what the theory behind 'soundwave' was.

Crystal found a list of employees that received payroll from Steamway and to her it was surprisingly small. Her father's name was still on the list! This also surprised her. She knew he'd retired years before and didn't know he still received a check from them.

What she found to be most strange though was the fact that all the people who worked at Steamway, except for a few security personnel, also lived on-site. Only five people were listed to live off the property. They were her father, Colonel Morgan, Cindy and Stephen Doster and Dexter Cleveland. When she saw the list, she recognized the name Doster from talking to Skipper earlier in the day and figured they must be related. As she looked through the list, she couldn't find Skipper's name anywhere. He didn't apparently live on-site so she figured he must still live with his parents. Another amazing thing she discovered is that all the people living on-sight didn't have a set salary rate. They just filled out requests for amounts of money that they needed, which in her opinion was very little for someone to live on. Then after a while she found out why. Steamway took care of all their bills including food and all room and board.

Stephen Doster was the highest paid employee at the company but she couldn't find a single check stub for Cindy. This was also confusing. She wanted to meet Skipper so she took down the house address and phone number and then decided to ask the Colonel about all she'd found.

She saw the Colonel hang up the phone and decided to question him about the other employees she hadn't met yet. When she entered his office, he held up a finger as to say wait a minute so she just stood there and bided her time. Once he was finished with his paper work she asked him about the requests for money and why no one received a regular check.

"Well Crystal, they need nothing we don't furnish for them," the Colonel said. "We just give them whatever they ask for. You'll soon meet all of them. You'll see they very seldom leave the plant."

"Why is that, Colonel?" Crystal asked.

"It's just policy. They can come and go as they please but choose to stay on-grounds most of the time. We've everything they need here. From entertainment to food and supplies. Most have no interest in the outside world. They have been with us since the start and going out just don't seem right for them."

"Well what about my father and the Doster's?" she asked.

"Your father and Stephen and Cindy just decided that they would live off-grounds."

"Well what about Skipper?" she asked.

"He's a new hire and will be asked to live here as well but I think he will keep his parent's house. They passed away a couple of weeks ago."

"So does Skipper live alone?" she asked.

"As far as I know yes. Why do you ask?"

"To be honest with you he sounded cute on the phone and I would like to meet him," she said.

"I see," the Colonel said. "Skipper's a good kid. He's about your age and I hope that you can do as good a job here as his mother did."

"I don't think that will be problem, sir. She kept very good records. It just don't seem like much product is going out of here to be able to support this kind of business."

The Colonel just laughed and said, "Our product is very expensive. We don't have money problems."

"Yes sir, I can see that. Can you answer me another question?" she asked.

"What's that, Crystal?"

"What is 'sound wave'?"

The Colonel looked puzzled and said, "Don't worry about that."

"I'm sorry sir, it just seems the government is paying a lot of money for research for something that we don't have any data on yet."

"We've got plenty. It's just classified. Just remember curiosity killed the cat Crystal. There are some things you don't need to ever do until you've a class-A clearance and the biggest thing is don't ever go through my files in those cabinets," he said, as he pointed to a set of file cabinets in the corner of his office, "those are class-A only."

"Yes sir. Will I be taking your calls or do all of them come straight to you?"

"You're very observant Crystal. No," the Colonel said, "you're not a secretary. I handle all my own calls, you only handle plant business. Most of my calls are security anyway. You handle all advances for the employees and keep records of outgoing and incoming products. You set your own business hours and your pay stays the same no matter how long you work each day. I prefer if you live on-site but it's not necessary yet. Your father can explain more later. Right now I've got some security business to attend to, so if you'll excuse me."

"Yes sir, it's almost time to go home anyway. I guess I'll see you in the morning and maybe get to meet other employees."

"Ok Crystal, I'll see you in the morning at 0800."

Crystal turned to leave the room to go back to her office and glanced at the file cabinets that were class-A accessible and wondered what they held. Once back in her office she picked up the Doster's number and put it in her pocket. This guy 'Skipper' she had to meet.

"What do you mean not yet, Brandon?" Skipper asked.

"I'm not trying to sound like you guys are dummies or anything but this charm has a chip in it that is coded and can't be duplicated. I've never seen anything like it before and don't think I ever will again. We don't have this technology yet and it's probably 50 years in the future before we will. I don't know how to explain it. It's a key that should work some kind of computer system or maybe start up an advanced bombing system. You know the kind you hear about in sci-fi movies where two guys have to turn the keys at the same time to launch a missile."

"You think it's for missile launching?" Skipper asked.

Brandon thought for a minute then said, "No, more like to start a machine or plane or ship. It's too technical for just a bomb. Let me study it more and I'll let you know."

Skipper said, "I can't. I have to have it back to go to work tomorrow. There's a story behind it and I'm not supposed to ever take it off."

"I'll bet," Brandon said. "This stuff is more amazing than anything I've ever ran across."

"Well," Skipper said, "keep the droplets but give me my charm back for now. I've got to go home and I might need it at work tomorrow."

"Uncle Skipper, if you find out what it does, please let me know."

"Yeah no problem. But all we find out stays between us, understand Brandon?"

"Yes sir. No one would believe me anyway."

The call the Colonel had received was from Mark. He'd informed the Colonel about Billy's trailer being burnt which definitely made it a government job.

The Colonel said, "We definitely have an inside man. Now we need to figure out who it is."

"I have a pretty good idea who it is," Mark said. "I'll let you know later this week once I check him out better. But I've finished the check on Billy. It seems that he does have a connection to the plant."

"Oh," the Colonel said, "what is it?"

"He's Skipper Doster's best friend, Smitty's, cousin. We're going to check them out tomorrow if that is ok."

"Yes, that's what we need to do. Maybe Skipper's been talking already."

"No sir, I don't think so. He was here the same time Skipper was. He couldn't have told him. Not while he was in the plant."

"You're right of course. Let's just concentrate on finding the leak."

"Yes sir," Mark said, and he hung up the phone.

When Skipper got home, he had a surprise waiting on his answering machine. He had a message from Crystal wanting to meet him tonight. He was on cloud nine. She'd left her home phone number and told him what time she could be reached so he decided to give her a call to see if she might want to go have supper or maybe a drink. He was still pondering all the things Brandon had told him earlier about the droplets and his charm. Why would his father give him a key to something but not tell him what it's for? How could Steamway make clear metal? And what about what Brandon had said about the droplets. Could they really be used to make a suit that would render the wearer invisible? This made him also start to wonder about Crystal. Why would a new hire answer Colonel Morgan's private phone? Was she how Colonel Morgan intended to keep an 'eye' on him? Were these invisible suits already being used? That would explain why he kept getting the feeling he was being watched when no one was around? And would also explain why he'd heard the front door close but no one was in the house even though the dead bolt was unlocked.

He wondered if Crystal was really a new-hire and if so how did she get his phone number? Things just didn't add up to him. He was starting to think like Smitty? Damn, he still wanted to meet Crystal. She sounded incredible to him so he decided to take a chance and call her.

By the time it was time for him to call he decided to play around with the idea that she was there to spy on him so he wanted things to happen on his own turf. If she wanted to meet him, she'd have to come over to his house. He dialed the number she'd left on the machine and he noticed it was a local number not one where the plant was so he already knew she didn't live on sight. When the phone was answered, it sounded almost like the Colonel who had answered but Skipper played like he didn't notice.

"Is Crystal home?" he asked.

"Yes, who's calling please?" the voice said, but before Skipper could answer he heard Crystal in the background scolding her father for snooping in her private life.

She took the receiver from her father and said, "Skipper?"

"Yeah it's me. How're you?"

"I'm fine. I'm sorry about my father. He always asks who's calling me like I'm still a child."

"He sounded a lot like Colonel Morgan," Skipper said.

"If you'd worked together as long as these two have you might sound like him too," she replied.

"Your father worked at Steamway?" Skipper asked, with curiosity in his voice.

"Yep for years and years."

"That's strange," Skipper said.

Then Crystal said, "I was hoping I could meet you. When I was at work today, I saw your parents worked for Steamway too. That's how I got your number. I hope you don't mind me being so forward."

"Not at all, to be honest with you I couldn't get you off my mind all day," Skipper said.

He could almost hear Crystal blush on the other end of the line."Why don't you come to the house for a drink?" Skipper asked.

"Ok," Crystal said.

"Great, Here's my address. It's…"

"I already have that too," Crystal interrupted him, with a laugh. " e don't live too far apart. How about 8:00 p.m."

"That would be great," he said. "I'll see you then."

Her voice was so soothing to him. He'd never been wooed by anyone before let alone by someone he'd never met before. Skipper spent the next hour cleaning the house and getting ready for his visitor. He couldn't wait to see the face that went to the voice of an angel.

Crystal was in her room getting ready to go meet Skipper when her father's voice startled her, "You know I used to work with his parents," George said.

"You scared me Daddy I didn't hear you come in."

"I thought the world of his parents. They were wonderful people. I didn't mean to eaves drop on your conversation but he sounded just like his father and it startled me when I answered the phone."

"It's ok Daddy. I haven't really met him yet. I'm kind of nervous."

"I'm sure he's a good kid if he's anything like his mom and dad."

"How long did you know them?"

"Oh I guess about 30 years."

"Daddy can I ask you something?" Crystal asked, as she stood and hugged her father.

"What's that angel?"

"Why didn't you ever tell me you were in the military?"

"It wasn't the military. We were a—well let's just say we worked for the military, kind of like civil servants."

"But Daddy, I saw a picture of you and Colonel Morgan in uniform in a picture on my new desk. It looked like you were standing in front of a plane."

"Yes I know the picture. Man, that was a long time ago when we took that."

"Yeah I could tell. You were much younger then. You never spoke of it at all. At least not that I remember."

"I know, we were a group kind of like NASA is today. We did experimental work for the government."

"Have you kept up with the people in the picture besides the Colonel?"

"Yeah, I probably shouldn't tell you any of this but you're about to go out on a date with the son of two of them and will meet the rest at Steamway."

"Steamway?" Crystal said. "You mean they all work for the Colonel still."

"Something like that. You'll find out much about my past as time goes on."

"Daddy, why wasn't mom in the picture?"

"She wasn't part of the group. I only met her after we settled in Alabama."

"Where were you before that?" She asked.

"Very far away."

"What does that mean, that's no answer."

"That's the best I can do for now. I told you, you'll find out a lot more as time goes on, now go and enjoy your date. We'll talk more about this later. Oh by the way, you don't need to discuss any of this with Skipper. He knows very little about his parents past and right now the less the better."

"Mark, come up to my office. We need to talk about what to do about Skipper's friends."

"Yes sir. I'll be there in a few minutes."

It only took Mark about five minutes to get up to the Colonel's office. When he arrived, the Colonel was waiting and Mark had brought all the information he'd dug up on Smitty and his family.

"I figure if we can find out about Skipper's friend, then whoever killed Billy Smith can also," the Colonel said.

"I've been thinking the same thing sir. Would you like me to post a guard at their house just in case?"

"That's not a bad idea but let's do it quietly ok?"

"Of course sir."

"Now who do you think the government's inside man is?" the Colonel asked.

"I'm still not positive sir, but I've a pretty good idea that it's Dexter Cleveland."

"Why Dexter?" the Colonel asked. "I hand picked him myself and we ran a thorough background check on him before I hired him. I know he's not one of us but just because he didn't arrive here with us doesn't mean he's the informant."

"Yes sir, I know but he's one of the only few that didn't and I don't think someone with the original group or their kids would be a traitor. Let's keep watching him and the other two that live on the grounds. Bug their rooms and get Twan to follow Dexter around for a while."

"Don't we already have his place bugged and his phone tapped?"

"Yes sir, we do but I'm thinking along the same lines as you. If he's the informant, he wouldn't use his home phone so following him would be a good idea."

"Anyone else besides the three that didn't come here with us that you might suspect?" the Colonel asked.

"No sir. I might be wrong Colonel, but everyone here's as anxious to get home as we are."

"Yes I know," the Colonel said. "I'll be glad once we get Skipper and Crystal up to speed so we can get back on schedule."

"Yes sir, me too. I'm ready to get started back home."

"I know Mark. We all are."

After Mark left the room, the Colonel smiled to himself thinking that his plan with the government informant must be working well. Mark was usually very thorough and in most cases would have figured it out by now.

"Mr. Secretary, you had another coded message arrive right after your left your office today. You told me to call you if any came in, right sir?"

"That's right. I'll be right there."

On the way back to the office John Collins was trying to figure out what the message might be about. He knew that the problem with the intruder at Steamway had already been taken care of. He was hoping that it would be some more information on 'soundwave'. This was why he kept on letting Steamway run their own company and not go in and take it over to make the 'Liquid steel' themselves.

The message was waiting on his computer when he made it to his office. After he decoded it, he found out that it was from Clark Johnson, the agent that handled Smith. He'd found out which one of Smith's cousins had used his truck and visited Steamway.

The message read: "Sir, we've found William Smith's cousin. It wasn't hard. He's the only living relative. How would you like us to continue? Will be awaiting your response. Clark J."

As the Secretary sat at his desk and contemplated what to do he wondered how much this guy could know and why he'd be there. Did they have any connections at Steamway? If so who? When he sent Johnson a message back, it read: "Check to see if they have any connections with Steamway. Don't act until you've reported back to me. We've had to interfere too much lately already. I don't want to draw any more attention to ourselves than we already have. If we do decide to act, let's take care in doing so like we did before. Make it look like an accident. Respond ASAP J. Collins."

Chapter 9

The doorbell rang and Skipper knew she'd arrived. His hands were sweating and shaking like a 16-year-old boy on his first date. He'd put on his favorite black jeans and a white button up with a western collar. He stopped by the hall mirror to check his hair and make sure he hadn't gotten anything on his shirt. He'd already started preparing supper for them. He'd chosen steaks and salad with baked potatoes.

He crossed the living room and decided to look at Crystal through the peephole in the door. But she was ready for him to do so. She'd placed her finger over the peephole and when she heard him at the door she said, "That wouldn't be fair. You can't see me before I see you" and she laughed. Skipper shook his head and started laughing too.

He opened the door but Crystal wasn't what he'd expected. She was more. He was speechless and just stood there and stared at this angel dressed in white shorts and a blue shirt with a bottle of wine in her hand.

"Well, aren't you going to let me in or would you like to have supper out here?" she asked, and laughed again.

She was stunning was all Skipper could think. Then his manners came to the rescue. "Please come on in," he said, blushing as he waved his arm for her to pass.

After they were in the house, Skipper said, "Why don't we go to the Florida room to get acquainted before we eat? I hope you like steak."

"Well to be honest with you, I'm a vegetarian. I don't eat meat," Crystal said.

Skipper's jaw dropped and he said, "Well I fixed a salad and baked potatoes too."

She just smiled and said, "Gotcha. Just kidding."

They both started to laugh and Skipper said, "I see we'll get along fine." He held out his arm for her to take, as he led her to the Florida room.

"Dinner smells great," she said. "I stopped and got us a bottle of wine. I hope you like it. It was the finest Winn Dixie had to offer."

Skipper could tell she had a great sense of humor and he loved it. She was beautiful, funny and apparently smart if she was working for Steamway.

After he'd poured both of them a glass, they sat down and started discussing Steamway. She was the first to bring up the subject and Skipper again became leery that she might be sent to see how much he'd reveal about what he'd seen.

Crystal asked him, "So what do you do at the plant?"

He looked Crystal straight in the eye and said, "If I tell you I would have to kill you."

Both looked at each other for a second then burst out laughing. She said, "Well I don't even know my official title yet but I guess I'm in management. I've got an office off to the right of the Colonel's."

"That's my mom's old office," Skipper said.

"Oh yea, Skipper, I'm sorry about your parents. My father told me that they were wonderful people."

"Your father knew my parents?" Skipper asked, surprised.

"Yea, he worked at Steamway with them for years."

"What's his name?" Skipper asked.

"His name is George."

"I don't guess I've ever heard my parents speak of him. I'm surprised we haven't met sooner."

"Skipper, before I say too much. If you don't mind would you tell me your security clearance?" she asked.

This actually made Skipper feel better. He said, "I have a class-C clearance what about you?"

"Me too. I guess we can talk more I just didn't want to cross any lines."

"Yea," Skipper said, "to be honest with you I was wondering if you were sent here to spy or rather see what I might say about the company."

"No not me. We both have the same clearance so I think we're ok," she said.

While they were talking, Crystal noticed a picture on the end table of Skipper's mother and father. She said, "Is this your parents?"

"Yea that's my mom and dad," Skipper said.

"I thought so. I saw a picture of them on my or rather your mom's old desk today."

"A picture? What kind of picture?"

"You know the one with them and my father, Colonel Morgan and the rest of the employees in front of the plane."

"What plane?" Skipper asked, as he shook his head.

"Maybe I've said too much," She said. "I don't think we should discuss things about Steamway until after we've been there awhile."

"Well we aren't discussing Steamway. We're discussing my parents."

"I know but I also know we've both been warned about talking about Steamway right?"

"Yea, I guess so but a lot of strange things have happened since Steamway became part of my life."

"Like what?" Crystal asked.

"I know you went to the second floor of the building if you were in my mother's old office right? Then you've to know it can't be seen from the ground right? Well what else do they do on the three floors below ground?"

Crystal thought for a minute then, she said, "One floor has to be for the apartments, the rest for research. Why don't we've dinner now then we can talk more?"

"Ok," Skipper said, "but I've got more questions I want to ask. You may not answer but I'm going to ask."

"That's fine. Maybe we can both enlighten each other," Crystal said, and smiled that wonderful smile.

Colonel Morgan's phone rang at 6:30 a.m. the next morning. He looked at his caller ID and knew right away that it was Mark calling.

"Good morning Mark," he said, as he answered the phone. "What can I do for you?"

"Sir, we need to put a guard on Smitty and Lisa Smith's house right away. We've got a problem."

"Oh? What's that Mark?" the Colonel asked.

"Well sir, I've finished my check on them and they're very very vital to our operation."

"How so Mark, we don't even know these people. I mean we've got a responsibility to protect them from the government because of us being here but besides that I see no reason to use our security personnel to take care of someone just because they're a friend of one of our employees."

"They aren't just friends of Skipper's sir."

"What do you mean Mark?"

"Well sir, they're the parents of Brandon Smith."

"Our Brandon Smith?"the Colonel asked, very surprised.

"Yes sir, the one and the same."

"How could that be Mark? Are your positive that he's the same Brandon Smith?"

"No doubt about it sir. I went by last night and saw him myself. It's Brandon!"

The rest of the night went perfect for Crystal and Skipper. They talked and laughed as they ate supper and drank wine until they both were nearly drunk. Both had finally agreed to wait to discuss anything more about Steamway until they'd spent more time at the plant. The only other question Skipper had asked was what she meant by the rest of the people in the picture being at Steamway and she'd told him that all the people worked at Steamway somewhere. She told him she hadn't met any of them but she knew she would before long. She asked Skipper what kind of service that they were all in and Skipper had told her that his parents had never been in any branch of the government that he knew of. She'd told him that all the people in the picture wore the same kind of uniform and her father had told her that they were like NASA. Skipper didn't understand but he knew he wanted to see this picture so he planned on being in the Colonel's office the next morning and he had a few questions he wanted to ask.

Skipper asked Crystal if she was ok to drive home and she said that she thought she'd be fine. Then Skipper let her know that he'd asked for her safety and not as a move on her. He told her he'd plenty of extra rooms to stay in but she said, "I better not. I'll just go on home."

He walked her to the door and she turned toward him and said, "I had a wonderful time I hope we can do it again soon."

"Me too," Skipper said.

She leaned to him and gave him a kiss and said goodnight. He stood at the door and watched as she drove away, the kiss still lingering on his lips and in his mind.

As she drove home she thought to herself, "I wish he'd have made a move on me," and she giggled at the thought.

The next morning at the plant Skipper arrived at around 7:30 and Crystal's car wasn't there yet. He was a little concerned but as he started toward the building he saw her coming through the security gate. He waved and waited until she'd parked then walked back to her car so that they could go in together.

"Hey how're you doing this morning?" she asked, as she got out of her car.

"Oh I've been better. I didn't get much sleep and I'm pretty hung over."

"I didn't sleep well either," she said, as they started walking toward the plant.

"Why didn't you sleep well?" she asked him.

"Well, I was just wondering about all we talked about and to be honest with you I couldn't get you off my mind."

She blushed then looked up at him again and kissed him more passionately than she'd done last night.

"I couldn't get you off my mind either," she admitted. "I've thought about what we talked about too and if it's all right with you I don't want you to say anything to the Colonel yet. Let me do some snooping around first. Besides I don't think he'd tell us much yet. Why don't you go and do whatever it is that you do and I'll do the same for a while then let's just keep quiet about what we find out until we can compare notes. I know that this place ain't on the up and up but I don't want to bring any suspicion to us yet."

Skipper thought about what she was saying and after a few minutes he agreed

"United we stand," she said, as he placed his hand on the scanner that opened the door to the clean room.

Skipper and Crystal both tried the scanner to the elevator that led to the top floor of the building. Neither was able to get the door to open. They were standing at the entrance to the elevator. They heard the swoosh of the clean room door open into the plant. They both looked toward the direction they'd heard the noise and saw the Colonel coming their way.

"Good morning you two," he said. "I see you've met."

"Yes sir, we've been getting acquainted," Skipper said.

"Well that saves me the introductions," he said.

"Crystal, why don't you wait over here in the lounge until I get back. I need to show Skipper where he will be working."

"Yes sir. Colonel, where's the lounge?"

He pointed to a small room just behind them and like all the other doors it had a scanner next to the door. She placed her hand on it and unlike the elevator it opened.

"Come with me Skipper, I'll take you down stairs and let you meet a few people you'll be working with."

They walked all the way across the plant to another elevator behind the workstations that you could see from the clean room. The Colonel didn't speak as they walked across the room but once they got to the elevator he told Skipper to try the scanner. Of course it worked fine. They both stepped into the elevator and Skipper felt it drop as they started to descend to the lower floors. They passed the first floor and Skipper asked the Colonel which floor he'd be working on.

"Well the floor we just passed is where most employees of Steamway live so you shouldn't need to stop there even though your clearance will let you. Research and Development is on the Third floor and is a class-A clearance only. You won't be able to access the elevator to open past the second level. The elevator to my office is a class-A clearance as well. There's a phone in the lounge that you can call me from and I can access it for you if you need to come up and see me for anything."

"Doesn't Crystal work up there with you Colonel?" Skipper asked.

"Yes she does, why?"

"Well, how will she be able to get to her office if you aren't in or if you're late one day?"

"Everything can be done by remote. All you or she has to do is contact me and I can access the elevator from anywhere I am. I'm always where you can get in touch with me if you need to. Always. You'll be provided a number that can reach me or my first-in-command Mark. Either of us can access any part of the plant by remote."

The doors of the elevator slid open to reveal a room twice the size of the ground floor. Skipper couldn't believe what he was seeing, "This place is as big as two football fields sir. How many people work here?"

"A few," the Colonel said, "but you'll be working with only two in your department. As you can tell, the whole place is sectioned off. Your class-C access will only allow you in the first six rooms. After that someone with a class-B or-A rating must be with you at all times."

"Here's where you'll start." The Colonel pointed to a door to the right and just like all the rest it had a scanner.

Once inside, Skipper found himself in one of the most extravagantly filled labs he'd ever seen. There was no one insight.

"Skipper, just make yourself at home. The rest of your crew will be here before long."

"My crew sir? I'm the new guy that seems kind of backwards."

"Yes but you've got the training. I want you to start going over all your father's files in those cabinets there and familiarize yourself with his work. See me before you leave work today and we'll talk but right now I've got to get back to Crystal. Use the blue phone to contact her office and the red phone to get me."

"Yes sir. I'll get started right away. How long before anyone else shows up?"

"Not long, everyone is ready to leave...I mean to get started," the Colonel said. Then he turned and started back to the elevator

"Mr. Collins, you've got another message. It's coming across right now from Steamway."

"Patch it through to my computer, Mrs. Evans." The Secretary of Defense reviewed the message and as he read through it he wondered what was truly going on at Steamway. He'd been sponsoring their program for more than twenty years and in that time only five new hires had been made. There had been two in the last week but he understood that they'd had to replace the Doster's.

His inside man had informed him that things were back on schedule as expected but that they'd shown no new progress on the work of the 'sound wave' project. As he read through the coded message, he learned that the liquid steel project was back in operation but no one seemed to even be working on the new weapon 'sound wave' His man told him that most everyone except for the two new people was working on the third floor where he'd not yet acquired access to see what was being developed there. The secretary wondered how much longer it would be before he had to take control of Steamway. He'd planned to from the beginning but he knew time was growing near. He'd had a man on the inside for almost sixteen years but he didn't seem to be able to gain access to the most important parts of the plant. He knew he had to gain control very soon!

Crystal was waiting in the lounge as the Colonel had asked her to do when he returned. "Come with me Crystal," he said as he opened the door. She followed him to the elevator as he explained to her as he'd done to Skipper about the blue and red phones. Once they were in his office he told Crystal that any question she had throughout the day to just ask and he'd try to help. Crystal could tell a difference in the way that he'd been acting since she'd met him. He seemed pre-occupied with something and she'd figured it had something to do with the breach in security that had happened earlier in the week.

Crystal started once again going over billing and shipping and receiving to try and understand the system that Steamway used. She'd found out that their only customer was the war department and it made her wonder why that the government didn't simply make the "liquid steel" themselves. She made a mental note to ask the Colonel about it. As she worked at her desk she noticed that the picture of the original group was gone but she didn't want to ask the Colonel about it. He'd seen her and Skipper together and even though he hadn't seen them kiss she knew that he felt the vibes between them.

"Crystal, let me see you in my office please," the Colonel said, over the intercom. Crystal stood and started toward his office when his other door opened and Mark walked in.

"Just in time Mark," the Colonel said. "This is the young lady I've been telling you about"

"Hello Crystal, I've heard much about you but I tell you, you're much more beautiful that your father had described you to be."

Crystal just blushed and said, "You knew my father?"

"Well yes. Everyone at Steamway knows everyone else. Your father was one of our finest. I'm sorry he retired."

"Well sir, after mother's death, he just wanted to stay as close to home and her memories as he could."

"Yes I know. She was a wonderful woman. I'm sorry he won't be going with us," Mark said.

The Colonel looked at Mark sharply as he changed the subject quickly and said, "Crystal, we've got a small shipment going out in the morning. I'll need you to have the paper work ready for 60 gallons of liquid steel and try to have it on my desk before you leave today."

"I don't think I'll have a problem with that."

As she turned to leave the room she saw Mark look toward the Colonel and say, "We're in place over at the Smith's," and she closed the door.

She could tell by the expression on Mark's face that he was getting scolded for the slip he'd made but now they'd raised her curiosity even more. She and Skipper had to find out more about these people they worked for. She thought of Skipper and smiled. She knew from the first time she'd seen him that she loved him.

Chapter 10

Skipper was going over the notes and files that his father had left. He couldn't see any reason he was even needed. His father's work was complete and well documented. Anyone could follow these directions to make the chemical that kept the glass clear and clean. He discovered that it was not something that you applied to the glass but instead it was an additive to the production of the glass so you never had to actually use it again after the glass was made. Or rather the metal he thought and smiled. He wasn't far into the notes when he ran across a file marked liquid steel. He was thinking he was about to read a file on mercury but once he opened it he knew immediately that he wasn't even close. According to the notes in the file it was almost the same product that the droplets were made of except it was in liquid form where it could be sprayed like paint on almost any surface. This didn't have the electrical conductors that would allow something to be invisible but he didn't see why it couldn't be added to it.

As he read further, he found out that this was the main product that Steamway made, and it was made exclusively for the war department.

As he thought about what he was reading he realized that the purpose of this 'liquid steel' was a shield or armor. Then he realized that is why the government had such an interest in this stuff. It could be only $1/100^{th}$ of an inch thick and stop a 60-caliber round without any damage to the structure it coated. Now he started to understand why

Steamway used such extreme security measures. About the time Skipper finished the file two people entered the room. One was an older gentleman about 50 to 55 years old, wearing a standard Steamway uniform and lab coat. He had a light beard and mustache and was tall and slender with silver hair. Skipper could tell that the younger man with him was his son. They both wore identical clothing and were almost the same build. The younger man had dark hair but no facial hair. Neither had seen Skipper yet standing at the file cabinet and they were talking and laughing about a trip that they were about to go on. They both walked past Skipper and neither looked his way.

"Hello," Skipper said, and the older man dropped his coffee.

"Damn Skipper, you scared the heck out of me," he said, as he smiled and started walking toward Skipper with his hand extended to be shaken, "I'm Allen Cook and this is my son Ray."

They shook hands and Skipper asked, "How do you know my name?"

They both looked at each other and Allen said, "You look just like your dad, plus we knew you were supposed to be here this morning."

"It's good to finally meet you," Ray said. "I've been waiting ever since I heard you were coming. I look forward to working with you. Your father was my mentor and I've already heard how skillful you are. He spoke of you often. I'm sorry for your loss."

"Thank you but I feel out of place here with everyone looking at me like I should know how to just step in. My father never spoke of his work at all to me."

"Yes that's right son," Allen said to Ray. "You have to remember they don't live on sight, Skipper only has a class-C clearance."

"Yes sir, I know but I don't understand how he can help us without a Class-A."

"Well that's not for us to decide. The Colonel will move him up quickly, I'm sure."

"Skipper, we'll be glad to show you what we do here. You'll see it's not much to this part but once you get a higher clearance the projects get more difficult."

"I've been told that we're to just get the next shipment ready for tomorrow and then we'll be informed what to do from there by the Colonel."

"I can't believe you look so much like your father. I miss him very much. I knew both your parents for many years," Allen said.

"If you don't mind me asking Allen, if you were so close to my parents why didn't you or anyone from Steamway show up for their funeral?"

"We weren't allowed Skipper, but you'll have to ask the Colonel to explain why."

"Ok, well I've got a few questions you should be able to answer since I've found the files here and was told by the Colonel I could study them. What is 'liquid steel' and where can I see some of it?"

"That is exactly what we're going to do today. We can prepare a whole shipment in a few hours."

"Then why do these files show only a small shipment a month and they seem to want all that they can get?" Skipper asked.

"We've got other projects we work on as well that the government doesn't know about yet. We just tell them it takes a lot longer to prepare the 'liquid steel'. That way they won't bother us about our other projects."

"You mean like being able to make the top floor of a building disappear" Skipper said sarcastically.

"Yeah but there are four projects here, two you know about liquid steel and bending light but the other two are Class-A classified. You'll work on them as well but only after your clearance is raised."

"Well then let's get started so I can have time to speak with the Colonel before I leave today."

Crystal was in her office hard at work getting all the paper work ready for the shipment of liquid steel that had to leave the plant tomorrow when the Colonel called her over the intercom and told her that he and Mark were going down to the lounge for lunch. He asked her if she'd like him to bring her back anything but told her it would be an hour to an hour and a half before they came back.

"No sir, I've brought a lunch with me, I'll be fine," she said.

98

As they left the top floor, Crystal decided to go through some more files just to familiarize herself with all she'd be expected to do. She'd already been through most of them but she knew there was still a lot she hadn't seen. She wanted to learn more about 'sound wave' as well. As she was going through the files on the computer, she couldn't get her mind off Skipper. He seemed to fill most of her thoughts all day. As she went to close out the file program on the computer, she accidentally brought up a screen that said 'Time files'. She didn't know how she'd got onto this screen but she needed a password to go any further.

She'd only been given the password to allow her into the Class-C clearance files but she wondered about where Mrs. Doster might have kept her passwords. She thought that they were probably just in her head but knew how hard it could be to try to guess the right one. As she sat there at her desk, she thought about "time files" What could that mean. Crystal had already been all through her new desk but she thought she'd look again to try to find any keywords that she might try as a password. She knew she'd an hour or so before the Colonel came back so she thought she'd just try some simple codes to see if she might access the file. If not when she went home she could ask Skipper if he knew what it might be. First she tried Steamway, nothing. Then almost without thinking she tried Skipper and wham the file opened. She couldn't believe that she'd managed to open the file on the second try.

Time files were a list of events that had occurred in the past. She thought that she'd just stumbled upon some of Mrs. Doster's personal documents. Things that she personally was interested in. There was a main menu that had a list of twenty events. One that first caught her eye was a file called "Birth of Jesus" She started to open the file but changed her mind. Instead she just decided to open them one by one starting with the first. It was labeled area 51 which she knew was Roswell, New Mexico. She'd always been a trecker so to speak. She loved Star Trek and anything to do with UFO's.

What she found, when she opened the file, shocked her so bad that she almost had tears come to her eyes. She only read a few lines then out of fear or just shock she simply turned the system off. The file read— "On our fifth jump, as we were coming out of the warp something happened to the electrical system. The pilot and Colonel Morgan tried to regain control but couldn't manage and we crashed. Most of our ship was badly damaged. We knew we were in trouble. We had made this jump to New Mexico according to our schedule to find out what the government was hiding at area 51."

The Colonel and Mark had gone to the lounge, then to Mark's office to discuss what kind of security they needed to put on the Smith house to protect Brandon.

They decided on a 24-hour surveillance under the cover of the light suits. No one needed to know they were there and with the suits on they couldn't be seen. Skipper had guessed right about them. They'd developed the same technology for flexible suits that they had on the top floor of the building.

"Let the men all carry sound wave guns. Tell them to set them to stun only. But at all cost protect Brandon," the Colonel said sternly.

"Yes sir. I'll handle it myself and use my best men to help me. I know how important he is to us."

"Whatever we do we don't need him hurt and keep in mind we don't need the light suits or sound wave guns discovered. Pick your men as best you can. Let them know that destroying the suits and guns are acceptable if necessary. They're all risking their own lives and need to be aware of it before they go, so do it on a voluntary basis. The government surely knows about the connections with the Smith's and we can't have them getting their hands on either the suits or the guns, understand?" the Colonel said.

"Yes sir. I understand. How do you think Skipper is involved with all of this?" Mark asked.

"I don't know yet but I'll see him soon and I'll question him some on it. We need to get the men over there ASAP. I don't want to take any chances on losing Brandon."

"Yes sir. Right away," Mark said.

"Mr. Secretary, we've been watching Billy Smith's cousin's house since early this morning and again sir, they don't look like the kind of people we need to worry about. We can't find any connections with any other government agency and I personally think that they were just there by coincidence. Not any type of spying. We can't find any connections with Steamway but we're still checking on that."

"There has to be more. Keep checking but again before you make any move inform me ok?"

"Yes sir, we will. We have them under 24-hour surveillance and should have some answers soon. All their phone lines have been tapped so I feel certain that we should have an answer by the end of the week."

"Stay on top of this Clark, I'm holding you personally responsible for this. Understand what I'm telling you. Your career is on the line with this one."

"I understand sir. I'll handle it."

"Do that Mr. Johnson, and keep me informed on any changes"

"Yes sir."

4:00 p.m. finally rolled around but Crystal never opened the file "time files" again. She was too disturbed by what she'd read. She believed that her father had been working for some kind of alien species and that Skipper's parents were involved somehow. She didn't know how to approach Skipper or the Colonel with what she'd discovered but she knew she'd have to discuss it with Skipper tonight. They might be working against the U.S. government. She decided to re-open the file but just as she started to try the Colonel returned to his office. Crystal didn't know whether to question him about it or not since it was above her clearance. Not long after the Colonel arrived, she decided to ask him about sound wave, and why so much money was poured into it by the war department.

She opened her door and walked into the Colonel's office with a solemn look on her face. "Yes Crystal, what can I do for you?" he asked.

"I have the invoices ready for the shipment tomorrow but I've a few things I need to ask you about sir."

"Well go ahead don't be shy."

Just about the time she started to ask his red phone rang. He said, "Hold on just a minute Crystal. I'll be right with you."

He took the call. It was from Skipper and he was in the lounge down stairs and told the Colonel he needed to speak with him before he left. The Colonel authorized the elevator to allow him to come up and told Crystal to wait until Skipper arrived because they might both have the same questions. "Kill two birds with one stone," the Colonel said, with a smile.

Once Skipper arrived, he opened the door to the Colonel's office and when he saw Crystal standing there he couldn't help the smile that spread across his face. Just as Crystal couldn't stop her face from lighting up as she saw him. It was obvious to the Colonel that there was something between them.

"Well why don't both of you've a seat and I'll see how many of your questions I can answer. I know that all you've learned over the past few days is a brain overload but I'll answer all I can."

Skipper looked at Crystal as if say "You first" so Crystal started the conversation. "Sir, what is 'sound wave'? I've found some files on it and our government is dumping tons of money into it without any apparent results."

This surprised the Colonel. He knew that sound wave was a class-A clearance. "Where did you find out about 'sound wave'?" he asked, "I guess I should have checked all that out before I let you in the system,"

Skipper just looked puzzled, he'd never heard of 'sound wave' and awaited an answer.

"Crystal, I can't discuss that with you yet. It won't be long until both of you've got the clearance you need to know all but not yet. It's not that we don't trust you we just have to be careful for security reasons."

"Well sir, if I'm going to bill the war department for something then..."

"You won't be billing them Crystal," the Colonel said, as he interrupted her. "I'll handle it for now."

"Any more questions?"

She just dropped her head and said, "No sir." Not wanting to mention the time files yet.

"Well what about you Skipper, what's eating you?"

"Well Colonel, why wasn't any of the employees of Steamway allowed to come to my family's funeral?"

"I knew this question would arise," the Colonel said, as he shuffled papers on his desk. "Most of our people never leave the plant. Everything they need is here. We don't allow them to be in the public view much. That's why we hire only family members of older employees with very few exceptions."

"Why?" Skipper asked

"We can't afford for any information leak Skipper, that's why we pay so well."

"Also sir, you have me working with two people that can handle the production of liquid steel without any of my skills. I don't see why I'm needed there."

"You are Skipper, you'll move up to the next level soon. The one you heard Crystal just speak of. After that your skills will be put to the test. Have I answered all your questions?" he asked. Once again Crystal looked at Skipper and they both nodded. "Ok now I've got a question for you. As you can tell, we here at Steamway are as tight a group as any family so I hope it doesn't bother you for me to ask but are you two seeing each other, shall I say, romantically?"

Crystal blushed and Skipper smiled. The Colonel said, "Well I guess that's answer enough. I was pretty sure this morning but now there's no doubt. Congratulations."

Chapter 11

As Skipper and Crystal walked to their cars they decided to go straight to his house to discuss what they'd both learned. Crystal seemed withdrawn since they'd left the Colonel's office but Skipper didn't question her why. He figured he'd have time after they got home.

As they left the main road that led to the plant and turned south on highway 231 Crystal was following behind him and he couldn't help but notice how beautiful she looked even through his rear view mirror. Just before they got back to town, Crystal started flashing her head lights at him and motioned for him to pull over. Skipper pulled into the next service station he came to. After he pulled in, he got out and walked back to her car. "What's up babe?" he asked.

"I don't think we need to go to your place Skipper. What I have to tell you is really important and they might have it bugged. Why don't we just get a motel room instead?"

Skipper put his hand on his chest as if he was shocked and said, "Is this a proposition?"

They both had a good laugh and Crystal replied, "Never can tell."

Skipper agreed so they went to the nearest one. Crystal went in and got the room.

"Isn't that what the man is supposed to do?"Skipper joked.

"Chauvinist!" Crystal said, as she opened the door to the room. They both went inside and Crystal flopped down on the bed and kicked her sneakers off. "This has been a heck of a day, "she said.

Skipper sat at the foot of the bed and started to rub her feet. "Why, what all happened?" he asked.

"You won't believe what I found out."

"Well don't keep me in suspense. Let's hear it," Skipper said, as he looked into her beautiful eyes. Crystal didn't say a word at first. She just sat and looked back at him.

"What!" he said.

"I'll tell you on one condition," Crystal smiled.

"And what is that one condition?" Skipper asked, with a twinkle in his eye. "Would you like to see my clearance pass?"

"No, you can take that pass and trash it. I want a kiss," she said, as she sat up and wrapped her arms around him.

This time Skipper was the one who blushed but he was more than happy to oblige her.

They kissed passionately and Skipper loved feeling the warmth of her body next to his. Then she said, "Skipper do you know who our parents were working for?"

Skipper looked at her with a puzzled look on his face, and said, "Trick question right?"

"Right," Crystal dropped her head and said. "I got into a classified file today. It scared the heck out of me."

"Why?" Skipper asked. "What was in it?"

Again she wrapped her arms around him and said, "How long were your parents with Steamway?"

"Since they began," he said, "but what did you find?"

"I'm getting to that, but first I want to tell you something and I think you feel the same. I'm in love with you and have been since the moment we met. I know we've only known each other a short while but I've never, never felt this way about anyone before."

This brought a tear to Skipper's eye and he said, "You hit the nail on the head angel. I do feel exactly the same way about you. I love you too."

"Then what I'm about to tell you is going to be hard for you to believe but..."

"Nothing at this point will surprise me," he interrupted her.

"Remember the picture I told you I found on my desk," she asked him, "the one with everyone standing in front of some kind of plane?"

"Yes of course," Skipper said. "What about it?"

"I think our parents went to work for, well aliens!"

"Aliens!" Skipper laughed. "What do you mean aliens?"

She stood and walked to the bathroom mirror and leaned on the counter which was stained with cigarette burns and said, "I opened a file today marked time files. It was on the crash at area 51 in Roswell, New Mexico. Do you know about it?"

"Sure it's where our government tried to cover up a crash of an alien space ship right?"

"Yea, well according to the file I opened we're now working for those aliens."

"Mrs. Evans, I'm going to Alabama. I'll have my pager and phone with me but if we get any messages in from Steamway send them to me coded."

"Yes sir will do. You expect anything to come in?" she asked.

"I just received one from our man there. That's why I'm going but I'm not sure if he'll try to contact me again. Call our office in Montgomery and have Clark Johnson meet me at the airport. There's something going on down there that I need to check out personally."

"Yes sir. When can I expect you back?"

"You don't, I'll let you know," he snapped, a bit impatiently.

"Yes sir."

The Secretary of Defense gathered his papers up and started out the door to the airport. He knew that things were going to go bad for Steamway and he figured that he could get the man power he needed from the office in Alabama, so he didn't intend to take any extra help with him. The message he'd just received said that his inside man had finally gained access to files on the 'sound wave' project and in his opinion it had been completed for some time. He was wondering if Steamway was trying to sell the project to another government. There had been too many new changes in the last few months for something not to be going on and now this new information about 'sound wave' being completed. This bothered him. He'd known that Steamway had other secret projects that they were working on and it was time he found out what they were. He knew in his heart that the Smith family had something to do with Steamway but he was not sure how. Once he got there, he could take control of Steamway and then if they had to eliminate the Smith family, so be it.

He'd never met with Mr. Morgan face to face and he thought it was about time he found out who was truly in charge. He'd let this project go on too long without military control. This was on error he intended to correct right away.

Colonel Morgan's phone rang and when he answered it Mark said, "Sir, we're at the Smith house but we're not alone. There are defense people watching the place just as we expected."

"What're they doing?" the Colonel asked.

"Nothing right now, it just appears to be a surveillance team. How would you like me to handle this?"

"Don't make a move yet Mark. But if they move on the house stop them at all costs. We need to get Brandon to a safe place soon."

"What about his family sir?"

"Mark, don't you remember what Brandon told us had happened to his family?"

"Yes sir but…"

"No buts we keep Brandon safe but his family has to fend for themselves. I'll make a decision soon on when to move him, but for now just watch them. If the defense department moves stop them understand?"

"Yes sir," Mark said, then he hung up the phone.

As the Colonel sat at his desk he wished he could help Brandon's family but he knew that there was no way.

"Do you really believe that Mr. Morgan and our parents were aliens?" Skipper asked.

"No, not our parents. Here's my theory. I've been thinking about this most of the afternoon. You can't tell me anything about your parents or mine before they went to work for Steamway right?"

"Well yeah, I guess so," Skipper said.

"I can't either with my father but my mother didn't work for Steamway so I knew my grandparents on her side. I also knew about her past."

"So what is your theory?" Skipper asked.

"I'm getting to that," she said as she paced the room. "I believe your parents and my father worked at area 51. That's why they were all in the picture together. I think that after they worked there for a few years they became friends with the Colonel and the rest of the aliens. Most likely our parents helped them escape and left with them."

"Why would you think that?" Skipper said. "If what you say is true then why couldn't our parents be aliens too?"

"Are you, Skipper?" she said, as she looked at him.

"Are you?" he responded.

"Not that I know of and I don't believe so."

"Me either," Skipper answered.

"Let me tell you why I don't think our parents were with them when they crashed."

"Well let's hear it. So far you've got me convinced."

"Well our parents didn't live on sight but as best as I can tell besides our parents only a couple of others didn't."

"I never knew that. I met Ray and Allen Cook today and they were getting ready for a trip. I wonder if they're planning on. I can't believe all of this!" Skipper said, as he cut his self off. "I mean we're talking about extra terrestrials right?"

Crystal stopped pacing and looked at him, "I know what I saw Skipper, and it was an entry your mother had made. It said we crashed but I just believe she meant they crashed or maybe the aliens had recruited them to help and that is why they were all in the same uniforms in the picture and why my father said it was like working for NASA. I believe the aliens were trying to train our parents to use the craft but instead of training them they stole the ship and came here and set up Steamway. My father loves Colonel Morgan like a brother so they have to be good aliens or whatever they are, but don't we have some kind of loyalty to our country?"

"Yeah but baby, you haven't heard about Billy yet."

"Who's Billy?" she asked.

"Billy Smith, my best friend's cousin. See the first day I came to the plant Smitty, my best friend, followed me to kind of keep an eye out on me. I didn't know he was following us because he used his cousin Billy's truck. Smitty got spotted but made it back to the truck without any incident but I guess they got his tag number. The next morning Billy was murdered."

"I heard about that on the news. Didn't they burn his trailer down around him to try to cover it up?"

"Yeah, but I found out through Smitty he'd been shot four times. The police say he got off one shot with a 12-gauge shotgun and apparently hit whoever he was aiming at. They found blood out in the yard. Have you heard of anybody at Steamway going to the hospital?" Skipper asked

"No, but with all the secrecy they probably got an infirmary at the plant. They have everything else there. You think Steamway had something to do with Billy's murder?" She asked.

"I don't know but it sure looks that way."

"Why would they do that? What did Smitty see?"

"Nothing, he never got inside the fence and according to him you can't even see the plant from there."

"Then why would they kill him?"

"I'm not sure they did but if what you say is true it would make a whole lot more sense than just trying to cover up experimental secrets."

"Skipper I'm scared," she said, as she put her arms around his waist and pulled him close to her.

"Listen to me honey. I don't think you or I have anything to worry about. They need both of us. Why, I'm not sure yet but like you said our parents loved it there and they were smart people. They had to have known about all of this right?"

"I think so," she said.

"Well let's just keep playing it by ear. As long as we keep watching them then one or the other of us will know when something is about to happen. Since you work next to the Colonel, why don't you try to copy that file. What did you call it? Time file? And let's go over it throughly. Maybe it will give us some more information. How do you know my mother made the entry into the file?" he asked

"Because of you," she said. "The password was Skipper."

"Allen, this is Colonel Morgan, sorry to bother you after hours."

"No problem sir, what can I do for you?"

"I just need an update on what all happened with Skipper Doster today."

"Nothing unusual sir. We finished the shipment and got it ready to be sent off."

"Did he ask any unusual questions?"

"Nothing we weren't expecting sir."

"Good, I want to move him up a couple of steps tomorrow. We just got word that the Secretary of Defense is on his way down here and that may mean trouble. He may just be coming to check up on the progress of 'sound wave'. That's why I want you and Ray to introduce Skipper to it tomorrow. Make it look as if the project is close to finished. Even plan them a low range show with the small stuff. But I want the Secretary to know nothing of the high range equipment."

"Yes sir. Do you want me to move it to level three?"

"Yes and get one of the technicians to take off the panels in the elevators to show we have only two levels, then have them to do the same to my personal elevator. I'll use the old office on the ground floor. Have some people to make it look like I still use it. Put a computer back in there and all the files on sound wave and liquid steel except for the Class-A files."

"Yes sir. When do you want it done?"

"Now," the Colonel said. "they should be here tomorrow or the next day."

"What about Skipper sir? How much do you want him to know?"

"Let's hold off on letting him see level three. I don't want him or Crystal to see the ship yet. But give him full access to 'sound wave'. Let him know not to say anything about high frequency equipment if they question him. We also need to show him the light suits. I don't mean the suits themselves but slowly show him how it could work and let him figure out the rest by himself. When he does, he will question me about them but by then the war department should be gone. I only want the minimal amount of people available to be questioned. Keep everyone else on the third floor and explain why."

"Yes sir but sir, shouldn't Mark be doing all of this?"

"I have him on another assignment. He won't be available for a few days. Can you handle this for me?"

"I think so sir. Can I ask you a question that might be classified?"

"Of course Allen. If it is, I'll let you know."

"Well sir, are we planning on leaving early. I mean we're letting a lot be known that I don't feel should be known yet."

"No we're only planning for it to be known if we must but as far as leaving early. It's very possible."

"Skipper, let's don't go home tonight. Let's stay here,Crystal said, as he held her close to him.

"What makes you think I want to spend the night with you?" he said jokingly.

She smiled at him and kissed him passionately again.

"What will your father say? Won't he worry about you?"

"I'll call him and let him know I'm not coming home. He understands. I'm a big girl now. Besides I would like to meet your friend Smitty and his wife. We could go over and visit them if you don't think they would mind us dropping in."

"No, they wouldn't mind at all. I'm sure he'd love to meet you after all he has heard."

"What have you told him? We haven't known each other long."

"Yeah, but he's Smitty and he knows all without me saying a word. But why don't we stay at my house instead of here."

"Because they might be listening in at your place right?"

"Yeah I guess you're right. I'll call Smitty. He should be home by now. I'm sure they would love to have us over for dinner," Skipper said.

Then Crystal noticed an unusually sneaky smile come across his face, "What?" she asked.

"Nothing," Skipper said, and he blushed more than she'd ever seen him do before

"What!" she demanded, smiling and tickling him.

"Well I was just thinking dirty thoughts," he said.

"Oh yeah, what kind of thoughts?" she said, seductively.

"Dinner," he said, as he looked into her eyes.

She pushed him back on the bed and fell on top of him and said, "When the time comes I'll keep you fed well don't you worry." They both had a good laugh then Skipper decided to call Smitty to see if they were going to be at home.

Smitty answered on the first ring and Skipper told him that he wanted to bring Crystal by to introduce her and that they would bring steaks for supper if that was ok with him and his wife.

"Of course," Smitty said, "you know I ain't gonna turn down a steak dinner even if I have to sit through meeting another one of your girlfriends."

Skipper laughed and told him that they would be there around 7:30 and Smitty said that would be fine. Crystal and Skipper decided to go by his house for a shower and a change of clothes then on the Smitty's.

They arrived at Smitty's right at 7:15 and as they pulled in Skipper noticed a black Ford LTD sitting just down the road from Smitty's house.

"Let's not get out yet," he told Crystal. "Just sit here a minute."

"Why?" she asked

"Did you see those two sitting in that car back there?"

"Yes but what has that got to do with us?" she asked, as she looked back at the Ford.

"They have government plates on it. Let's circle the block again. I want to see something," Skipper said.

"Won't it look funny? Us pulling in and just leaving again?" she asked

"Your right let's go in. Me and Smitty will check them out once it gets good and dark."

They got out of the car and Lisa met them at the door. "You must be Crystal," she said, as she shook Crystal's hand. "You look like a nice girl whatcha doing with this bum?" pointing to Skipper.

"He kidnapped me," she said laughing, as Lisa moved aside and let them in. Smitty was in the living room and Skipper introduced Crystal to them.

Skipper handed Lisa the steaks and Lisa just looked at Crystal as Smitty and Skipper sat down on the couch.

"Women's work I guess," Lisa said, as she looked at Crystal. They both laughed as they headed into the kitchen.

"Not bad man, not bad at all," Smitty said.

"We may have a problem," Skipper said.

"Already?" Smitty joked. "You just met her."

"Not with Crystal you nut, I think she's the best. I mean you have somebody watching your house."

This got Smitty's attention, "Who, Steamway?" he said, angrily.

"I don't think so. They have government plates on their car. I want us to take a walk after it gets dark and see if they're the only ones watching you. If they are, maybe it's time we found out what they want."

"Sir, this is Mark. Skipper Doster and Crystal Watson just showed up at Smith's house."

"What're they doing?"

"It looks like they had some groceries. I think they must be planning supper or something."

"What about the surveillance team? Are they still there?"

"Yes sir. Two cars, one in front and one behind the house."

"Watch them close Mark, they could easily connect Skipper or Crystal to us. Stay on guard yourself. Ok?"

"Yes sir. I'd already planned on staying until they left."

"Where's Brandon?" the Colonel asked.

"Somewhere in the house but I'm not sure where."

"Check it out. Use the light suits and find him. I want a guard within reach of him 24 hours."

"No problem sir. I'll watch him myself."

After dark Smitty and Skipper told the girls that they were going for a walk and that they would be back in a half an hour or so.

"That's great," Crystal said, "use us then lose us," she laughed.

They both left out the back door and as soon as they got into the alley behind Smitty's house they saw the other government car. They both just kept walking and talking as if nothing was going on and as they passed the car Skipper said, "Hey you guys ok?"

The man sitting in the car said, "Yeah, we're fine just waiting on a friend. He's supposed to be here soon."

Skipper noticed that the man had a bandage on the side of his face and right away knew it must be the guy from Billy's. After they passed on by Smitty said, "That's the son of a bitch Billy shot! I"ll bet you anything."

"Be cool Smitty," Skipper said."Let's just get back to the house. I don't want to leave the girls there any longer by themselves."

When they got back Crystal met them at the door. She said, "I'm glad you two are back."

"Why?" Smitty said. "Where's Lisa?"

"She's in the kitchen but she's pretty upset."

"What's going on?" Skipper asked, as they rushed into the kitchen. There they found Lisa sitting at the table crying.

"What's wrong honey?" Smitty said, as he put his arm around her.

"I went downstairs to check on Brandon and he was busy as usual but as I turned to leave I walked right into something."

"What?" Smitty asked.

"I don't know. Nothing was there. Nothing!"

Skipper looked at Crystal and they both knew it was Steamway's doing. Lisa had bumped into Mark.

Crystal said, "Why don't you get the kids and stay with us tonight? We have a room and it'll be safer."

"No way," Smitty said. "These bastards ain't gonna make me leave my own home."

Skipper thought about telling Smitty what had happened but he knew that Steamway's people could be standing right there and they wouldn't even be able to see them.

Skipper decided that he and Crystal should go ahead and leave hoping that Steamway would follow them. He whispered in Smitty's ear where they would be staying and told him to stay put and he'd call him later but to stay on his toes. He wanted to tell Smitty about Steamway but he couldn't figure out a way of doing so without them knowing and figured as long as he and Crystal were there that Smitty's family was in more danger. They said their goodbyes and Skipper said he'd see them tomorrow.

"Is everyone in place?" the Secretary of Defense asked Clark Johnson when he arrived to pick him up at the airport.

"Yes sir. We've got two cars there."

"Good. Anything going on there?"

"Yes sir, I just got a report that Skipper Doster and some girl just showed up there."

"That's our connection then. His parent's must have told him something about us before they were eliminated."

"Maybe sir. But I don't think so. He was at school when they had their 'Accident'."

"I don't care. His parents wouldn't work with us so I doubt he will either. Let's keep an eye on them. If they start to leave, I want to know about it."

"Well sir, they've already left."

"Dang, did you get anyone to follow them?"

"No sir. We had only two cars there. I didn't want to chance losing Smith."

"Ok, tomorrow let's take care of the Smith's. Plan them an accident. I don't care how but don't make a mess of this."

"Yes sir. We have something already planned for tomorrow night. It'll all be over then," Johnson said.

Chapter 12

As Skipper and Crystal started back to the motel Skipper wondered if Crystal wouldn't be safer at home with her father. He wanted nothing more than to spend the night making love with her but he didn't want her in any danger. They didn't say much while in route but once they arrived back at the motel Crystal started to get out of the car but Skipper just sat behind the wheel.

"What's wrong?" she asked disappointedly.

"I just wonder if you wouldn't be safer at home. They could've followed us here and there's no way we could have even known."

"You think we're in danger now?" she asked, worriedly looking over her shoulder.

"I don't know Crystal but I know you'd be safer with your father."

"I want to stay with you," she said, as she took her hand and lifted Skipper's face to hers.

"I just have a bad feeling about us staying here together."

"Well we can't go to your house Skipper. We know it's watched."

"I know. Why don't you go home? I mean I want to spend the night with you more than anything else I've ever wanted in my life. But this could be dangerous."

"Don't worry," she said, jokingly. "I'm on the pill."

Skipper smiled but shook his head, "No baby, you go home and let's just meet back at the plant tomorrow."

"No, I want to stay with you," she said, with a pout.

This almost broke Skipper's heart then she said, "Why don't you come home with me?"

"Are you kidding? Your father would flip out," Skipper said.

"Yea, he probably would but he'll just have to understand," she said sternly.

"Crystal, I don't want to start off on the wrong foot with your father. Let's just start over tomorrow."

Crystal stared at Skipper for a few seconds, "I guess you're right. Besides," she said, keeping things light, "they say anticipation makes everything better."

She kissed Skipper as she got out of the car and told him she loved him.

"I love you too. Be careful going home and I'll see you tomorrow ok?" Skipper said.

"Yea ok, "Crystal said, as a million questions ran through her head. She had no answers to them but once she got home, she fully intended for her father to answer some of them. She wasn't going to let him off with any excuses. As she pulled into the driveway, she noticed that her father's bedroom light was already off. She'd called him earlier and told him she wouldn't be home so she figured he'd turned in early. She went into the house and discovered she was right. He'd already gone to bed. She looked in on him as he slept and thought to herself, "You got off lucky tonight daddy, but tomorrow is another day."

Skipper decided to stay at the motel but he couldn't sleep. He'd thought about trying to get back to Smitty's house or get him to the motel so he could explain what had happened to Lisa but the more he thought about it the less he liked the idea. He figured that if Smitty knew too much it might be even more dangerous for them. Skipper had decided to go into work early in the morning and confront the Colonel about Steamway watching Smitty's house and to try to find out about Billy before Crystal got there. He couldn't think of an approach to use so that the Colonel wouldn't know Crystal had accessed some classified files. I'll just go in at the regular time and try to give Crystal time to copy all the files she can. Then if we need government protection they would have the proof that they needed. Only one problem he thought, who is the bad guys here Steamway or the government? "So many question so few answers," he said out loud. He was worried about Smitty and his family. He knew Steamway was behind Lisa's scare but he still wasn't sure if they were the ones behind Billy's death and the people watching Smitty's house.

"Daddy, I wish you were here to help me figure this out," he thought, as a tear formed in the corner of his eye. He didn't know if his parents had ever met Crystal or not but he knew he loved her with all his heart. He was scared for her safety and felt a little selfish that he thought he might lose her before he could show her how much he loved her.

He started having second thoughts about her staying with him but he knew it would be for the best if she were home.

His father had always told him tomorrow's another day and as Skipper thought about him saying that he said, "Yea it's gonna be one heck of a day at Steamway." If only Skipper knew, Steamway wasn't where trouble awaited.

That night Smitty couldn't sleep either. He'd taken all three of his kids and made them sleep in their room with him and Lisa. He couldn't comprehend what had happened to Lisa in the basement but he knew he was going to protect his family at all cost. He was an avid deer hunter and had taken his .308 rifle down from the gun rack and loaded it. He was sitting in Lisa's makeup chair by the dresser thinking about what he should do next. He knew he'd placed his family in danger following Skipper to Steamway.

He had a friend or rather an acquaintance that dealt in black market weapons and was considering going to see him in the morning to get a more specialized weapon. He wasn't sure what it would be but he was sure that his acquaintance would recommend something. He knew no sleep was awaiting him tonight so he made a list of things he thought he might need. He used his hunting scope on his rifle to occasionally check to see if the cars were still watching him. They hadn't moved. Around midnight he noticed another car pull up beside the car parked out front and they sat side by side for a few minutes. He guessed they were updating one another on the status of his house. Then the first car left and the second took its place. There were still two men in the car out front and Smitty could see them clearly through his scope because of the street light behind them. Smitty was so angry. Each time he placed the cross hairs in the scope on one of the people in the car he wanted to pull the trigger. He knew from hunting that it would be an easy 70-yard shot and he could probably get both of them before they could even radio any help But he also knew the car out back would hear the shots and call for help then he wouldn't have a chance. He decided to wait until morning and try to sneak away with his family to take them somewhere safe. He knew he would have to out run the feds but he was a good driver and felt like he could do it without much trouble. After all he grew up in this area and knew more about the back roads than the local road crew did.

He knew if anyone came in the house tonight he could stand a pretty good chance of stopping them But out in the open they'd have the advantage. He thought about calling the investigator on Billy's case and letting him know what was going on but he didn't think the local police could even help. Besides they would side with the government anyway. No, he thought, wait until morning and he'd be safe. Daylight had its advantages. There would be many more people on the road and the people watching them was less likely to try anything. He wondered if Skipper and Crystal were ok. He felt pretty sure they were. "Daylight," he thought.

At 6:30 the next morning the phone next to Skipper's motel bed rang. Skipper was lying in bed but hadn't slept a wink. He wondered who would be ringing the phone. No one should have known where he was "Except Crystal," he thought. He started not to answer it but then he didn't want to miss a call from her. He picked up the receiver but didn't say anything instead he just listened.

"Skipper?" Crystal said, "is this you?"

"Yeah babe, it is. I just wasn't sure you'd be calling."

"I didn't wake you did I?" she asked.

"Are you kidding? I haven't slept a wink."

"Me either," she said. "Why don't I come back by before we go to work. I'll bring some breakfast with me. How does McDonald's sound?"

"I don't know if it's safe or…"

"It's safe enough," she said, as she cut him off. "I'll be there in 25 minutes or so."

"Be careful babe. I'll be watching for you," he said.

"I love you. See you shortly," she said and hung up.

Skipper looked out the window to see if he saw any odd looking cars or maybe somebody from Steamway. Nothing, but he wondered if Crystal might be followed.

It didn't take Crystal the full 25 minutes to get there. When he saw her drive up he thought McDonalds must not have been very busy. When she stepped out of her car Skipper smiled. He thought to himself that God had never made a more perfect woman.

He opened the door and let her pass without speaking. He just looked out behind her to make sure she wasn't followed then closed the door. When he turned around Crystal was no where in sight.

"Crystal," he said.

"Yeah," came her voice from the bathroom.

"I was just wondering if you'd vanished on me or what," he joked.

"No I'll be out in a second. Breakfast is on the night stand."

Skipper sat down to hash browns, two egg Mcmuffins and coffee. He'd nearly finished his coffee and sandwich and Crystal still hadn't come out of the bathroom.

"You ok in there?" he asked.

"I'll be out in just a second. Be patient. You should know how women and bathrooms go together," she said.

Skipper snickered but didn't say anything. He decided to start getting ready for work himself even though he didn't have to be there for a couple of hours. As he was standing with his back to the bathroom putting on his pants, he heard the bathroom door open but trying to finish buttoning his pants he didn't turn around. Then Crystal said, "That'll just be a waste of time."

As he turned to see what she was talking about he saw her standing in a see-through negligee and his chin almost hit the floor. He couldn't believe the angel standing before him almost naked. He was speechless and just stared at her.

"Well?" she said. "Do you like it?"

Nothing. "Skipper?"

"Huh?"

"Do you like my outfit?" Again nothing.

She started walking toward him and he felt like a sixteen-year-old boy seeing his first naked woman. Nothing he'd ever seen had compared to what he was seeing

"You're the most beautiful woman I've ever seen," he finally said.

"Well it took you long enough to say something," she smiled. "For a minute I thought you were going to ask me to leave." He walked to her and took her in his arms.

They kissed for what seemed like an eternity then Skipper's shock finally wore off and he said, "I can't think of but one way that outfit could look any better."

"Better?" she said, sarcastically. "How?"

"If it was crumpled up beside the bed," he said, as he started to undo the top buttons to the over vest. He gently slid it off her arms exposing a white bra and panties. As Skipper kissed her, he picked her up in his arms and laid her down on the bed. It didn't take long till she was helping him take his own pants back off. She tugged at the zipper but it was stuck

Skipper said, "I'll get it," and stood up but instead of trying to use the zipper he just pulled his pants straight down. He stepped out of them and threw them over the back of the nearest chair. Then he slowly slid his hand up her leg until he touched her panties.

She looked at him and said, "It don't bite."

He smiled and she pushed his hands away and slid out of them herself. Skipper climbed on the bed with her and as he was kissing her stomach he reached around behind her back and tried to undo her bra. Crystal starting laughing and Skipper looked at her and said, "What?"

"The clasp is in the front," and she laughed again. After Skipper finally managed to undo it he exposed what he considered the most beautiful breast any woman could ever have. From there it wasn't long until they were making love like they'd been lovers for years. Their bodies moved in perfect union. Skipper wanted to be tender and gentle but after a short while Crystal rolled him over and sat up on top of him. She was much more passionate than he was. Each time she'd push down he could feel her hip bones hit against his pelvis and he knew he couldn't stand this long. This woman was incredible. He'd never had any woman please him in this way before and he could tell she was just as pleased. After they'd finished making love, Crystal laid down beside him with her arm across his large chest.

Skipper said, "I love you Crystal," and she noticed a tear in his eye.

"What's wrong?" she asked, concerned.

"Nothing. That's just it. Everything's perfect."

Then Crystal, joking as usual, said, "Don't worry I'll still respect you in the morning."

Skipper looked at her and couldn't help but laugh again.

Smitty had his whole family up and dressed by 8:00 a.m. He wanted them to get out of the house while traffic was at it's most busy. He was downstairs looking out the back window drinking his morning coffee watching the men watching him. He noticed that "old bandage face" had also traded places with someone else. He was no longer in the car and figured these new men must have relieved him in the middle of the night like the ones out front had done. Just as he started to sip his coffee his phone rang and he spilt coffee down the front of his shirt and cursed the phone for startling him.

"Hey buddy, I see you made it through the night," Skipper said.

"Yeah but these bastards are still here."

"Don't say anything. They're probably listening in," Skipper told him.

"Good!" he said. "If you suckers are listening, be ready I ain't going down like Billy did."

"Smitty hush and listen to me."

"I'm sorry. I'm still angry about all this."

"Yeah well I came up with an idea that might help us both so hear me out. Do you remember where my apartment is?"

"You mean…"

"Don't say it!" Skipper interrupted him.

"Yeah I know."

"Meet me there this afternoon at 4:30."

"Why whatcha got in mind?" Smitty asked.

"Never mind just be there and bring the whole family."

"Ok but we're going to try to get the kids somewhere safe."

"They'll be safe just come to my apartment at 4:30."

"We'll be there," Smitty said, and they hung up.

Smitty couldn't help but want to get his family out of the house because he knew trouble could break out at any time.

Once Lisa came downstairs with the kids dressed and ready to go he told her what Skipper had said.

"I want to get out of here now!" she said, angrily

"Let's just give him a chance. He knows something and he ain't telling me. We'll be safe here until then. I'm sure but just to make sure I'm going to see an old friend of mine. He's someone you don't know but he deals in black market guns."

"Why," she said, "you have a gun now."

"Yeah, but he can sell me something much more effective. I might get off five rounds with this rifle but he'll sell me a gun I can shoot about a hundred times a second. We might not need it but I don't want to take any chances."

"Ok," Lisa said, "but what're me and the kids gonna do while you're gone?"

"I'll show you how to shoot this but I doubt seriously you'll need it. They won't move on us in the daylight. Besides I can sneak away without their knowing if I'm alone. I'll be back in about an hour and a half. You'll be fine."

"Please hurry Smitty. I'm scared," Lisa said, as tears began to roll down her face."I'll keep the doors locked."

Smitty left out the back and went under the fence on the left side of his yard which led into his neighbor's yard. From there over a couple more fences until he was out of sight of his house. He had in mind a pretty good list of what he wanted and hoped that Bruce had everything in stock. Smitty knew if they saw him return with the new guns that there would be trouble so after he'd made the purchase he went straight to Skipper's apartment and left everything but one teck-9 there. This gun was small enough to conceal and had four, 30-round clips that came with it. It would do until he could get back to Skipper's.

Skipper and Crystal dressed for work after taking a shower together. The water was hot and Skipper found that he loved to be bathed and he in return bathed Crystal.

"So what's the plan for today?" she asked.

It was a question he'd been expecting but wasn't quite ready for.

"Well babe, I'm going to work," he said, with a smile.

"I know that silly," she said. "What do you want me to do?"

"Keep an eye on the Colonel and copy any files you can. Tell the Colonel you and I are going to meet for lunch and we'll go from there."

"I'm going to try to go into the system and upgrade our clearance as well," Crystal said.

"Can you do that?" he asked excitedly.

"I think so. Your mother had everything set up pretty simple."

"Well then let's get started. I want to be back to meet Smitty by 4:30."

Chapter 13

"Yes sir. They know we're watching them. I've got a recorded phone call this morning from Skipper Doster talking about it," Clark Johnson was telling John Collins.

"I don't think that's a problem Clark. If any locals show up, we'll just tell them the usual," the secretary said.

"Sir, I don't think it will be that easy. You need to hear the tape. Smith knows we killed his cousin or at least he suspects we did."

"Bring the recording to me. I'll decide what to do then. For now keep a close eye on the place. If anyone comes or goes I want to know right then, understand Clark?"

"Yes sir."

"I also want you to get me together twenty or so men, arm them and plan on taking over Steamway by the middle of next week. Can you handle that?"

"No problem sir but..."

"No buts, Clark. Just do it. Also, put a surveillance team on the Doster House. I want to know every move he makes from now until this thing is done."

"I've already assigned someone there sir. When we lost him last night, I sent a team to wait for him at home but he never showed up."

"Keep them there. He'll be back and when he does show let me know. I want to speak to Mr. Doster personally."

"Yes sir."

"Colonel Morgan, we've had some movement at the Smith's house this morning sir."

"What happened, Mark?"

"Well sir, just mostly routine but I saw Mr. Smith sneaking away from his house this morning. He knows he's being watched by the government. I overheard a conversation with Skipper this morning and then with his wife. Apparently he's going to a black market arms dealer to buy some weapons. Then he's supposed to meet Skipper back at his apartment at 4:30 this afternoon."

"Where's Brandon at?" the Colonel asked.

"He's upstairs. His mother won't let him come down and she's standing guard over the kids with a rifle. I couldn't get very close but I know they're safe for now."

"Good, don't leave them alone. Do you have anyone with you to help in case they try to come in?"

"Yes sir Twan Golson is with me. He's the best I got if things get tight."

"Yes Twan is good at what he does. Keep him close to Brandon as well."

"We've got another slight problem sir."

"What's that Mark?"

"Well sir, I was standing guard over Brandon last night and his mother came down to the basement to check on him. They talked for a few seconds. I was standing near a pile of clothes on the floor and she abruptly turned to pick them up and bumped into me."

"What! Mark, how could you let that happen! You know to stay clear of any chance of that happening."

"Yes sir, I know but I was clear. It was just a freak accident."

"Did anyone else see it happen?" the Colonel asked.

"Only Brandon sir then, she grabbed him by the arm and ran upstairs with him. Not long after that her husband and Skipper came home from an after supper walk and she told them all about it. I think Skipper and Crystal put two and two together and it added up to Steamway."

"Did they say anything to the Smith's?" the Colonel asked.

"No sir, but I know somehow Brandon knew. He didn't say so but I could tell by the look in his eyes he knew."

"I guess things are going to happen faster than we wanted with Crystal and Skipper now. I'll need to talk to them today. It's time they knew where we come from and why we're here. It's apparent they won't say anything to anyone or they would've told the Smith's about what happened to her in the basement yesterday. They should be here around 9:00 a.m. but I've got a feeling we're going to have visitors today. So I'll speak with them after our company leaves."

"Mr. Secretary, how're you doing?" the Colonel asked, "I heard you were in town." Beating him to the punch, he said, "Why don't you try to take time to drop by our facility and see what you've been spending all your money on?"

"That's exactly what I had in mind Mr. Morgan. How about sometime this morning?"

"That's fine with me sir. I had some previous plans but it's nothing that can't be changed. How is around 10:00 a.m.?" the Colonel asked. He knew this would give them enough time to finish preparing for his visit.

"Yes that's fine. I'll have a couple of my people with me. We'd like to check on the progress of 'soundwave'," the Secretary said.

"That's fine. I think you'll be impressed sir. I'll have a little show set up for you when you arrive and after a small tour we'll demonstrate one of the most powerful weapons you've ever seen. I'll have my secretary let you in just tell them who you are and they'll be expecting you sir."

"That will be fine Mr. Morgan. I'll see you around 10:00 a.m.," he said, as he hung up the phone.

The Colonel sat at his new old office desk and hoped they could pull this off without any catches. The ship wouldn't be ready to leave for at least another week. He knew that if Collins smelled a rat he'd bring the whole army down on him. "Today Skipper," he thought aloud, "you'll earn your trip home."

Skipper and Crystal decided to use separate cars to go to work just to be safe. Skipper followed her to the plant and this time as they went through the clean room no privacy screen was needed. They both went straight to the employee lounge and got coffee. They still had time before they had to be at their work stations but nothing was said about last nights events.

Crystal stepped out of the lounge behind Skipper and almost right away noticed an out of order sign on the elevator door.

"Skipper look," she said.

He turned to see what she was pointing at and the Colonel came out of an office right next to the elevator.

He said, "I've been waiting on you two." They both looked at each other shocked. Then the Colonel said, "We've got some important visitors coming today and I don't want them to know about our little secret up on the second floor. The elevator still works we just changed the plates."

This gave Crystal and Skipper a sigh of relief.

The Colonel said, "Crystal, take everything you'll need up with you including food and drink. I don't want this elevator opening about the time the Secretary of Defense walks by. You won't be able to come down all day and no one will be coming up either."

This was the opportunity Crystal needed. She knew if she had all day she could copy most all the files that Steamway had.

"Skipper," the Colonel said, as he turned to look at him, "did you ever play with fireworks as a kid?"

"Of course sir," Skipper said, with a smile.

"Did you ever make any of your own?"

"Sir. I'm a chemical engineer. I could make any kind of explosive you needed," Skipper joked. Then he noticed a glimmer in the Colonel's eye.

"Good," he said. "I have a project that should challenge that mind of yours. Oh and by the way you both have been given a Class-B clearance as of this morning."

Crystal headed for her office and Skipper to the lab. Skipper wasn't sure of what the Colonel had in mind for him but he knew if Steamway was behind Billy's death then he wasn't about to make them any kind of explosive. Once he arrived at the same floor he'd worked on the day before he was met by Allen.

"Hello Allen" he said. "What's on the agenda for today?"

"Well I've got a surprise for you. It's something else your father and I've worked on for years."

"What's that?" Skipper asked.

"It's best I just show you," Allen said.

He led Skipper down to the end of the hall where they stopped at a scanner and told Skipper to try it.

"I already know my clearance has been upgraded," Skipper said. "I talked to the Colonel this morning."

"That's good. Did he tell you what we were in for today?"

"All he said is you'd show me and that we were expecting important visitors. He also mentioned something about me designing some fireworks whatever that meant," Skipper added.

"Did he say when he wanted us to start on them?" Allen asked, with surprise.

"No I'm just supposed to work with you again today getting ready for our visitors."

"Well first things first then let me show you a light show," Allen said, as he smiled and led the way into a large room where several other people were working.

"Skipper have you ever heard of our project 'sound wave'?" Allen asked.

"No, I can't say I have. Why? What is it?"

"Well, we make four major products here and sell one to the government. The other three we use for ourselves. Soundwave is a government-funded project that they will never see the use of."

"Why would the government fund something that they weren't going to be able to use?" Skipper asked.

"They don't know that they're not going to get it. With it they would be unstoppable."

"Let's have a look," Skipper said.

"Not so fast. First you must understand that we're going to give a low range demonstration for our visitors today. What you'll see is simply a stunner. The weapon on full power would destroy a building and you can hold it in your hands like a rifle. Here's the amazing thing about it. You can calibrate it to fire 'sound' at a high velocity the size of a bullet or the size of a car."

"Sound?" Skipper said. "How could you compress sound to make a projectile out of it?"

"That's the whole secret. Let me show you how it works."

They walked into the room and Allen went to a cabinet near a cinder block wall and took out what looked like some kind of laser rifle with rings of glass around the end. It appeared to be made mostly of glass. To Skipper it looked like something from Star Wars and made him think more about what Crystal had told him about aliens.

"You know about liquid steel and now soundwave. Now I'll show you an addition to liquid steel but I'm not authorized to show you our prize project yet. I think this will keep your excitement level up for a while."

"What do you mean an addition to liquid steel?" Skipper asked.

"Well it can be converted to a solid with a conductible base."

"You mean like the top floor of the building is coated in right?"

"Yes and no. That is a solid sheet, this is flexible," Allen put down the soundwave gun and opened the next cabinet. The second Skipper saw it he knew what it was.

"A light suit," Allen said. "This can be worn like a set of overalls with a hood."

"In other words," Skipper said, "you can walk around invisible?"

"That's right," Allen said.

But Skipper wasn't shocked. He wanted to learn more about soundwave. "When are you going to show me how that rifle works?" he asked.

Allen just tilted his head as if to say "I really mean invisible" but instead just closed the cabinet and picked up the gun and said, "See that watermelon in front of the cinder block wall? Watch this."

Crystal was busy in her office trying to figure out how that she'd accessed time files. Finally she found what she was looking for. She put in a floppy disk and copied the file. Once she was finished, she stuck the file down in her bra. She then tried to find the access to finish upgrading her and Skipper's clearance. She hadn't had any luck in finding the upgrade but while trying, she discovered most of Steamway's files. It was almost lunch by the time she'd finished copying all the files she found. Then she noticed she had more than ten discs and there was no way they could all be hidden in her bra. She laughed at the thought of what she'd look like if she tried. Crystal knew by now that the Colonel had to be giving his guests a tour of the plant and she wondered how long it would last. Around 1:00 p.m. she got a call from Skipper asking her how she was doing and if she'd found anything new.

"Yeah. I got what we need but now I don't know if I can get out with it. I've got more than ten discs. Have you seen the Colonel yet?" she asked.

"Not yet, but I'm told they're on their way here now for a demo of sound wave," Skipper said.

"I have the files on that too plus something called light suits and the ship but I haven't taken the time to read them. I was scared that the Colonel would walk in and catch me but there's something else I need to tell you. I found a file called industrial spies. It had three names listed. You won't believe what they were."

"Who?" Skipper asked.

"Billy Smith, Cindy and Stephen Doster."

"That's not possible Crystal. No way were my parents spies!"

Skipper thought about all that he and Crystal had learned over the past few days and said, "Maybe they found out the things we have and were going to the government with it. This soundwave thing alone in the wrong hands could be devastating for our country. You wouldn't believe what this thing can do. I'll tell you more later babe, they just walked in and I'm gonna watch this show."

"Soundwave is everything you said it would be and more, Mr. Morgan," the Secretary said. "I'm very impressed. When can we expect to see production of these for our use?"

"Soon sir, there are still a few kinks we need to work out. Maybe as early as June."

"That would be wonderful. I believe our money was well spent but my time is short and I really need to be getting back."

"All right sir. If you'll just follow me and I'll show you to your car."

Skipper thought about Crystal and the discs she had. He knew the government would never take control of soundwave but he couldn't just blurt it out to the Secretary of Defense. He noticed as the Colonel left with Mr. Collins that everyone was leaving for a late lunch and Allen told him that they would return in an hour or so. This gave Skipper an idea. He decided to use one of the light suits to get Crystal and the discs out of Steamway. He put the first suit on and was learning how it worked and decided that this would be a final move for him at Steamway. He took two suits and hid them in the lab where he first worked then he returned to the soundwave room. When he got there, he discovered that the Colonel had left his security radio on the table where they'd demonstrated the guns at. Skipper picked it up but discovered that it had been turned off. As soon as he switched it on, he could hear Twan call the Colonel. He knew the Colonel couldn't reply because he had left his radio. He thought about answering him and pretending to be the Colonel but decided he'd better just listen. Then Skipper heard the elevator doors open and someone started walking his way. He quickly replaced the radio on the table and peaked into the hall to see the Colonel headed his way. Skipper didn't want to talk to him until he'd gotten a look at the files that Crystal had taken from his mother's old computer. Skipper stepped into the men's room to wait on the Colonel to leave but instead of going back to the elevators he picked up his radio and stepped into the men's room. Skipper had stepped into one of the stalls just in time. The Colonel hadn't seen him. The Colonel said, "Go ahead Twan, I'm alone now."

"Sir, we've got a problem with Crystal's terminal upstairs. It seems she has downloaded all our classified files. I caught her doing it on the surveillance cameras," Twan said.

"I'll be right there," the Colonel said.

Skipper knew they had trouble. Crystal must not have known she was being watched. He quickly went to the lab and put on one of the light suits and activated the second and just carried it as he ran to the elevator. He knew he had to get to Crystal before they did. Once he was back on the ground floor he ran to the elevator just in time to see the Colonel go into the lounge to meet Twan. He knew they couldn't see him so he walked right past the lounge to the elevator. His clearance wouldn't allow him to operate it so he decided to just wait for the Colonel and Twan. He knew once they got in the elevator that he could simply step in with them and hope neither of them bumped into him. To his surprise he over heard the Colonel tell Twan to call Crystal down to the lounge. This made Skipper's job easier. He waited for them to make the call to her but it seemed to take forever. Finally the call went out and Crystal came down.

As she stepped out of the elevator Skipper grabbed her around the mouth so she couldn't scream. He whispered in her ear that it was him and she quickly calmed down.

Skipper said, "We've to get out of here. They know you copied the files. They have you on camera. Do you have the files with you?" he asked her.

She said, "No, I left them in my top drawer."

"Here," Skipper said, "put this on," and he deactivated the second suit so she could see it. Once inside the suit he showed her how to activate it and told her to stay right here that he was going to follow the Colonel back up to the second floor and get the files. "I'll call you when I get back down. Be ready to go. We'll have to make a run for it."

"What about our cars?" she asked.

"I don't know yet. We'll work that out once I find you again. Listen for me to call out for you. Why don't you wait on me in the entry locker room?"

"Ok baby," she told Skipper, "please be careful."

"I will. Now go," Skipper said.

As Crystal walked away, she felt as if someone had stabbed her in the stomach. She didn't want to leave Skipper but she knew he had a better chance alone.

Skipper waited by the elevator for the Colonel and Twan to come out of the lounge. He could overhear them talking but couldn't make out what they were saying so he decided to get as close as he could to the lounge. Just as he started in their direction they both came out and he froze in his tracks. As they passed him, he could have easily touched either one of them. He turned to follow them back to the elevator and as he did Twan stopped. He slowly turned and looked straight at Skipper. Skipper thought for sure he was busted. The Colonel opened the elevator and stepped inside then turned to look at Twan.

"What's wrong?" the Colonel asked.

Twan turned and followed him into the elevator and said, "Just jumpy sir."

"Well it's been a long day for all of us. Once we get upstairs and get Crystal straightened out then we can both relax a little."

Skipper slowly moved into the elevator with them. He was scared to even breath. He knew Twan had sensed his presence but he knew he needed the files. The elevator ride seemed to take forever but finally the doors opened and the Colonel and Twan stepped out and went straight to Crystal's office.

"No one's here sir. She's gone."

"Call the front gate and make sure she doesn't make it out of the plant," the Colonel said. "Tell the gate guards not to hurt her at all but she must be stopped."

Skipper walked past them both as they were preoccupied with stopping Crystal and eased her top drawer open and picked up the packet of discs. Skipper wished he had taken one of the sound wave guns as well as the suits. He wasn't sure how he could hide the discs without deactivating the suit and putting them inside so he ducked down behind Crystal's desk and switched the suit off. It only took him a second to place the pack of discs in his suit then he quickly re-activated it. When he stood back up, he saw the Colonel and Twan way ahead of him headed back to the elevator. He knew he couldn't activate the elevator once it closed and he also knew he couldn't make it into it before the doors closed so Skipper quickly knocked over the chair behind Crystal's desk. This stopped Twan and The Colonel in their tracks. As they headed to investigate, he went to the elevator to wait on them to return. Twan was now more suspicious than he was before. He was smart and felt something wasn't right.

"Sir," he said to the Colonel, "I believe someone is in here with us."

Skipper thought to himself that he had to be very careful not to get caught. He'd be at a big disadvantage in the elevator so he thought about staying upstairs instead of getting in it with them.

The Colonel and Twan knew something had knocked over Crystal's chair. But they'd no way of just feeling around the room and they knew Crystal had to be stopped.

"Skipper," the Colonel said, "I know it's you. What do you think of our light suits?"

Skipper neither moved nor replied. As the Colonel talked to who he believed was Skipper, Twan was moving slowly back to the elevator.

Once he stepped inside the Colonel said, "You realize you'll be trapped up here until I return so think about what you two are doing and realize these people you're working with are the same one's your parents died trying not to reveal any of our secrets to."

Then the elevator doors closed. Skipper didn't understand what he'd heard. Did the Colonel have his parents killed for sneaking the government secrets or did the government kill them? One thing was for sure. They were murdered. This made Skipper furious. As he scanned the room, he discovered an old walking cane that the Colonel once used after an accident years ago. Using the cane he tried to pry the elevator doors back open but had no success. He went to the Colonel's desk and dug through his drawers until he found a screw driver. Again he tried to pry the door open and again failed. "Damm," Skipper said and picked the cane backup and smashed the scanner. The second he hit the scanner he heard the elevator activate and start back up. He backed away thinking, "Some security scanner one lick and open sesame."

Once the elevator reached the top floor Skipper stepped into it. The elevator quickly descended to the ground floor and the door re-opened to reveal Colonel Morgan, Twan and Allen all three blocking the exit of the hall. They'd given Skipper a second to step out of the elevator and for the door to close behind him before they stepped into sight. The three of them had the exit into the main floor blocked. The only way Skipper knew to go.

"Skipper," the Colonel said, "we know it's you and we can't let you leave son. Do you have Crystal with you or is she already gone?"

To Skipper the three of them looked like a defensive line of football players standing side by side blocking his touch down

"You killed my parents!" he yelled angrily, then like the running back he was, he plowed right through the three older men. He'd played football for the best college team in the state and no way could three older men stop him but Skipper made sure to center Twan head on. He appeared to be in the best physical shape and knew he didn't want Twan chasing after him and Crystal.

As Skipper ran toward the exit locker room, he started shouting Crystal's name even thought neither of the three men had managed to get off the floor yet. As he ran into the room that exited the building Crystal turned her suit off long enough for him to take her by the hand.

"I have an idea," she said then turned her suit back on. "Don't say a word just follow my lead."

"How can I follow something I can't see!" Skipper said.

"Hold on. It's pretty simple," she placed her hand on the scanner but nothing happened then she realized she had to do it with the suit off. As she turned it off again, they both saw the Colonel and the other two men coming toward them but they were still in the plant and had a ways to go before they reached them. Crystal quickly placed her hand on the scanner and the outside door slid open and once again she turned the suit back on. Skipper started pulling her toward the door and Crystal said, "No" and pulled him to one side. The Colonel, Twan and Allen all ran into the room just as the door slid closed.

"Open it open it!" the Colonel shouted. As Twan placed his hand on the scanner the door slid open and all three men ran out.

Once the door closed again Crystal said, "See their just men. Easy as pie to fool," and she laughed.

"So girl genius, what's next?" Skipper asked. "Now we can't get to our cars."

"Yeah I know so I thought we'd call a cab," she said, as she snickered again.

"Whatcha got in mind now."

"Come with me," she said, as they exited the building.

Once in the parking lot guards were standing all around their cars and Skipper knew that there was no way they could ever make it to them but Crystal was pulling him by the hand in the opposite direction. Once they rounded the corner of the building, he knew what she had in mind. There sat the Colonel's car and no Amos.

Chapter 14

"Follow them. Don't let them out of your sight," Andy Tillman told his partner, as all five of the Smith's got into their car. "I have to call Clark. He needs to know they're on the move."

"Sir, did you see the gun he was carrying?"

"Yeah, it looked like an Uzi. Where in the heck did he get something like that?" Andy said, as he radioed Clark. "They're on the move sir. We're following them now."

"How many of them," Clark Johnson asked.

"All of them. They're headed south."

"Do you think you can over take them without any witnesses?" Clark asked.

"Sir, he's carrying a fully automatic Uzi"

"An Uzi?" Clark said.

"Yes sir. We probably need to hold off for now and just follow them."

"I agree. Just watch them and stay in touch. I want to know if they stop to piss understand?"

"Yes sir," Andy said.

Clark placed a call to the Secretary to let him know what was going on. The conversation was almost exactly like the one he'd just had with Andy.

"Do nothing just follow and stay in touch," the Secretary told him.

About the time they hung up Andy radioed Clark again, "Sir, your not going to believe where they went," he said.

"Where Andy. We don't have time for games. Just tell me."

"They just went into Skipper Doster's house."

"Ok don't let them leave there. Call everyone in and let's get ready to settle this today."

"Yes sir. When do you want it done?"

"The sooner the better. I want this over today or no later than this evening."

"Crystal, we can't just drive past the guards," Skipper said.

"I know, we wait here until Amos comes back. We'll already be in the car. You know where the Colonel sits and I'll sit up front by Amos."

"It won't work Crystal. They'll see our impressions in the seat."

"Then let's just take the car," Crystal said, "maybe we can just drive by them, who knows."

"They'd shoot us before we got to the second guards. But you do have something. Let's wait in the car until they both get in, " Skipper said, "then I'll tell the Colonel I've got one of the sound wave guns pointed at him. We'll make them take us out."

"Do you think it'll work?" Crystal asked.

"I don't know but right now I don't see any other way."

As they waited on the Colonel, they discussed where they would go and who they would talk to. Amos came out of the building but the Colonel wasn't with him.

Amos sat down in the car and leaned back on the head rest. Crystal and Skipper thought he was waiting on the Colonel but then he cranked the car and started out of the plant. No Colonel in sight. He drove past the first gate then the second but they had no idea where he was going. Then the call came in. Amos answered the phone with a sigh.

"Yes sir," he said. "I'm on my way there now. No sir. I don't believe it either. I thought both of them were great kids. Is George going to be waiting? Yes sir. Thank you sir," then he hung up.

Crystal knew Amos was going to get her father. After they'd left the plant. Crystal saw Skipper appear in the back seat. At first she didn't think of doing the same but when Amos hadn't seen Skipper she shut her suit off. Amos jumped all over and the car swerved badly. He placed his hand over his heart and said, "You two scared the crap out of me! What're you doing in here? Everyone at the plant is looking for you."

"Yes Amos, we know. That's why we decided for you to give us a ride," Skipper said.

"The Colonel says you've stolen all of our files and intend to try to sell them to the Secretary of Defense. Why would you two do that? Steamway will always give you all the money you'll ever need."

"We're not selling nothing," Skipper snapped. "We're just using them to stay alive. I know that you guys killed my parents and probably Billy Smith as well. You have people over at Smitty's house now watching his whole family."

"Skipper, we didn't kill anyone. We're there to protect Brandon and we all loved your parents dearly."

"You mean loved them to death! No, I don't buy this crap anymore. I'll keep the discs until I know me and Crystal and the Smith's and Crystal's father are safe. Then you can have your dirty little secrets back."

"We can't let those files get away, Skipper. You don't understand what you're doing," Amos said.

"Area 51. The crash. I understand more than you think." Skipper said.

"Then why would you think we're the ones who killed your parents?"

"Just shut up Amos. Take us to my house. You and I are going to go over these files and see just what's going on. Crystal's dad better not be harmed either while we're there."

"Let me call the Colonel and he can explain more than I can."

"No way. This is just our ride Amos. I don't need anyone knowing where we're headed. Remember Amos, I've seen the sound wave project and I know they could knock out the whole house or completely destroy it with one shot. No we're going in alone. You can park in the garage where no one can see the car."

As soon as they turned onto his street Skipper spotted the black Ford LTD waiting just down the street from his house. He quickly told Crystal to activate her suit so they wouldn't be seen as they passed the surveillance team.

"You see Amos. They're watching my house now!"

"Those are not Steamway people Skipper," Amos said, "see they have government plates on that car. We need to inform the Colonel."

"No, not until I look over these files. Now let's get inside."

When they pulled into the drive Skipper had to get out to open the garage door because he'd left his remote in his car back at Steamway. Once they stopped Skipper told Amos to get out and open his door so it wouldn't look crazy for the door to open on its own. And for him to act like he was retrieving something from the back seat.

"Amos," Skipper said, "don't try anything funny while I'm opening the door. Crystal has a sound wave gun pointed at you as we speak."

"Skipper you and I both know that's a lie," Amos said, "but I'm not going no where with those goons watching your house. I may be your only protection."

"Protection?" Skipper said.

"Yes," Amos repeated. "Protection," as he placed his hand under the front seat and removed a pistol, "Now Skipper, as you can clearly see I could kill both of you now but I've to prove to you who you really are. Let's get inside." Amos got out and instead of opening Skipper's door he went and opened the door to the garage. To Skipper's surprise there sat Smitty's car. Amos returned and drove into the garage. As all three exited the car Smitty came out of nowhere. He had the Uzi pointed at Amos and Skipper shouted at him to stop. This startled Smitty. He hadn't seen Skipper or Crystal and he knew Amos had the pistol in his hand.

"Skipper?" he said, shocked.

"Yeah it's me," Skipper said, as he turned his suit off.

Smitty almost fainted at the sight of Skipper seeming to materialize out of thin air. "We've got a problem old buddy," Skipper told Smitty, as Crystal appeared.

"Yea well, we're now a little more prepared that you think," Smitty said, with a laugh.

Mark had been following Smitty and his family since they'd left their house. He knew that the Smith family was being tailed and he'd prepared for anything to happen. He'd wanted Twan with him because he knew Twan was the best man he had and the most experienced. He'd tried to use the light suit and enter the Doster house but the Smith's had barricaded the doors. He had his key but they'd used chairs under the door knobs and other things to stop the windows from being opened even if somehow he could manage to unlock them. As he watched the government agents watching the Doster house, he saw the Colonel's car approaching. He didn't understand what was happening. He saw Amos get out of the car and open the door to the garage then return and drive in. He knew Amos was supposed to be going to pick up George so he could help round up his daughter and Skipper.

"Colonel, this is Mark. Your car just pulled up at the Doster house. I thought he…"

"Mark, listen to me," the Colonel said, interrupting him, "it's a good chance Skipper and Crystal are with him."

"Sir, he was the only one in the car, "Mark said.

"They have two light suits Mark. Stay on your toes. We're on our way. I'll stop and get George then we'll be there."

"Yes sir. We'll be waiting."

"Go ahead and set a man at each government car ready to move. I don't want any of them hurt. Especially Brandon. When we get there, I'm sure they'll try a move on us. Use the sound wave and set it to stun but wait until they move on us first. Understand?"

"Of course sir. Why don't you have Twan tap into the transceiver we have in the Doster house so we can hear what is going on? I've got my transceiver with me but it has to be activated from the plant office."

"That's a good idea Mark. We haven't used those for years but they should still work."

Twan switched the listening devices on, then he left with the Colonel going to pick up George. Mark sat listening to the conversation he could hear in the house. He could hear Skipper telling Crystal to boot up his computer and Amos started explaining that Steamway had never killed anyone.

Smitty told Skipper, "I went out this morning and armed us a little better." He handed Skipper the Uzi he'd been carrying and took a second one from the shelf in the corner of the room. He had Lisa and the kids in the basement and she was armed as well.

"Smitty, let's check out these files before you try anything crazy."

"Skipper," Smitty said, "you knew it was someone in our house from Steamway yesterday and you didn't tell me. You have a suit like they must have been wearing when Lisa bumped into him. They're the one's that's crazy if they think I'm not going to protect my family to the fullest of my abilities."

Then Crystal said, "Skipper, look at this."

When he walked over to the computer, she was reading the files with his mother and father's names on them the files read: 'Today Stephen and Cindy Doster were killed in an automobile accident. I believe that this was no accident. Stephen came to me yesterday and told me some people from the war department had approached him and at first offered him a large sum of money for information on Steamway but when he declined they threatened his family. Then the next day they were killed. His son, Skipper, has not been hurt but we're afraid for his safety so over the next few weeks we're going to keep a light suit guard on him 24 hours a day. I'm even going to offer him his father's job to keep him at the plant as much as possible where we can protect him. We have to keep him safe until our departure date. Colonel Morgan.'

This really shocked Skipper. He'd known he was working for the bad guys, now he finds out that they've been protecting him and his friend's family for weeks. He let Smitty read the log entry then said, "Go get Lisa and the kids. Let's get everyone down to the plant. We'll be safer there."

As Smitty called Lisa and the kids from upstairs, he told her what was happening. Skipper told Smitty to get them ready to make a break for it once they were in the cars. That he and Crystal would go and flatten the tires on the government cars with the use of the light suits.

Just as Skipper finished telling Smitty the plan, Smitty went to the window and pulled down the shade to see if all the government agents were still in place. Just as he opened the blinds, the glass shattered with the impact of a bullet that hit Smitty right in the chest. Then instantly the room was filled with gun fire. Skipper saw Smitty go down and he tried to make his way to him. He saw the next burst of bullets hit Lisa as she tried to get to Smitty as well. She went down hard and Skipper knew both of them were dead. Skipper turned to check on Crystal. Amos had Brandon over his shoulder and Crystal had the other two kids one by each hand, and headed for the garage door. Skipper had noticed that the automatic weapons had stopped firing. He jumped up and tried to follow Crystal and Amos as they entered the garage. Just as he made it through the door, he saw Amos fall first but heard no gun fire. Then Crystal and both other children seemed to buckle and fall to the floor. None of them including Brandon moved at all.

Skipper screamed as loud as he could and dove back into the house. He spotted Smitty and Lisa lying on the floor in the bullet riddled room. Lisa was bleeding badly from a wound he could see in her shoulder. She was lying on her stomach and he knew like Smitty, she'd been hit several times in the chest. Then he spotted the Uzi Smitty had held in his hand. He grabbed for the Uzi and just as he did the front door exploded open. He aimed the gun toward the door and started to squeeze the trigger but he knew he was too slow firing the weapon. As he fell, he thought it was strange he hadn't felt the bullets as they'd hit him. He knew as the room turned black he was dead as well.

"Sir, they're dead. It was an ambush. They were waiting on us. I don't have a single man left standing."

"What about the Smith's?" he asked.

"Well sir, I know both parents are dead. I saw them go down myself. I'm not sure what happened to the children."

"And what about the others?" the secretary asked.

"I'm not sure."

"What do you mean you're not sure? You had ten men against a couple of armed civilians. What happened?"

"We don't know, sir. Some of my men never made it out of their cars. There wasn't two armed civilians. They had help. Lots of it. We saw the first target open the blind in the front room and took the shot. After that everyone knew to just spray the house from all directions, once we started firing. Something, I'm not sure what, happened. My men just fell dead. I don't, I mean, I didn't see anyone or hear a shot. I saw them fall without a single wound. Nothing, but they're down and I never saw anyone."

"Clark, have you checked to see if they were dead?"

"Sir, I saw them fall…"

"No listen to me go and check to see if they're dead or just unconscious."

"Yes sir," Clark said.

"I think I know what happened to your men, "the Secretary said, "and if I'm right Steamway is behind it."

"Have we got everyone picked up?" the Colonel asked Mark.

"Yes sir we do. It looks like Brandon's mom and dad were…"

"Yes, I already saw them. Let's not say anything to anyone. Have the house burnt now. Let's get this mess cleaned up. How's Brandon?"

"He's fine sir. We took him and the other kids to George's house but sir, for everyone's sake I don't even think Skipper or Crystal should know they survived."

"They can't come with us and George is staying behind anyway. Let's get Crystal and Skipper back to the plant. If I know the war department, they'll want an explanation of what happened to their men. Twan took down ten men without a single bullet fired and the Secretary just saw the soundwave demonstration. He'll know we're behind it. We need to prepare. How's Amos?"

"Not so good, sir. The soundwave had a pretty bad effect on him but he'll survive," Mark said.

"Ok, let's get him on the ship to the infirmary. He can stay there until we leave. Mark, as far as anyone knows Skipper and Crystal are the only ones that survived. Everyone else but Amos dies in or before the fire. Understand?"

"Yes sir. Only you, Amos, Twan, and I'll ever know differently. Those kids will be safe with George. But sir, Skipper and Crystal will be devastated with this. They'll blame themselves for their deaths," Mark said.

"Not for long. We'll be home soon and then they'll know the truth," the Colonel explained.

"Home," Mark said, "that's so hard to believe."

"Skipper. Skipper. Can you hear me?"

Skipper's eyes fluttered as he tried to open them.

"Skipper," Crystal said, "can you hear me baby?"

Skipper jumped as if shocked and Crystal and Mark tried to hold him. Skipper being a football player, was strong and fit. He pushed both of them back across the room. Once to his feet he started to regain his senses.

"Crystal," he said, "what the hell's going on?"

"We're ok, baby," she said.

Skipper shook his head and said, "I saw you go down. Then I got shot too. What the hell's going on here?"

"They shot us with the sound wave guns. They just stunned us to stop us from getting hurt or you shooting someone with the gun you got from Smitty."

"Smitty," Skipper said, "is he ok too?"

Crystal didn't say anything she just walked over to him and placed her arms around him then said, "I'm sorry. I know you loved them but Smitty and Lisa were both shot by our fabulous government before Steamway's people could intervene. After you, Amos and I were shot with the soundwave guns the kids ran outside and were shot as well. We were the only one's to survive. After they got us out and safely back here we heard that they'd burned your house."

This held Skipper in such shock he couldn't say anything. Skipper hated himself for bringing Smitty's family into this. Now they were all dead. He couldn't believe Smitty was gone.

"Skipper," Crystal said, "we need your help. You have to put your losses behind you and come with me to the Colonel's office. He's got something you've got to see. We have to hurry now. When the government attacked your house, Steamway's security totally wiped them out and now the Colonel feels they'll come try to take over the plant."

"You have to know the truth about us."

"What do you mean the truth Crystal?" Skipper asked. "What truth?"

"Where we really come from. The Colonel can best explain but I'll be there with you. We've got to get you up to his office so he can tell you the whole truth. Then remember the fireworks he wanted you to work on? You have to get started. We'll be leaving soon," Crystal said.

"Mr. Secretary, you were right all my men were unconscious. They've all came back around but we've got local police all over us. We're gonna need some help cleaning this up."

"Why did you burn the Doster's house down Clark?" the Secretary asked.

"We didn't sir. That wasn't our doing. I guess Steamway did it to cover their tracks."

"Did we lose any people at all Clark?"

"No sir, not one. They'll all recover."

"Ok, let's meet at your office in two hours and we'll discuss what we'll do next."

"Sir, how could they have taken out ten men without being seen and no one be hurt?"

"Don't worry about that now, Clark. I'll explain when we meet. I'll need at least thirty heavily armed men ready for an assault on Steamway day after tomorrow."

"Thirty sir. I don't know if I can have that many ready from the office here or not."

"That's ok Clark, I'm calling in a specially trained group out of DC to handle this. I can't have another screw up like this. Your men have done their job the best that their training would allow. Now it's time to bring in the big boys. I fully intend to take over Steamway's operation completely. They have a lot more going on there than they're letting us know about. What I want your men doing is combing through the ashes at the Doster house. Look for any clues that might help us. Go over every inch. When they burnt the place, they were covering up something. I want to know what! How many bodies have the police taken from the ashes?"

"None sir. Not yet anyway."

"I thought you said you knew you got the first target. Why haven't they found him?"

"I don't know sir. They must have carried the bodies with them."

Why would they take the bodies out of a house that they intended to burn? The Secretary thought to himself.

"I don't buy this Clark. Don't leave a square inch of those ashes unchecked. When you were checking your men to see if they were dead or alive didn't you see them leave?" the Secretary asked.

"Well no sir. I didn't see anyone leave but they might have left during the time I placed the first call to you."

"Six people and Steamway employees left without being seen. Check with the surrounding homes. See if anyone saw them leave. I want a report on my desk by tonight."

Chapter 15

"George, we have some new friends," Twan said with a smile. "We'll bring them by soon but the Colonel is scared that the government will put us together with you so he wants you to go up to the lake property. There's no way they can trace that place to us and if everything goes as planned, once we leave, there won't be anyone looking for you anyway."

"Who's my new company?" George asked.

"It's the Smith family. I'm not sure if the Colonel's said anything to you or not but Brandon is one of your new guests."

"Brandon who?" George asked.

"Our Brandon, George," Twan said, excitedly, "looks like you get to be his mentor or at least his body guard until he starts to work on our project."

"No way," George said, in total disbelief, "how could this happen? He's not even from around here."

"Who else is with him?" George asked.

"His sister and brother. We had a pretty bad time at the Doster's house and we may have to leave a lot sooner than we've expected to so the Colonel wants you to meet us at the lake house ASAP. We've already got you a full change of credentials and we'll soon have the kid's credentials done. Nobody will know who you or they are. We've got one other problem George."

"What's that?" he asked.

"Do you remember what Brandon told us had happened to his parents?"

"Yeah Why?"

"It's true, they were both shot today."

"It's hard to believe we couldn't stop something we knew was going to happen," George said.

"Hello Skipper," the Colonel said. "I guess I owe you an explanation. Sit down and let us have the talk you and your father should have had years ago. Crystal if you'd like to wait, your father will be here soon. We relocated him to our safe house and he wants to see you again before we leave."

"I've already heard most of the story before Skipper woke up sir. So you can go ahead since our time is short."

The Colonel stood up from his desk and walked over to the window placing his hands behind his back, "Skipper, this is going to be hard for you to believe..."

"Sir, nothing you can tell me will surprise me anymore," Skipper said.

The Colonel turned and looked at Crystal then to Skipper. He started to speak then Skipper said, "I already know most of it sir."

"Oh do you? Well let's hear what you know," the Colonel said, as he smiled.

"Well sir, I know about your crash at area 51 and how my parents helped your escape from the government there."

"Well," the Colonel said, "Crystal told me that much but this might shock you. Your parents not only helped us escape. They arrived with us."

"What're you saying sir? That my parents are aliens?"

"To this time maybe but we're all from earth same as you. Your father and mother and many others left in a ship in the year 2041 bound for the past."

"The past!" Skipper said.

"Yes Skipper we're time-travelers not aliens. We're historical research scientists and had planned a trip to our past to confirm historical events one of which was the alien space ship that crashed in Roswell, New Mexico. Only to our surprise it was us who crashed not aliens. But our wonderful government wouldn't believe any different. Your father was 23 when we crashed. He was 27 by the time we escaped and had already married your mother. You see Skipper you were born almost 40 years before your father was! We were here just to observe. We used the light shield on our ship so we couldn't be seen. By the year 2038 no space craft had ever been proven to exist so one of our stops was to check out Area 51 or the exact date and time the space ship was supposed to have crashed. What we didn't realize was when we came out of the time warp, we had a bad power shortage, lost our light shield and then crashed. We had already made four other jumps before and Area 51 would've been our last on this trip before we returned home."

"What were the first four?" Skipper asked.

"Well the first was the birth of Christ. The second was."

"Wait you mean you actually saw Jesus born?" Skipper asked.

"Let's just put it this way Skipper," the Colonel said, "Pray, pray, pray every day. We also wanted to see events in history that were unproven. So our second was the Resurrection of Jesus. The third…"

"Well?" Skipper said.

"Well what?" the Colonel asked.

"Don't leave me in suspense!"

"In time Skipper, but for now I've got to get you prepared on what's needed of you and to do so I need to finish the story. So if you can possibly control your curiosity for just a little longer," the Colonel said with a smile, "the third was the disappearance of the people on board the *Marie Celeste*. Do you know the story of the *Marie Celeste*?" asked the Colonel.

"Yes sir. It was a ship where all the people disappeared. Not one person was ever found but the ship was. It was found in perfect working order. Nothing missing but the life boats."

"That's correct. Then our fourth jump. This is something that will shock you. It has yet to happen. You see on September 11, 2001, four

Jumbo jets were stolen by the AlQueda terrorists headed up by a man named Osama bin Laden. Then two were crashed into the World Trade Centers in New York City and one crashed into the Pentagon. On the fourth plane the passengers tried to take it over and it didn't make it to its destination. It crashed in upstate Pennsylvania. Both of the twin towers will be completely destroyed. More than 10,000 people will die in the attack. We had seen it on film but to actually see it in person was unbelievable. It's hard to believe that man can actually do that to another man," the Colonel said, as he seemed to stare at his feet, "anyway on our final jump we crashed. As you can imagine, we couldn't tell the government who we really were. They assumed we were from another world. We let them believe what they wanted. They helped us repair our ship under the impression that they would keep total control of its technology. After we were there for almost four years, we had managed to piece our ship back together enough to jump we thought. But instead of landing in 2041 we landed here in Wetumpka, Alabama in 1979. The year you were born. Our light shield still worked so we were undetected. That was the year we all started Steamway. We figured we could sell the government the secrets they would soon have anyway and use the money to supply us with what we needed to complete repairs to our ship and to keep us alive. We needed food and shelter. Soon we bought the land and started building Steamway. It really wasn't as simple as that though, first we had to hide who we really were. We had some historical files from our own time that we managed to salvage but most were lost in the crash. We knew approximately when our government started using soundwave equipment and liquid steel so we just helped them along a little. Your father, from memory, managed to redesign liquid steel. It was a primitive form of what we used in the future but it managed to land us a government contract and from there he improved his formula each year slightly until we thought they would try to start manufacturing it themselves. Then to stop them from doing so, we introduced them to the plans for soundwave technology. It was in the form of what you'd call a hand gun but we managed to build it into rifles and then a couple of good cannons, one portable and one that we can use in flight if we need it when we start to leave."

"Sir, if you don't mind me asking why didn't the people you worked for in the future just send another ship to intercept you before you could crash or rescue you after you did?"

"Well those are two very good questions we've asked ourselves many times. First we'd have returned back to our own time only 15 minutes after we left even though those of us on the ship would be close to three months older once we returned. So you see they don't know yet we're even in trouble. That 15 minutes has not passed for them yet. Once we get our ship completed and return it will still only be 15 minutes later than we left even though we would've aged 40 plus years. That's one theory. The second is we were the first. If we've somehow changed history then our people in the future won't even know it. But to them we simply disappeared in the sky when we left. They don't know if we jumped back in time or if we've been lost in time forever. So they wouldn't have risked a second ship doing the same. Besides it would've taken years to build one."

"Man," Skipper said, "won't it be a shock to ya'll's family when you return and instead of being three months older you'll be forty years older."

"We had taken certain precautions for things like that to happen. Most on board, like your mother and father, were young couples. Married around 20 to 25 years old and no children. Only after we arrived here did any of you come along. We had an older scientist that helped us with many ideas along those lines. He was a genius and the one who invented the light shield which made time travel possible. He also invented the light suits as well. When we left, he was 55 years old. Once we return, I'll be older than him by ten years even though I was only 25 when we left."

"Now you know most of the story behind Steamway's secrets. Do you believe me?" the Colonel asked.

"How can I not? I mean I saw the disc entries where after my parents were killed you had someone protecting me 24 hours a day and I know my father was a very big part of all of this but I wasn't, so I see no reason for you to have taken such precautions to keep me alive. I mean it's obvious you don't truly need me. My father's records are very complete and a 10-year-old could continue his work. So it must have been out of loyalty to my parents right?"

"We've promised everyone that has ever been part of Steamway, no matter the cost, all of us that wanted to and were able, as well as their families, would return home. It's our greatest hope and dream," the Colonel said proudly.

"How did you come up with the name Steamway?" Skipper asked.

"When we first were forced to land here in this town and time, we picked the most secluded spot we could find within walking distance of town. You see we had no transportation yet and we knew we'd need all kinds of different supplies. After we gained the government contract, we bought the land around the ship, which at the time was still simply sitting on top of the ground right here in this small clearing. Then once funding started we built this four-story complex as you know three underground and one at ground level."

"And one above," Skipper added.

"Yes but that came much later. We incorporated a hanger in the basement floor for the ship and built a lift which will bring it to the surface directly in line with the plant road when it's time to leave. You see it's truly a runway not a road. We need its length to get up the speed to get airborne, then once up to full speed we can jump back to our time."

"When can I see the ship?" Skipper asked excitedly.

"Soon" the Colonel said. "But your father was working on a very important project for us that we fully intended you to complete even before his death and we need you to begin work on it as soon as possible."

"What project?" Skipper questioned. He thought he'd seen all his father had been working on by now but he could tell in the Colonel's voice this was important so he sat up in his chair to pay close attention to the contribution he could make.

"Well," the Colonel said, "you remember me asking you did you know how to make fireworks?"

"Sir, your people are going to be here first thing in the morning. Are you sure you don't need any of our people to help with the assault on Steamway?"Clark asked the Secretary of Defense.

"No you keep your people combing through the ashes at the Doster's house. We'll handle this. Have my people to gather at the location you and I discussed yesterday and tell them to be ready for the assault to begin at noon. How're all of your men doing?" the Secretary asked concerned.

"Totally recovered like nothing had happened to them sir. None of them seem to know how they were knocked out. The all guessing it was some kind of gas but sir, that was my field in the military and I know of nothing, not any gas anyway that could knock a man unconscious that fast. The ones who did manage to get out of their cars fell in their tracks. We just don't understand what happened sir and to be frank I was hoping you could shed some light on the subject for me. I know you said Steamway was behind them being taken down but I don't understand how a 'Glass Plant' could have taken out my best men."

"Let's just say that they're working on some 'special equipment' for us and leave it at that Clark."

"Sir I need to kno…"

"Clark remember in our business curiosity killed the cat so watch how you meow."

"Yes sir, I understand, Oh sir, your man at Steamway called me a few minutes ago. He needs to meet with you today. He said you'd know where."

"Did he say when?" the Secretary asked.

"Yes sir. 8:00 p.m."

"Thank you Clark. Let me know if you find anything in the Doster house."

"Yes sir."

As Clark left the room the Secretary thought about the meeting with his man at Steamway. He needed to get him clear anyway before they took over tomorrow. He'd been a good informant but he no longer needed him there. Even though his informant didn't officially work for the government, he'd been paid well for years. Now the Secretary thought, do I put him to work for me or have him silenced. Either way his job at Steamway is over.

"Daddy!" Crystal cried, as George came into the room. She ran to him and he held her in his big arms.

"Well hun, what do you think of your old man's past now? I'm sorry I could never tell you but living off-site it would've been dangerous for you to know."

"I understand daddy. Did mom know?" She asked.

"Some," he replied, "but not all. I swore the day I married her I'd never leave her so you'll be going home without me. Besides I've got a couple of new friends that,"

"George," the Colonel said, "can I speak with you alone for a second?"

Skipper and Crystal exchanged looks as the Colonel stood up and George followed him into Crystal's office and closed the door.

"Whatcha think that's all about?" she asked Skipper.

"I don't know and I'm not sure I want too!"

"Me either now that we know what all is going on."

"George," the Colonel said, "we let them believe that the Smith's were all killed in the fire."

"Why?" George asked, "they'll be worried sick!" he snapped back

"Because we can never again expose Brandon to anyone from our time! It'll be strictly up to you to point him in the right direction and besides Skipper would want them to come with us. You know that can't possibly happen," the Colonel said.

"Yes of course you're right. Once again I'm sorry for the slip of tongue. I guess I'm just getting old."

"Nonsense my old friend, no harm done."

"Well Colonel, what's your next move?" George asked.

"To get Skipper to make the incendiary explosives for Steamway's destruction."

George, looking past the Colonel toward the window behind the

Colonel's desk, noticed that it was raining outside. "Colonel, have you ever explained to the kids why we call this place Steamway?"

The Colonel smiled and said "No but Skipper asked me about it just today. I just haven't had a chance yet."

George pointed past the Colonel to the windows. The Colonel turned to see where George was pointing and he also saw the rain falling hard outside.

"Good idea George," the Colonel said, "let's take them out and show them."

They both turned and walked back into the main office and the Colonel said "Skipper you asked me earlier why we call the plant Steamway. Come with us and we'll show you something that, even in our time, we're very proud of."

As they took the elevator to the ground floor no one spoke much but George noticed the looks that were cast between Crystal and Skipper. Out of the blue George looked at Crystal and said, "You love him don't you Crystal?"

Blushing Crystal said, "Yes daddy, I love him very much."

"And I love her" Skipper said, as he looked at George.

"Then let me give her to you before you leave here going home. She's my angel," George said, his throat clogging with emotion, "and I love her with all my heart. I knew your father well and have no doubt you'd make her a fine husband."

Crystal looked at Skipper embarrassed but said nothing as they exited the elevator.

"Well," George said, "are we gonna have a wedding or not?"

"Daddy," Crystal said, "don't you think you should give Skipper time to ask me himself?"

"We or rather you two, don't have time. It's now or 40 years from now and I won't be able to be there then."

George still seemed to be waiting on an answer when the outside door opened and Skipper and Crystal saw it was still pouring rain.

"Walk over to the employee parking lot with us and we'll show you Steamway" the Colonel said.

Skipper removed his lab coat and placed it over Crystal's head and they all ran through the rain. Once they made it to the gravel the Colonel and George said, "That's far enough," and Crystal and Skipper stopped. The Colonel turned and pointed to the second floor on the building. What they saw held them both in awe. As the rain fell the computer tried to keep up with the changes in the position of each raindrop and the way the wind made the trees sway behind the building. The effect it had was almost a blue but as you looked at it appeared the whole top of the first floor was putting off large amounts of steam. "Steamway," the Colonel said proudly.

Even in the rain you couldn't tell the building had a second floor. It simply looked like the plant was being used at full speed and emitting a lot of steam.

"This is incredible," Skipper said, as he watched the steam or what appeared to be steam rise off the first floor of the building.

At 7:30 that night the Secretary of Defense, John Collins, remembered he had only 30 minutes left until he had to meet his informant at the safe house they'd established many years ago. He took a government car but had no driver to drive him there. He knew his informant had to remain a secret and he wanted no one but himself to know who he was. Once he arrived at the safe house, he saw no other car waiting on him but he still had ten minutes.

As he opened the door to the house, he could hear another car coming down the road. It was a long dirt road and no one else lived past the entrance. The only other cars that ever ventured down here were either lost or looking for some place to hunt. Deer hunting was a major sport in Central Alabama and more than once there had been people stop in and ask the caretaker about hunting. It wasn't long until John Collins saw the champagne-colored Rolls Royce and the caretaker coming down the road.

"Good evening Amos," the Secretary said, as Amos got out of the car, "what news do you have for me today?"

Chapter 16

There were about sixteen or eighteen people milling around the ship when Crystal, Skipper, Colonel Morgan and George arrived. Skipper recognized Ray and Allen Cook right away. They both waved as the Colonel led them past.

"I never thought it would be this big," Skipper said.

"Well when we left there were thirty of us now there's only seventeen. Eight died in our crash at Roswell and the rest after we got here. Some of the security didn't arrive with us and know nothing about the ship or our missions. Mark and Twan both arrived with us but most of the others are from here," the Colonel said, "Skipper, take time to look over the ship but afterwards we need to get you started on the project I spoke with you on."

"Exactly what is that sir."

"You need to make enough incendiary explosives that once we leave, will completely destroy Steamway. I mean leave nothing but ash. No evidence of what we did here. It needs to totally melt everything."

"I'll need some supplies sir," Skipper said, "but it shouldn't take long to make all we need."

"I think you'll already find everything you need in lab number three. According to your father it should be well stocked."

"That's great sir. Then I was hoping that tonight we might have time for a wedding," Skipper said, as he looked toward Crystal, "That is if I can talk this angel into marrying me."

Crystal stepped closer to him and kissed him passionately the said, "Nothing would make me more happy," as tears rolled down her cheek.

"I just wish Smitty could have been here to be my best man," Skipper said "but whether he's here or not he still is." You could tell Skipper was broken hearted but at the same time he knew his best friend would've been happy he'd found his true soul mate.

Skipper and Crystal toured the ship arm and arm. To Crystal it seemed much like the inside of some type of large fighter plane but Skipper could see many things that couldn't have came from this time.

"Hello Mr. Secretary, it's been a while since we've seen each other in person," Amos said.

"Yes it has Amos. What do you have for me tonight?"

"Why don't we go into the house and we can speak there sir," Amos said.

Amos unlocked the door to the house he'd lived in from the time he moved off site. Soon after that he went to work for the Department of Defense. The house was small, only five rooms consisting of a kitchen, two bedrooms, one bathroom and a living/dining room. Amos asked the Secretary to have a seat at the small table while he poured them a couple of glasses of tea. "I found out today that Steamway was behind the attack on your men at the Doster's house," Amos explained as he sat the tea down on the table, "how many men did you lose?"

"None," Mr. Collins said, "they were only knocked unconscious. I believe they must have used the sound wave guns on them. Did we get our targets?" Collins asked.

"Most sir," Amos said, "but Skipper Doster and Crystal Watson made it out. I figured you already knew." Amos told Mr. Collins.

"No, we couldn't find a single trace of anyone left in the fire. They're still looking though. The rain storm has held them up some but tomorrow is another day" Collins said, "listen to me Amos. I don't want you to go back to the plant. We're taking it over tomorrow and I don't need you in harms way. You've served your country well and my men won't know you from Adam. They have been instructed to take the plant at all cost."

"I have to go back," Amos said, "they're holding a wedding for Skipper and Crystal there tonight then I can return here afterwards. I really hate to know you're going to take over now. I know the soundwave project is nearly finished."

"It's finished enough for us now. Besides we'll keep the necessary people there to finish even after we take over," Mr. Collins said.

"What makes you think they'll cooperate?" Amos asked.

"Oh they will whether they want to or not. We've got our ways Amos."

"Yes I'm sure you do. And what will become of everyone else if you don't mind me asking? I mean the Colonel is my friend and has been for many years."

"We won't hurt anyone that don't put up a fight. I'm not going to let them know we're coming until we have the place totally surrounded. Now, can you help me with the layout of the plant and the grounds so no more lives will be lost than is necessary?"

"Yes sir. I'll draw you a diagram but you know I never got the clearance for the lowest level so I can't help you there at all."

"I know Amos, let's get busy so you can get back to the wedding and I can get my troops ready. They won't arrive here until morning and we plan on starting the takeover at noon."

"No problem sir. Why don't you let me make sure the Colonel's not there tomorrow when you come in? That way I'm sure he won't be hurt"

"I don't want to spook him Amos. Let's just get this diagram finished. Your Colonel will be fine."

"Daddy, I can't actually believe I'm going through with this. I've only known Skipper for a few days."

"Are you having second thoughts? I thought you were sure you loved him?" George said.

"Oh no, no second thoughts and I've never loved anyone like I love

Skipper. I know he'll make the perfect husband but I still don't understand why you won't go with us."

"Because honey, I want to stay with your mother and I don't want to be buried 40 years after her. I'll stay and be buried by her soon. I know when you leave it will be the last time I'll ever see you but I couldn't leave you in better hands. Now finish getting ready, we've got a wedding to get started."

"I love you daddy," Crystal said, and threw her arms around him.

He returned her hug and said, "I love you too my angel."

"Now I got to go have my talk with Skipper. I can't let him get away with you without laying down the laws to him."

Crystal smiled as he left the room.

It wasn't long before her father returned. He opened the door and said, "Honey, I almost forgot to give you this. It was your mother's. I hope it fits you ok," George came on in the room carrying the most beautiful white wedding dress Crystal had ever seen. Once he'd taken it off his arm Crystal could see that it had a train that must have been ten-feet long and the lace work was incredible. It had a criss-cross, shoe string open back and a lace veil. He also had a pair of elbow length gloves made of the same lace.

She stood and took it from George and with tears in her eyes and said, "Thank you daddy, this is the most wonderful gift you could have ever given me."

"No your gift is yet to come. This is from your mother. My gift is 40 years in the future."

"What do you mean daddy?"

"Never mind you'll understand once ya'll make the jump. Skipper is waiting in the chapel so hurry now and finish up. He's got lots of work to get done tonight before he can, well let's just say your honeymoon might have to wait 40 years or so."

"Oh daddy," Crystal said blushing. George laughed as he left his daughter to finish putting on her mother's wedding dress.

"Colonel Morgan, I need to see you right away," Amos said, "it's very important.""Amos, we're about to start the wedding can't it wait until after that?"

"Yes sir it can but we got some preparing to do. They're coming tomorrow!"

"When?" the Colonel asked.

"Noon sir. I gave them the info you told me to. The Secretary still doesn't suspect anything. He still thinks I'm bringing him the information he wants. He has never been hard to fool. Even after all these years," Amos said, "he's got the false layout of the plant and they're bringing 30 to 40 men heavily armed."

"Did you try to get him to put the attack off for a while?" the Colonel asked.

"Yes sir, I done just as you told me but he wouldn't wait. They'll be here noon tomorrow and in full force."

"Well come on in and let's marry these kids then we'll have a surprise for them when they arrive tomorrow. Mark and Twan are already preparing the ambush from the top of the second floor. No one will make it in without we want them to."

"Sir," Amos said, "they plan to kill almost everyone. The Secretary said he wouldn't hurt anyone who didn't force him to but I could tell he was lying."

"What're you saying Amos?"

"I don't think we should just use the stunners on them tomorrow. If we do, they'll be back in even bigger force."

"Then you think we should kill them?" the Colonel asked.

"Well sir that's not for me to decide. I don't know what kind of effect it would have on the future. But that would be my suggestion. If we don't kill them, we'll have to fight them again in a day or two and they will be more prepared than ever. They might even make an assault on us with the use of aircraft and Twan and Mark might not be able to handle that unless we're airborne."

"Well," the Colonel said, "let's just get past this wedding then we'll call the council together and discuss our next move. We have until noon tomorrow. Amos, you've been more than valuable to us. You played the roll of a double agent perfectly."

"Thank you my old friend," Amos told the Colonel, "I'll see you shortly."

Skipper, George, Amos and the Colonel awaited Crystal to call for her father to escort her down the small isle where many of the Steamway couples had gotten married. "I hope she's not much longer," the Colonel told George, "we need to have a council meeting ASAP."

"I'll go check on her," George said, but as soon as he turned to go he saw the door open and his daughter waved for him to join her.

"I'm sorry Skipper, to have to rush through this. We've got some very important things to prepare for. I want you to take your father's seat at the council meeting tonight. You'll also have his vote," the Colonel said in a low voice.

"What's the meeting about?" Skipper asked, as the wedding march began.

"We're going to be attacked tomorrow at noon by the war department. They're going to try to take our plant away from us. We'll have to fight them to stop them but Amos has been working as a double agent for us for many years and has found out all the details about tomorrow's attack"

Crystal and her father drew close as the Colonel finished speaking with Skipper. Skipper couldn't believe how beautiful she looked. She never ceased to amaze him with the way she looked. Each time she changed clothes she seemed to grow more beautiful and that smile. It was mesmerizing to Skipper.

The Colonel made the usual speech and told Skipper he could kiss his bride. He raised her veil and there stood the angel that had truly stolen his heart. After they'd kissed, the Colonel told Skipper that he had one hour before the meeting would start and then he apologized to Crystal for the rush. No one but Amos, George, Skipper, Crystal and the Colonel were there.

Skipper told Crystal what was going on at the meeting and she told him that she'd been invited to sit in on the council meeting as well.

The meeting was going to be held in the Colonel's office on the top floor and they'd been told that the head of security would be addressing the council. Amos had already informed Mark and Twan about all the Secretary of Defense had told him.

"First," Mark said, "I want everyone to stay near the ship and ready to leave. It's not likely they will make it past the perimeter fence. Twan will be manning the main cannon on the roof and I'm going to be on patrol on the ground in case anyone gets by him. There's only supposed to be between 30 and 40 men coming and we should be able to handle that many blindfolded. Skipper you need to start tonight on the incendiary explosives. I don't think we'll be leaving tomorrow but more than likely we'll have to leave the next day. Ray and Allen, you both need to be working on duplicating the time key. We've never recovered the second one and without it we can't make the jump. All we could do would be simply move to another location and hide again. Now we need to have a vote on what kinda force we should use on the assault team tomorrow. We can set the sound wave cannon to simply knock all the attacking troops out or kill them. If we only knock them out, we'll have them to deal with the next day. If we kill them, we could be changing history. Everyone think this over tonight. Consider all the pro's and cons and let us know first thing in the morning. Everyone stay busy tonight. Skipper, be careful with the explosives and Allen, you and Ray try to have the key ready. I know it's going to be hard and we won't be able to test it but do your best."

"Any questions?" Mark asked. "Good let's adjourn until the morning."

After everyone had left the meeting Amos, George and the Colonel remained in his office. The Colonel walked over to his bar and poured three glasses of brandy and offered one to each of his old friends. "I can't believe what I'm seeing," George said, "I've never saw you drink anything stronger than a beer."

"Well George, this is the last time I'll probably ever see you and as for Amos here he's a double agent and we'll just kill him later so who ya'll gonna tell," and they all had a good laugh.

"What do you think will happen after the attack tomorrow sir?" Amos asked. "Do you think they will come straight back or wait a couple of days?"

"That all depends on the council's decision on whether to use lethal force or not. If we don't, we'll be hit again by night fall. If we do and clean up after it's over there won't be anyone but some bureaucrat in the office to report a special op's group missing. It'll take a day or two for them to regroup."

"You sound in favor of the lethal force Colonel," George said.

"I am. You know I don't think it's possible to change the future by us coming to the past. I mean, how does it go, if I go back in time and kill my grandfather then how would I be born and if I'm never born how would I go back in time to kill my grandfather. It's just like our crash at Roswell. We knew the history of a ship crashing there but when we got there, hours before it was supposed to happen, we crashed. I mean it was us all along. No way that we can alter the future but that's just my theory. That's why I wanted to keep Brandon safe at all costs. Just in case. A toast gentlemen," the Colonel said, as he raised his glass, "to our past, present and future, may the God who's birth we all witnessed be with us."

"How's it coming honey?" Crystal asked, as she entered the lab.

Skipper turned to see his new bride coming toward him. "Well not too bad considering you just scared me and if I would've dropped this KABOOM," he said. He was holding a glass beaker full of a clear liquid.

"I'm sorry I didn't mean to startle you," she said, with a smile.

Skipper took the beaker and sat it down on the counter next to where he was working and took her in his arms.

"Whatcha think is going to happen tomorrow?" she asked.

"I don't know. It's just a matter for the security to handle. We were told to stay below remember. Besides I've seen what that soundwave equipment can do and 30 men don't stand a chance. They couldn't help Smitty and Lisa with it though," Skipper said.

"You know they can't interfere with the people of this time. If they could have, they would have."

"Yes I know but I still miss him. It still don't seem right. If he wouldn't have been spying on Steamway, who ain't supposed to be here anyway, then he'd still be alive. But they couldn't use their forces to save him or the kids. Something's not right with all of this. In Smitty's words 'this stinks'," Skipper said, "I've got a lot of work to do here but if you want to stay and help I sure could use you to help me mix these chemicals, "Skipper picked up the beaker he'd sat down earlier.

"Sure I'll be glad to help," Crystal said, "I didn't want to leave you here anyway."

"Good. Here, hold this while I go get an empty beaker."

Crystal took the beaker that held the mysterious clear liquid in it and stared at it like it might explode any second. Skipper returned with an empty beaker and took the first one back from Crystal. She was shaking as she handed it to him. He poured half the liquid into the empty beaker and handed her the first back. Then Skipper took and walked over to the refrigerator and took out four cubes of ice and put two in his beaker and as he dropped two into Crystal's she almost had a heart attack. "Cheers hon," he said, as he took a drink of his. She looked at him very puzzled as she still held onto hers with both hands.

"Vodka on the rocks. Helps calm the nerves," he said, as he began to laugh.

Crystal realized he'd been playing a joke on her the whole time. She pinched him on the arm as he turned to run away.

"I'll get you back you just wait and see Skipper Doster!"she exclaimed, "You scared the hell out of me!"

Chapter 17

It was close to 4:00 in the morning when the Colonel entered the lab where Crystal and Skipper had been working most of the night on the incendiary explosives.

"How's things going?" the Colonel asked Skipper, as he made his way to the computer on the desk in the far corner of the lab.

"Fine sir," Skipper replied, "we're just cleaning up now. Everything is finished."

"That's great! Why don't you get with Mark? He's a structural engineer in our time and he designed this building. He can show you just where to plant the explosives so that they'll have the best effect."

"I kinda figured Mark would be busy most of the morning sir. I mean the government still plans on attacking us don't they?"

"Skipper," the Colonel said, "with the equipment we have there probably won't be a battle. Nothing like you're expecting anyway. You've seen what a sound wave rifle can do right?"

"Yes sir."

"Well as I've mentioned before, we have two cannons. One for in-flight use and one already placed on top of the building. We'll simply wait on them to come into the perimeter fence then one or two shots should take them all out. Not one man should get off a shot. We've lost enough people to our government. I don't intend to lose one more person."

"Anyway to a lighter subject," the Colonel said, "I got those files Crystal copied that were lost in your house when it burnt. I thought you and Crystal would like to see what we did the first couple of months we were here."

"Yes sir we'd love to know what all ya'll found out."

"Well let's get started," the Colonel said, as he slipped the first disc into the computer. Once the computer booted up, on the monitor appeared the words, 'The Birth of Jesus.'

"Now here's the strangest part of our trip. We have some of the most advanced equipment for filming that there is and like the sound wave guns, it can be hooked into the light suits so we were undetectable while we filmed all these historical events. But on our first and second jump we couldn't get any of the cameras to work at all. When we checked the equipment between jumps, it was working perfectly. Now in time-travel you can never visit the same place twice because if you did, you might actually see yourself there and create what is called a paradox. It's like an earthquake in time. So we can never try to witness these events again. All we were able to do is simply take notes."

"I'll scroll down until I get to the interesting parts," the Colonel said, "most biblical history is very accurate. Mary gave birth to Jesus and he was placed in a manger of straw. It was an extremely cold night but the atmosphere around the Baby Jesus almost seemed warm. Most of us were historians and could make out part of the language that was being used. I could show you all this file but you couldn't do any better than to simply read your Bible," the Colonel explained, as he changed screens to get to the second jump. It was labeled 'The Resurrection of Christ'.

"We jumped close but were off by almost a week. At least we were early and actually got to see Christ Crucified. You kids think people are cruel to each other now days. You should see a man that had been scourged. They beat him with a whip that had about ten or fifteen straps of leather on the end. Each piece was dipped in lead just on the tip. So as Jesus was being whipped, these pieces of lead would tear his flesh. A man named Simon was called by one of the soldiers to carry Jesus' Cross for him when he no longer had the strength to carry it for himself.

169

This man, Simon, didn't believe Jesus was Christ and actually refused to do as he was ordered by the soldiers but after they'd threatened him he picked it up and carried it the rest of the way to the top of the hill. Jesus was being spat on and dirt kicked in his face as he crawled up the hill to his death. Very few people were there weeping for what was about to happen because they feared for their own lives. Once at the top of the hill…"

"Colonel," Skipper interrupted, "we were both raised very Christian. We know the story. What we don't know is the same reason you went there. To see if Jesus truly rose from his tomb in three days."

"I know you and Crystal both know the Bible Skipper, but it truly don't describe the torment our God went through hanging there on that cross, but you're right. To answer your question we watched the stone or the front of Jesus' tomb from the day his body was placed inside we also had our video equipment running thinking we were filming the event and yes in a blink of an eye the stone was moved and our God arose from his sleep. It was spooky. He looked directly at us even though we were using our light suits. He knew we were there. Then we saw two women coming up the trail to the tomb and heard a rustle in the bushes behind us. I turned just in time to see Simon of Cyrene the cross bearer running away. We already knew who the women were but had no idea Simon was there. Our job was finished even though I wanted to stay. I knew it was time for us to leave. Once back on board the ship we tried once again review the film we had made and there was nothing. It was once again blank except for the second we stepped back on board it started filming again."

"You think Jesus had something to do with the camera not working Colonel?" Skipper asked.

"Yes I do. In order to be saved you must have faith not proof. If we'd have been allowed to make a film of his resurrection many would still not have believed but some would have only because they saw it. Jesus wants us to believe because we feel him. To actually feel his presence in our lives. Do you understand?" the Colonel asked.

"Yes sir we do," they both said.

"Before we go any further why don't we pray together then and let our God know we have that faith," the Colonel said, as he bowed his head.

After they finished praying the Colonel said, "now for the *Marie Celeste.*"

Then he opened the file.

"This was a personal project for me," the Colonel explained, "I've always been interested in ships lost at sea. And the disappearances in what is known as the Bermuda Triangle. One of the most famous was a ship that was recovered but as you know had not a single soul on board.The *Marie Celeste* was launched in Nova Scotia in 1860. Her original name was *Amazon.* She was 103 Feet over all, displacing 280 tons and listed as a half brig. Over the next ten years she was involved in several accidents at sea and passed through a number of owners. Eventually she turned up at a New York salvage auction where she was purchased for $3,000.00. After extensive repairs she was put under American registry and renamed *Marie Celeste*. The new captain of *Marie Celeste* was Benjamin Briggs, 37, a master with three previous commands. On November 7, 1872, the ship departed New York with Captain Briggs, his wife, young daughter and a crew of eight. The ship was carrying a cargo of more than one thousand seven-hundred barrels of raw American alcohol bound for Genoa, Italy. The captain, his family and crew were never seen again. This mystery had always intrigued me and so when my rank gave me one choice event in history to observe I chose the *Marie Celeste*. The best theory behind the disappearing crew comes from the understanding that despite his years of sailing experience, Captain Briggs had never before shipped crude alcohol. His puritanical nature obviously made him suspicious of his cargo. Unfortunately the temperature during the ship's voyage would've caused the alcohol casts to sweat, leak and eventually pop their lids due to pressure. This would also explain why the cargo hold hatches had been blown off. Panicked by the evil powers of alcohol and fearing that his ship might soon explode, Briggs may have ordered his family and crew into the life boat. The sea was clearly calm when they boarded the life boat. So Briggs did not take care to rope the lifeboat to the larger ship. As evidenced by the torn and missing sails, the *Marie*

Celeste soon encountered a storm or two. So everyone believes that the lifeboat was cast hopelessly adrift toward a doomed fate."

"Well we now know," the Colonel continued, "that most of this is true except the fact that Captain Briggs did think to rope the life boat to the *Marie Celeste* but he did make a fatal mistake. He used a rope that was close to three inches in diameter and even though they were being towed along behind his ship at a good pace, when the first storm hit it caused the *Marie Celeste* to surge forward hard and instead of snapping the rope it tore most of the front of the life boat away and it sank rapidly. Then came our dilemma," the Colonel said, "should we rescue them or let the past be the past? We had all decided and been trained to let it alone and just observe but we couldn't. We had to try. What we didn't know is that the prevailing storm wouldn't let us any closer than we were. Each time we tried, we'd receive some kind of electrical interference. Lighting was our only excuse but I still believe that you can't change the past. At least our cameras worked this time and we now have a full record of what truly happened to the crew of the *Marie Celeste*."

"After this we all decided to take a break. We had planned a small vacation during our trip anyway so we put down on an uncharted island not far from Hawaii. It was a tropical paradise but not long into our stay we found out that we were not alone on the island. George, myself, and your father, Skipper, were doing a little exploring when we ran up on a young man named Gilligan."

Skipper looked at Crystal and the Colonel just burst into laughter.

He said, "you should have seen the look on ya'll's face. I just thought I would break up the dreary past I've explained so far and throw in a little fun."

Skipper and Crystal both joined in on the joke too. Skipper said, "So is Ginger really as good looking in person?" Crystal pinched him again and they all had another good laugh.

"Now on to our next stop," the Colonel explained, "this year on September 11, four planes are going to be hijacked by a group of terrorists called the Taliban. Its leader was Osama Bin Ladin and even as of today we're still not sure of their exact goal but they managed to crash two jumbo jets into what is now the World Trade Center. One plane in each building totally destroying both of them. The first plane hit at 9:10 a.m. and the second around 10:00 a.m. Both buildings held more than 50,000 people each but due to a large traffic jam not even half the people were at work that morning. The third plane crashed into the Pentagon but actually missed its target by several hundred feet and only managed to do minor damage. On the fourth plane the passengers tried to take it over. They didn't succeed but managed to crash the plane in up state Pennsylvania in an abandoned area. Here's some amazing statistics. The planes were scheduled to hold more than one thousand people only 260 had made their flights. The rest were somehow stalled and unable to catch them. The twin towers held more than 100,000 employees total but only 20,000 had made it in to work that morning. In my personal opinion, that was God's hand at work. The twin towers stood for more than two hours after the planes hit them and according to structural engineers that in itself was impossible. Now I'm not sure if I should even be showing you this footage because it's actually still possible to be in your future but I'm pretty sure you'll be going with us so it will actually be in your past."

"My God," Skipper said, "I can't believe what I'm seeing. This is terrible." Crystal just sat and stared at the screen with tears in her eyes.

"Where were you when the planes hit?" she asked.

"About 10,000 feet above the twin towers and just arriving at the Pentagon when the third crashed. We didn't make it to the fourth in time to film it."

"I can't imagine what kind of impact this all had on our economy," Crystal said.

"Well," the Colonel explained, "your or rather our president George Bush Jr. swore to the public that he would completely wipe out all terrorist activity world wide and not stop until it was done."

"In his own words *'you're either with us or you're against us! Choose sides'*. Then he declared war on the Taliban terrorists. In the year 2041 when we came back, terrorism still existed but Bush wiped out 99 percent of them. The U.S. was at war for more than twenty years.

Most of the superpowers sided with us, even China and Russia. But it still took a very long time to root them all out."

"I can't believe we were attacked on our own soil," Skipper said

"Believe it, it's coming and we have to be home by the time it does. If we're still here, it could cause a paradox. It's not likely because we won't be in the area but still possible."

"Now on to the good stuff. Roswell, New Mexico. On July 4, 1947 according to the history books. Something crashed just outside Roswell, New Mexico. As you both know now, it was us, I'll review the reports as was given by the government first then I'll tell you what truly happened."

"A farmer named Mack Brazel was working his fence line with his neighbor's son. They came across a debris field where something had crashed. They found what appeared to be aluminum foil but to their surprise they couldn't tear it or destroy it in anyway. Brazel said he could wad a piece of it up and it would unfold back to its original shape."

"Your liquid steel coating," Skipper said.

"Exactly. He, Brazel, took a large piece of it home. Then on July 7 he finally reported our crash to the local sheriff who in return reported it to Major Jesse Marcel of the 509th atomic bomber group. On July 8, 1947, they sent out a press release stating that the wreckage of a crashed disk had been recovered by the commander of the 509th William Blanchard. Hours later he finally convinced them to tell everyone that what they'd found was just a weather balloon."

"From then on it was simply a cover up. The local coroner Glenn Dennis was notified that we were in need of some air tight coffins and needed to know how to preserve a body for the longest period of time possible. We had planned on taking our dead back home with us. The coroner misunderstood and thought that the government was trying to hide alien bodies to be studied later."

"Now," the Colonel said, "onto what really happened! As I said, the 509th was an atomic bomb group. What they were doing on July 4, 1947 was testing some of our first nuclear devices. As you might know, when a nuclear weapon is detonated it causes a bio-electrical surge to be emitted. Shutting down or shorting out everything electrical for miles."

"Even time ships," Skipper once again said.

"Yes, that's correct," the Colonel said, "just as we came out of the time warp and appeared in the skies over Roswell, even though no one could see us at the time, they set off an underground nuclear bomb. It shorted our light shield and all of our other instruments. We went crashing to the ground in a ball of fire or so it would've seemed from the ground as the shield shorted out. We hit where Brazel found parts of the liquid steel but had enough speed up that we bounced almost four miles away to some cliffs where we stopped. It was like skipping a flat stone on the surface of a pond. It took the military only three days to find us. We had several injured and a few already dead. We lost our pilot and several others by the time we were found. Thank God there are others of us who know how to fly. Our ship was then loaded up and hauled to nearby Roswell, New Mexico to a hanger where we remained for almost four years. The government, believing we were extra terrestrial or what they called ET"s, wanted our technology very badly. They fell in love with the liquid steel because it could be so simply applied and how strong it then became. But we never let on that we could produce it. They tried but failed. They helped us nurse our people back to health and repaired our ship. We had them believe that the repairs weren't even near ready for flight but we thought we already had the bugs worked out. They also loved the stealth design of our ship and used it in designing your stealth fighter. They wanted to know how our propulsion system worked but once again we played dumb and told them we weren't technicians just crew. The whole time we were repairing it on the sly. Once we thought we were ready, we used the sound wave pistol we had, knocked out a few guards, slid the hanger doors open and rolled our ship outside for the first time in four years. We knew it was not in tip-top shape but this was our chance to jump home. As we started to roll down the runway we turned on our light shield which we had repaired and to our surprise it actually worked. We vanished right before their eyes. Once we were airborne, we prepared for a jump because we knew they could track us on radar even though they couldn't see us. We set our time and destination and went into the time warp. What we didn't know was that the equipment used to make a jump had been damaged as well. Instead of ending up in our test sight in Virginia in 2041, we ended up here. The jump had fried all our time warp circuits so we needed repairs once again. What we weren't ready for is the structural damage we had sustained during the jump from 1951 to now. Our light shield and liquid steel wasn't as strong as we had produced in the future and most of the liquid steel had peeled away even though the light shield was still functional. Here we are twenty years later just finishing up the repairs but this time we know it's been done right."

"So Colonel," Skipper asked, "you don't see any problems with this trip?"

"Nothing if Ray and Allen can duplicate the time key. It was that triangle-shaped piece of glass I first asked you about after your parent's died."

Skipper's face went pale. He knew he was wearing the key as they spoke but he thought to himself that was all he had left of his family and if they could duplicate it, then let them.

"Well kids, that's our history. Now the ship is complete and as soon as everyone is packed and ready to go we'll be leaving. We still have some minor repairs to do but it's only two days away. Crystal, your father will be back this morning to say goodbye. He asked me to tell you to have some of those wonderful waffles cooked you make. It's no wonder he's getting fat. All he wants to do anymore is eat," the Colonel said, as he smiled at Crystal, "and Skipper you need to get with Mark and get those fireworks ready."

"Mr. Secretary, your special op's group is here. They're in route to the safe-house where you told them to meet you," Clark said.

"Tell them that I've got a caretaker there and for them to wait in the yard. I don't want anyone in the house. I'll be there within the hour. Clark, have you finished going over the remains of the Doster's house?"

"Yes sir, but we've found nothing to indicate any bodies were in the fire sir. The only things we found that might be useful to us were two Uzi's and two bullet proof vests. They were burnt beyond recognition but our people in the lab tell us that is what they were. We did find two small pieces of bone that were determined to be human though not enough to say there was a body there. It could have been just a bad wound."

"Could your lab tell if the vests had been hit or not?"

"No sir, they couldn't tell. I'll have them double check though."

"No, That won't be necessary. If anyone survived, they will be at Steamway, and after noon today, well, let's just say it wouldn't have mattered if they did."

The Secretary hung up the phone and told his driver to take him straight to the safe-house. Once he arrived there, he was greeted by several familiar faces.

"Sir," one man said, as he snapped him a salute, "all present and accounted for."

"Well Master Sargent, it looks like you came ready for a war. It's just going to be a simple sweep operative."

"Yes sir, I know but you can never be too prepared"

"Yes of course you're right. Let's you and me and your top few people go inside and we go over the layout of the building."

"Yes sir."

"Oh, by the way, have you seen my caretaker. His car is not here."

"No sir. No one has been here since we arrived at 0500."

"That's not good," the Secretary said, "I told him to come back here last night after the wedding at Steamway. You see he was also my inside informant."

"You don't think that Steamway is holding him captive do you sir?"

"No, no he was worried about us harming his people. He might have warned them we were coming."

"Still sir it shouldn't matter. They're only civilians and I have 38 men here fully armed," the Master Sargent said.

"Yeah I know but you don't have 'sound wave'," the Secretary said, "come inside and I'll brief you."

"Come on Romeo," Mark told Skipper, "let's get these toys of yours planted."

"Yes sir."

"Sir? No I'm just plain Mark," he told Skipper.

"Ok Mark. Where do we start?"

"By telling me how stable this stuff is. I mean I don't want to drop this stuff and get blown up."

"No, it's very stable. It's kinda like C-4 but burns more than explodes. Once the building comes down this stuff will burn hot enough that it should re-separate the concrete. I'm sure the temperature will reach somewhere around fifteen- to twenty- thousand degrees Fahrenheit."

"Damn! That's hot," Mark said.

"Well that's mainly what we were shooting for right?" Skipper asked.

"Yeah I guess so. How will you set it off?" Mark asked.

"You've two choices. Either on a timer or by remote. Now what I suggest is to set the timers off by remote. That way we can be airborne. If we just set the timers and something happens where we can't leave right away then we're dead. If we set it off by remote then we're sure to be leaving already," Skipper explained.

"Agreed" Mark said, "let's get this done."

As they left the lab, Mark helped Skipper push the two 55-gallon drums he already had on a small cart toward the elevator. They went down to the basement level where Mark showed Skipper that there were eight columns that held the entire building's structure.

"We should place two drums at each column. That should do the trick, "Skipper said.

"How easy is it going to be to set them all off at once?" Mark asked

"Not hard at all. All we have to do is detonate the center most drums and the rest will go with it."

"Are you sure?" Mark asked, as they placed the second drum near the center column.

"Oh yeah very sure. The drums are plastic but even if they were metal it would still go all at once. We just need to be sure to be out of the blast zone when it goes."

"How far?" Mark asked Skipper, concerned.

"One mile," he told Mark, "anything under that and we could still receive the shock wave from the blast. It's mostly going to blow straight up because of the depth of the charges but anyone close as half mile don't stand much of a chance. Not just because of the shock wave but the heat is going to incinerate everything within a half mile circle of the building."

"That's great," Mark said excitedly, "we don't have to worry about anything on the grounds we might have forgotten. Let's get finished up. I have to go tend to some business on the outside that should be getting here in an hour or so."

Chapter 18

"Is all the 'sound wave' gear ready?" Mark asked Twan, as they walked into the secretary's office.

"Yeah everything's ready. Our man on the roof has already spotted people moving through the woods on the backside of the property. This may not be as easy as we planned," Twan said.

"How many did Amos say we were to expect?" Mark asked.

"30 to 40 special-ops personnel. He really didn't know much more but if they're special ops they'll be Delta or Seals so we better be careful. They're due to start the attack in less than one hour," Twan said, as he started placing his light suit on.

"Well they're conventional hand-held weapons won't be able to penetrate the light suits so we don't have that worry. Just look out for explosives. I doubt they'll have time to use any but just in case they do get through the perimeter fence let's make sure all the motion detectors are working and have a man in here monitoring them. If he picks up any movement let us know where on the radio and you can use the roof cannon and just sweep the area," Mark instructed, as he placed his light suit helmet on and activated it, "everything seems to be working. I'll use a hand-held rifle and help cover the main entrance in case anyone gets past you and that cannon."

"Nobody will sir," Twan said, with a slight smile, "I've been waiting 20 years for a little payback and after they killed Stephen and

Cindy Doster, well all the more the better. Will the Secretary be with them?" Twan asked Mark, as they left the secretary's office and headed for their assigned locations.

"No, I don't think so. He'll probably just be in radio contact with them. That's why I want you to hit anything that looks like radio equipment first then start on anyone who might be trying to make it to the trees. Just do a sweep around the whole plant after you hit the convoy. I don't want them to know what hit them. If they do make it past the perimeter fence, I'll take it from there. Just radio me and tell me where they're coming in at. You should be able to see them from the roof and I'll be more mobile with the rifle than you'll be with that cannon. Ok." Mark said, "this is it. Let's get it over with."

They parted ways as Twan went up onto the roof and Mark went outside to await anyone who might get past the fence. They felt pretty safe that no one could see them with the light suits on and the soundwave equipment should stop anything they brought with them.

"Let's move out," the Master Sargent told his troops, as they started down the plant road. He already had twelve men placed all around the outside fence to Steamway but they'd reported no movement as of yet.

"Is anyone there?" the Master Sargent asked the scouts.

"No one we've seen so far sir. Even the guard house is empty."

"That's strange. They must be expecting us. Let's stay on our toes people. You were all informed this morning about this new weapon they have. Once you spot it concentrate all fire on it. Don't let up until it's destroyed."

As they started to move down the plant road, Mark could hear them coming but knew Twan had them covered good from the roof so he walked out to the fence and started making his rounds. Then he thought about what he'd told Twan, after the convoy, sweep the area around the fence. This sent a tingle up his spine as he made a hasty retreat back to the safety of the plant walls, He could watch the back fence from there.

There was a total of six vehicles when they finally came into sight. Twan waited until they stopped at the gate before he fired the first burst from the sound wave cannon.

The humvee at the rear of the pack had what appeared to be a small satellite dish on top of it so Twan assumed it was the communication equipment. When the blast from the cannon hit the humvee, it seemed as if it had been slowly blown to pieces from the inside out. Like a balloon that you'd overfilled with air. At first it seemed to swell then burst into a million pieces. Twan just simply swept the cannon forward and one by one each transport vehicle did the same. After the third on, the men from the first three started to scatter in all direction. Twan brought the cannon around and he could tell as the sound wave hit each man. All he could see from his location, even using the screen that was built atop the cannon, like a telescope, was a burst of bright red as the wave passed each man fleeing the fire that was created as he finished off the last of the convoy.

Once the convoy was gone, he started receiving small arms fire but nothing was even hitting close to him. Everything was being fired at the ground floor, this didn't surprise Twan, He knew that none of the soldiers could see him on the top floor of Steamway. After he'd finished off all he could see with just the screen, he switched the setting on the scope to thermo imaging. This meant he could track the men that did get into the woods using their body heat. It didn't take long till he started finding men hiding behind trees and in small ditches. When Twan would fire the cannon at the one's behind the trees, he could see with his naked eye parts of the trees flying straight up into the air. Some as high as fifty feet above the rest and some just as splinters the size of toothpicks. As he spotted the ones in the ditches he couldn't see much of what happened to them except that their thermo image simply grew in size to a circle of about eight feet then slowly went out. He could only guess what a blast from the cannon set on full power would do to a man's body.

It wasn't long before he asked Mark if he'd spotted any of the early arrivers.

Mark said, "Yeah I got two who had cut a hole in the back fence and made it through. I still want you to do a complete thermo scan of the area."

It didn't take him long until no more readings were found.

"Base to Delta Elite 1 come in! Base to Delta Elite 1 come in!"

Nothing. The Secretary was at the safe house with one communications officer and had tried to reach his special-ops group since just after noon. No reply had been received.

"Nothing sir. It's like they don't even have their equipment with them. I've got G.P.S. tracking on the convoy and once they got to Steamway something shielded the G.P.S. from picking them up," the communications officer told the Secretary.

"Shielded them or destroyed them," the secretary said.

"That's not possible sir. One of our men would've gotten off a distress call. All of them couldn't have been destroyed at the same time."

"Let me ask you this. If there was a huge surge of sound like could be produced at a rock concert but concentrated, could it stop our men from transmitting to us?"

"Not likely sir. It would take something ten times as strong as that to break our satellite link communication."

"Keep trying to raise them and if you can't, call me in twenty minutes. I've got to call the President."

"Colonel, it's over," Mark said, with sadness in his voice, "we're gonna need a big cleanup crew. The soundwave cannon did more damage than we had expected. There won't be enough of the men left to pick up so I suggest we just use some type of flame thrower and simply burn the ground around where they were. As far as the convoy, we can use one of the Doziers from down in the basement to dig a hole and drop what's left of them in and cover them up. There won't be much."

"I'm sorry Mark, you had to go through all of this," the Colonel said.

"It's my job sir, and they would've done the same to us. They'd no intention of coming in peacefully."

"How many men were lost?" the Colonel asked.

"All of them sir or at least we couldn't find any more with a thermo scan. I went to see for myself the damage that the sound wave had done and besides a heck of a lot of blood I couldn't find a single trace of a man, No bone no skin nothing. It was like it obliterated them."

"Ok Mark, how's Twan taking all of this?"

"That's what scares me sir. He doesn't seem to be bothered at all by it. To him it was payback for all they put us through over the past 23 years."

"Let's get started cleaning all of this up right away. I would imagine that they'll want to know what happened to all of their people and soon, so use all the resources you need to get it done quickly."

"Sir, do you expect another attack?" Mark questioned.

"Yes, not today but soon, so after the cleanup is finished let's start loading the ship. I want everyone on board and ready to go except for Ray and Allen, let them keep working on the second key. Pray they finish it in time or we'll simple relocate but still be in this time."

"I know everyone needs rest," Colonel Morgan said, "so when the cleanup is over give everyone five or six hours then have them to ready the ship. Tell Skipper I need to see him and Crystal before they take their break. I'll be in my office and also tell Amos to get in touch with George and tell him to be expecting Skipper, Crystal and myself this afternoon. I'll treat him to supper again at the same place and time as before. I want to say good bye in person."

"Mr. President, this is John Collins calling. We've got a problem with our project down in Alabama. It seems we've lost the one of our special ops groups."

"What do you mean *Lost the group?*" the President asked.

"Well sir we sent in 38 men according to our plans but none have been recovered. All of our equipment was lost as well."

"Are they dead or lost or what? Explain exactly what you're saying," the President said.

"I don't know sir. No bodies have been recovered and we lost all communication with them the second the takeover started. We lost all satellite communication with them and we can't seem to find a single person or vehicle. They just disappeared sir."

"Nothing just disappears John, find out what happened to those men and get back with me."

"Sir, I've already sent men over there and all they have found is burnt circles on the ground and places in the road that indicate that our convoy was destroyed as soon as they arrived. They never even had a chance to get out a distress call."

"Ok John, this has been your project from the start so it's in your hands. Here's what I want you to do. Call up the head man there. What was his name, Morgan I believe, and set up a meeting between you two and see if he can be bought-out. If not let him know that our next force won't be 40 men. It will be a couple of bombers understand."

"Yes sir, but I'm not sure he'll meet with me or not."

"Then call him John, and find out. That's not too hard, is it?" the President asked, sarcastically.

"No sir, I'll get right on it."

"John, we don't need this technology getting away. If it's necessary, I meant what I said. Call me back and I'll blow that place off the map. It's a matter of national security now. If you can't buy him off then tell him flat out, he won't see the sunset tomorrow night."

George arrived at Red Lobster as Amos, the Colonel, Skipper and Crystal were arriving.

"How's everything at home?" the Colonel asked George, who greeted him with a hand shake.

"Fine," George said, "I'm getting settled in well."

"Amos," the Colonel said, "join us tonight. We've got much to celebrate and you're a big part of the reason Steamway has existed as long as it has."

They entered the restaurant to find it fairly empty so they were seated right away. They all ordered and sat down to drink and to wait on their lobster.

"I guess this is a goodbye dinner as well as a reception for your wedding, "the Colonel said to Crystal and Skipper.

They hadn't been eating long when the Colonel's cell phone rang. He knew few people had the number and he figured that there must be something wrong at Steamway.

"Colonel Morgan here," he said, as he answered the phone.

"Colonel, this is Mark. I'm sorry to bother you but I felt this was important."

"What's wrong Mark?" he asked.

"Sir, you just received a call on your office phone from the Secretary of Defense. He wants to meet with you first thing in the morning."

"I'll bet he does," the Colonel said.

"He said he'd be alone and he left a number for you to call him back."

"What's the number Mark?"

"It's the number to Amos' house."

"He must still be there. Ok Mark, thanks. I'll give him a call and see what he wants but I want you and Twan to stay on alert. There ain't no telling what he's up to."

"We will sir. Tell George goodbye for me."

"I will Mark. We should be back in about an hour or so. I'll see you then."

As they finished supper the Colonel told the others about the call and said that once again they needed to cut dinner short. Crystal walked with her father back out to the car and told him how much she was going to miss him.

"I'll miss you too Angel, but Skipper is a great man and who knows we might meet again one day even if we've got to wait till I see you in Heaven."

She kissed him goodbye and they told each other how much they loved the other. Skipper just stood back and waited till they were done. Then he walked up to George and shook his hand and said, "Sir I'll protect her with my life."

"I know you will Skipper. Just try to keep her happy."

"I'll do my best sir," Skipper said.

"That's all I ask," George told him, "and when you get back to 2041 there will be a surprise waiting on you there. I've left my home there to you as a wedding gift."

"I hope you'll be happy honey, "he said to Crystalm, as they said goodbye for the last time.

Chapter 19

They arrived back at the plant with Crystal crying about not being able to see her father again and Skipper holding her in his arms and telling her everything would be fine.

The Colonel hadn't said anything since they left the restaurant. He knew he had a difficult phone call to make, and an even more difficult meeting to plan. He also knew as long as the Secretary of Defense was at their plant they wouldn't be attacked and security had already said that he'd meet there.

The Colonel wasn't sure what to expect. He didn't know if it was some kind of trap or if he was simply looking for more information about what actually happened to his people. Mark had watched two other men, whom he figured were from the government, sneak all around the outside fence but they never tried to enter. They checked out each spot that they could find where the soundwave cannon had done its job. The Colonel had given Mark orders to simply watch them and to let them leave when they were through unless they found something incriminating.

Once they arrived back at the plant, the Colonel told Skipper and Crystal that he had a few calls to make and he'd see them in the morning. They'd been assigned a small apartment on the second level and even though barely furnished it was much better than the motel room they'd rented earlier.

The Colonel went to his apartment and went through his usual routine. First he got a beer from the refrigerator and then sat down in his favorite recliner. After a few seconds and a long cool swallow of the beer, he picked up the phone and dialed Amos's home number.

"Mr. Secretary," he said, as John Collins answered the phone.

"Colonel Morgan, I've been waiting on you to call. We need to sit down together and have a good long talk," he said, with a tone in his voice like a father would use to a disobedient child, "Seems we had some trouble at your plant today and I need to find out what happened to my men."

"Your men," the Colonel said, trying to sound shocked, "I'd no idea those were your men. All I knew is Steamway was under attack from an outside force and we had to maintain the integrity of the plant and the secrets it holds. None of them identified themselves as your men."

"Well they were. Why don't I come down to the plant tomorrow morning? I'll be alone and we can discuss it further."

"That's fine with me John, but there's one thing I want you and the government to remember. This is Steamway and no one is going to take it away from us," the Colonel said firmly.

"Don't worry Colonel Morgan, like I said I'll be alone and by the way, tell Amos I said hello."

"What do you think the future will be like?" Crystal asked Skipper, as they lay in bed wrapped in each other arms.

"I don't know hon, I don't guess we've bothered to ask anyone that. The way the Colonel talked about the killings at the World Trade Center, most wars don't exist and I'm sure by then they have had to do some cleaning up of the environment. I don't think we'll be living in a bad time or all of these people wouldn't want to go back so badly."

"What if we don't like it once we get there?" Crystal asked.

"Then we'll steal a ship and come back," Skipper joked.

"It's not funny Skipper," she said, "I'm serious, do you think they would let us come back?"

Skipper thought for a minute then said, "I doubt it. You see we, that is you and I, aren't supposed to be here anyway. We could possibly alter the future in some way."

"I'm supposed to be here or at least half of me is," Crystal said, "My mother is from this time remember."

"Well honey, you and I are both from this time. I really wish I knew more about how all of this really works then maybe I could answer your questions."

"Well even if we do get stuck in the future and don't like it at least I'll have you," she said, as she leaned over to Skipper and kissed him.

It had been a long and stressful day for Skipper and he knew making love to his new wife was out of the question but Crystal, being the aggressive one, wouldn't take no for an answer, even though she wouldn't give him a chance to say no. They made love for the second time since they'd met and for both it was better than the first time. In the afterglow of their lovemaking they fell asleep in each others arms. Skipper dreamed of flying cars and clean oceans. Crystal dreamed of her father and of the house he'd left them in the future. She could only imagine what it looked like. He'd never told her much about it but she was sure she'd love it. She knew her taste in homes and her father's was much alike. It was still hard for her to believe that he came from their future.

At 9:30 a.m. Skipper and Crystal finally crawled out of bed. Neither wanted to move. The last few days had been the most tiring of their lives.

"Why don't we go to the cafeteria and have some breakfast?" Crystal asked.

"Ok," Skipper said, "let me get a shower first."

"Us," she said, "let us get a shower first."

Once again Skipper thoroughly loved being bathed and loved bathing Crystal. He thought to himself that this could end up being one of his favorite pastimes in the future.

As they dressed Skipper said, "Do you think the Colonel has met with that guy from the Department of Defense yet?"

"I don't know but I'd about bet they won't meet until around lunch."

Once they were dressed, Crystal came to Skipper and placed her arms around his waist, "Tell me again that everything is going to be all right," she said.

"I'll do one better than that," Skipper said, "when I was sleeping last night I had dreams about our future and what it was going to be like."

She looked up at him awaiting the rest of his story

"I'm positive you and I'll be fine and even though our parents crashed when they came back. I believe that their trip will be considered a success. Therefore more trips will be made most of the people here have made several jumps but have grown old so we're the next generation. I don't know why we can't visit our future past. I mean why can't we return next week and visit your father. We would've never been there before so we could return here one week or one month or one year from now and not create a paradox."

"Yeah," Crystal said, "but will they let us?"

"Crystal, you and I together could conquer the world. When we get there, we'll start studying all we need to know about time travel and who knows."

"Good morning Colonel," John Collins said, as the Colonel answered the phone, "are you about ready for me to come by for our meeting?"

"I guess so Mr. Secretary. Now is as good a time as any. Are you near the plant now?"

"As a matter of a fact I'm turning in on the plant road now."

"I'll have my guards show you to my office sir," the Colonel said, as he hung up.

Colonel Morgan walked over to his office window and watched the Secretary of Defense approach and his guard, Cleveland, meet him at the employee parking lot. Earlier in the week Mark had told all of the security staff that was not part of the original group that today would be their last day. He'd already made their severance checks and today he'd say goodbye to several good friends he'd made here. Cleveland was one of his favorites. Once Cleveland had escorted Mr. Collins to the door of the plant, Mark met him there and finished the escort to the Colonel's office. Mark was still not sure what the Colonel had in mind to tell Mr. Collins but he'd been invited to sit in on the meeting and just for security measure Twan was there as well in a light suit armed with a sound wave pistol.

The Colonel knew that John Collins knew nothing of the second floor on Steamway but they'd planned on leaving the next morning anyway so he saw no reason to hide it anymore, besides he thought who would believe him anyway?

"Welcome Mr. Secretary," the Colonel said, as Mark and John Collins entered his office. The air in the room was tense with anger and you could see it on the Secretary's face.

Colonel Morgan offered his hand to be shook but Mr. Collins simply placed his brief case on the Colonels' desk and said, "Colonel Morgan, I'll get right to the point. First do you want your guard in here with us because what I have to say to you'll be in the strictest of confidence."

"He's my second-in-command Mr. Secretary, what I know he knows."

"Fine," Mr. Collins began, "I, as a representative of our government, want to purchase Steamway and all it's workings outright. No longer do we just want to buy the product that you make but we want the whole operation. All I need from you is a price. We know from our scouts that you killed some 38 of our men yesterday and we don't want another incident."

Colonel Morgan just leaned back in his chair and put his hands to his chin as if he was praying. Then he said, "Mr. Secretary your men came to take Steamway by force and you know it. I can't and never will part with it for any price. Now I can guarantee you that none of our secrets here at Steamway are sold to anyone but our own government."

"Yes," the Secretary said, "but there are many you haven't sold us. Like the one you used to destroy my Delta Elite group yesterday. Those were some of the best trained men in the world and they never got within sight of your plant."

"As I told you before sir. No one has the capability of taking Steamway. Even though we may be a small company, we have big weapons."

"Colonel Morgan, you don't understand my offer. If you're not willing to sell the U.S. Government Steamway then we must, for national security, take it by force."

"No sir Mr. Secretary, it's you who don't understand. You can't take us by force. Let me show you an example of the advanced capabilities we've here."

The Colonel looked at Mark then walked over to the windows and started opening the blinds. Until this moment John Collins hadn't even noticed that they'd went up in the elevator and not down. Once the Colonel had the blinds fully raised, the Secretary just stared out in shock. At first he didn't say anything at all. He walked over to the window and looked out down the plant road and past his own parked car. The Colonel and Mark could tell he was astonished. Then he turned and said, "This doesn't change anything. We must still have this place. If you think that being able to make a building unseen can stop us from taking it over your are mistaken."

"Mr. Collins," the Colonel said, "you need to think of what you're saying. We could have twenty buildings unseen and an entire fleet of ships and tanks that you don't even know exist and you know they will all be coated with a much stronger version of the liquid steel than we sell you. Our capabilities allow us to have any equipment we used, airplanes, ships, cars and whole bases be totally undetectable."

"Still Colonel Morgan, that's more the reason we must take Steamway over. If you're not willing to sell it to us then we'll be forced to do it the hard way!" the Secretary said, "We may have to use a thousand troops but we'll have this complex!"

"How can you expect to fight something you can't see sir?"the Colonel asked, "Your troops will be destroyed as before. Now, we can continue to work together but there's no way you'll ever and I mean ever have Steamway!" Colonel Morgan said.

"Colonel Morgan, how many people do you employ here 30, 50, 100. How can you think we can't take this place by force. We could use aircraft with simple gas explosives to just kill everyone in the building with minimal damage to the complex."

"They wouldn't make it in. The soundwave devise can be broad cast in a large circle and would be like a force shield. Any aircraft missiles or bombs you sent at us would be destroyed miles before they got here. And as you know if you sent people in on foot they don't stand a chance."

"If I sent enough they could destroy this place," the Secretary said, angrily.

"Again sir you can't kill something you can't see. Twan," the Colonel said.

Twan turned his light suit off and he was standing between the Colonel and Mr. Collins. Collins almost fell backwards as Twan appeared out of thin air only a couple of feet from him.

The Colonel said, "This meeting is finished. Mark, show the Secretary to his car. Mr. Collins, think long and hard about what you've seen and heard here today. If you attack us again, I'll be forced to send a group of men wearing these suits to visit your superiors and 'explain' to them in person why you can't have control of Steamway. Now, next time we speak, let's make sure it's for your next shipment and not about taking our company away from us. Am I clear sir?"

The Secretary didn't say anything he simply closed his briefcase and started toward the door. Mark smiled at the Colonel and turned to follow him out.

"That was perfect timing Twan," the Colonel said, "I think we bought us enough time to finish loading the ship and get everything ready."

"I don't know sir. He seemed determined to take Steamway soon. I just hope he bought the bit about having planes and tanks."

"Me too," the Colonel said, "why don't you go down and let everyone know to expect to leave first thing in the morning, say around 0800."

"Yes sir, but I don't know if Ray and Allen will have the key ready by then."

"If they don't, we'll stay as long as we can but I still want everyone prepared to go on a moment's notice. Just in case we do come under attack."

"Yes sir, I'll have them ready."

"When you see Mark, tell him I need to speak with him."

"Yes sir, I'll just radio him and let him know to come back up to your office."

Twan left the room and the Colonel could hear him enter the elevator. He sat back in his chair hoping he'd made the right decision by showing the Secretary of Defense their light bending capabilities. He knew one thing, he'd had a good laugh out of seeing the expression on John Collins face when Twan suddenly appeared right in front of him. As the Colonel looked around the room he knew that all he'd worked for would soon be gone but he had the hope, as did most of the others, that he'd soon be home.

Mark watched John Collins as he drove down the plant road. He knew he wouldn't have to worry about another attack for a while but he knew it was inevitable. The ship was ready all but the time key and even if they had to leave before it was finished, they could hide somewhere in a jungle until Allen and Ray could finish it. He was ready to go back home and just be Mark Norris again.

As Mark started back to the building, he received the call from Twan that the Colonel wanted to see him right away so Mark headed back up to his office.

"You wanted to see me sir?" he said, as he entered

"Yes Mark, how do you think all of that went?"

"I thought you were wonderful sir. He can't help but believe we're a force to be reckoned with. They won't attack for a couple of days at least."

"How're things coming with your security team? Are most of them taking everything ok?"

"Yes sir, none of them want to leave but the severance pay you offered them seemed to help. They haven't made that much money the whole time they have worked for us."

"Well," the Colonel said, "I don't see we've a need for it anymore after tomorrow. Why not give it to our trusted people,"

"What about George sir," Mark asked.

"George will never need or want for anything. Neither will his guests.

He was left the remainder of Steamway's funds, mostly in cash so that they couldn't be traced back to us. He will die here a very rich man."

"I wish he would leave with us, "Mark said.

"Me too but this way we've got somebody here to watch over Brandon that understands how important he's to us."

Crystal and Skipper were in the cafeteria finishing breakfast when Twan walked in. As he held up his hand and said, "Can I have everyone's attention please."

The room grew silent as he continued, "The Colonel asked me to convey a message to everyone. He wants all of us on red alert. Be packed and ready to leave in the morning around 0800. Now we're not sure if we'll be leaving then but he wants us ready. As you all know we were attacked yesterday and now we fear we may be attacked again by an overwhelming force. We must be ready to leave in a moments notice. Have all your children already on board and make sure that everything you're taking with you is securely in place. Now we may see some combat here again but it's unlikely we will before we leave. More that likely what will happen is they will try to attack us once we're airborne. As you all know we can easily out run them once we're in the air. They will be able to track us on radar until we jump so we might have to do some air to air combat. Be ready people. I want to see the pilot and flight crew on the bridge in twenty minutes for a warm up check and everyone in charge of the air lift make sure your equipment is working. I want the ship to be able to surface in 30 seconds. We'll do a trial run tonight on the lift. Are there any questions?" Twan asked.

No one said anything. Skipper and Crystal just looked at each other.

"Good," Twan said, "let's go home."

"Mr. President, this is John Collins. Things didn't go so well at Steamway. They wouldn't sell and practically dared us to try to take their compound over again."

"What happened to the Delta Elite you sent in John? Did you find out?"

"Yes sir. It's as we thought. Nothing remains of them. Steamway has some unbelievable technology that I'd no idea they had. Colonel

Morgan assured me that we were and always would be his only customer but sir, I saw things there that is very much a threat to national security!"

"What type of things John. You know I don't like you to beat around the bush when it comes to telling me something like this."

"Well sir. I don't believe you've ever seen Steamway. But it appears from the outside to be a single story building. Now we knew it had two lower floors underground but sir I went *up* in the elevator to the top floor. Sir you can't see a top floor from outside at all."

"What're you telling me John?"

"It's invisible sir. The whole top floor is invisible."

"That's not possible John," the President said.

"I know what I saw sir, and that's not all. Colonel Morgan made references to planes, ships and tanks with the same cloaking capabilities. They must have used the soundwave equipment to stop our troops and then burned what was left of them. The Colonel also told me that this new soundwave technology created a force field around the plant that when activated nothing could penetrate."

"Do you believe him John?" the President asked.

"Yes sir I do. They definitely convinced me sir."

The President thought of all he was hearing and wondered if the man was delirious.

"Sir, there are other things as well. I knew that they can make a building invisible but as our meeting was ending he had one of this men materialize out of thin air standing between us. He'd been there the whole time but he was wearing some kind of suit."

"So what you're saying, John, is that this power if invisibility can be used by a single man and he can be mobile with it on? "the President asked.

"Exactly sir. He told me that if we tried to attack them again that he'd send one of his own teams, using these suits, to pay my superiors a visit and let them know personally why we shouldn't try to take their plant from them."

"Are you telling me he threatened me?" the President asked, angrily.

"Only if we attack sir," John Collins said.

"Then this man is truly a threat to our country's security and should be dealt with swiftly."

Chapter 20

It didn't take Crystal and Skipper long to realize that they'd nothing to pack and nothing to secure in place for the flight. They'd left everything behind including their families.

It gave both of them an empty feeling inside like they hadn't eaten for weeks. Everything they loved was in this time and as bad as they wanted to see the future, both were having second thoughts about leaving but neither said anything to the other.

There were many of the people milling in and out of the ship carrying things that they'd collected over the years. Skipper heard an announcement over the intercom asking everyone to clear the launch pad for a test fire of the propulsion unit. People began to scatter and head for the doors as the hatch to the ship closed. He and Crystal followed the largest part of the crowd to a view window that allowed them to watch the test. To Skipper's amazement he couldn't hear any roar of an engine or see any flames or exhaust. The first thing that happened was the pilot checked the light shield of the ship and Skipper was still in awe when a plane the size of a stealth bomber trembled as the propulsion unit was accelerated. The only sound was wind displacement and he could see the shields behind the ship begin to bend slightly just before the pilot cut the engine.

"Ok everyone our check is complete," the pilot's voice came again, as the ship reappeared, "you can complete your boarding."

Skipper and Crystal had no idea where they were supposed to be on the ship when it took off so Skipper decided to try to get in touch with the Colonel and ask him.

Skipper and Crystal found that their clearance had been extended to a class A because when they tried the scanner which operated the elevator leading to the first floor, it worked. They found the Colonel sitting quietly behind his desk and staring out the front window.

"Come in you two. I've been expecting you."

"You have?" Crystal said, surprised, "we didn't even know we were coming until just a few minutes ago."

"Well I figured you were worried about leaving and wondering about the future," he said, as he turned toward them and smiled.

"Well sir we were mainly wondering where we were supposed to be when the ship took off," Skipper said.

"You'll be on the bridge with me and the crew. You get to see the view once we engage the time warp. It's one of the most beautiful sights you'll ever see. There's so much you two haven't had the time to learn yet. But I'm sure you're curious about where you're going so if you'll have a seat I'll try to answer any questions you've got."

Skipper and Crystal both sat down and the Colonel turned and walked over to the bar. Even though it was only about 1:30 p.m., he poured himself a drink. "Would either of you like one?" he asked.

"No sir, it's a bit early for us," Skipper said.

"Yeah, it's normally early for me. I don't usually have anything stronger that a beer but I haven't had much sleep lately and I fully intend on going to bed after our talk today."

"To be honest with you sir, we don't know where to start. We both have been having second thoughts about leaving. Not knowing where we're going, if we'll like it, and if we don't, will we be allowed to return," Skipper said, as he took Crystal by the hand.

"Here's what I can do. I'll tell you what is now your future and will soon be in your past then you can decide. As you already know on September 11, 2001, the US was attacked by terrorist. The United States retaliated and declared war on all and I mean all terrorist organizations and anyone who supported them. Within five years we were involved in another full scale world war. Mostly the US had been able to keep the battle off of our home soil except for small things. We had received mail with anthrax virus un it and this was only in small quantities and to random locations. It killed a few people but only a few were lost. Then in April of 2007 we were attacked again. This time our adversaries were more successful. They did as they'd done before and hit several places at one time. At almost the exact same time. This caused a nationwide panic and killed more people over the next year than has ever been recorded in history. One third of the world's population will be lost to these attacks. But here's where they made their mistakes. They planted bombs in places like New York City, Washington, Chicago Dallas Richmond Indianapolis, Buffalo and of Course Atlanta. Almost every major city on the east side of the Mississippi River was hit with a number of explosions at the same time. Now the terrorist, Thanks to our governments relentless attacks on them, didn't have any nuclear capabilities, but the bombs did their damage and most of the cites were almost completely destroyed. Their mistake was two things. One, the time of year the attacked us, April is the US most rain-filled month. We had a steady NE wind all of our weather moves ENE and That April it moved fast. Second they hit their main target with success. It was the Center of Disease Control in Atlanta, where we house some of our most volatile virus'. There was stuff stored there that once vaporized and put into the air killed millions in the US alone but the prevailing winds carried the virus right straight back to our attackers and finished the job the attacking US forces had started. Most of the middle east was affected and many died. But now for the good news. Most every country in the world learned from this. All biological viral and nuclear weapons were destroyed and it became against the laws of the UN for anyone including the US to manufacture any of them. This at first was hard to enforce but after losing half of the people on the planet to disease in only one year. Then the infection that followed from the massive amounts of bodies that had to be destroyed. Finally everyone agreed. Now anyone caught in the act of trying to build a nuclear or biological weapon will have their county taken away and it becomes part of the un and they distribute it among the rest of the world powers to control. So far no one has even tried. The US was lucky. We had a strong east wind the day the CDC was hit and by the time the virus could circle the globe most had died off so our west coast suffered minor losses. We had the fewest deaths due to the CDC being bombed that nay other country in the world. After 20 years of cleaning the world back up we now live in a most spectacular place of peace and beauty. But bear in mind before you decide. The bible speaks of 1/.3 of the world being destroyed then a great peace that follows. We may be living out part of the prophecies of the bible. Our air is now cleaner than it has been in a hundred years and our water as well. Your future, the one you'll soon see, you two will see anyway if you're killed in the up coming war. So my advice to you is come, go home with me and let me show you some of the most wonderful sights you've ever seen. Many cities that you know no longer exist. But a few were rebuilt. But most everything for the Mississippi River east is back to an unpopulated or mostly unpopulated region. It's now more wilderness than anything and it's beautiful. Small towns still exist all throughout but nothing like it used to be. During this time three-fourths of the US population is on the east side of the Mississippi River. In my time there's only one-fourth on the East side."

"As I said before, we were fortunate that we were not attacked with nuclear bombs or we wouldn't be able to even visit the area. That's when we, The US, started working on the soundwave equipment. Non nuclear it can be used to simply stun and in 2041 we've it mounted on our satellites. If necessary, according to the UN, we can immobilize an entire city without killing a single person. No loss of life. But also if necessary it can be very deadly as well. The simple threat of being the only country to have the soundwave technology is enough to deter any others from trying to develop nuclear or bio weapons. If the UN suspects it's being done, zap, we'd knock the whole city out for enough time for the Un to investigate and no one would be hurt. If someone did manage to manufacture a nuclear device and use it the UN would use the soundwave to destroy everyone involved."

"Now in my time the light suits and shields are still very experimental. Even though I work for our government, only a small portion knows about it. The soundwave on the other hand is known world wide. Our government is once again ran by the people not by a bunch or bureaucrats and most everything is voted on. I'm not saying the general public knows about things like the light suits but any major political move like war must be voted on and not decided by a small group of representatives. Now or rather then you can vote from your home. Everyone has something like your telephones that is used. You simply dial in your security number then vote. It was another incredible invention that came after the great war. There's so many things that I could talk about for years and never cover all of them but for now I hope I've answered some of your questions," the Colonel said.

Skipper and Crystal just sat where they were not moving like they were watching a great movie.

"Do either of you have any questions I can answer for you that might help ease your minds?" the Colonel asked.

Neither of them knew what to say. They'd just found out that the world as they knew it was soon to be almost completely destroyed but the Colonel showed no emotion about it. Of course it was something he was taught in as history class. But to Skipper and Crystal he was talking about their friends and family. The Colonel seeing the concern in their eyes said, "there's nothing you can do to change what is about to happen. Even if you could warn everyone in all the major cities who would listen to you. Who would believe you? You can't change the past, future. I've tried," the Colonel said, as he hung his head and stared at his shoes.

"Can't we warn our—?"

"NO, no one must be told of any thing to come," the Colonel said, "besides you don't have time. We'll be leaving in the morning and besides who would you warn. Crystal your dad already knows and Skipper you only have family in the future and from what I gather most of your friends are gone."

"I understand your point," Skipper said, as he and Crystal stood up. "I think we'll go back to our quarters and mull over all you've told us. We'll let you knew whether we decided to stay or go later today."

"That'll be fine Skipper," the Colonel said. "I'm gonna get some rest. Tomorrow's going to be another busy day."

"That's a very populated area sir. All except about one mile around the plant itself. Here's the satellite photo of the area. As you can see there's a dam within four miles so any large weapon is out of the question," John said, as he spread the photos out on the conference room table. He wasn't expecting a visit so quickly from the president.

The President wanted answers and he wanted them now.

"Why wasn't 40 men able to take this plant?" the President asked, as he pointed to some of the satellite photos.

"It's like I said sir. They've been developing a weapon for us known as the soundwave project and we suspect it was used against our own troops when they tried to secure the plant. None of our men even got off a distress signal."

"How much do we know about this soundwave?" the President asked. "And can we mount any kind of a defense against it."

"Not much sir, except that the weapon uses compressed high frequency sound as a projectile or as a beam like a laser and can be magnified with the turn of a dial. As far as a defense, I've got people working on that right now. They believe anything can be sound proofed therefore they should be able to design some kind of a shield against it."

"If they used sound," the President said, "why didn't the whole city near by hear it? I mean it had to be extremely loud to destroy our men let alone the whole convoy."

"Well sir, from the test I've seen it makes no sound at all or not any that a human can hear, it's kind of like a dog whistle."

"John, I want this over now. How long will it take your people to develop something to shield that kind of power?"

"I'm not sure sir, maybe only a couple of weeks."

"Weeks! No! We're going to finish what your Delta group started tomorrow. I want-."

"But sir"

"Don't interrupt me John!"

"Yes sir"

"I want you to mobilize another force. Post it on all the local news channels that we're going to be doing some large scale testing in the area. I want two fighter-bombers ready and have me a group of say a thousand ground troops."

"Sir, if we announce it on the news they'll know we're coming."

"John, they already know we're coming. Wouldn't you? Now get this done. I want you to have the men and the fighters ready to go in the morning. Don't use the men to begin with. Keep them back out of range of that soundwave thing. Have them on stand by ready to move in. I'm gonna give this Colonel Morgan a call myself after the news announcements and try to talk some sense into him. If I can't, we'll have the bombers use a couple of light weight bombs to hit the building and then after the initial shock, send in the troops. We'll use enough men to simply overwhelm them. They should be mostly immobilized after the bombing but the ones that are left shouldn't resist much. We should still get by with minimal damage to the complex."

"Sir," John said, "with all due respect, you haven't seen the things I've seen there. We should, in my opinion, try to work with Colonel Morgan and not attack him. I don't think twice that many men would stand a chance in hades of even scratching his plant let alone taking it over."

"We will see," the president said, "we will see."

The Colonel awoke to his bedside phone ringing. He looked at his clock and saw it was about 5:45 p.m. He'd planned on sleeping most of the night away but once he answered the phone he knew no sleep was in store for him tonight. The Colonel was still half asleep when he answered and the first thing he deciphered was Mark saying to turn on the TV to the news. The Colonel reached for his remote control and turned the tv to channel 12 news. It was a station out of Montgomery. He saw hundreds of troops and vehicles moving down the highway through town.

"Mark, what is going on?" the Colonel asked.

"I've only caught half of it sir but the governor is saying that there's going to be some major exercises going on in our area in the morning.

You know that there isn't going to be any exercise. They're coming for us in full force sir. And there was talk earlier about F-16's doing practice bombing runs."

"Mark meet me in my office now. Let's catch the 6 o'clock news and get the whole story."

"Should I have everyone on board the ship sir? Or would you rather wait and see if it's just a threat or if they really plan on attacking us again?"

"It's no threat Mark. They're coming. Have everyone on board by 4:00 a.m. Announce it now then meet me up here. It's time to go. Does Skipper have all the incendiary explosives in place?"

"Yes sir. I helped him myself. That stuff should melt a hole in the ground the size of two football fields and Lord knows how deep."

"What about our shields? Will they hold if we're attacked?"

"The ship is as solid as ever sir. But we need to be airborne. We could defend ourselves much better."

"Is the lift ready to go?" the Colonel asked.

"We haven't tested it yet. We were going to test it after dark. But I see no problem with it. We should be able to surface the ship in thirty seconds or less."

"What about Ray and Allen, have they finished the key?"

"No sir, they haven't been able to duplicate it. We just don't have the technology here to form the chip inside it. They said with a little more time they might be able to get it to work."

"How much more time Mark, we only have until morning or we're just in for a fast flight to some other secluded place till they get that warp key finished."

"I don't think they'll be ready by morning sir."

"Then come up to my office and let's talk about stopping these jerks from attacking us again. It looks like they would've learned the first time."

Skipper and Crystal both heard Mark's announcement over the loud speakers. He'd instructed everyone in the plant to be on board the ship and strapped in by 0400. He'd made it very clear that this was a must.

Neither Crystal nor Skipper had seen the news yet but as they made their way back to their room Skipper noticed the unsettling way the other people moved past them He'd over heard some of them speaking of the local news showing troop movements. As soon as they were inside Skipper turned on the 6 o'clock news and right away he knew what all the fuss was about. He saw the news anchorman standing in front of a whole convoy of national guard troops and pointing behind him a t two f-16 aircraft. Skipper finally managed to find the sound button on the tv set. He heard the announcer saying that this was the biggest exercise that this particular unit had ever done and that it was actually a combined effort of four local national guard units. Skipper and Crystal just sat and watched as the anchorman described exactly where the exercise would take place and for all the local people not to worry. He explained that they would hear explosions and see lots of smoke and also there would be a few bombing runs by the local air unit.

The anchorman said that no one had to leave their homes or worry about any repercussions from the bombs. What scared Skipper is that the location they were describing was Steamway. Which the anchorman called an abandoned research center that the government no longer used. Skipper thought they used a good coverup plan. No one from anywhere around had ever been let into Steamway and he guessed anyone who knew that it existed figured because of the way it was guarded it was a military complex.

"They're going to come after us again in the morning," Skipper told Crystal, as she sat on the foot of the bed next to him.

"What're we going to do?" she asked him.

"I think we should leave with the rest of Steamway. If we stayed, they would find us but if we go maybe we can come back to visit like I said before."

"By the time they come in here in the morning we'll be gone and nothing else will be left of this place but a hole in the ground. They said that the exercise would start in the morning and I think that's why Mark wants everyone on board by 0400."

Mark took the elevator up to the top floor where the Colonel was waiting on him. "Come on in Mark. They've already started the news coverage again."

As the Colonel and Mark watched the troops being organized on the tv Mark asked the Colonel, "Are we going to stay and fight or are we going to run into another location?"

"I don't know yet," the Colonel answered.

"I don't want to hurt any more people," Mark said.

The Colonel just looked at him and Mark hung his head as if he was ashamed of what he'd just said.

"Mark," the Colonel said, "I'll defend these secrets till the end but we'll avoid a fight at all other costs. I'm like you. We're not truly fighting men and never have been. We've done here what we had to. Now I think it's time we left but I don't just want to go to another location in this time unless we've to. They could almost track us anywhere now so if we can't buy enough time for Allen and Ray to finish the key then we'll have to fight."

"But sir, we're altering the…" the phone rang and interrupted what Mark was saying. The Colonel walked over to his desk and picked up the receiver.

"Yes," he said, "yes Mr. President, I've been watching. I'm totally surprised that you'd be the one to call instead of John Collins. Yes sir, I know you're serious but you must understand I told John that we wouldn't surrender Steamway. Sir, your forces don't stand a chance. I don't want us to fight but as I explained to John our technology is so far advanced that we can stop any attack even before you get near the plant."

"Colonel Morgan, that very statement is a threat to our national security. No one can have the type of equipment that you claim to have and not know your company itself is dangerous to us."

"Sir, our company is devoted to serving only the U.S. and have no interest whatsoever in selling any of our secrets to anyone else." the Colonel explained. "But we can't give up even to our own government incomplete equipment and as I've said we can't allow it to be taken away by anyone."

"Colonel Morgan you must try to understand—."

"Mr. President I've already explained to you the only way Steamway could respond to another attack. I pray you see we're here to serve our country and only our country and you'll recall the troops you're sending this way. I don't want any more loss of life but you're forcing my hand. Call your troops back, let's keep doing business as usual and al will be well but if you insist on going through with this assault on Steamway then you're about to lose a thousand men"

"He's being stubborn," the President told John Collins. "We'll have to take the plant by force. He seems to think he can stop a thousand of our troops and our planes from taking Steamway."

John Collins hung his head without saying a word.

"What's wrong John?" he asked.

"Sir, with all due respect he can stop a thousand probably 10,000 or more. You haven't seen the things I've seen."

"Tricks John, nothing but simple tricks. The technology you've told me you saw I've checked with our best people and I'm told that it's many years into the future before those things could possible be."

"Sir, they also told you the same thing about the liquid metal we purchase from them now! I wish you'd reconsider sir. I've already lost enough men and—."

"Listen to me John, we must, must take this plant. If we don't then they'll be ten more just like it in a year and before long we, the government of the United States, will no longer run this country. We'll have plants like Steamway telling us what we can and cannot do."

"Once again sir, with all due respect, there are not and never will be any more plants like Steamway."

Chapter 21

"He's not going to listen to me Mark. Have everyone ready to go by morning! Rush Allen and Ray up. Tell them we need that key ready by sunup."

"Yes sir but if they don't finish it, Colonel, then what?"

"We're leaving Mark. I'm not going to kill another thousand Americans because some bureaucrat wants to make a name for himself. We'll find somewhere safe to land till they can finish the key. Have everyone on board by 0400. At the first sign of trouble we're gone, understand?"

"Yes sir, and Colonel thank you for not putting us in the position to take another life. I would rather run than kill another man."

"Well Mark, there are many places we can hide that they couldn't possibly find us. I've been thinking about it a lot lately and we could simply fake another crash except this time, do it over the ocean, somewhere very deep. Our ship can survive underwater as well as on the surface. So if we can't jump we'll simply all go for a swim. But Mark, we've got to defend the plant till the ship is lifted and everybody is on board. I figure you, Twan and I'll stay off ship till we're ready to take off and hold off the oncoming troops then we can board at the last second"

"Sir, you don't need to be off ship. Twan and I can handle it without you. You're much too valuable to take a chance on losing."

"Well just the same, we'll stand together in the morning as we've done for the last 25 years. I'll be fine."

Skipper and Crystal wanted to watch to see how the ship lift would work so Skipper called Twan and asked him about where would they be safe.

"Skipper, why don't you and Crystal go up to the Colonel's office. You'll be able to see the gates from there when they lift open. It's really amazing. Half the fenced lawn on the left side of the building is artificial. It folds open to form a very large hole where the lift raises the ship three stories to ground level. We'll be testing it shortly so why don't you call the Colonel and ok it with him. You'll really be able to get a good look at our ship from there."

"Thanks Twan, I'll call him right away. That is if you don't think he's too busy?"

"I'm sure he'd be glad for you to see all of this happen. Only I have to double check with him first before we make the lift. We don't quite have enough power yet for the light shield to be used without using some of the stored power. We'll need for tomorrow's flight. In other words, you'll be able to see the ship. It won't be cloaked."

"It's almost 10:00 p.m. Twan who'd be around to see?" Skipper asked.

"Big brother," Twan said, "satellite recon. They'll be watching us. You can bet on it but I don't think it will matter. We'll be gone in a flash in the morning. They don't have anything that could come close to keeping up with our ship. We only have to be at half power to make a jump and that's twice as fast as any plane they got but they got some pretty fast missiles on those F-16's. We'll have to be careful even with the ship fully armored. We don't need any other setbacks."

"Yeah I'll bet," Skipper said.

"I'll call the Colonel now Skipper and let him know you're coming up to watch."

"Thanks man, I can't wait to see this thing in action."

"Ok," the President said, to himself, "I think they're taking the bait." He walked over to his desk and pressed the intercom button and said, "get me Alex Hall on the phone please and get my plane ready. I'm going to Alabama tonight to visit an old friend."

"Yes sir, right away," a young lady replied.

"Yes sir, Mr President. What can I do for you?" Alex Hall said.

"You know the project that we've been watching in Alabama."

"Yes sir"

"I think we'll have to go ahead with our plans. The War Department has screwed up again. I'm glad we stepped in when we did without them knowing. The loss of our people could have been astronomical. How's the 'reflective shields' coming? Are they close to completion?"

"They're ready for use sir. The testing was completed this morning. They should withstand a blast from their soundwave gun with no problems. We used the gun that you got for us to test how well it would hold up. We only found one problem."

"Oh and what was that?"

"Bounce sir."

"Bounce?"

"Yes sir, as the wave of sound hits our shield it's diverted or reflected away from us but it 'bounce's' we can't control its compression or the direction it's reflected in. It loses its strength rapidly but if there's anyone caught in the 'bounce' well to be honest with you sir. We're not sure what will happen to them."

"Have your people ready to leave for Alabama tonight. We need to be ready to intercept our friends from the War Department by daylight. And Alex I'll be there when you arrive."

"Sir?"

"I have my reasons. Just remember you report to me only. Understand?"

"Yes sir."

The President opened his desk drawer and took out a picture. He stood it on his desk then sat back in his chair and laced his fingers behind his head and smiled slyly "Bounce," he said out loud, "is that the name they've given to wave dispersement? "

He leaned over to his small bar which stood beside his desk and pulled out a bottle of beer and twisted off the cap. He held the beer up with his arm fully extended in a toast and said, "here's to you Colonel Morgan. I've been waiting on this day for a very long time."

"Ah Skipper. You and Crystal come on in and enjoy the show. It's a sight to see something so large rise up out of the ground."

"I'll bet it's sir," He replied. "I can't wait!"

"Well Skipper there's something else that I've wanted to tell you for a while and now is as good a time as any."

"What's up Colonel?" he asked.

The Colonel opened a drawer on his file cabinet and pulled a picture that Crystal had seen on Skipper's mother's old desk. "Take a look at this. Look closely and see how many people you recognize. I think you'll be surprised."

Skipper took the picture from the Colonel. He looked at Crystal and she knew he was almost afraid of what he might see in the photo. Then slowly his eyes left hers and focused on the picture.

Right away he recognized his parents, The Colonel, Mark and a few others. Then as he scanned down the line of people in uniform, a young man standing on the end caught his eye, "is this who I think it is?" Skipper asked, as he looked back up at the Colonel.

"Yes it is," the Colonel said. "He was just much younger then. That's the President of these United States."

Chapter 22

"Colonel, you mean to tell me we've the President on our side?" Skipper asked, with a smile.

"No!" he said, as he started to laugh, "he's on the other side."

"I don't understand sir," Skipper replied.

"See Skipper about three years after we got to this time we had a few people who wanted to leave and go out on their own. One of them was a young hot-headed man you now call your president. We managed to convince most of them to stay but nothing could stop him. He knew as much about our technology as any of us did and wanted to use it to become rich and just live in this time forever."

"We all knew he shared the same name as the president of this time but we didn't have a clue it would be him. When he left, there was a small confrontation between him and Mark. Things got a little out of hand and now because of that he doesn't exactly like us. He stole a sound wave pistol and he also has the ability to build a shield against it. Our only advantage over him is he doesn't know we're ready to go back home. We shouldn't have ever been able to leave."

"With his knowledge of the future it didn't take him long to advance in our government. Now we've to guess how far he has taken that knowledge That's why we're gonna try to leave before he gets here tomorrow. We don't know what he's capable of. I'm going to try to talk with him again but I don't think it'll do any good."

The light in the office flickered slightly and the Colonel said, "look the show's starting."

"Mr. President."

"Yeah Alex what's up?"

"You said to report to you personally sir."

"Yes"

"Our satellites are picking up some movement at Steamway."

"I'm sure they are Alex, what's so unusual about that?"

"Well sir, it's hard to describe. The ground is moving or rather it's opening up. The hole that has formed is huge sir! You could put Yankee Stadium in it."

The president sat upright in his chair where he'd been napping. Wiping the sleep from his eyes he said, "are your men in place?"

"Yes sir. We're here and ready to move in sir."

"Ok as soon as the sun rises we'll go in."

"Sir, Sir!" Alex interrupted.

"Yes What is it?"

"There's some kind of plane rising from the hole."

"Calm down Alex. They ain't going anywhere yet. They 're just testing their equipment. It's just procedure to check everything out before they plan to leave. Now I'll see you at 0400 just as we planned understand?"

"Yes sir."

"No, Colonel Morgan," the President thought, "your not gonna run and hide again. This time your going to fight me and Mark won't be able to step in and stop us. You're slipping in your old age. I can't believe you raised the ship where it could be sen uncloaked!"

"So whatcha think Skipper?" the Colonel asked.

"It's enormous sir. You can't tell how big it really is till you see it out in the open."

"Well we're not the only ones looking at it. I'm sure our government sees it from above so I want you two on board ASAP," the Colonel said, as he opened the door to his office to let the young couple out.

"I'll see you two on the ship in the morning," he said, as they passed him headed to the elevator.

Just as the elevator doors closed, the Colonel's phone rang.

"Sir we've got a problem," Mark said.

"What's that Mark?"

"Power failure. We can't lower the ship. It'll be exposed at daylight if we can't get the power back on."

"Do we've enough to take off Mark?" he asked.

"Yes sir but barely."

"We have enough to get off the ground but we can use either the shield or the time drive. We can't use them both."

"Then can we use them in sequence?" the Colonel asked. "First the shield then the time drive?"

"I'm not sure how that works sir, but I'll find out for you."

"Do so Mark and tell Cook to get that key ready now!"

"They're trying sir."

"Without the key, the time drive is useless anyway. I guess we better just plan on a relocation for now. Have the pilot to concentrate all power to the shields and we'll go from there."

Just as Mark started to leave, his radio crackled to life.

"Mark," Twan said, "we got movement on the outside of the fence. Our motion detectors are going crazy all around the plant."

"Get everyone on the ship Mark, "the Colonel said. "They won't move in before daylight but it never hurts to be prepared."

A few hours passed as Steamway came alive. It was buzzing like bees in a hive. Everyone there was scrambling to get all their personal possessions on board. Mark and Twan were watching the monitors and motion sensors to keep up with the force of men and equipment that was building around the outer fence.

Helicopters had buzzed by a few times with spotlights shining bright but the Colonel had already told everyone not to worry about them. Just to smile and wave as they passed by.

The Colonel stood at his window watching all the activity below at the ship when his private line rang.

"Colonel Morgan," the President said.

"Yes sir, I've been expecting your call. What can I do for you?"

"Surrender the complex," he replied.

"You know I can't do that sir."

"Then you and all your people will die there."

"Oh I don't think so," the Colonel said, in a very calm voice. "We have the ship outside and are ready to leave as I'm sure you know."

"Colonel, I'll shoot you down as soon as you lift off if you try to escape in that pile of junk," the President said, "we're here and awaiting your first move. You can give us Steamway or we'll take it from you. You know I know how to get around your defenses and we're prepared for your soundwave attack."

The Colonel reached over and picked up the radio on his desk and said, "Mark they're coming. Is everyone on board?"

"Yes sir except for Twan, you and me."

"Ok then," still speaking into the phone, "Mr. President bring it on."

Chapter 23

"Mark," the Colonel said, "meet me at the side door. Have Twan spray the perimeter fence with a burst from the sound wave gun on stun before we go out. That should give us safe passage to the ship. Is everyone on board and ready to go?"

"Yes sir," he said.

"What about the remote to detonate the incendiary device for the complex?"

"Skipper has it sir."

"Then let's make our way to the ship."

"Fire," Mark told Twan on the radio.

Twan smiled as he pulled the trigger on the soundwave cannon. As he moved the cannon side to side, he noticed that all the soldiers at the perimeter fence just stood there without moving.

"Mark, Mark!" He yelled over his radio.

"Go ahead Twan. What's wrong?"

"Soundwave," he replied, "it's not having any effect on them."

Then with a loud swoosh and a trail of while smoke the complex lit up with a large explosion.

"I bet that got their attention," the President said, as he watched the explosion on a closed circuit monitor. "So much for Steamway and their precious soundwave."

"Colonel," Mark said over his radio, "are you ok?"

"Yes Mark, get Twan and you two get onboard. I'll meet you there," he replied, as he ran for the ship.

"They're coming sir," Twan said to Mark, as they ran toward the ship.

Bullets started riddling the side of the building just over their head. The soldiers had stayed behind the shield that the president had made for them and now that the soundwave cannon wasn't manned they could move in.

As Mark, Twan and the Colonel ran for the ship another missile burst thru the side of the building knocking them to the ground. Once they made it back to their feet, with the troops closing, they ran as fast as they could to the steps of the ship.

Twan was the first to make it. He turned to see Mark and the Colonel being chased by a soldier. The soldier stopped and aimed his rifle at the Colonel. Just as the Colonel made it to the steps, the soldier pulled the trigger. From out of no where Mark dove in front of the Colonel. As he fell the Colonel could see blood pouring from his side where the bullet just passed through.

Twan ran back down the steps screaming Mark's name. The next burst of bullets from the gun hit Twan twice in the upper chest but before he could hit the ground, the Colonel caught him under the arms and started up the steps with him. As the Colonel made his way up, Skipper was coming down. Bullets continued to hit the ship all around them as the soldiers came closer.

"Skipper," Mark said, "what the hell are you doing?"

"Saving your behind!" Skipper said, as he grabbed Mark up and slung him over his shoulder. Skipper bolted up the steps so fast he almost caught up with the Colonel before he made it to the top.

"Get us of the ground!" the Colonel screamed, as he entered the door.

The pilot was already expecting this order and was lifting off. As they rose up off the lift Skipper asked the Colonel if he was ok.

"Yes I'm fine but these two ain't doing so well."

Skipper looked over to the corner where Crystal was sitting. She was crying but what caught him by surprise was she was talking on her cell phone.

All he heard was "Good bye Daddy" and he knew that she had just spoken to her father for the last time.

"Turn the shields on," the Colonel said, as the ship began to gain altitude and speed.

"Shields activated," the pilot said.

"Shields?" Skipper said to the Colonel. "I thought this ship would be coated with liquid steel sir."

"It is but remember when the President left he took a sound wave pistol with him. I don't know how far he'd taken that technology. If he has developed a cannon, he could bring us down it with. The liquid steel, as you've seen, can stop small arms fire. But we'd be lucky if we could withstand multiple air strikes. I also noticed some of those bullets penetrated the hull of the ship. We've been selling them liquid steel. I guess they've started making bullets from it and if they have done the same with heavy arms we could be in trouble."

"Sir they ain't working," he said, as he looked back at the Colonel. "They must have taken a hit by some of those bullets."

Out of the blue directly in front of them two F-16 fighters appeared.

"We got to get out of here!" the Colonel said. "We're sitting ducks without the shields."

The Colonel turned to Skipper and said, "Blow it! Blow the complex."

Skipper removed the remote from his pocket and pressed the detonation button. The complex seemed to fall into itself. Seconds later you could see an orangish-yellow glow coming from what appeared to be a volcano.

"It's gone sir," Skipper said. Just as he finished speaking, he could see the F-16's fire two missiles

"Oh my God," the pilot said, "we're dead!"

"Engage the time drive," the Colonel said.

"I can't sir. We're still missing the key."

Skipper overheard what he said and remembered what Brandon had told him in the Smith's basement 'This is some kind of key'. He thought of what his father had told him as a child. 'This could save your life one day'.

"Colonel," Skipper shouted.

"Not now Skipper," he snapped back.

Skipper took his charm out from around his neck and held it up for him to see.

"The time key," the Colonel said.

Chapter 24

"Sir we're picking up a signal," the young lieutenant said, as he stared excitedly at the blinking blue light on the computer console. "They're coming back!"

"Take your stations everyone," shouted an older gentleman standing near the rear of the room. "They should be coming out of the barrier in three minutes."

His hands were shaking like they'd never done before. In the last hour he'd sent his son and several people he'd come to love back in time. Until he heard the signal and saw the blinking light he wasn't sure that they would ever return.

He'd wanted to tell his friends what they were in store for before they left but he knew that they would find out soon enough.

"Have the emergency medical team standing by," he shouted.

"Sir?"

"You heard me. They're coming in with two men badly wounded."

Everyone in the room turned to look at him as he started walking toward the landing platform. "Move!" he shouted again.

"But sir. How could you know they have wounded people on board?" asked the young lieutenant.

"I just do," he said.

"It's gonna be a bumpy landing," the pilot said, as he turned and smiled at Colonel Morgan.

"I don't care if we crash again," he replied, "as long as no one else gets hurt. I'm ready for this adventure to be over. I'm tired."

"Me too," Mark said, as he tried to stand.

"Don't move my old friend," Colonel Morgan said, "we don't want that hole to start leaking again."

"I'm fine sir," Mark said. "It went clean through."

"Yeah I know. I'm sure they'll fix you right up as soon as we land."

"I know they will, I just hope it's soon. The others ain't doing as well as I am."

"They'll be fine Mark," the Colonel said, as he patted Mark on the shoulder and smiled. "I can't wait to see Skipper's face when he meets my father again."

"You and I both sir. Won't he be surprised."

"30 seconds sir," said the lieutenant, as the medical team made their way down to the landing pad.

"10-4 lieutenant," the older gentleman said, as the lights in the room started to dim slightly.

"It's gonna be a lot different from when they left people. We're not sure how well this re-entry will be but everyone stay at your assigned post till I give the all clear."

Just as he finished speaking the building started shaking. Slowly at first then gradually worsened then the lieutenant said, "In 3, 2, 1."

A whirling wind engulfed the room blowing wildly and the power surged even more. On the landing platform, which wasn't much more than a concrete pad with three pedestals coming up from the center, a bright ball of light started to form. It increased in size with each second and what appeared to be small streaks of lighting started to form all around it. Suddenly the room was filled with a blue haze and the air temperature dropped ten degrees. The building was enormous and only one end of it contained the equipment necessary for time travel. All at once in a bright flash of light, which made everyone there turn their heads, the ship appeared on the platform.

The hull was smoking and all types of what looked like gas escaping from under the bottom of the half-frozen ship. A hush came over the room. The only sound was made by the buzzing of the computers. Not one person was moving.

"Here we go everyone. Hold on," the Colonel said over the loud speaker.

The ship started shaking slightly and as quickly as it started it stopped with a sudden jolt.

"Raise the shields," the Colonel said. A deep glow filled the bridge of the ship as the shields slid slowly open. Nothing could be seen, the room seemed to be full of smoke.

"Skipper," the Colonel said, "why don't you lead the way. There's someone here who wants to see you."

Skipper just looked at him without saying a word. He knew all the people he knew were dead but he'd also learned to just take the Colonel at his word. Skipper took Crystal and the Colonel by the hand and said, "we're gonna do this together sir."

"Welcome to 2041," the Colonel said, as the outside door slid open.

Standing there was the grey-haired gentleman. Tears fell down his cheeks as Skipper, the Colonel and Crystal walked down the stairs.

Skipper stopped in front of him and stared into his eyes.

"Hello Uncle Skipper," Brandon said. "It's been a long time, for me at least."

"And I see you met my son, the Colonel."

The End

KARL B. FRIEDMAN

THE
PROFESSOR

Black Belt Publishing
Montgomery, Alabama

This is a work of fiction. With the exception
of a few actual people, the characters, names,
incidents, dialogue and plots are the product of
the author's imagination or are used fictitiously.
Any resemblance to actual persons or events is
purely coincidental.

ISBN 1-880216-58-2

Printed in the United States of America

With grateful appreciation and with all my love, respect,
and affection to my beloved wife and lifelong friend,
GLADYS COHEN FRIEDMAN,
who has been a wonderful companion, a stable and supportive
influence, and a marvelous mother to our three children,
MARK H. FRIEDMAN, TRACY FRIEDMAN STEIN,
and LOLLY FRIEDMAN MILLER.
There is no gift that could fully express my commitment to her. The
publication of this book is at least an effort in that regard.

Contents

Prologue

T he two most virulent plagues of a very old person will always be boredom and loneliness. Having outlived all of my friends and most of the people with whom I have associated in life, I find myself, for the first time, wondering if there is any value in the present, or any need for a future. If I should decide that there is something here and now, what am I going to do about it? If I decide that I have had enough and that time has run out and there is no future and no future quality of life, what am I going to do about that?

My life began in the aftermath of slavery when the mere survival of any black person fulfilled every day with needs and demands and pushed aside anything having to do with quality of life or activities or even dreams. We were locked in a chamber of hopelessness, every generation of us, from great-grandparents to great-grandchildren. There was no joy, no pleasure, no personal or spiritual growth, only a struggle to live.

As I grew out of my formative years, I came to face the basic conflict of the races. It seemed that from every direction I was besieged with the concept that I was something less than equal, that I was inferior, probably incompetent, and certainly nearly worthless. I did not seem to be valuable in any sense, nor did I think anyone else thought I had value, yet I sensed that there was something more to life. There had to be.

As I moved into my years of education and came in contact with a variety of people, I could see that some type of struggle was in order, that I was

11

unwilling to consign myself to being a non-entity, a non-person, and I could feel a challenge rising within me, and that challenge drove me toward something which I neither understood nor anticipated, but I drove on, nevertheless.

Certainly through those years, and into the years of my higher education, war after war throughout the world, man's inhumanity to man, my life became filled with significant and important events and activities and thoughts. I don't remember ever having a time for relaxation or peace or serenity.

In college, for the first time, I began to feel a sense of identity, that I was someone, that other people might look upon me as someone. The light of the future began to shine and glow, and my struggles seemed to be reaping rewards. Certainly in college and law school there was no opportunity to be bored or lonely. In fact, there was not sufficient opportunity to fulfill all the needs of the moment. Life was a mad scramble, many places, many faces.

Litigation was both a frightening and illuminating experience, mortal combat in the courtroom, adversarial relationships prevailing and pervading, a fierce loyalty for my clients and their causes, and an angry antipathy to all who opposed. Once again, never enough hours in the day, never any time alone.

Then, I knew what my dream was, and I realized it, and in my teaching years, I loved every moment of every day, and I began to realize that the quality of life did in fact involve something other than struggles and labors, and that the brain functioned beyond one's talents into one's dreams and plans. Those were glorious years, with meaningful relationships.

As I grew older and older, life was better and better, financially, personally, and the rewards were many and often. Perhaps I was already old when I reached the apex of my life. Yet, in retrospect, I do not see many things that went by the wayside which I had wished to retain, nor many things that I desired that I did not accomplish.

Now I am old, quite old. For the first time I sense there is a possibility of nothingness. I have certainly left behind me a trail of litigation, a host of admirers, what many might believe to be huge wealth, and a record of my life

which may last, and be interesting, for decades into the future, but it, too, shall pass.

I sit here alone. No one calls. No one comes. My daily needs are met by others. While I am enchanted by new technology and the huge expansion of society and the activities within it, I am not really touched by anything or anyone. I guess I am like the seed that is planted, fertilized, grows, attains stature and beauty, wanes, falls, and fails, dust to dust.

Introduction

L adies and Gentlemen, welcome to the Constitution of the United States. There are no notes for you to take, nothing of lasting value to be retained, but I do want your undivided attention. You and I are going to be together on many occasions and for a lot of hours. This first session is going to be composed of three different categories, you, me, and the curriculum.

I am quite confident that each of you is a near genius, or you would not have excelled in your undergraduate work to become qualified into this great university law school. You undoubtedly have a competitive spirit, and an anxiety to win and be successful. I encourage that. On the other hand, I am going to start with you on the assumption that your mind is a blank, an empty container, unskilled, unschooled, and unprepared for the knowledge that you are about to acquire. You may remember that many years ago, there was an over-the-counter medication of a pink liquid, which, if swallowed, would coat the lining of your stomach, shut out everything else, and make you free of pain and discomfort, and at the same time, completely empty. In my hands, today, that is the condition of your mind, empty. Don't have any preconceived notions. Don't leap to any unwarranted conclusions. You have your other obligations, to your law courses, your social life and extracurricular activities, but to the extent that you let anything other than your commitment to this course interfere with your diligent pursuit of your

obligations here, you will suffer a detriment.

It is not necessary for you to attend class. I do not keep rolls. It isn't urgent that you try to impress me with your progress because your entire endeavor will be evaluated in your final examination which I, personally, will examine and grade and publish, without ever knowing which of you has succeeded completely or has succeeded to a lesser extent, or, perhaps, even failed. You have heard many things about this course, and about me, most of which are probably true, but I find that each class adds its own interpretations and therefore some of the myths continue to grow. Enjoy yourself in that regard.

I do not require that you pay attention in class. If you choose to listen to music or read a novel, feel free to do so. You must, however, do so in a fashion that does not disturb others who wish to devote their full attention. Your grade will not be affected by your behavior, and, unless you choose otherwise, for personal reasons, you will remain completely anonymous insofar as I am concerned. Since you are freshmen, just entering, you are going to be bewildered and uncertain and full of self-doubt. If not, I will have failed in my efforts.

Now, let's next talk about me. If I live until my next birthday, this coming May 23, I will be ninety-two years old. I promise you that I will make the effort so that your class and course will not be incomplete. You are the thirty-ninth class to come under my surveillance. I am the oldest law professor in the United States. I am the most senior employee of this great university. Fifty-seven percent of the active practitioners who are licensed to practice in Alabama respect me for having taught them constitutional law and for having given them the direction for the successful practice of law. I have sat on many judicial commissions. Governors have requested me to accept appointment to the Supreme Court. For many years, and many years ago, there was a constant movement to have the President of the United States appoint me to the Federal District Court which sits here. I have refused all of these overtures because I have everything in life that I want. I am happy. I am successful. I am very powerful throughout the State of Alabama, and elsewhere. My time is my own. I do as I wish. I pay homage to no one

except the lovely lady who has shared more than fifty years of my life. While it is not remarkable to you, it was once very remarkable in the State of Alabama. As you can see, I am black, a native born American who has never accepted any addition or clarification to that title. My mate is white, the most beautiful woman in the world, ninety-three years of age, and my constant companion, from one of the most prominent white families in the State of Alabama. We have no children. We are not married. There is more to these stories, for a later time.

Now that we know each other so well, let's talk about the course. I love the Constitution of the United States, every paragraph, every sentence, every word, every punctuation mark, every statement, every nuance, its very own atmosphere. When I wake up in the morning, I think about the Constitution. When I leave home, I think about this course in Constitutional Law and you. I read the newspapers and watch the television, read a multitude of periodicals, and study the law, constantly. With the exception of my beloved companion, it's my whole life. I happen to be very rich, financially, but the riches of my life are in the law and the Constitution. You are going to be enveloped, circum-scribed, excited, and challenged by this course. You can make of it what you wish, each to individual choice. Priority every day will be what's going on in the law that very day. We will discuss the cases and the characters and the Constitution. There is no law that fails to be tested by the Constitution. We will pass briefly by the Constitution of the State of Alabama, and its multitudinous amendments, all of which is a big mess, and proclaims the stupidity of our elected leaders over the generations, but we will dwell most of the time on the pristine Constitution of the United States of America. I will select cases which have been so tested and discuss them with you, and permit you to discuss them with me. Don't ever agree with me. Be suspicious. Be wary. I may smile and go on to the next case, or I may attempt to make a fool of you.

Let it be known, now, that the four most important cases to which you will be exposed in this course are as follows: A. *McClung v. Katzenbach*, a serious adventure in interstate ketchup; B. *Joseph Jasper Smith*—incidentally, that is who I am—*v. The Alabama State Bar*

Association and the Supreme Court of the State of Alabama, which case will not only teach you a considerable amount of law, but will further teach you who I am, and why I am here; C. the *O.J. Simpson* cases involving a well-known athlete, charged and convicted of murder, appealed and reviewed, and who was sued for damages, appealed and reviewed. These cases involving O.J. Simpson tested the law and tested the lawyers. Finally, the cases of President William Clinton.

This is a bit of information that you need. You may purchase a new book for this course, as designated in your literature at the school book store. The cost is fifty-five dollars. It is looseleaf because I add and subtract cases, as I choose, from year to year, and even in mid-year. If you have an economic problem, you can buy one at a much lesser cost from students who have already taken this course, and to the extent that it is not complete, I will personally supply you with photostats of the missing cases. At the end of this course, I will expect each of you to have a book which contains all of the cases that I have required during your year with me, and you can pass it on as you choose, thereafter. Some have chosen to save theirs, and have prevailed upon me to autograph theirs, and I have consented to do so.

I will see you tomorrow morning, those of you who choose to come, at eight a.m. in this very room. Eat what you will before you come, relieve yourselves in the restrooms, and be prepared for two hours of mental stimulation, remembering that if at any time any of you are bored, or have conflicts, you are free to leave, but try not to disturb those who choose to remain. Spend as much time as you choose, tonight, reading, *McClung v. Katzenbach* which is cited at 379 U.S. 294, 13 L.Ed.2d 290, 85 S.C. 377, decided on December 14, 1964, and be prepared for a discussion of the case and its ramifications and what it means in the law today. There is a world of literature about that case and I will begin tomorrow's lecture and discussion by telling you of my relationship to Mr. McClung. Good day, friends.

First Class

Neophyte students, make yourselves comfortable. If my previous introduction startled you or seemed arrogant, both were intended. I told you to read and study *McClung v. Katzenbach* and I assume that everyone did an analytical study in order to get off to a good start in this class. The case itself, as reported, is rather simple and direct. Before we get to it, however, I need a reaction from several of you.

Why do you think this case was chosen as the first case for you to analyze and deliberate? Anyone who wishes to respond, please raise your hand.

NUMBER 71: I believe you chose this case because it was personal to you, it happened in your community, and you had some familiarity with it.

PROFESSOR: Next—Number 83.

NUMBER 83: It seems to me that you wanted to accentuate the race issue, not only because it has been so prevalent in litigation, but because you have probably suffered discrimination in your own life.

PROFESSOR: Next—Number 12.

NUMBER 12: The *McClung* case is obviously an early piece of litigation which partially dealt with commercial discrimination but which has been modified and amplified over the period of time to teach

us that a single case at a single moment might at some later date be not so significant.

PROFESSOR: There is merit in all of those points. Before we get to the substance, however, I will tell you why I chose the case, and I will give you some facts and information which will make you look at it from a different standpoint. The Constitution is a living thing. It was created by man, modified and adjusted by man, and is implemented and enforced by man. It is a living document. You know from your history books when it was born, and that the Constitution, in its basic form, was a relatively simple document, but the amendments which were added, the first ten, breathed life into the instructions, and the many amendments which have been enacted since have spread these meanings throughout our society and in every walk of life. Today you walk side by side with the Constitution of the United States. It is yours to love or leave. If you touch it and feel it and share life with it, you will be enriched, and you perhaps might be enabled to add something constructive to our society and to our great nation. You will begin to think like a lawyer, and a citizen. When a news release takes place, and it captures your interest, part of your evaluation and consideration will be the Constitution of the United States. When you are faced with legal research or preparation for a trial, always in the corner of your mind will be the constitutional questions that might be insinuated into the case. You will learn not to make assumptions, and certainly not to assume a status quo that once was. In your personal, social, and community life, you will constantly wonder how the Constitution and its amendments apply to what happens to you, what you do, and what you think and plan. It's a marriage. Today is your wedding day. Your bride or bridegroom is the Constitution. I am your priest, minister, or rabbi, and I declare you in political and personal matrimony. I leave to each of you to make your own selections as to Holy Matrimony. There are people—scholars—who approach the Constitution as one might the New Testament, which accepts every word as the word of God, fixed, immutable, thus not living and growing. I must tell you that every day of my life, in my waning years, there are constitutional thought processes. Even today, I concern myself not only about teaching

the Constitution to you, but whether or not I have the right to do that, and the extent to which I am privileged to persuade or indoctrinate you. After all, I am in total control with full power. You are a simple and new student with desires and aspirations which I may affect or disaffect. I am entitled, merely because I am hired and employed to teach you, and at the same time to influence and develop your thought processes. Is that a constitutional question?

Each of you is here with some type of a public stipend, in some fashion supported by the general public. You may think that you pay a very substantial tuition, and you do, five times what was paid when I entered, or more, but this school exists because it is supported with public funds. You are privileged to utilize those funds as part of the cost of your education. Is that equal taxation? I have a domestic servant at my home. She comes, cleans up, takes care of ministerial duties, and she is handsomely compensated on the general scale of domestic servants. She owns her own home, and she pays real estate taxes. Some of those real estate taxes go into education, and some of the education funds are assigned to this great university. Does it shock you to learn that my domestic servant is helping you get a law education? Is that a constitutional question? She probably understands this constitutional question better than you do, right now. Well, that's the first reason that I selected the *McClung* case, to challenge you and to make you think and realize that the Constitution is alive, and that real, live people were involved.

I want to tell you a lot about these real, live people. I will start by telling you about the *McClung* family and the McClung restaurant known as Ollie's.

Re: *McClung v. Katzenbach*

I never was a guest in that restaurant because in my earliest years, black people could be employees at Ollie's, but not diners. There was a small door at the back where a black person could walk up, order, pay cash and leave with the food in a brown bag or a Dixie cup, but absolutely forbidden entrance to the main emporium. If you looked in the window, however, you saw several interesting and somewhat startling things. All

over the walls there were plaques and posters about Jesus Christ, about humility, about caring and worshiping, and there were Bibles for sale and other religious literature to be handed out to customers, and it appeared that there was a very holy presence inside, a presence, of course, for white people. In addition, almost all of the employees were black, neatly groomed, in white aprons with the word "Ollie" on the front and a baker's cap on the head of each. There was one tall, handsome white man—his name was Howard. Everyone seemed to gravitate toward him, and he was somewhat of an underboss, and all of the rest of the servants were black women who waited on tables, arranged the food, cleaned the floors, reset the chairs, and generally were the lowest level of servants that a restaurant could have. From the day each went to work, the waiter or waitress was taught to memorize the menus and the customer's orders, no notepads, no scratch notes, nothing, just memory, and I'm told that they were perfect, and in fact the regular customers would find their orders delivered immediately, without even calling upon someone to wait upon them. Through a side window, by the parking lot, you could see into the kitchen area. There was a large table. Behind it was a barbeque pit of brick and steel, a furious fire going and delicious things being cooked, but at the preparation table stood the McClung family, father, son, brother, uncle, whatever—they prepared the food according to the orders, likewise, from no notes or memos. Mr. McClung frequently went out on the floor and greeted the customers as though each one was a friend. He seemed to be a pleasant and humble man. That's what people said about him. He was very religious. They said that, too. Apparently, however, he found no religious problem in the separation of the races, and he was probably typical of a Southern gentleman of those days, kind, considerate, affable, hard-working, generous and religious, caring for the downtrodden, but not black people, for, I assume, they were considered something less than other human beings. It is not to damn the McClung family. That was very much the way of life in the State of Alabama in those days. If McClung was to be damned, so would all of his patrons and customers, for they undoubtedly enjoyed the personal privacy of being waited on by black people, but not sitting to eat

with them. The Civil Rights struggle changed that, but it was the acceptable mode of the day, not different from the fact that black people lived in one place and white people lived in another, nearby.

The McClungs lived in a very fashionable part of Mountain Brook, where the rich and the elite lived, and they had a swimming pool. I understand it was open to all their friends and neighbors. I believe if I had known Mr. McClung, we could have been good friends. If I had worked at his home, as I did for a family known as the Ragsdales, I am certain that I would have been treated in a kindly fashion, generously compensated, and I would have been able to work with dignity. The reason for this dissertation is so that you will look at the law in the light of the people involved, and the McClungs became involved with Mr. Katzenbach.

Because I know that you have read and analyzed and studied the case, and every line, sentence, clause, phrase and punctuation thereof, I will not dwell too much on the stated facts of the case. Remember, however, the year of the Supreme Court decision was 1964. To get the case in the proper perspective, read your history books and find out what was happening in the world in 1964. Israel was becoming the dominating influence in the Middle East. China was a sleepy, remote, misunderstood nation, the largest population, the largest land mass of any nation in the world, and it mattered not although it rattled sabers, pretending to be a military power. Civil Rights wars were just as devastating, in some ways, as the Civil War, itself, in the South. I recall that it was 1954, ten years earlier, that the Supreme Court integrated the schools, with all deliberate speed, so to speak. The USSR was the other super power in the world, but it was a frightening specter, and an ominous, fearful opponent in the Cold War. Referred to as Russia, it dominated from the Baltic to the Mediterranean, from Berlin to the Far East and included in its hegemony were the Baltic nations, a major portion of Germany, Egypt, Afghanistan, all countries that at different times have been the focus for the concern of the citizens of the world, but in those days, the specter of the communist giant hovered over a quarter of all the people in the world and kept at bay nations like China, Japan, Korea, and even Pakistan and India. Space travel was the electrifying event, accompanied, however, by

long range missiles and new scientific adventures. The truth is that the world was very busy and very concerned, and only a few selected people and organizations cared about Mr. McClung's business, and for the most part, no one in Birmingham, Alabama cared about it except Mr. McClung and his guests.

Enter the awesome power of the United States of America through its then serving Attorney General, Nicholas Katzenbach.

Will someone tell me how in the hell Mr. Katzenbach, and others, became concerned with this tiny, little, unremarkable barbeque serving café. Number 60—give it a try.

NUMBER 60: There was clearly racial discrimination by restaurants engaged in interstate commerce, and under the commerce clause of the Constitution, Section 8, the Federal Government is empowered first to provide for the general welfare of the United States, which would include all of its citizens, blacks, others, and, further, to regulate commerce.

PROFESSOR: Whoa! Stop right there! Recite for me from the Constitution, verbatim, where the Federal Government is authorized to regulate commerce.

NUMBER 60: It says "to regulate commerce with foreign nations, and among the several states and with the Indian tribes."

PROFESSOR: Indian tribes?

NUMBER 60: Well, not Indian tribes in this case.

PROFESSOR: Foreign nations?

NUMBER 60: Well, not in this fact situation.

PROFESSOR: Then, I assume you conclude that Mr. McClung's little old business was some kind of commerce among the several states.

NUMBER 60: Yes I do.

PROFESSOR: Elaborate.

NUMBER 60: Well, according to the facts of the time and this very case people come across the borders of the State of Alabama and do business.

PROFESSOR: Wait a minute—It says "*among the several states.*" What's that got to do with people traveling back and forth?

NUMBER 60: That's what commerce is, buying and selling and traveling and going into shops, and eating barbeque.

PROFESSOR: Aren't you reading a lot more into that clause than it really says—were there several states involved, is the State of Alabama involved with another state, or don't you think that that particular clause merely offered an opportunity to negotiate treaties between the states, treaties of commerce?

NUMBER 60: No, I think it includes people.

PROFESSOR: Well, I think you are adding fertilizer and moisture to tiny seeds, but I can't damn you because the Attorney General of the United States tended to agree with you, in part. However, what was the commerce?

NUMBER 60: Well, the headnote, #17, says that the power of Congress to regulate interstate commerce is broad and sweeping; where it keeps within its sphere and violates no express constitutional limitation the Supreme Court will not interfere.

PROFESSOR: I concede that's what it says. That's not what I asked you. I want you to describe the commerce among the states.

NUMBER 60: There are admitted facts in the case to the conclusion that about $70,000 worth of food was moved in interstate commerce.

PROFESSOR: Did Mr. McClung move it?

NUMBER 60: He bought it.

PROFESSOR: Was it shipped by common carrier?

NUMBER 60: I believe so.

PROFESSOR: Well then Mr. McClung didn't do anything in interstate commerce, he didn't go to Atlanta and buy provisions and bring those back in his truck to Birmingham.

NUMBER 60: Well, the goods moved in interstate commerce, across the borders.

PROFESSOR: How significant is $70,000?

NUMBER 60: Well to me that's a lot of money, but I don't know what percentage of the sales or business of Ollie's that amount of money would represent, and I guess it would not be significant in the overall picture how much interstate commerce would be done between Atlanta and Birmingham.

PROFESSOR: I think you are on thin ice. Pick up a few words out of the

Constitution, and expand them and broaden them, and then you decide
that the few bottles of ketchup that came on a freight train is commerce
among the states. Don't you think that's stretching the point?

NUMBER 60: Somewhat, but I think the whole Constitution is dealt
with in that light, growing to meet the changing times and to cope with
the laws that Congress passes.

PROFESSOR: Well said, son, although there are differing views about
the perfect world. You think it was a great victory for black people?

NUMBER 60: It was part of the building blocks and, yes, I think it was
a giant step forward and it added to the common welfare and the good of
the general population by stopping violence and demonstrations in
Birmingham, and elsewhere, in various restaurants and eating facilities.

PROFESSOR: How old are you?

NUMBER 60: Twenty-one.

PROFESSOR: In your whole lifetime you have never seen a restaurant
facility where black people and white people, and people of all types and
sorts, could not sit down and enjoy a meal together. You find a *fait
accompli*, things like they are, and you may consider that to have been a
handsome amount of progress for our great nation, but what about the
rights of Mr. McClung, and others like him, to be left alone, to choose
their own comrades and patrons. I guarantee you that Mr. McClung
never thought he would be hung by a bottle of ketchup, nor did he think
that he was doing anything wrong or evil, nor did he consider himself of
such moment as to be engaged in interstate commerce and he and his
representatives thought, contrasted to your view, that it was not only
stretching a point, it was a ridiculous and absurd conclusion. You ought
to go to Ollie's and visit some of that interstate ketchup and see how
dynamic it is, how it has powerfully moved this nation into another less
stressful generation of eaters. Nevertheless, you neglected to mention the
Heart of Atlanta Motel which I told you appeared at 379 U.S. 241, 13 L.
Ed. 2nd 258, 85 Supreme Court 348 decided on December 14, 1964, at
the same time, same day, same argument session as McClung. Didn't
you think that was material?

NUMBER 60: Yes but that's not the question you asked me. *Heart of*

Atlanta Motel dealt with a different issue, but similar and parallel about interstate commerce, and this had more to do with the travel of people from place to place, on the highways, and on the streets, supported by public funds, than it did with the food consumed in a restaurant. I believe it had to do with housing and renting hotel rooms.

PROFESSOR: I agree. Let's suppose Mr. McClung did $1,000,000 worth of business in 1963 and he only bought $40,000 worth of ketchup and other provisions, would you have considered that interstate commerce? And, before you answer that, suppose he only bought $10,000 worth of ketchup?

NUMBER 60: I suppose it could become ridiculously small.

PROFESSOR: But you're willing to put an amount on it—like $70,000—or draw the line, somewhere?

NUMBER 60: Well, I don't know.

PROFESSOR: Well you didn't tell me about the interstate nature of the commerce. Suppose I agree with you that if Mr. McClung got in his truck and drove over to Atlanta and bought some food and raw materials, and drove his truck back across the line to Birmingham, that he had done something in interstate commerce. I'm not saying that I agree with that, but suppose, for the purpose of this intelligent discussion, those are the facts. Would it be different if he ordered his ketchup from a distributor in Birmingham instead of going to Atlanta to get it?

NUMBER 60: No, I don't think that would make any difference, because the ketchup moved in interstate commerce even though it may have come to rest in another place of business before it went back en route to Ollie's.

PROFESSOR: That's interesting. Suppose you were a patron at Ollie's, enjoyed a wonderful meal, paid the cost of the meal, and bought a bottle of ketchup to go, and you took it home. At that point were you engaged in interstate commerce?

NUMBER 60: Well, I didn't do anything to cross lines. I didn't order anything. I didn't buy anything from a distributor. I bought at a retail establishment.

PROFESSOR: What's the difference between your buying a bottle of

ketchup from Mr. McClung and his buying that same bottle of ketchup from the XYZ distributorship?

NUMBER 60: Well, I guess it hadn't come to its final resting place until it got to McClung's.

PROFESSOR: It didn't rest at McClung's, it went home with you.

NUMBER 60: That's what, hmmmmm . . .

PROFESSOR: Well, Number 60, I'm not judging you right or wrong, good or bad, but after you read cases and try to harmonize them, it's time to engage your own brain and spin out other alternatives or conclusions. I bet, if you had a conversation with the attorneys representing Mr. McClung, they had a whole package of other ideas and alternatives to try to sell to the Supreme Court, and the fact that they lost does not damn the other ideas which didn't sell. The point I'm making is this—on the way to a win or a loss, you have to exhaust every possible effort and thought and conceive of every idea, ingenious or creative, to give your client the best shot at a win, and still, you're going to lose some. You'll lose some that you ought to win. You'll win some that you ought to lose. I guess that's a tribute to our system of justice, the absence of perfection.

To conclude this discussion with you, however, let me say that you and I could drift down to Ollie's barbeque, enjoy a meal together, black and white, with interstate ketchup, and not an eyebrow would be lifted. In 1963 they would have hauled your ass off to the city jail, and you'd have had a lot of company too. They might have taken me out in the back to the woodshed, same justice system.

After Class

As the Professor departed from the law school classroom area and started down the front steps of the building, he noticed, at a side point, that there were four or five white students, boys and girls, and one young black boy. As the Professor observed, the black boy was entertaining the white students. The little boy would sing a song, do a dance, and the students would throw coins in his hat. He then played a game of songs that he made up while drumming a rhythm with spoons. The Professor continued to watch as another student threw a crumpled one dollar bill onto the ground and the little boy picked it up with his teeth and put it into the hat. The students cheered and clapped, and tried to get him to pick up a coin that was laying flat on the ground, but he couldn't. The Professor was infuriated at the demeaning of the little black boy. He stepped over and joined the crowd.

PROFESSOR: Young man, what is your name?
BOY: Donnie.
PROFESSOR: What is your last name?
BOY: Sometimes it is Brooks and sometimes it is Jones.
PROFESSOR: Explain that to me.

The students sat silently and observed.

BOY: Well, Brooks is my dad's name, but Jones is my mom's name, and it depends on where I am living. When I go to school, it's Brooks.

PROFESSOR: Do you do this for a living?

BOY: I sure do. I come here sometimes and all around the campus and I entertain people and they give me money.

PROFESSOR: Young man, let me borrow a little bit of your time and have you come to my office, now, and I will provide you with lunch, too. As to you students, I want to see the five of you in my office at 2:00 p.m.

The students remained on the steps, hushed, silent, and worried, as the Professor took the little boy into the front of the law school and up to his office. The conversation continued.

PROFESSOR: Do you enjoy what you do like this?

BOY: I sure do—I make a lot of money. I do much better on the school campus than I do on the streets downtown, but sometimes I go to the bus station, and I always go to the football games, and sometimes outside the auditorium when they are playing basketball. Those games are when the students are most generous, and sometimes they give me a cold drink or a sandwich.

PROFESSOR: Do you think that they may be laughing at you?

BOY: Yes, sure. That's what makes them want to help me.

PROFESSOR: Do you think that they are looking down on you and making fun of you?

BOY: Yes.

PROFESSOR: Does that bother you?

BOY: A little.

PROFESSOR: Sometimes are you ashamed of yourself?

BOY: I think so.

PROFESSOR: What do you want to be when you grow up?

BOY: I want to play in a band or act on a stage or be a comedian or a singer.

PROFESSOR: Are you doing anything about that?

BOY: Not really. I go to school and I do pretty good in school and then I get out on the streets.

PROFESSOR: Do you play ball?

BOY: No.

PROFESSOR: What do you do to entertain yourself and to make yourself happy?

BOY: Nothing, really, but I like to make people happy, and I like it when they cheer and clap for me, and I really like it when they give me money.

PROFESSOR: Would you be interested in a job that might be something where you can earn a steady amount of money on a regular basis and not have people laugh at you?

BOY: I think I would, but I'm doing pretty good this way.

PROFESSOR: But you aren't doing anything that would head you toward the entertainment industry.

BOY: I think I'd like to do that.

PROFESSOR: I have two ideas in mind, but let me tell you why I want to help you, first. I was once a little boy like you. I had to struggle every day to exist. I didn't have the talent that you have to entertain people, but I did learn how to get along with white people, and I found that studying hard and learning was the most important thing. I had a job and it led me to a career. I really hate to see any young black boy making himself laughable or pitied when he can find a stronger way to go in life.

BOY: What's in it for you?

PROFESSOR: Nothing, except that I want things to be better for young, black people than they used to be, and I don't like the image of people laughing at us or talking down to us, or treating us like animals in a show. Sooner or later, you have to stand up and be yourself, and behave in a manner so that people respect you and will be kind to you because you are a good person, and I think that what you are doing is like begging, rather than earning.

BOY: What kind of a job?

PROFESSOR: Well, I want to think about that because I have to get you something that you can do that will not interfere with your schooling. I

have an idea. I am very close to the editor of the local newspaper. I am sure that at your age I could get you a newspaper route where you could deliver papers in the afternoon, after school, and make more money than you are making this way. You would get a chance to meet people and, in effect, have a little business of your own. If you decide you want to try that, I can also tell you that the newspaper has an entertainment section and they have people who go out to the concerts and the athletic events and the plays and other productions to report about them. Those people get to meet the stars and the performers. Perhaps I could get them to take you along, say one evening a week, or maybe more, and then you could see people perform and maybe someday you would find a contact that will get you where you want to be.

BOY: I like the idea, but what do I have to do for you?

PROFESSOR: Nothing, absolutely nothing, except stay in touch with me. Take this piece of paper and write down your name and your home address and if you have a telephone number, put that down, too. Give me your mother's name and I want to talk to her, first. If she agrees, I will have someone from the newspaper call you or come to see you. I will want you to stay in touch with me and let me know how you do. When something good happens, tell me about it, and if something bad happens, let me see if I can help. You see, son, someone did that for me. I had no future until a person reached down and picked me up and pointed me in the right direction. That's a long story that I am not going to tell you, but someday, if you do what I am suggesting, you will be able to reach down and pick up someone else, and then you will really feel good about that.

BOY: Please call my momma first. I don't want to do anything until she agrees.

PROFESSOR: That's the right thing to say and do. Good luck.

After lunch, the Professor met with the five students in his office. He began as follows:

PROFESSOR: I don't want your names and I don't want to know who

you are, at least not now. I want to tell you that what I saw you doing was terribly embarrassing and humiliating to me. You picked up a little waif off the street who is struggling for groceries and treated him like a monkey with an organ grinder. Do you think he enjoyed being humiliated? Would you be willing to tell your parents what you did? You must have considered that he was something other than a human being, or that if he were a human being, he was not equal to you. Life has been that way, in the past, and a long time ago, and it still exists in our society, today, but I cannot stand it.

You are law students. Hopefully, one day, each of you will be an officer of the court and each of you will have the responsibilities for the lives and the finances and the welfares of your clients. I hope you will not then determine your relationship with a client based on the color of skin or the method of worship, but I also hope that you will mature to where you believe that a human being has dignity. You have taken away his dignity, or at least you have painted him into a corner where he doesn't require dignity anymore. Throwing that dollar bill on the ground required him to grovel in the dirt, not different from if you threw a piece of bread to a pigeon. Would you be proud if that were your son? What would you do if you came upon a scene like this and it was your son who was being treated in that fashion?

I have to tell you that I am utterly ashamed of you. It may be a passing moment when you lost your good senses, or perhaps it was easier to follow the others as a crowd because that is what someone else is doing. Well, it's not easy. It is treacherous to fall into a pattern like that, particularly when someone is being injured in the process. I think that if you share this event with your preacher, your minister, your priest, or your rabbi, or any other confidant, you would not bring pride to them, but you would find them with my feelings, perhaps multiplied.

Some day along the way, you will probably be in my class of Constitutional Law, or some other seminar that I teach. I probably will not recognize you because I am not going to make an effort to do that. I think this day is a black mark for each of you and all of you. It is something that you need to bear in your mind and your hearts the rest of

your lives. So, having given you as much hell as I can for the moment, I want to give you a challenge.

Think of yourself as a very successful, prosperous individual who has all that one needs and all that money can buy, and a glorious lifestyle. Think of yourself, then, as one who might share that with someone less fortunate. I don't suggest that you make a major sacrifice if things are important to you. But, if you enjoy your blessings and feel that you have had good fortune, society demands that its leaders put out a helping hand to those who need it. Having said that, think long and hard about this. Sometime during this next year of your school, look and search for someone who is in need, however minor the need might be and extend a helping hand and see if that doesn't make you feel better than the fun that you have just had. Help an old lady across the street. Help a blind man into a taxicab. Watch a hungry kid in the grocery store and buy him a candy bar. Notice someone in your class in tattered clothing and buy him or her a shirt or a scarf, and do it without identifying yourself. From this moment on, you are at a crossroads in your life, and you can choose yourself, first and exclusively, or you can choose yourself as a part of society. I will forgive you the injury which you have done to me, but I hope you carry away from this conference something that will be meaningful to you for the rest of your life. You are dismissed.

Second Class

You have often said and heard it said that one is entitled to a trial by his peers, based upon constitutional privilege. Let's talk about that. First, I want to call upon you, young lady, sitting in seat number five in the first row. Please stand. Obviously, you are white, beautiful blue eyes and long golden hair, medium size and stature, with an excellent prior education and an eager attitude to succeed. Please describe for me, now, who constitute your peers.

NUMBER 5: The word "peer" generally means equal, or equivalent—perhaps one who is equal.

PROFESSOR: Well, I think that's a pretty good dictionary definition. Does anyone in the class dispute it or wish to add to it or detract from it?—Hearing no further comment from others, let's proceed.

Will the gentleman in seat number seventeen please rise. Thank you. You are tall, handsome, black, athletic in appearance, with excellent academic credentials. Do you consider this lady your peer?

NUMBER 17: I certainly do.

PROFESSOR: If you were on trial in a capital murder case, as defendant, would she be such a peer as you would choose to sit on the jury?

NUMBER 17: I certainly would.

PROFESSOR: Would she meet the test of a peer under our Constitution?

NUMBER 17: For sure.

PROFESSOR: I know that you don't know this lady. Let me tell you some things about her. She is from an extremely wealthy and very prominent family. Her father is a very successful businessman, very active in his community, but he has long been associated with far right causes including financial support of the Ku Klux Klan, the Skinheads, and certain armed self-designated militias. Is she still your peer?

NUMBER 17: I would expect my lawyer to strike her off the jury, or move the judge to strike her for cause.

PROFESSOR: Why?

NUMBER 17: I think it would be obvious that she was probably influenced by the political and social views of her father and that she would not and could not be fair to a black person.

PROFESSOR: Her parents were divorced before she was born. In fact, they were only married for eleven months. Her mother was then the Executive Director of the Alabama Civil Liberties Union, and still serves on its Board of Directors. The cause of the divorce was the serious nature of the differences about social and political matters. Has she requalified as your peer, constitutionally?

NUMBER 17: Yes.

PROFESSOR: Describe to me the constitutional right to a trial by peers, as you see it and understand it.

NUMBER 17: There are probably hundreds if not thousands of cases decided in various jurisdictions which interpret or deal with the question of what constitutes a peer under the Constitution, and obviously, I could not be familiar with all of them, but I would think that the general trend would be someone from the same community, without substantial prejudice or bias, not easily subject to influence by extraneous matters, open-minded, fair and reasonable, regardless of their race, color, or previous condition of servitude.

PROFESSOR: Well, the latter part of your comments dovetail well with the Fifteenth Amendment which gave you and other blacks the right to vote, but I am sure you are also aware that the Fifteenth Amendment does not deal with the qualification of jurors or what constitutes a peer. However, having enumerated all of those tests that you would apply, or

that you would think the law describes, have you any idea how you would go about getting answers to those questions? Do you think that the average person would answer those questions truthfully, or in a fashion that would be pleasing to the interrogator?

NUMBER 17: Admittedly, the inquiries and the interrogations would be very difficult and sometimes not very rewarding. It's an imperfect system.

PROFESSOR: Indeed it is. Let me add, too, as I said once before in an earlier lecture, do not be easily led, and do not accept statements or make assumptions until you are on solid ground. Tonight when you go home, get out the Constitution, again. Tomorrow morning, point out to me carefully and in detail where you have been granted the right to a trial by your peers. You won't find it. I would also like for you to memorize the Sixth Amendment, as I have:

> In all criminal prosecutions, the accused shall enjoy the right to a speedy and public trial, by an impartial jury of the state and district wherein the crime shall have been committed, which district shall have been previously ascertained by law and to be informed of the nature and cause of the accusation; to be confronted with the witness against him; to have compulsory process for obtaining witnesses in his favor, and to have the assistance of counsel for his defense.

When you have failed in your search and concede that you have been led astray, be prepared to tell me what you would consider an "impartial jury" as contrasted to your assumption that trial by your peers is in the Constitution.

PROFESSOR: I want both of you to remain standing. Number 17, I want you to know that I have never seen Number 5 in my life, to my recollection, until she appeared here at the first day of class, and I have no idea whatsoever about her background, her parents, their political and social philosophies, and anything other than that she is an academic scholar, or else she would not be here.

Finally, since this is the end of today's session, I want Number 5,

Number 17, Number 21, Number 52, and Number 79 to select a companion of your choosing, and the ten of you are invited to have dinner with me at my home on Saturday evening at 7:00 p.m., and you will meet my lovely friend and we will get to know each other a bit. Dress as you please. Tomorrow we are going to discuss O.J.

An Evening with the Professor

The home of Professor Smith and Cindy Ragsdale was a beautiful and elaborate mansion that was off the campus of the University of Alabama, approximately a mile, and sat on the highest plateau in the area. The entrance was off of Bear Boulevard through a gated entrance that was activated from the home. Guests would arrive at the gate, blow the car horn, and receive a voice answer from the house, identify themselves, and the gate would open and the car could enter, and then the gate would close again. The entire premises were surrounded by a high chain-link fence that protected the property. The premises consisted of about four acres of land, wooded around the perimeter with gardens and outbuildings behind the home. There was a long roadway which curved in front of the home, made a loop, and returned to the gate. The house was two stories, thirteen rooms, with brick and marble exterior. The entire property was lighted with lanterns along the roadway and spotlights in the perimeter trees. As the guests approached the front door, they were met by Professor Smith.

PROFESSOR: Good evening, ladies and gentlemen. Welcome to the humble abode of the arrogant professor. Follow me into our family room. Let me first present to you my beloved, Cindy Ragsdale, whom I have known almost all of my life and who is my constant enchanting companion. You are going to learn to know her better and know a little bit more about her, but first I want you to introduce yourselves, your

guest, and a little bit of your family background. Let's start with you.

TOM: Professor, I am Tom Brown. My guest is Mary Lou Brown, my lovely and beautiful wife. We were both born and raised in Birmingham, Alabama, but before we started school, our families moved into the same neighborhood in the City of Mountain Brook which was a very young city at the time, incidentally, not far from the old McClung home. We had two grammar schools, Crestline School and Mountain Brook School, which I understand were soon before that acquired from Jefferson County, Alabama. We both lived in the Crestline area, in fact, just a block or so apart. My father was an insurance executive in a very prominent Birmingham based insurance company, and my mother was a dutiful housewife, and together they raised three children. I was the oldest. Mary Lou's father was a Methodist minister, and she was, likewise, the oldest of three children. We started Crestline Grammar School together. And, together with three or four other children, we gathered on the corner to walk about two blocks to the school and onto the playground where we began our days. By the time we were old enough to continue elevating our education, we attended the Mountain Brook Junior High School and then the new Mountain Brook High School, and we were regularly classmates. Our families occasionally took trips together, down to the Alabama coast or to the Florida Panhandle, or to Calloway Gardens over in Georgia. On one occasion, we went to New Orleans. As a result of this close contact, Mary Lou and I became very good friends, but in the early years we did not realize what we would someday mean to each other. We parted company when I went to the University of Pennsylvania, and the Wharton School of Finance, and she went to the University of Alabama, School of Commerce, once known as Bidgood Hall. She excelled in accounting, got a Masters degree, and got her CPA privileges on the first effort. While we were in separate colleges, we corresponded, occasionally showed up at each other's home during vacation. The relationship grew, and soon we were married.

I wanted to be a lawyer. She had not decided exactly what she wanted to do, but she wanted to be engaged in the business of finance. On a lark, not really expecting it to happen, we both applied for admission to the

University of Alabama Law School. We were both accepted. I was fully intentioned, and remain so, to practice law, and she was just experimenting to see if that is what she wanted. Needless to say, now, she is also a member of this class, and is one of your students. I guess that is enough background. It tells you somewhat who we are and where we have been. We were raised by strict parents, in a relatively affluent society, at one of the most impressive periods in the history of the world. We look forward to sharing the beginning of our law education with you."

PROFESSOR: Well said, young man, and I am pleased to meet you, Mary Lou. Next.

HARRY: Professor Joseph Jasper Smith, I am pleased and honored to introduce myself. I am Harry Blackmun, Jr., one of your prime exhibits from your previous lecture, and I am more than pleased to present to you my beloved mother, Mrs. Harry Blackmun, Sr. Like Tom, I have a valuable female companion, and she will probably meet you in due course, but it is such a privilege for my mother to have this opportunity that I chose her, above all the women in the world. Before I tell you about my father and my mother, let me tell you about my grandparents, on my father's side. I never knew the grandparents on my mother's side. My grandfather was born deep in the Black Belt of Alabama in a little town named Clio. It's only real claim to fame was that the former Governor of Alabama, George Wallace, was born and reared in that community, but my grandparents lived a few miles out of town and raised cotton. They labored long and hard, but their primary goal in life was to see that their children were educated. My father went to grammar school, high school, and technical school in Montgomery. He became a welder while the Industrial Revolution still prevailed, and he did quite well financially. My grandmother was an orphan, abandoned by her parents and raised by some neighbors until she was fifteen years old when she married my grandfather. She gave her life to her children. My father was similarly committed to education, and he chose as his bride, some thirty years ago, this wonderful lady who stands before you today. She was in the early years a high school teacher, teaching history and English, until she became an assistant principal in a high school where every teacher, every

administrator, every student was black. My parents lived constantly in a two-color society, doing well financially, owning a home, having many friends, but staying within the appropriate bounds. My mother not only reared me and nurtured me, but she charted the course of my life, and she decided long ago that I was going to be a lawyer, and more specifically, a civil rights lawyer, and even more specifically than that, a lawyer who would work for the good of the common man without regard to economic consequences. I was taught about the Constitution as a child, as a youth, and I have never been permitted to step aside from it. Even though my mother was very active in racial causes and in civil rights matters, she never exposed me to any danger or risk, and I thought that at this stage of my life the only reward that I could truly give her would be to be a part of this evening, and my mother said that she would like to say a few words.

MRS. BLACKMUN: Professor, I am humbled to be in your presence. I have known of you for most of my adult life, I am pleased that you will be a mentor for my son, and I would very much appreciate having a picture of you, my son, and myself, together.

PROFESSOR: Mrs. Blackmun, what a charming lady you are, and I am pleased to have you in our home, and I promise not only the picture, but to cherish the remarks that you and your son have made. On the other hand, as is my custom, I will struggle with all of the vigor within me to treat your son to an education, but to no favors. You would not want it otherwise, would you?—Next.

DOUGLAS: I am Douglas Chancellor, and, like all of the others, I am truly grateful to have this opportunity to meet you in person. Like them, I certainly expect to reap the benefits of being a student in your class. I guess that is what all of us look forward to more than anything else when we consider this law school. On the other hand, I have no tradition of southern involvement. I was born in the Bronx, in a mixed neighborhood, where everyone had to struggle to survive, and my parents did not make it. I have two brothers and a sister, and all four of us ended up in an orphanage in the Bronx when our parents split up and went their separate ways. None of us have ever heard of or seen them since, nor do

we have much by way of recollection since the oldest of us was only seven years old at that time. That was my sister. I was not among the fortunate ones to be adopted, and I lived in various institutions until I was eighteen years of age. The institutions did manage to keep me in touch with my sister and brothers, but mostly we shared correspondence and an occasional telephone call.

Other than recognizing our mutual existences, we are not much of a family. I spent nine years in military service, beginning as a volunteer in the infantry, and finishing as a major in the Air Force headquartered at Maxwell Field in Montgomery. Alabama became my home state. I have retired on a full and total disability pension, and I have managed to sustain myself by teaching seminars for the handicapped through the Department of Industrial Relations of the State of Alabama. My life has not permitted me to make friends easily or of a lasting nature, and I have been pretty much of a drifter. Last night I had dinner at the little Chinese restaurant a couple of blocks from the law school, and this nice young lady, Lin Ye Song, is a waitress there. I would like for her to tell you a little bit about herself. Lin?

LIN YE SONG: Sir, I am privileged to be here. I do not have a college education, and pardon me if my English is not too good. Many lawyers and law students come to our restaurant which is owned by some of the members of my family. Often, in my free time, I have wandered about the campus, and I have been in the law school, and I have watched the students in the library, and I have listened to them talk about law cases. I have had discussions with Douglas, and I am grateful that he brought me here to meet you.

PROFESSOR: Well, you are certainly an interesting couple, and so far we have found a variety of backgrounds in our guests for the evening. Douglas, some day I will sit with you, just the two of us, and I will exchange stories about the tragedies and difficulties in our lives that made us who we are today, because every person is the end product of all of the experiences of life that that person has had. Adversity is a good part of training to be a lawyer, and I hope you have the resiliency to practice law in the same fashion that you have survived the misfortunes of life. For

you, Lin, I welcome you to my home. I am pleased that you might be interested in the law, and I hope that you will find life here in America, near this campus, to be rewarding. You might even think about and search for a program through this great university where you might begin more formal training, so now let's move on until we know everybody better.

Let's take advantage of Cindy's hospitality before we meet the rest of you fine young people. Before the evening is over, I promise you that Cindy and I will also tell you a little bit about ourselves and our lives together. First, but not foremost, she is an excellent cook and a great home manager. That's not the only reason that I took her into my life many years ago. Please help yourselves by passing through the dining room, picking up a plate, and you will find an assortment of attractive selections that Cindy has prepared herself, and then we will gather outside on the patio to enjoy each other's company. Cindy is going to insist that you go back for seconds. The bar is set up on the patio and you can mix your own.

The Professor, Cindy, and the ten guests moved quickly through the line, picking and choosing their meals and carrying them through the dining room, returning to get drinks, and back to the patio. The wrought iron table would not seat twelve people, so some of the students seemed to gravitate toward seats away from the table, large chairs with side tables, and some sat on the floor. The Professor and Cindy, Tom and Mary Lou, Harry and his mother sat at the table. There was a small floral piece in the center. Cindy had gathered the floral arrangement from her garden outside. The dining room windows were open to display the beautiful gardens and trees of the side yard. A gentle breeze swayed the see-through draperies, and it was a beautiful and serene setting. Initially, there was only the clinking of the silverware and the rattling of the ice in the drinks until the Professor spoke.

PROFESSOR: I hope everyone is comfortable. Let's enjoy our meal together, but let's continue with meeting each other and give a chance to those who have not spoken yet. I promise you that at the end Cindy and

I will give you a chance to learn something about us. So, young lady, will you please come forth and speak.

ESTHER: Thank you. I guess I am a little bit timid to present myself, but I will have a go at it. My name is Esther Halevi. My parents were Morris and Esther Halavitz, both of whom were born in a small town in Poland by the name of Minsk which had a substantial Jewish population and which was known for Jewish scholarship in the last century. My father's real name was Moshe which liberally translates into Morris. Esther was my mother's given name because she was to be like Esther in the Bible. When I was born my original given name was Sabata. I was born on a Saturday, the Jewish Sabbath, and that's why I was given that name. I hardly remember my earliest years because there was constant turmoil. We had lived in our own home on the outskirts of the city and my father was a tailor. I was an only child. We then began to move. We left our home at first to go stay with relatives in a nearby city, Pinsk, and after a few months there, our family, who lived there, and my mother, my father, and I started to leave to find our way to Warsaw, many, many miles away, but we were captured by Polish people who were sympathetic toward the Nazis, and we, along with several hundred others, were loaded into cattle cars and sent to a concentration camp, Auschwitz, or Oswiecim. The trip was a miserable experience: no food, no water, no sanitary conditions, not even a place to sit down. It seemed to me that it lasted for days until we were unloaded, like cattle, into a courtyard, and as we got off the train, my father was sent in one line, and my mother and I were sent in another, in different directions. I was just five or six years old, and really did not comprehend what was happening to me or to them, nor did I understand what was being said by the camp guards. I never saw my father again.

I lived with my mother in a barracks for almost two years. She was both a cook and a seamstress, and she worked all day long, and I stayed in that barracks, sometimes alone, but my mother would always bring food and drink to me at the end of the day. I guess she had eaten before because everything that she brought was given to me. Then she got sick. I didn't understand then what dying was, and I had no concept of the

concentration camp life or Hitler's final disposition of the Jewish people. I guess I was destined to be part of that final solution. My mother made many friends in the barracks and she was often able to do favors for others. Then she died of dysentery. One of her best friends, Zelda Yoffie, took me to be her daughter. She had never had children and she had never been married. She wanted me to change my name to Esther, and I did, and after that I have always been called Esther.

I won't bore you with all the details, but Zelda had relatives in the United States. She arranged to send me with another family who lived in Charleston, South Carolina. There was some difficulty in my entry into the United States. In Charleston I was first placed into a home and school that was supported by the community. I stayed there, in fact worked there, and helped others as I grew older. I did get a good education at the orphanage school in the beginning, and in the public schools of Charleston. When it came time for me to graduate from the institution and seek higher education, that community provided a place for me to live with another Jewish family and to go to the University of Charleston where I received scholarships and grants. I guess it is fair to say that I owe my life to the City of Charleston and to my mother's friend who got me there. I think because of this somewhat unusual background, the University of Alabama Law School was anxious to have me and has enabled me to be here as a beginning law student. So much for me.

I am living in a dormitory and this is my roommate, Deloris Stein. Just by happenstance we were assigned to room together, both being Jewish. Her nickname is Dixie. A few years ago she had a serious cancer problem develop in her throat and her vocal cords have been removed and she will never speak again, but she hears well and she communicates in sign language well. I thought coming here with you would be a wonderful experience for her, too. That's who we are.

PROFESSOR: That's a very moving story and I am sure it both depresses and lifts up the spirit of all of us.

CINDY: That really is sad. It's impossible to know what such tortures of life and such misadventures can do to a person, but I would have been glad to have you as my daughter when you were six years old, when you

first got to Charleston, when you first went to college, perhaps even now, but we need to talk more about that. Welcome to you, too, Dixie.

PROFESSOR: Well, let's move on to our last couple.

A.J.: I am A.J. Kay. I know it's a funny sounding name, and what's worse is that the "A" and the "J" don't stand for anything, so I guess my parents got my name out of alphabet soup. I don't have any electrifying stories to tell or any unusual background. I was born right here in Tuscaloosa. I went to Tuscaloosa High School. My family was comfortable from a financial standpoint, very much involved in the Tuscaloosa community, and in fact in campus life because my father is an investment counselor, and he assists in managing some of the university funds, but also helps the professors and staff at the University who need his services. He and my mother are regularly invited to attend social events and scholastic events that are open to the public, so I am no stranger to the campus.

I think I was born in a red and white jersey because the Crimson Tide has always been a significant part of my personal life and my family life. Whenever possible, we travel to the football games. Whenever there is a home game, we have excellent seats, extra seats, and I can take my friends. That's an expensive luxury now. After high school my parents thought that I should get a business education and I went through the Commerce School. I have an adequate academic record, good enough to get into the law school, and I have been fortunate to be involved in a lot of other campus activities of an extracurricular nature. I have continued to live at home until just recently, and I now live in my own apartment, just a few blocks from the law school. I guess you would say that I and my background are plain vanilla, with one possible exception. I have been exposed to the law a lot. I had been studying law long before I was admitted to law school. My goal may result in the active practice of law, but my preference is to teach. I would like to be a law professor, and I think it's great that I am getting my first exposure to you since you are obviously a legend here at the University.

Now, my guest. She is Betty Smith. We went through high school and commerce school together. She has lived here with an aunt while she has

gone to school. Her parents are separated and both live in different communities, and she has an excellent relationship with both of them. Her father is a lawyer and her mother is a doctor, but she chose business, and she is now a beginning executive at a local bank. She expects to be president of that bank someday, and I think she will. With the blessing of our parents, she and I are going to be married on Valentine's Day, next year. So I present to you my bride-to-be. I hope she will make a lot of money and support me through law school and that we can both not only have successful careers, but a large family. I have not said that to her before.

There was a moment of laughter and light-heartedness with the students and their guests exchanging comments and huddling together and continuing to eat and return for more. Everyone seemed to be relaxed and enjoying the companionship and the meal. It soon came time for dessert.

CINDY: Ladies, please give me a helping hand and let's clear the table. I won't ask you to wash the dishes. I have taught Joe to do that and he is very good at it. He takes pride in it and he doesn't like anyone to interfere with his expertise.

The students and guests begin to shift around, the ladies helping and carrying and scraping, and the guys just huddling together, getting to know each other and asking questions. Then Cindy brought to the table two huge containers, one of chocolate ice cream, and one of vanilla, two scoops, a bowl of hot fudge, a bowl of marshmallow sauce, nuts, and other ingredients, all for the purpose of making hot fudge sundaes. She invited everyone to dig in and they did. Some had second portions, mostly the men. The Professor then invited everyone to follow him out past the patio, to a small picnic area under two giant oak trees. There were permanent tables cemented to the ground with wooden benches on each side and room for everyone to sit and face each other. The tables could have accommodated several more people, and on the tables Cindy spread an assortment of fruits—bananas, oranges, apples, pears and grapes. Everyone sat down and relaxed, and the Professor began to speak.

PROFESSOR: Well, I guess it's time for you to hear from Cindy and me. As you perhaps suspect, we have done this before, so I am going to give you a few highlights of my life, and then I will let Cindy tell you about hers, and then we will open ourselves to questions. But, I really want you to understand the purpose of this. My life commitment is to teaching students constitutional law. I don't believe that a professor can teach as well to strangers as he can to friends, nor do I believe that a student can gain the maximum from the teaching without knowing something about the background of the professor. I am always curious to hear what questions you might ask, not just from those of you who are students, but those who do not propose to become lawyers. Every one of us has a different background, and as I have said many times, each of us is the end product of all of our experiences. That's who we are—a composite of who we have been—that's how we are—the product of the things which have happened to us. You can apply that to yourselves and do a self-analysis.

I was born and raised by unmarried parents, and I lived in a ghetto on the south side of Birmingham. My education began in a very simple and not a meaningful way until I met Cindy. Early in life I learned to read and to inquire and to expand my horizons. I am not sure when I decided that the law was my future, but it came early in life. Through the help of Cindy's family, I was able to go to good schools, to graduate and become a lawyer, to practice law for awhile, and then to move on to this career. I have never forgotten my humble beginnings, nor have I removed from my mind and my emotions the fact that I was not only a minority person, but a subclass individual in a society where blacks were not only not equal, they didn't matter. Cindy and I have been together for a very long time, actually from childhood, but she is the only thing, the only person, in all of my life, who has been more valuable and more meaningful to me than the law, and particularly the Constitution.

I have very few friends. I have a multitude of acquaintances, and as you perhaps suspect, some admirers, some supporters, some detractors. I am no longer considered a controversial person, but I once was. I am

very much at peace with myself, and Cindy, and my life, and I have no desire ever to quit teaching. It is interesting and challenging and rewarding, and on the side I sometimes counsel and advise with lawyers who have constitutional problems, and that's invigorating and fulfilling. That's my story and that's who I am. So, let's hear from Cindy.

CINDY: Well, I really prefer to remain in the background because this is his show. This is his life. We have done this before, and I enjoy telling about my life because it is so much in contrast to the description of the life that you just heard. I was born into a very well-known family in Birmingham, wealthy, successful, perhaps even powerful. I lived in a large and beautiful home on Highland Avenue, a very fashionable part of the City of Birmingham. Today you would say that I was raised in the lap of luxury, or with a silver spoon in my mouth, but it didn't seem that way to me when I was young because so many of our friends were in equivalent positions. Our families were members of country clubs, the major community organizations, active in whatever was going on in the community, and my home was frequently filled with guests, including famous people. I was exposed to politicians, musicians, intellectuals, radicals, people of every faith, color, and persuasion, and therefore my young years were filled with diversity. I had no early plans for my life, but I knew that I was in step with high society and would receive all the rewards that came from that status. I was certainly among the very privileged few.

My parents were avid about education. Nothing short of excellence would be tolerated for me or my siblings. We not only were required to be at the top of our classes academically, but to have extracurricular activities like sports, music, literature, and the arts. We had a vast library in our home, full of all of the greatest books of time, and there was a different section where the things of the day appeared, newspapers, magazines, best sellers, but we were not encouraged to spend our time with fiction. At the dinner table we talked about things of interest to each of us, things that were important to our community, to our nation, to the world, and we discussed things that were controversial, and we were encouraged to express controversial views. Some of our discussions were

heated, but never with anger. My parents very clearly outlined the parameters of our lives, what we could and could not do, and the fallout from what we did do that was unacceptable. I would like to say that we stayed within those parameters, but we didn't. Sometimes we were mischievous. Sometimes we were unwilling to account for where we had been or what we had done, but the one feature that was never a part of our lives was disrespect. We never talked back to our parents or raised our voices against them. We treated our school teachers, the ministers, in effect, all adults, with a lot of respect. In fact, we were generally expected not to speak to adults until they spoke to us first. I guess you could say that we were strictly disciplined, but our home was full of love and caring and togetherness. Whenever one of us accomplished something special, we all celebrated. We took many great vacations together. My father owned a very fine home on a lake where we would frequently go on weekends to swim, fish, cook out, and such things as that.

I had an excellent education, the best that money could buy. I spent two summers in Europe, one in London, one in Paris. I could have made any of several choices as to my undergraduate studies. But, oddly enough, the biggest influence that persuaded me to become a lawyer was Joseph Jasper Smith, the Professor. He had finished law school and was beginning the practice of law, and he was very excited about what was happening to him and the different avenues that were opened because he was a lawyer. I must add that I have known Joe almost all of my life, or at least I hardly remember not knowing him.

I practiced law for a few years with a large law firm. Joe practiced with a large law firm, but it was the law firm that represented my family, and I did not want to be employed by that law firm, but rather to strike out in my own direction, so I applied at several other law firms, had a few offers, and chose one which was headquartered in Birmingham, but had offices elsewhere, as well. It was a very prominent and successful law firm, and it still is such these days. As a beginning lawyer I was exposed to everything, no particular specialty, but took a liking for domestic matters. After several years I decided that the domestic area was a segment of the law that I wanted to be in full time. For the last several

years I have had my own shop, just myself, with a small staff, and I enjoy very much what I do. I guess you would say that I am a full-time practitioner, but I go and come as I please, pick and choose the cases that I want, and it is not imperative that I generate a huge income from my profession. I guess that's enough about me.

PROFESSOR: It's your turn, who's up first?

TOM: I have a lot of questions and your resumés are thrilling to me. You seem to come from such different backgrounds, and I would like to know how you came to share your lives together.

PROFESSOR: I think we both need to respond to that, but I will reply first. I lived with my mother, just a few blocks away from Cindy's home. My father was a regular employee of her family, and he was responsible for the landscaping, helping clean and maintain the interior, serving as a butler when needed, and occasionally as a chauffeur. That was his nearly full-time job, and his primary source of income. When there was a big party at Cindy's home, sometimes my mother came and washed dishes and helped clean up and things like that. She was not asked to serve at the tables. They had others who did that. As a result, our family was very close to Cindy's family, but, obviously a very different status. You could not say that we were friends, but rather servants, but Cindy and I became friends, and I will tell you why, and this is one of the best things that ever happened to me in my life.

Cindy was full of vitality. She was always doing something active. Many times my father would bring me to work with him, when I was not in school, or on the weekends, and I helped him, and part of my duty was to stay out of everybody's way. Sometimes I did my lessons at their home. In the back yard there was a beautiful greenhouse that had not only flowers and shrubs and other growing things, but a sitting area, almost like a separate apartment. I remember the first time that Cindy came into that apartment when I was there studying. I really did not know how to read, and I guess I was coloring pictures and learning my alphabet, or something like that, but she sat down with me and began to teach me how to read. That's what we now call phonics. She taught me to pronounce every letter and every combination of letters and the variation

of the use of letters, and then to understand the meaning of the words. As time went by, several occasions like this took place, and she taught me how to make sentences, and how to use punctuation marks, but she always forced me to learn to spell. That was very important to her, and in fact she was a contestant in spelling bees, regularly. She thought that was the most important thing I could learn. Remember, we were about the same age, she being just a little older, but she had had a much better education than what I was getting. We later moved on to multiplication tables and finally to read things and discuss what we read together. She was really an inspiration although I did not fully realize it then. Now, as I look back, those sessions in the greenhouse were probably what launched me toward my career. My parents insisted on my schooling, modest as it was, but Cindy made it beautiful and meaningful.

Then as the years went by I began to assume more responsibilities, and I worked inside the home. In the basement of the home there were living quarters where, if need be, my father and I could stay overnight. There were bathrooms and showers available. The family hardly ever came into that area, but we kept it as clean as if it were upstairs. We took pride in having access to be there. Whenever the day of work was done, my father insisted that both of us go into the basement, shower and clean ourselves, and change into better clothes. He actually kept some of his there, different kinds, but when I came to work, I came in work clothes and brought better clothes to change into later. You could say, then, that I really grew up in Cindy's family, and as I became a teenager and a young man, her father began to assign specific duties and responsibilities to me. He trusted me. Upon occasion he would sit and talk with me about important things, not just what we learned in school, or heard on the streets, but really important things about the world and what he was doing and what was happening in the big picture. He was a very intelligent person. The most important thing that I remember is that he never treated me like a servant. When he told me to do something, it was with kindness, sometimes firmness, but when we sat down for a chat, he treated me like an equal. He really did not have an awareness or an appreciation of the fact that Cindy was my dearest friend. That would be

unheard of, and it would have ruptured the relationships between our families.

As we grew older, there were opportunities when I could repay Cindy, somewhat. I frequently ran errands for her, drove her someplace in the car, took care of personal things, and she was always very gracious about what I did. She never paid me, because that was not within the relationship that we shared, but she gave me many kindnesses and much appreciation, and handsome presents.

After she graduated law school we saw each other regularly, in the courthouse, or in the law firms that we attended. We even corresponded when she was away, like the summer in Paris. I looked forward to her letters and the little gifts that she sent, and the many pictures which she took.

Then there was an event in my life that severely altered the direction, having to do with my practice of law, and you are going to be exposed to that somewhat in the classroom, but it drew Cindy and me closer together. We maintained our relationship on a very personal but not intimate basis, and we did not come together to live together until both of her parents and both of my parents had passed away. Even at that late date, there was a certain amount of wonderment that a black man and a white woman could share this type of companionship. But, I think it is the best thing that has happened to both of us. It has certainly extended our years and brought joy to us, and I think I have said enough.

TOM: Ms. Ragsdale, can you top that?

CINDY: No, but I will fill in the blanks. First let me tell you that I always enjoy Joe's recollections, and as the years go by, some of the things that he remembers are somewhat different from my recollections, but just as he is in the classroom, he is very convincing and persuasive, so I wonder if my recollections are truly correct. Be that as it may, most of the things which he has said about me are true. I was born into the lap of luxury, silver spoon, all of that stuff. Because education was so important in my family and in the lifestyle of my family, all of us did very well in school. And, from time to time, I found topics that were particularly interesting to me. I am sure I read more books than anyone else in my

class. In fact, one of the great weekend pleasures was when my mother would take me to the downtown library, to the children's section, and help me select books to read during the coming week, maybe six or seven. I knew that she was choosing books more advanced than my age required, but she was pushing me along, and since I was inquisitive and curious, I just fell in love with reading. When I learned that there were a lot of people who could not read or write, it was distressing to me because I did not know any of those people, firsthand, until I met Joe.

He was always a perfect gentleman, perhaps shy, but he said that he was "keeping his place." He was very responsive to anything that anyone in my family requested, and we had absolute trust in him which was very unusual in race relationships in those days.

I guess I enjoyed our study sessions together because I felt that I was the teacher and he was the student, and that we were making great progress. I began to share with him things that happened in my school and in my classrooms that were not available where he went to school. He quickly picked up on reading, and when we would meet, sometimes, he would tell me something that he read, and where he read it, and who wrote it, and he loved new ideas and things about life that were different from his. He had some difficulty getting along in writing. First, he didn't write well. He did pretty well printing letters, but quite poorly with cursive. So, I launched him on a career of writing and it was amazing to me how quickly he could develop ideas and create thoughts and put them down on paper. I still have dozens of letters that he wrote me in those early years, and he would bring them on the weekends when he came to work. Let me say that there was no sign of affection or personal involvement, but mostly reporting on his progress and his life and events which took place during the week. Through those letters I learned about his parents, the deprivation of living in the Block, and the despair or hopelessness of substantially everyone who lived near him. That made me want to help guide him out of that wilderness into a life more nearly like mine. In looking back to those days, that was a pretty mature thought for a young girl who had not even herself reached maturity.

Time goes on and Joe and I drifted apart as we schooled in different

places, but whenever there was a vacation and we were both in town, we would find some time together and catch up on the things that had happened. Then, my father took a greater interest in Joe and began to encourage him with loftier horizons and challenges. There were one or two occasions that I remember very well when some scholar or otherwise noted person would be in our home for a social event, to make a speech or to raise money, and my father would ask Joe to work that evening and then come and sit with the others and listen, so Joe got exposed, far beyond his years, to intellectual and worldwide matters of interest. We stayed in touch with each other all through his schooling and, honestly, I do not think that I would have gone to law school except by his encouragement. There were many other avenues open to me, but I had a desire to be independent and self-sufficient and make my own lot in life rather than to follow in the ways of my family and relatives. So, I was somewhat of a renegade.

We ended up in different law firms, both large and prestigious, and we talked regularly about what we were doing. We were in entirely different fields of law except that there was also some trial work in what I did. By then, it was becoming socially acceptable, or as a matter of law, for the different races to eat in the same places and perhaps eat with each other, so we had many meals, lunches, quick snacks, in the courthouse cafeteria, sitting at the same table.

I don't know when I really fell in love with Joe. I know that I cared for him deeply from the earliest days, but when it became a matter of love and affection, I just can't say. I also don't remember that there was ever a turmoil in me about sharing my future with Joe, although both of us knew that it would be shocking to many others who were not yet ready for interracial relationships.

I knew for a long time that Joe really wanted to teach, but he was a damned good trial lawyer, and he was very successful. He was unquestionably the most outstanding black young attorney in the community. I know that he had offers from other law firms, but he stuck where he was and he was working his way toward the top. Before it was time for him to be a partner, a conflict of a serious nature developed. As a result of that,

Joe left the practice of law, somewhat reluctantly, but went on to realize his real dream of teaching. When that happened, we decided that we belonged together, and we moved in together, and we have been together ever since, and we will be together the rest of our lives. I am proud of him. I guess that now concludes everything that you ever wanted to know about Joe and Cindy, doesn't it?

MRS. BLACKMUN: I don't believe I have ever experienced a more enjoyable or challenging evening than this, and I am truly intrigued and impressed, but with my background, and the background of each of you, I am curious how you were persuaded to cross the line and join each other with the racial concerns that then existed and still exist in this community. If I am not too presumptuous, tell me how you could do that.

CINDY: It wasn't easy. I was never myself concerned about my relationship with Joe. Once I had reconciled in my mind that I truly loved him and considered him something more than a friend, I wanted to be with him all of the time, and I guess I was strong enough where the opinions of others wouldn't bother me, but I did not want to offend my parents or my family or embarrass them. I believe that if Joe and I had talked marriage, it would have been a scandal, and I am not sure that our families, his or mine, would have been ready to accept that. Was it easy? Not really. Remember, too, that the Constitution of the State of Alabama forbade the marriage of people of different races. The Supreme Court changed that, but it didn't change in Alabama. Well, anyway, we didn't make any formal announcement, but word soon got around that we were living together, and those friends which he had and those friends which I had who were truly friends had very little trouble mixing, but some of their friends were aloof, as to them and as to us. Let me assure you, however, that whatever sacrifices there were, and whatever we might have given up has been returned to us manifold. Life could not be better for us, nor do we want for anything, nor is there anything in life nearly as important as what we feel for each other. Would I recommend it to someone else? I don't think so.

PROFESSOR: My reaction comes from a different direction, but I have no objection to the question or the comments, whatsoever. Part of what

is suggested by your inquiry was difficult to resolve within myself. In the young years I never even envisioned more than a distant relationship, and I had to be very careful, and I wanted to be very careful, and I never did or said anything that could offend Cindy or her family, or anyone else, for that matter. I am sure neither of my parents would have permitted me to get "out of line." I was a courageous young man and the mountains didn't seem too high for me. My life became full to the extent that Cindy might have been the most important single relationship, but she was not all of it, and sometimes not any of it, depending on where I was or what I was doing. I am sure I knew far earlier than Cindy did that I intended us to be united, but I never would have said that to her, nor would I have said or done anything to suggest it. I would never have taken the risk that I might lose what we had together. It certainly was a bold stroke. I think I can probably pinpoint the moment when we crossed the line, when we came to know that we loved each other, and that we felt life together would be worth any risk. I had just finished a trial in which my law firm was successful. It was one which had some community notoriety, and as we left the courtroom, there were a lot of congratulations and cheering for me and the senior partner who was my supervising attorney. As we left the building, I saw Cindy coming into the building in a rush. I stopped her to talk for a moment, but she said for me please to wait, that she was on a deadline. So I sat outside on the courthouse steps as the sun went down and waited almost a half hour until she returned. She had a brief that had to be filed that very day and she wanted to be certain not to miss the clerk. We sat and talked, and she shared with me the exhilaration of the victory. I remember what she said—"Joe, this calls for a drink, let's go to the Tavern." The Tavern was not far from the courthouse. A lot of law-type people ended up there in the evenings, finishing up their work, drinking, dining. I positively remember that walking into that place it was obvious to me that we were the only interracial couple there, but they found us a table in the back near the kitchen, not a highly desirable place, because there was a lot of traffic and noise. We did our "catch-up" as to what she had been doing and what I had been doing, and she reached out and put her hand on mine and told

me how proud she was of me, and how much she wished for my future. I remember saying to her that whatever my future was, it would include her. We looked into each other's eyes, without saying a further word. I don't know what interpretation she put on that, but I knew the one that I did, that this was going to be forever. The truth is that neither one of us had ever established a firm and personal relationship with another person, that involved intimacy, or even semi-permanence, so there weren't other people to talk about, no debris behind either of us. Before we left that evening, I asked her if she would like to join me at an Alabama/Auburn basketball game the next evening and she said she would, and I told her that I would pick her up, early, and we would have a bite to eat, first. When I left, I wondered what I had done, if I had really made some progress on my dream, or if I had risked alienation, because her response was not as enthusiastic as I had wished. However, the next night was great in every respect. When that evening was over, I kissed her for the first time, and she responded, and I am sure I saw the sunset, heard the waves on the beaches, and the other things that one gains at a moment of intense serenity. On the other hand, contrary to Cindy's final view, I would say that anyone who is bold enough to measure the gains against the risks and find an overwhelming support of the gains, ought to try and make the relationship regardless of race or religion or any other diversity. Yet, at the same time, you would have to go in with your eyes open, anticipating some disappointments, because they will be coming. Even today, after these many, many years that Cindy and I have enjoyed, I don't see much of this type of mixing. So it takes the right people, and we're the right people.

MRS. BLACKMUN: I wish I had a tape recorder, but I am not sure that either of you would like to be taped in this setting. I'll remember every word that you have said. I do have to add one thought of my own. I have often wondered about the "mixing of the races" which was hellfire and damnation most of my life, and just as Cindy's parents would have been concerned, perhaps shocked, I, too, would have been terribly frightened about such a union in my family. My anxiety would have extended beyond the interracial marriage to a concern about the children, and

that's one the two of you have not had to face, or at least, have not chosen to.

CINDY: True. We never planned around children, but that would really have complicated our lives. But, let's go on.

DOUGLAS: I have told you that all of my life I have been a loner, and so being alone may not be pleasant, but one can grow accustomed to it. It makes one emphasize other facets of life. Mrs. Ragsdale suggested some type of an event which brought about your departure from the practice of law and led you into teaching. Could you share that with us?

PROFESSOR: I'm going to give you a bird's eye view of that, but it is going to be part of a class responsibility soon to come for you and the other members of your section. You might remember that in my opening remarks on the first day of class I enumerated some cases that would be of interest to you and which we would discuss. One of them is known as *Joseph Jasper Smith*. I am that person. I concluded the settlement of a lawsuit and I will give you substantially all of the background of that case in class. Following the settlement which was accompanied by strict non-disclosure agreements, all parties concerned, there were disciplinary proceedings that went to the Supreme Court of the State of Alabama. Those, by rules and understandings, are confidential. I then ceased the practice of law. I had resigned from my law firm, and I took this wonderful position with the law school. You will hear considerably more later, but that series of events culminated in my becoming Professor Smith. So much of that.

Later That Evening

JOE: Let's call it a night, Cindy, dear. I have finished all the dishes, but I have left some pots and pans for tomorrow. I think you have done enough cleaning to be released from your chores.

CINDY: I agree. I'm worn out. I love these events with your students, and I love to make new friends, but it gets harder every year. I really do enjoy it, mostly because I see what pleasure it brings to you.

JOE: Right. It is a pleasure. I guess I keep in touch with my youth by spending time with young people. Some of them are very special and I see something special in Tom. He's a born leader. On the other hand, as I have told you, and the classrooms, I have to watch out to avoid any favoritism. During the course of the year I learn a lot about the students. Those who speak up seem to get identified, and I recognize them, and sometimes, honestly, I know who is writing the exam answers. It's a question of style. I know, for sure, too, that Harry Blackmun is going to amount to something. He's a gentleman, but he's got fire in his eyes and in his heart, and I thought it was beautiful that he brought his mother.

CINDY: I got the same reaction, but I guess you always look at the guys. I think I was most impressed by Esther, not only the tragic background that she suffered, but her willingness to share her life with an impaired person. I think she will spend the rest of her life paying back society for the kindnesses which were done for her. You know, you have generally tracked and followed all of the students with gross numbers like how many practice in Alabama, how many didn't practice at all, and how many gave to the alumni fund, all of those types of things, but it would be nice if we set up a mechanism to trace what happens in their lives. That might be something to keep us both busy for a few years.

JOE: That's a good idea. Let's think about how we will go about it. It will be easy to put together a format with this present class. We could probably have some kind of a regular mailing so that we could stay in touch and follow the changes of addresses, but I don't know how we would ever catch up with the students of prior years.

CINDY: Well, I think I'm sorry I said that, now. It's late and you've got enough on your plate to keep you busy, and I have to think about a couple of cases that are set for trial next week. Let's go up.

JOE: Does up mean go to bed?

CINDY: Certainly.

JOE: Does it mean anything else?

CINDY: What do you want it to mean?

JOE: Oh, nothing really, yet—let's go on up and I'll think about it. I'm going to take a shower and clip my toenails while you are putting all

that gunk on your face and rolling up your hair. Isn't that a romantic setting.

CINDY: You are romantic all the time.

JOE: Ain't you glad.

CINDY: Good night, dear.

Another Class Session

Good morning. It's time for us to move on to the practice of law because the Constitution is merely the basis for that. You know from your other courses that there are three sources of knowledge, wisdom, and presentation of our law, beginning, first, with the Constitution of the United States, and supplemented by the constitutions of the various several states. Then, in the infinite wisdom of our legislators, we have enactments, laws, rules, and regulations, and the process of having our government govern us and our money. Third, and finally, we have case law. That means, as you know, that someone has instituted some kind of a cause of action for a court, a tribunal, or an agency, in which parties are in opposition to each other, an issue exists between them, and the issue is resolved by the opinion of the hearing party. That body of law is far more complex and less specific than constitutions or statutory enactments because it involves creativity. If you read a statute and it says, "Thou shalt not . . ." then that's reasonably clear. When you begin to read about that law in the case books and the decisions of the courts, you may find a somewhat different interpretation than the words that you read.

I want to tell you an interesting anecdote. When I first entered law school, as a young boy, a beginner, not well trained or exposed to the ways of life, I did so with considerable trepidation. I had a good academic

record, but I never had the confidence that I was at the top of the academic arena. No matter how hard I worked, no matter how much time I devoted, I always fell short of the mark. That's the attitude that I had when I attended the first day of law school. My first professor was Dr. Hogan Masterful. Really—that was his name, and he had quite a reputation for being one of the toughest law professors. He explained to our class, somewhat along the lines that I have just explained to you, the derivation of the common law and how that came to be. He editorialized about the scriptures and the laws of ancient Rome, the laws of the British Empire, the laws of the colonies and how one was derived from the other over a period of time. To illustrate that point, he assigned several cases for presentation the next day. Of course, all being beginners, no one knew really how to present a case, hardly how to read a case, but I am sure that all of us trudged home, got out the books, and began poring over the contents. The first case was a fragment. It was in Latin, ancient Roman. Having suffered through Latin classes in high school, and having still retained my text books, I proceeded to translate what was there, which was very little, consisting merely of a short statement of fact and a decision of the tribunal. There probably were not more than fifty words. As you might expect, at this point, I was the first student called upon in my law class, and I am not so sure that Dr. Masterful picked me purely by chance. I stood and read the translation, followed by a moment of silence. "Mr. Smith," he said, "you have just ruined my day. In all of the years of my teaching, I have chosen this opportunity to taunt or tease a student, but no one has ever come forth to translate and present that case, and I will forever hold this against you." I was both startled and pleased, and I can assure you that in all of the several courses that I took under Dr. Masterful, I was his favorite student. That's happenstance.

The class went on to the next case which was several hundred years old, in an ancient, English court, presided over by a judge appointed by the Crown. The English was difficult to read or understand, like Chaucer. The next student chosen did an adequate job, but it was anticlimactic. The third case was to do with the title of land in New Amsterdam, New York, and how the ownership of that land was divested

from the British monarchy. That was an interesting bit of history. It did teach me a lesson, and I am passing that lesson along to you, that the law is as old as creation, and it will endure forever, and it's like a bowl of jello—you can't just grab a handful and squeeze and hold onto anything, because it is constantly moving and changing. Part of my task as your professor is to prepare you to deal with change.

Now, I told you that we were going to deal with the O.J. Simpson case. What you will find in your textbook is not reports of hearings or trials or judgments in court, but rather several excerpts of the testimony given at trial, in pivotal issues, the analysis of certain witnesses that testified, and the verdict and judgments. There are also interviews of jurors that were undertaken after the cases as a work project under the guidance of the Dean of the Tulane School of Law and used in the Trial Advocacy course at Tulane, first, now, elsewhere, too. The purpose is to give us a background to discuss cases that you read about in the newspapers and see how your legal minds work. My first question to you is this. If there is anyone in this class who believes that O.J. Simpson was innocent of murder, please rise. It's unanimous. This entire class has decided that he was guilty. Let's see.

PROFESSOR: Number 44, tell me what you know about O.J. Simpson.

NUMBER 44: I will start by saying that I have an avid interest in athletics, and I love football. I first knew of O.J. Simpson when he was an outstanding college player, and, then, when he became probably the most famous and most successful running back in the National Football League. He set records in many categories. He was handsome and articulate and exciting. He regularly appeared in commercials, running through airports, food supplements, but often, also, appeared in presentation of worthy causes, as a contribution to the efforts, such as the feeding of hungry children in Africa. He was often in movies, filmstrips, and on television, somewhat of an idol. I don't remember much about his personal life and his behavior except that there were stormy sessions described in gossip columns. I guess I have to say that I admired him and respected him and didn't want him to be guilty.

PROFESSOR: Well, you described a pretty nice guy—someone that

was great at what he did, and someone willing to sacrifice for others. What turned you against him?

NUMBER 44: I wouldn't say that I turned against him, but the overwhelming evidence made him guilty, and there were no good explanations of the facts that pointed to him as the guilty party. A lot of the things which were presented by the defense were just not believable. I think that was the feeling of almost everyone in the general public, except, of course, the jurors.

PROFESSOR: What did you think of the jury verdict?

NUMBER 44: I thought it was wrong, foolish, unacceptable.

PROFESSOR: I think you have enjoyed this exchange between the two of us, but I think you have departed substantially from my warning to you earlier in the year about being led astray, following the masses, or making stupid responses. O.J. Simpson was positively, absolutely innocent. You and I know that because that's what the jury said. It leaves no doubt that he protected himself with his constitutional rights. He had advice of counsel. They performed admirably, whether you like it or not. The decision, by virtue of our Constitution and our laws, was sound, proper, and final. How can you challenge that?

NUMBER 44: Well I understand that he was found innocent, but that doesn't mean that he was not guilty.

PROFESSOR: Don't play with words. When the jury comes in, you are determined to be either guilty or not guilty, and that leaves no room for doubt, and it is acceptable.

Now, let's talk about the case and the constitutional questions. There is no need for us to discuss the basic theory of law of presumed innocence. The defendant was innocent at every step of the way, which brings forward the analysis of the burden of proof. What you have read in newspapers, books, professional treatises, all have exposed fully everything that happened at the trial, the views of the jurors, comments from the court, so that there is no mystery as to what happened, and there is certainly no mystery about innocence. This must mean, therefore, that the prosecutors were never able to bring forth such strong evidence as would convince the jury that the defendant was guilty beyond a reason-

able doubt. I, too, have read everything that I know that has been published about the O.J. Simpson cases, including the civil case, which we will discuss later. However, this is a course in constitutional law. I would like a show of hands of any of you who might care to make a comment about constitutional rights of the defendant from what you have read about the trial. Yes, ma'am—you first.

NUMBER 6: I don't remember ever hearing or reading about the rights of the defendant, and the Miranda warnings. From everything that I have seen or heard, it is clear that the investigating officers, at the scene of the crime, had at least part of an intention to find information that would prove Simpson guilty. I know that during the trial of the case that issue was raised, and there was considerable testimony, from law enforcement officials, that they were concerned that there might be physical harm or damage to Mr. Simpson, in the same fashion that the two parties were murdered. I cannot help but believe, and there was testimony, that there was an effort to find and seize and capture Simpson before he could escape. To the extent that the latter aspect had any merit at all, Miranda warnings should have been given to Mr. Simpson before the first interview with law enforcement officials. I have read nothing and I have heard nothing to indicate that they did that.

PROFESSOR: Good issue, good analysis. You will remember that he was first interviewed by reporters on television, and it was in that first interview that the injury to his hand was exposed and discussed, and he made an explanation to the effect that he broke a glass and cut himself before he returned. There is also strong indication that he did in fact confer with his personal legal counsel, a good friend, but nevertheless his attorney, before he was interviewed. That was not illustrated at trial, but just in the public press. There is an interesting question as to whether or not Miranda warnings must be issued even when there is no evidence prejudicial to the defendant coming from such interview. Since there was no attempt by the prosecution to introduce a confession, or a statement adverse to the defendant's interest, by the defendant, the constitutional question of Miranda warnings did not arise. It is very significant, however, that you would have been alerted to the constitutional ques-

tion. That's the way every case should be approached.

PROFESSOR: Next, yes, the gentleman in the back corner on the left.

NUMBER 93: I remember a series of facts that follows this pattern. Early on, the defendant did in fact hire an attorney, an attorney who was skilled in such matters, and after a brief appearance by that attorney, he withdrew and apparently referred the defendant to the lead attorney that handled the defense. I surmise, and perhaps it's just a guess, that in the confidential and attorney/client relationship between that first attorney and Mr. Simpson, guilt was admitted. There was probably a discussion that Simpson would deny it by taking the stand and offering contrary testimony. I surmise, further, that the first attorney, being honorable and having foresight, told Mr. Simpson that the evidence was very damning, and that if Mr. Simpson would tell another good lawyer the same story, that good lawyer would not permit Mr. Simpson to take the stand and testify, publicly, contrary to the truth and the evidence that he would have provided to the second good lawyer, and therefore he would not be able to testify at the trial and plead his innocence, or, if he did, the second attorney would have to withdraw and report to the court his reasons. So, O.J. told the second lawyer that he was innocent. I could envision the prosecution calling the first attorney and exploring that area. Undoubtedly, the first attorney would plead the attorney/client privilege, and the second good attorney would present that view on behalf of the defendant. I see nothing unconstitutional, or in violation of the Constitution, that would prevent the calling of that first attorney because the jury would draw an inference from the assertion of the attorney/client privilege that there was something to hide.

PROFESSOR: That might be an excellent trial tactic, and I will discuss that, but I'm not sure that it's a constitutional question, but I am positive that the exploration into such an event should be appropriately made to determine if there is a constitutional question as in every aspect of any trial.

There is an old saying that an attorney should never pose a question to a witness unless he knows the answer, and certainly that is not always true, but at least it's a caution. Now, let's follow your scenario. You now

have the attorney on the stand, intending to have him infer that there is some secret that he is trying to protect, so you ask him if he was consulted, and the answer is in the affirmative, and if he had a conversation with the defendant about the facts, and his answer is in the affirmative, and then, having opened the door, you ask him to tell the substance of that discussion. That's where you would expect hell to be raised with the attorney/client privilege. However, defense counsel might not even object. You have probably put your foot in your mouth, or worse, because now the first attorney testifies as follows:

"We discussed the facts at length. Mr. Simpson clearly denied any responsibility or liability, or even knowledge. He was terribly shocked to learn about it and was very distraught and made immediate arrangements to come back to be with the family of the woman he loved most of all in his life, and he wanted to help search, and pay the costs, to find the killer. He positively convinced me of his innocence, and I observed his demeanor which was anger and frustration and revengeful. I told him that he had an excellent chance of winning the case, but he would undoubtedly be a target because of his personal notoriety, and the prosecution would like to bring down a great person, and that he needed a whole team of experts in his defense. I then told him that I would love to lead the defense and would do so with the strong commitment to the very personal relationship that he and I shared, but that I was already engaged in a matter of such significance, with constant court appearances, so that I could not give it my immediate attention, and it was my view that immediate attention was urgent. I referred him to my good friend, Mr. Shapiro, who is one of the most skilled and highly respected defense attorneys in this state, perhaps in the nation, and that Mr. Shapiro would assemble the rest of the team with the various skills that would be needed. I also told him that it would be terribly expensive, not only the costs of the litigation, but his personal attention in the defense of himself, time and availability. I finally told him that I was convinced of his innocence, but he needed to be wary of the prosecution, regardless of how thin the evidence against him might be."

Remember that the attorney/client privilege belongs only to the

client, and if the client has not asserted that privilege, the testimony comes freely into the record, and I believe what I have quoted as a possibility would be extremely damaging to the prosecution. Any other constitutional questions that you can envision?

NUMBER 55: Yes, sir. From the facts that I have read and heard, it is clear to me that there was a violation of the Constitution by unreasonable search and seizure, the invasion of the home of the defendant. Even though there is a suggestion, barely a hint, that the law officials went to protect the defendant from personal harm to him, they immediately learned that he was not there, but nevertheless proceeded, without warrant, and without emergency, to seize evidence. It would seem to me that the defendant's constitutional rights were infringed and that all evidence gathered after the moment of discovery of Simpson's absence should be eliminated from the trial.

PROFESSOR: That is excellent. That is positive thinking. That's exactly the type of constitutional question that should be raised and vigorously contested. I suspect it probably was. You will remember that there was a series of in chamber conferences in which the press was excluded. We must conclude that this constitutional question was discussed and that the court overruled the contention and allowed the testimony. The jury was not entitled to hear the discussions in that private conference, and so the constitutional issue was not raised in the presence of the jury, but it could very well be decided that it was an issue of law, and not an issue of fact, and it was therefore to be decided by the court and not the jury. You will notice that in one form or another, objections were made to every bit of evidence offered, but the defense counsel chose not to make a declaration in open court that the objections were made on constitutional grounds because that might have an undesired impact on the jury. But, let's move on to another question that is inferred. It is a constitutional question. What right is there for the judge, in a public trial, to have a confidential meeting with the lawyers or the parties and exclude the press. The press has a very positive right under the First Amendment, and almost every case that I have ever seen has sustained the right of the press and the media to be there, to observe, and

to report. It is often said philosophically that the freedom of the press is
the greatest protection in the Constitution for the American people
because it exposes everything. I will say that there could be cases in which
the press might not be included and particularly in respect to little
children and sex crimes, but those cases make hard law and sometimes
unfair conclusions. Enough of that.

The final question now has to do with whether or not, under our
Constitution, it is permissible to proceed in a civil claim against the
defendant who has been acquitted. The law has clarified more and more
as the years have gone by. The conclusions are almost universal that a civil
action can be brought where a criminal action was decided adversely to
the interest of that claimant because it is not double jeopardy. The
theories are different. One is a punishment for a crime; the other is a
recovery of financial damage. However, the question is much closer
when a defendant is acquitted of murder and then the federal government puts the defendant on trial for the violation of civil rights,
depriving one of liberty or property without due process, things like that,
double jeopardy. Incidentally, in a battle for custody of the minor
children between O.J. and the parents of his ex-wife, what is the burden
of proof and what is a constitutional question? Is the potential loss of his
children and the custody of them a second jeopardy? Think about that.
I will conclude on this note. I want you to study in considerable depth
and carefully analyze these last issues and research them up to this date so
that you will at least be aware. Through the course of this term, we may
very well find changes in the law on these subjects, and we will bring
them up and discuss them at the time. Some of the cases we have
discussed involve different races and racial problems, the enactment of
statutes, and the applications of those, but I don't believe that any of you
could have a true feeling or conception of how things were between the
races before you were born. In the processes of my gathering material and
producing various publications, and sometimes in public appearances, I
ran across an item in the archives of the Birmingham Public Library
which I think you will find meaningful and significant. The time was
after World War II, but before the open warfare of the civil rights years

or the civil rights legislation. The City of Birmingham made a sincere attempt to improve the racial relations and to forestall what obviously was coming, and did come. A meeting was conducted at the downtown auditorium in Birmingham to give some of the leaders an opportunity to express views and hopefully to create solutions. That meeting was recorded in some fashion, probably shorthand, and later transcribed into notes which were turned over to the Library by the Chamber of Commerce. I think it will be enlightening for you to hear me read to you, on tape, that transcript.

At your next class session, I will not appear, and it will be brief, and I will have a member of my staff present to turn on the recorder and play it for you, and to bring it back to me at the end of your class session. You may find the material helpful in the evaluation of other constitutional questions relating to discrimination, and it may cause you to wonder about the mentality and the purposefulness of those who authored the 13th, 14th, and 15th Amendments. I suggest that you read those amendments in preparation for this next class session. This class is now over.

The Next Class—
A Community Forum

The Professor's students listened closely as a small black recorder filled the room with disembodied voices of the past. The students passed the time in various positions of repose and with varying degrees of interest as the tape ran its course.

CHAIRMAN: Please come to order. Please come to order. Thank you. Will you be seated. This meeting was called to bring together the leaders and those persons most interested in the welfare and progress of the City of Birmingham and Jefferson County, Alabama. My name is Jamo Cabeza. I know many of you personally, and I am sure that some of you are aware of the fact that I have been involved in community affairs for most of my life.

This program was organized at the instance of three outstanding Birmingham organizations, Kiwanis, Rotary, and the Young Businessmen's Club. In the recent past, these three organizations found that they had some items of common agenda, and their presidents concluded that isolating the most important and creating an agenda for discussion would be beneficial to all of the organizations and to the entire community. They have asked me to chair this meeting and I am willing to do so.

Let me give you some background information. You will find pamphlets at your seats. The City of Birmingham has supplied us with its municipal auditorium for the purpose of this meeting, and perhaps other

subsequent meetings related to this one, and the City has likewise supplied soft drinks and refreshments during your stay here. This meeting was called and convened at nine a.m., and will terminate, regardless of the progress that we make, at 11:30 a.m.

There are many problems which face our community, but the sponsoring organizations feel that the most serious problems that we have relate to race and discrimination. We have invited various officers and leaders of organizations who have been confronted with racial issues, to speak to you, to report to you, and hopefully to help all of us, together, find common cause. Each of the speakers will be introduced solely by his or her title, although you will know most of them. Each will speak solely from the standpoint of the organization that he represents. If we are all enlightened from the various points of view, perhaps we can begin to delve into potential solutions. I will first call upon the Chairman of the Birmingham Chamber of Commerce.

COMMERCE CHAIRMAN: Ladies and Gentlemen, I very much appreciate the opportunity of appearing before you and serving my community. I am honored to represent the Birmingham Chamber of Commerce. We have done studies over the last few years, not only to determine where we have been, and where we are, but what we might do about the future of our business community. There are a multitude of problems to be confronted, but if we simply compare ourselves to our sister cities in the southeast, we will find that we have lagged far behind. Before World War II, this was a very vibrant community, recovering from the Great Depression years, and moving forward because we had all of the raw materials necessary for industry. We mined coal, made steel, built transportation, and attracted industry to our community. Like all of the other cities in the southeast, we prospered greatly and made considerable progress during the war years, of the necessity of the times. Shortly after World War II, however, we found ourselves lacking in dynamic leadership while our sister cities had plenty of it. The emphasis in the southeast shifted away from Birmingham, very much toward Atlanta, then to New Orleans and Mobile on the coast, to Memphis and Nashville and Knoxville and Chattanooga, to the north, and, to a certain

extent, Florida. We found that our city lacked sufficient cultural opportunities for newcomers, a very modest zoo, an insignificant museum, almost no musical complement, and a lot of old buildings downtown. That made us less than fully attractive. Studying the root cause, we found great conflict between the black community and the white community. The schism was so great that it was almost as if we lived in two different cities. There was no social intercourse. There was no substantial job availability for Negroes except common labor. The lines were drawn and tempers rose. We will always be cursed with the history of our nonperformance during that era. We were foremost among the communities that were condemned, and in retrospect, certainly, rightly so. Many of us are today ashamed of what we did and what we failed to do, and we left a serious fire simmering. It was very depressing for the expansion of business opportunities. White people began to move away from the inner city, into bedroom communities, and those who remained in the city were mostly the poor and the colored. That was not a good nucleus for business expansion. We sit here, today, years later, in the same atmosphere. The Chamber of Commerce believes, solemnly, that we will continue to lag and falter unless you, the people who are interested in this community, do something about race relations. The Chamber of Commerce is ready and anxious to help.

POLICE CHIEF: I am the Chief of Police of the City of Birmingham, and the remarks that I am about to make have been submitted to the Sheriff of Jefferson County and have his full approval and endorsement. We come to you in regard to law enforcement. Recognizing, as does the Chamber of Commerce, that prosperity and progress require mutuality and cooperation, we would be remiss if we did not report to you that the separation of the races in some respects, is warranted. We have statistics that reflect that sixty or seventy percent of the criminal activity in Jefferson County, Alabama, has originated in the Negro community. For reasons which we cannot fathom, we find that discipline is absent. Young children roam the streets. They steal automobiles. They break into business establishments. They fight and maim and injure and kill, and we simply do not have a sufficient law enforcement force to cope with the

massiveness of the misbehavior in the black community. On the other hand, the white community has removed itself from the fray. They have physically moved away, withdrawing themselves from the heart of the city and removing their children to private schools or other educational institutions. We have never had a black policeman in the City of Birmingham. There are several causes for that. The first is that no colored men are qualified. The second is that a few of them, who might be qualified, are unwilling to expose themselves among their peers. However, the most serious aspect is that white people would not recognize the authority of a black person, so we are locked in a mode with no evident opportunity for change. There are treatises from universities and other institutions of higher education that say that the races are different, that they have different talents and skills and that black people do better in industrial arenas while white people do better in business and the professions. Unfortunately, we have reached the conclusion that the separation is the safest mode in which to live. That sensitivity works its way down to the lowest ranking police officer or deputy sheriff and perpetuates the attitude which is negative to the black community. They justify it by proclaiming the need for the protection of the white community. Those of us who are in command feel that we are powerless to change the status quo, and most whites don't want to. As long as we use terms like "nigger" or "white trash," the separation will continue.

SUPERINTENDENT: I have served as the Superintendent of the Board of Education of the City of Birmingham for many, many years, back during the period that the Chairman of the Chamber of Commerce spoke of, the Depression, and the recovery, and the war, World War II. It has been common knowledge for all of my years of public service that the black community is not sufficiently educated and perhaps might not be educable to the extent that the white community is. We have had separate schools. Some of our white only schools are truly outstanding, the best in the State of Alabama. Very few of our black schools receive any recognition. They are warehouses for children who are unwilling to commit to learning, but more evil than that is the absence of the commitment of the families to insist that the children learn. So, today,

we continue to build brand new schools with new equipment, in fine white neighborhoods, and the same thing is happening in the bedroom communities over the mountain, and to the east of us. We are patching old schools in the Negro community. None have air conditioning. None have adequate heating. Drinking water is not safe. Food handling is grossly inadequate. Most white teachers who are properly certified are unwilling to serve in the black schools. Social promotion is the rule of the day. When colored children come to school, they move from grade to grade whether they learn or not. When they graduate from grammar school they are ill-prepared for high school. When they graduate from high school, they are not acceptable to colleges. We have had a sense of desperation about this for a long time, but we are always told that there is not sufficient funding available and the money needs to be put where it does the most good. I must confess, also, that the colored teachers fall far below the minimum requirements for sufficient skills. They, themselves, had inadequate education and they are granted teaching certificates when they have modest talents, at most. The combination of unwilling students and less than able teachers does not bode well for the future. It has been suggested that black children should be trained for the most menial jobs, with some having skills to become brick masons or carpenters, but mostly as common laborers. That puts a ceiling on almost half of our population because that type of training is a road to nowhere. Until such time as those of you who lead the budgets and finances of the City of Birmingham and Jefferson County are willing to make a dramatic move, we will have more of the same. The State Legislature appears to be less than interested in education in any respect. We think the time is critical, and members of the Board of Education are fine, decent, and devoted people, without the tools.

BANK PRESIDENT: I am not sure why I have been selected to participate in this forum, but if it is because of my position as President of the First National Bank of Birmingham, I am ill-prepared to deal with the concerns which have been expressed. There are no Negroes who are active in the banking community or in any financial institution of which I am aware. All of our institutions have black employees, porters, maids,

and service people. There is very little banking done with colored people. One of our smaller banks has a little banking system in all of the schools and the colored schools have the advantage of being able to make deposits and accumulate savings, but that is more of a teaching tool than an economic one. Black people do not apply for loans at banks, but rather at neighborhood pawn brokers or loan sharks. Apparently that satisfies their borrowing needs. Black people who have credentials and who are probably educated and prepared for banking do not move to Birmingham, and those who are invited do not choose to move here, regardless of the incentives. On the other hand, black people do work, earn, and spend money in the community, but they don't put it in banks. They trade with the grocer and the department stores. Therefore, the primary impetus for any improvement in this area should be coming from those merchants who deal with the black community. I don't know of anything that we, as banking institutions can do or should do. We cannot make bad loans. We cannot hire incompetent people. I have contacts with bankers in other major cities in the southeast and they have the same problems and perhaps the same lack of concerns. However, we do find that in those communities where the schools have improved and the jobs for black people have become more prevalent, there is a move toward establishing banking relationships with the black community. I must say, also, that our bank considers it very fortunate to deal with those few black families who have prospered and have become educated elsewhere, and we readily treat them as good as any customers of the bank. In conclusion, let me say that I believe that the direction of this group should be in the field of sociology rather than finance.

DEAN: I am the Dean of Southern University. I am the first woman dean of a major educational institution in the State of Alabama. I notice that our chairman for this morning said that each speaker would speak about "his" organization. I am in no manner offended by that, but I do think it is important to recognize that even in Alabama a woman can rise to a prestigious position if she has the talents and the opportunity. I emphasize opportunity. The individual who seeks a high position cannot at the same time create an opportunity. The opportunity needs to be

created within the community, or within an institution, so that an appropriate applicant can come on board. I have not been in this position long, and I know that I was chosen to be dean in order to do something about the very issues that you are beginning to discuss. On my staff there is a financial officer. He was born and raised in Chicago. He graduated from the public school system there and went to the University of Michigan where he not only acquired his Bachelor of Arts, but entered the graduate school and received his Masters in Business Administration. He is black. He comes from a prosperous family that could afford his education. He is here for the same reason that I am, to make this a better institution, and to make visible to the community that people of all skin colors can be valuable. This is the first year that we have had a teaching staff with Ph.D's—three of them—one is black. Our student body is open to all who are qualified academically, regardless of race, color, religion, and for that matter, there is no bias. I say there is no bias, but there is one. We are not willing to admit students into our student body who do not have the basic skills to learn. We therefore find almost no black students coming out of the Birmingham and Jefferson County school systems who are qualified for a college education. They do not read much. Their writings are terrible. Their speaking abilities are limited. Mathematics appear to be nonexistent. I said that we would not admit them to our student body, and we won't, but we have been fortunate enough to have an endowment, and this year we have taken thirt-six students, wholly unqualified for college learning, and we have installed a system of tutoring and training for one year, at no cost to those students, to test the possibility that they may be able to enter fully as a student the following year. I hope that when I appear before you again that I will be able to report that some, if not all of these, are fully qualified students at Southern. Yes, I am an outsider. No, I have not grown through your pains, but I do have some experience that I will share with you. What you have in this society is a disgrace. Perhaps the blame does not fall upon those of us here assembled, maybe it is our fathers or forefathers, or maybe it is the lethargy that causes us to leave things as we found them, but you are perpetuating a black community of incompe-

tence, and violence, as the Police Commissioner has said, with little or no future, and your city is going to be a breeding ground for trouble. I predict that unless you do something dramatic, you will soon be faced with the full strength of the federal government which will force it upon you. I will stay and I will discharge my responsibilities as long as I see progress and signs of help. If I determine that you have determined that there will be no change, I will use my talents elsewhere. I know these words sound harsh to you and probably they are not properly aimed at those of you who are sitting here today, but if you have the responsibility for this community, the burden is on you for the future. I am perfectly willing to serve on any committees or assist in any avenues where you think I or my staff can be of value.

PSYCHOLOGY CHAIRMAN: I am the Chairman of the Department of Psychology at the University of Alabama in Tuscaloosa. We have seventeen full time professors, Ph.D.'s, twelve in the progress of getting their doctorates, and twenty-six student assistants. Like the speaker before me, we have no black students. We have one black professor and he is positively outstanding, without a doubt, one of the best professors in the entire university. He loves teaching and he loves people and he has a wealth of knowledge and a lot of experience. Your children choose not to go to his class if they have an option. For some reason or in some fashion you have raised them to believe that black is inferior, and if you have a choice between a black professor and a white professor, you go with the white professor. Yet, I want you to know that those students who learn from that black professor are the most enthusiastic and excited youngsters I have ever had the privilege to meet. They hang around class and talk to him after the sessions are over. They question him about intimate things, about the difference in his life and history. They write him letters. They have yet to invite him to a home for dinner or to a family party, and that's your fault. Personally, I am quite secure in my position, tenured, well compensated, and much appreciated, but I sense a vacuum in the teaching process. It is as though we are taking one small segment of society and perpetuating them to advance ahead of all others. They may not even get a chance to mix with people of different

backgrounds, except to the extent that some of the students come here from the north and have a somewhat different culture. So much for the facts as they are, because I want to spend a moment talking to you about the psychology of what you are doing and what you need to do. When someone is born into a society and constantly taught that they are inferior and made to feel less than equal, they will in turn bear children and teach them the same philosophy. Being black in Alabama can be equated with being in a penitentiary. Someone else has control of your life. No one is accountable to you. There is no upward mobility. There is no hope and therefore no enthusiasm and no willingness to make sacrifices. Psychologically, your black community is underprivileged and trained to be comfortable with that. There is a sickness—perhaps I should say two sicknesses. Blacks are sick because they are hopeless. Whites are sick because they don't care that blacks are hopeless. I also have an opportunity to have private patients in the hospital and in the institutions in Tuscaloosa. I come directly in contact with situations that confront black people, because it is no different in Tuscaloosa than it is in Birmingham. Those who come to me for guidance are thoroughly entangled and distraught with their own lives. What they want is not guidance, but a magic bullet shot as if that could cure all their ills. Such people don't have a sense of reality. Almost everyone that comes to me for help would like to live somewhere else and start over again. I must say that I am more optimistic about the future than the other speakers who have proceeded me. I know that these are not mean and evil and twisted minds, prevailing within the black community, but rather untrained, uninspired, so if we supply the training and the inspiration, we are going to have different kinds of people. I would like to make a couple of specific suggestions. Energize your mental health community. Get them interested in the black community. Let them do seminars and teach classes and outreach into the black areas instead of waiting for the cries for help. Raise some money, through your churches or other charitable organizations and create an institution primarily directed toward the improvement of the mental health of young black people. We probably have already lost the senior citizens. If you will do things like that, there will

⸴ hope for all. Thank you for your attention.

CHIEF EXECUTIVE: A few years ago, the City of Birmingham and Jefferson County, through their elected bodies, created a small public organization to manage the public housing in this area. The management consists of myself, as the chief executive, a secretary, and five field workers. Interestingly, we are all black. I believe that we were chosen, all black, because the housing problems in this community are essentially those of black people. Just as in your school system, we have public housing for blacks, public housing for whites, and they are not anywhere near each other. The public housing for whites and the public housing for blacks began as exactly the same physical structures from blueprints supplied by the federal government and to be used throughout the country in poverty areas. While I was not here at the beginning, I know that everyone started from the same beginning point. As soon as the buildings were constructed, the applicants were awarded entrance and were granted apartments. The rent per unit was dependent upon the earnings and the income of the occupants, and the number of individuals in the family. Many of the occupants, black and white, though in separate communities, were welfare recipients. Some few had social security of an amount that mattered. Many had small jobs. The divergence began almost immediately and is particularly evident these days. The units in which white people live are clean, well kept, very presentable, with a lot of activities. In contrast, the black housing is run down, neglected, beaten up, and ominous. The whites seem to live at peace with each other. The blacks live on a battleground. I must give you two examples that point the way to the future. A new project was built on the south side of Birmingham in a very disreputable, evil, dirty section called "The Block." Run-down shanties with no plumbing and electricity or any conveniences were replaced with two-story apartments, four units to a building. All of the tenants were black, but someone inspired them to create a community committee. Of the occupants totaling about seven hundred or eight hundred men, women, and children, twelve took responsibility, and ultimately were approved and accepted as the leaders, and they had plans. Soon everyone had a potted plant on the front porch,

a few flowers growing around the edge of the lot, a door mat at the front door, a door bell that worked, and everyone took pride and behaved accordingly, and if some people chose to act in a different fashion, the committee called upon those people, not in anger, but in humility, and pleaded with them to join in the attitude of the others, and for the most part they were very successful. It turned out to be the nicest of all of the public housing units. Then, and this is the most important part, eight additional buildings were added, contiguous, and white people moved in. Lo and behold, they, too, took pride in their new housing and followed the leadership of the blacks who preceded them. Since it was one unit under management, applications were made to the same division and were scrutinized by the same representative from the housing authority. One of those gentlemen is still a part of my staff and he is probably one of the most respected men in the black community, and, fortunately, by the white community as well. He began to assign blacks into the white area and whites into the black area. That was not totally without problem. Resentment came from a few white people. The committee called on them and pleaded with them to understand and to try. He was a real inspiration. On one occasion, he got the Birmingham Electric Company, which owned the bus system, to give him, on a Sunday, the use of one bus and one driver, and he took a bus load of people in that complex, including some who were uncomfortable with the aspect of integration, and drove them all over town to the other projects. None was as attractive as theirs, and when they returned back to their project, they spread the word. Even white people got angry with other white people who raised racial barriers with the black community. That's a shining example of what might happen given the right leadership. The committee now has eight blacks and four whites.

That's the pretty part. Let me tell you the unpleasant part. For every guard or watchman at a white project, we have seven at a black project. That should tell you something. When the police speak of violence in our projects, almost all of it is in black communities. Therefore, we all must conclude, together, that if the right chance is provided to the black community and to black people, there is a good possibility that fine

results will come about. While we have an overall budget problem in the housing authority, it has nothing to do with race. It's just that the community has not been willing to keep and maintain these projects in a first class condition and pay the rent for those who cannot pay for themselves. We are continuing to struggle because we can see some light at the end of the tunnel.

CHAIRMAN: I can see and hear the rustling and the movement which indicates that all of you are uncomfortable. Perhaps that was the primary purpose. We are halfway through our goal, the first half being to alert you, to make you aware, and hopefully to have you buy in with the concept of doing something about racial disharmony in our community. All of the people who spoke today, and a handful of others from the three sponsoring organizations are going to begin to work on a format which involves solutions. We heard a few glimmers of hope, from the housing project, from the department of psychology, and even from Southern University. In the packet of materials before you is the name, address, and telephone number of everyone who has spoken here today, and all of the presidents and officers of the sponsoring organizations. They have asked me to beg you to call or write or offer assistance or guidance. It is not too late to start. If there are among us those who choose not to adopt a new philosophy, and a modern approach to racial relations, you can at least take away with you the spirit of what has happened today and pass it along to others. We have run out of time, and true to my promise, we are now adjourned.

In the Beginning—
Several Years Later

PROFESSOR: Welcome, Tom, it's a pleasure to see you again. It's been many years since you first came into my life as a student. Come into my new and humble abode. As you can see, I gave up the extravagant mansion which was my nest with my Cindy for so many years, for practical reasons. I am rebuilding my composure, here.

TOM: It's a delight to be here, Prof. I just want to hug an old man who has meant so much in my life, and I want to be able to report back to our many friends, and your admirers, that you are bright, alert, apparently healthy, and still contentious. I recall so well my law school years spent with you. It's hard to realize that's so many years ago.

PROFESSOR: All that is true. Let's sit in here and relax, and I am at your disposal. Tell me what you would like to do, today.

TOM: First, right down to business—here's a certified copy of the approval and declaration and existence of the Joseph Jasper Smith Philanthropic Foundation. We are now in business. In addition, this is a copy of the approval from the Internal Revenue Service that we are qualified as a 501(C)(3) organization and that, of course, gifts and contributions will be tax deductible under the present state of the tax law.

PROFESSOR: That's beautiful. I appreciate it. Tell me who is going to run this show.

TOM: Okay, let's start with nine people. Here's a list. Everyone of these nine, including myself, of course, worshiped at the shrine of your Constitutional Law course. Four are from your class that won the first

book award. Every one has been a successful attorney. All have previously exhibited support of our law school. They are a mixture of young and old, not so young and not so old, various shades and colors of skin and genders, truly a representative selection from some of your best classes. I take great pride in being a part of this group and serving initially as chairman.

I am giving you the bios of each one. You will notice that each one also has a personal note directed to you. We have chosen a course which takes your Foundation completely out of politics, and personal agendas, too. Let me tell you how that works. All nine are already elected and designated, and are constituted as trustees. We have no term limits. If one dies, retires, or resigns, or moves out of the State of Alabama, on a permanent basis, that trustee is replaced at the earliest convenience of the remaining trustees. The Board, however, must always be constituted with four who are past the age of fifty-five, four who are not yet fifty-five, and one whose age does not matter. This will probably result in the trustees having to choose younger and younger people, whenever there is a vacancy. There will be times when it will be impossible to maintain this age factor, but if several of the trustees are past fifty-five, and continue to serve, then all of the subsequent replacements will be with people under fifty-five so that the maintaining of the ratio is a best efforts. We think this is a way to show continuity and permanence.

PROFESSOR: What if one of the trustees falls from grace, as perhaps I did. Would that person continue to serve?

TOM: We have thought about that. We have tried to be careful in the original selection, and we hope that subsequent trustees will be just as careful, but it's bound to happen sooner or later. Rather than try to proscribe the conditions or the requirements to consider someone unworthy, it's better for that person to continue to serve, or perhaps that person would be persuaded by others toward self-removal, rather than have any hint of impropriety in respect to the Foundation, itself.

PROFESSOR: How about money?

TOM: Glad you asked. From these trustees, and perhaps a dozen other former students of yours, we have already raised nine million dollars in

contributions, and we have selected investment counselors who have already invested the money, on a temporary basis. We plan a massive campaign, beginning with all of your former students who are still living, and where not living, representative members of their families, perhaps heirs. After we have made a massive effort in that direction, which I know will be successful, we will then begin regular and periodic public solicitations as well. We will coordinate some of our activities with the law school chair which bears your name.

Of course, you are free to make a contribution, and since you have no one who relies upon you for the wherewithal of life, you may consider making a bequest or a gift, yourself. Everyone knows that you are wealthy.

PROFESSOR: Stop, there, because I have some plans about that, too, and I want to tell you of them later.

TOM: Now, to the third area of fund raising, and that's really the purpose of my visit. Sometime ago, you acquiesced in a request from the University which wants to do a study of your life, for many reasons, and publish your biography, and they would like for it to be as much of an autobiography as you will permit and in which you will participate. The time has come and we are ready to get started on that, immediately. All we need is a time for you to designate when you are prepared to begin unraveling your mysteries, and reporting your histories, and subjecting yourself to examination and cross-examination. Of course, you can preserve your constitutional rights, to a certain extent, but all of us are aware that there have been some mysterious times and occasions in your life that could be both interesting and revealing.

PROFESSOR: I did say that and I will do that, and I will do it, soon. I intend to be one hundred years old this coming May 23, and I am confident that I have the strength and commitment to reach that date. But, as to the allocation of my time and energy, I would like to get whatever is going to be done behind us not later than that date. That should give you plenty of time and I will give you as much of my time as is necessary. Take a moment, now, Tom, and remind me of the goals which you have established in the Foundation.

TOM: Well, in this package is everything in detail, but I assume, as you did in class, that you want a shorthand version with no B.S., just the core of the apple, as you used to say. I wish I could claim that the biography was my idea, but it came from the University. I do claim the authorship of the Foundation documents, but that claim is not for me alone. It involved the others of the nine trustees and three living deans or retired deans of the University law school, together with some of your former students who specialize in charitable foundations, and the like. Basically, this is what it is. First of all, the Foundation is dedicated to honoring you, your life, and your teachings, as well as to serve for a memorial to you after you are gone. The funding will be only as to income, so that there will never be a diminishment of the principal, except under certain extraordinary conditions which are outlined in the document. The trustees can distribute all or none of the income, as they choose, from time to time.

The distribution of funds will be for a broad series of purposes, the first of which is to establish a research library, bearing your name, into which we will accumulate as much material as we can gather, for the archives, with emphasis on writings, briefs, and other publications which do not necessarily appear in court documents. For example, several briefs were prepared in your behalf in your personal litigation. There are some cases which you continued to utilize in every course, from year to year, and those cases are being researched for the purpose of gathering similar documentation, not otherwise published or preserved. We will seek from all of the lawyers in the state of Alabama, with particular emphasis on the large law firms, various archive materials which they might have, which do not breach the confidences of their clients, yet constitute erudite, scholarly analyses of intricate, legal, constitutional issues which were not filed in court proceedings, but in preparation for trials or hearings. This is going to be an important research tool, not only the original documents, but accessible by computers. It's an interesting new concept.

While that's a very long term project, and an ongoing one, the more immediate types of distributions are first to aid, financially, qualified students, and perhaps some not fully qualified, to gain a law school

education at our university, and the distribution authorization is broad enough to provide for all costs of education, as well as other living costs, in a reasonable and comfortable style while in attendance at law school. The next category is one about which you have spoken often, and which we think is a worthy cause. You told us that in your early years, all lawyers were committed to pro bono work, to helping the poor and the unfortunate, and that you were displeased when the Bar Association began to distribute them to attorneys willing to help, and thereafter the Bar abdicated in favor of a federal government sponsored program where the taxpayers pay for sometimes incompetent and inadequate legal services for people who desperately need quality services and cannot afford them. So, there is going to be a new Legal Aid Society, bearing your name, paying its lawyers comparable community compensation, and providing necessary funding in cases where the absence of such would prejudice the rights of the needy litigant. As you could surmise, this could be a bottomless pit, financially, but it certainly represents the nobility of your approach to serving clients.

The final category is the cause of your life, the Constitution, as you have said. Funds will be available, at the discretion of the trustees, in any litigation involving the Constitution of the United States, with the trustees choosing the side of the issue which they are anxious to fund. We have no idea what the costs in that area could involve because once having entered a major piece of litigation, we will be in it until it is resolved. I think most of us share your philosophy of the law and would be able to decide, in most instances, which side of a case to take based upon what we learned from you as being your philosophy.

That's it. There is a catch-all clause for other miscellaneous stuff, but these are the primary directions. The unanimous vote of the then-serving trustees can add additional categories. That probably depends upon the availability of contributions and the growth of the corpus of the fund.

PROFESSOR: That's enough for right now. I have arranged a slight repast for us to share. Let's get to that, now.

TOM: Okay, thanks, but I need a little more time today to pick your brain of some details of your life.

Intermission—
Chit-Chat

My friends, I have done a lot of thinking about me, my life, and the fact that you are undertaking a permanent record, and I want to tell you some things that have crossed my mind. First, on the scale of things in life, I am pretty old. There is no one who gets old who has total recall of all the facts from years gone by. What happens is this. There are high points and low points in life that have an impact, and they create circumstances from which memories evolve, and as years go by, you talk about those particular memories, and so they become cemented into your brain, and become a part of your fabric of thought. That doesn't mean that the mind retains other things that happened at the same time or between events. You just can't have a whole and full recollection. In addition, memories fade somewhat, and even those high points and low points become blurred. Or, because of the change in my life, they may have had a different impression. After all, every one of us is the end product of all of the experiences that we have had. That brings me to the partial conclusion that it is impossible, really, to have a dialogue in which you can capture any kind of precision. Maybe this is a pseudobiography that we are talking about.

The other important thing, to me, and it's personal, is that I don't want to glorify myself. I don't want this to be some declaration that I am a hero, or that I'm a special person, because I'm not. What I am willing for it to be, Tom, is a history of the hundred years of my life, and the way

the history can be tied together is by using me as a tool, I would prefer that the final publication be a one hundred year history of the development and changes in the State of Alabama as seen through the events which happened in my life. That may be a subtle difference to you, but it's important to me. I have had my share of praises and awards and banquets, and things like that, and I am always uncomfortable, and while I have no intentions of leaving here at age one hundred, I would not want to feel personally responsible for preparing some magnification of me. I hope you find these guidelines and thoughts acceptable. To the extent that you might not fully agree, I did commit to assist in the writing, and I will do the best I can, and I will live with whatever you and the others produce.

I told you earlier that I would add some thoughts along this line. I have done some serious thinking, myself, about what I am going to do with my assets when I am gone. Frankly, I live quite comfortably with Social Security and my pension and my demands are not much. My health care needs are well provided, so I simply continue to accumulate, and it's not meaningful to me. What I am going to do when you and I are through with the effort is either to publish my will, with some thoughts which I have, or make an outright gift to the Foundation of substantially everything that I own. When do we start?

TOM: You know that I will take to heart everything that you have said, and it is just further proof of the character that we are going to illustrate in the biography. We have already accumulated a lot of material, some taped sessions of meetings and classroom sessions and speeches, many of your writings and articles, and things like that, some of which will be woven into the text and others simply put into the archives. I would like for you to do a search of your memorabilia, things, writings, correspondence, and make those available to us. I think we'll probably have several sessions, and I will try to prepare an agenda and give to you in advance of the areas and times that we will cover because it will probably be easier if we start at the beginning and progress through each major event in your life, at the same time weaving in your philosophies. If you agree, then let's have our first session consist of the story of your early

childhood, if that's okay, and as far as we are concerned, you pick the time. I would like to bring some other trustees with me.

Early Childhood

PROFESSOR: Well, friends, I have tried to do what you have asked of me. First, I want to tell you a little bit about history and recollections. The truth of history is a combination of facts. The facts are immutable. They are so. They are fixed. When someone, like myself, reports the facts, however, it is generally with additional adjectives and adverbs which flesh out the fact and make it personal. For example, if I say "I went", you realize that I moved some direction in the past. If I add that I went upstairs to visit my ailing grandmother who was living away her last moments, just as the sun was setting, the fact takes on a new meaning. If I say, "I loved my girlfriend," that would be a very positive fact, but if I elaborated to say—"but she was the meanest, ugliest human being on earth and I could not tolerate her for long"—well, you get the idea. The facts that I am going to report to you about my early years are naturally going to be amplified by my personal history and emotions and reactions which might differ somewhat from others who traveled the same road.

Before I tell you about my family, and some events, I need to tell you where I spent most of my young life. Most of you are familiar with Birmingham. I was born and raised in a ghetto, almost one hundred years ago, which is a very long time in your lives. My ghetto was called "The Block." There were many others like it, all around Birmingham, encircling the city and constituting areas where all of the black people lived, with the exception of a few farmers who lived way out, and some of the very poorest people lived, even though they were not black. These were slums of the worst order. What you have seen, some of you, in India or Mexico, and which shocked you, well, these were certainly no better and probably considerably worse.

My block was south of downtown, less than a mile. All of downtown Birmingham and most of the immediate areas in every direction were laid out on a square grid. Downtown Birmingham began at 1st Avenue

North, 2nd Avenue North, etc. Downtown Birmingham began at 20th Street, and in one direction was 19th Street and 18th Street, and in the other direction was 21st Street and 22nd Street. It was easy to find one's way around. South of town, the streets began in the same fashion, 1st Avenue South, 2nd Avenue South. Well, the Block began really at 8th Avenue South, which is now University Boulevard, and proceeded to 10th Avenue South, and it spread from 24th Street to 26th Street. All of the streets around the Block were paved, hard surface. On the outer rim, facing the hard surfaced streets lived poor, white people, mostly in small, multiple-unit apartments, a few houses, very modest. In contrast to our living conditions, all of those perimeter housing facilities for white people had water and electricity and heat. The heat was called radiators, wall-mounted, cast-iron boxes that were filled with hot water to make the rooms warm.

I cannot guess how many people lived in the Block, but hundreds and hundreds, maybe thousands. The Block was really a massive, flat field with rows and rows of little houses. Going east and west, there was something called "the alley" which divided the Block and which constituted a pathway for most people to travel. A little way south of that was a very small alley, called South Alley, and, in like form, there was a North Alley. There were no yards, front or back. There were no flowers, no greenery, but the very basic simple living facilities. First, let me tell you about water. No house had water. From one end of the alley to the other, and about every two or three houses, there was a vertical water pipe sticking up out of the ground. It had a screw top and a faucet. If you wanted water, you simply took your container out there, put it under the faucet, turned on the faucet, and took as much water as you wanted. In cold weather, the pipes often froze and there was no water. Sometimes the pipes burst and there was water everywhere. There was no such thing as electricity except that there were telephone poles running throughout the Block that carried lines for electricity and telephones, but they didn't touch ground in the Block. On the southside of South Alley and the northside of North Alley, there were what we gentlemanly like refer to as latrines, if you were in the service. Actually, they were very rudimentary

outhouses. They were small cubicles, like a toolshed, with an open swinging door on hinges. Inside there was a board about two feet off the ground. I say ground because there was no floor. Some of these boards had two holes and some had three. There was no gender assignment. When you had to go, you went. You can add whatever adjectives or adverbs in that sentence that you choose. When it was cold, it was very, very cold in the outhouse. When the weather was bad, the ground was mushy, muddy, and wet, and sometimes cold, making it difficult to get back and forth. Sometimes some of our own hoodlums turned over an outhouse or two. That was a mess, but then when we had to go, we went to the next one up the street. It was up to the landowners, whoever they were, to correct the problems.

Let me tell you about the houses. They were all alike. Each house was about the size of this apartment, divided in two, a wooden porch with three steps, boards, one front door. When you came into that front door, you could turn left into Apartment A, or turn right into Apartment B, each of which consisted of two rooms. The front room of each family, on each side, was where everyone sat or slept. The back room was where everyone went to eat, or be washed, or help cook, or clean up. Remember, no bathroom, no running water, no electricity.

I am sure you have laughed about the Saturday night bath, but that was true. Let me tell you how it happened. In each of these little apartments which, incidentally, my mother told me cost five dollars a month, a side, to occupy, there was a fireplace and a potbelly stove. You have probably never seen one of those, but even white people had them. It was a big, iron pot, with a metal tray below. You put some chunks of coal under the pot and you took a little bit of old newspaper, or some kindling wood, and you lit a fire in the tray below, and the fire started the coals to burn and flame up under the pot and heat the top of the stove. If you were cooking, you just set everything on the top of the stove that needed to be heated, but if you were getting ready to wash all of the children and some of the adults, on Saturday night, there was a different procedure. Everybody owned a washtub, a big, round, metal container, and I think it was galvanized steel. Two guys would take that washtub out

into the street and fill it halfway with water and bring it back into the house. Whoever was doing the washing also had a mop pail, and you would put the mop pail down into the washtub and take out a full pail of water and sit that on top of the stove until it was boiling and then it would be poured back into the washtub to heat the water and mix the hot and cold. Well, one didn't make a lot of trips back and forth to the water faucet and to the hot stove, so when one or two of the little ones got in and out, some of the bigger ones went. So, disgusting as it may seem, the whole family bathed in the same tub of water most of the time.

Air conditioning was unheard of in those days. Our air conditioning in the summer was open windows, open doors, and a hand-held fan. Our heating in the winter was to put newspapers over the windows, keep the doors closed, and keep heat in the fireplace and the potbelly stove. It really wasn't very costly. Just a few blocks away there was a coal yard, and you could buy a shuttle of coal for five cents. You could buy a large bundle of kindling wood for the same price. That was enough kindling wood to last a couple of weeks, but the shuttle of coal only lasted a few days. I made many trips back and forth to the coal yard. You people have read about and studied the Great Depression which really began with the collapse of the stock market in 1929, and hit the bottom when Franklin Roosevelt became the president in 1933, and closed the banks. There were stories of people running away, jumping out of the buildings, selling their wedding rings, all types of panic, for white people. There was no depression for black people. It was business as usual. In the flourishing and prosperous times of the 1920's, white people dressed nicely, had automobiles, went to the movies, gave parties, everybody went to work, kids went to school, good times. It was abject poverty for black people and the poverty didn't change with the good times or the bad times or the Depression. It was all the same, misery.

If you were sick, there was no doctor around. There was no such person as a black doctor. Sometimes in an emergency, you could go down to the old Hillman Hospital which, incidentally, was the nucleus for the University Medical Center and the University of Alabama at Birmingham. That's where it all began—a small, redbrick hospital on

the southside, about six blocks from where I lived. During the week, if your medical condition was extreme, you could simply wait and be served and doctors would see you and try to help you. On Saturday night, it was different. The Emergency Room was filled with injured people, from fights and wrecks, and guns and knives—it was a sideshow. Some of the white people used to go down there and watch the Emergency Room just for the excitement. Sometimes, if you knew what medicine you needed, you could walk up the street to 10th Avenue, where there was a little shopping center and a drugstore, Woods Drug Company. Dr. Woods was kind, and sometimes he would simply decide what was the best medicine and what the parent ought to do with the child.

There was another avenue of relief. Right across 26th Street, sitting on top of a huge mountain, was St. Vincent's Hospital. It towered over everything in the neighborhood. It was a three-story red, brick building, in the beginning, and it had an elevator, and it was operated by the Catholic Church, and there were many nuns who lived there in their blue habits and white hats. Years later, they built a nursing home with a nursing school. It was several stories high. At night, the young boys could sit on the curbs of the street or the wall of the hospital grounds and watch the nursing home to see if some of the nurses were changing clothes without pulling down the blinds. Sometimes that was an exciting evening.

I was never a religious person, and I'll explain that later, but I thought God lived at St. Vincent's Hospital, because when the sun came up in the morning, the first thing I could see out my window was the sun shining on a huge cross on top of the hospital, and that's how my day began. The hospital was for white people. If a black person was fortunate enough to be close enough to a white family, or work for a white family, the white family could take a black person up to the hospital for help, but the white person had to pay the costs or agree to pay the bill, whatever it was. That was for two reasons. First, blacks didn't have any money. Second, black people who made promises had no way to fulfill them.

I said I was not religious. That doesn't mean that I am not a God-fearing person. There was no religion around us that was meaningful to

me. Across 9ᵗʰ Avenue South from the Block was a little store where black people could go and shop, and next door to it was a house which had been converted into some kind of a church called Holy Rollers. When they got together during the week, or on Sunday, they raised hell, hollering, screaming, praying out loud, hugging each other, and if you stood outside, you could hear the preacher. He spoke beautifully. We had no background or training or knowledge about the Bible or Biblical history, so most of it didn't make sense. We did learn the tales and the stories of the Bible, but those were told to us at home. Besides, no one in the Block could afford to put any money in the charity plate, so there weren't any churches for us, and there weren't any preachers coming around.

Let me tell you about school. There were laws about truancy. When you reached six years of age, you were obligated to go to school, and if you didn't go to school, they could put your parents in jail. The truth is, no one cared whether black children went to school or not. In the Block, in one of the little houses, on one side, little children, six and seven years old, could go to begin to learn to read and write. The teachers were nuns from up on the St. Vincent's hill, and they came every morning, five days a week, from nine o'clock in the morning until noon, and they brought pencils and paper. They had a blackboard with chalk and an eraser, and we learned the alphabet and block printing and we sang religious songs. We looked forward to going to school. Very few of the parents who lived in the Block could read or write, but all of them were anxious for their children to learn. There was no snack served, and that was why school was out at noon. I'll tell you later how I got my education, but you do need to understand the background and the history of the times and the impact on people like me.

There wasn't much to family life. For most families, these little apartment units were home to a mother, maybe a grandmother, sometimes, a father or an uncle, and several children. Apparently all the adults knew how to have children, and none of them knew how to keep from having children, and so there were children all over the place. Most of the children didn't know who their father was. Most of the fathers did not live in the Block, so it was essentially a matriarchal society. I had a

wonderful, marvelous mother, and I am going to tell you a lot about her, and I was one of the fortunate few who knew who my father was. In my house, in addition to my mother, there was an old aunt, and my mother's sister, and seven children. Of those seven children, six were children of my mother and my aunt. I knew who my father was because he came to visit often, and he developed a relationship with me. He was married to someone else and lived with that family on the north side of town. I am going to tell you about him, later, too. I just want you to get the flavor of my earliest years.

Almost all of the women who lived in the Block had jobs. They worked in homes of white families. Many worked in the apartments that bordered the Block. My mother worked for a Jewish family in an apartment that faced on 26th Street, upstairs. There was a father and a mother and a daughter and a son. My mother went to work every morning at six a.m. after first seeing to it that all the children in our house were fed and clothed in some fashion. She went in the back door of their apartment. Nobody locked the doors, and most people didn't even have locks on their doors. She went into the kitchen and prepared breakfast. The father, the mother, and the children got up around seven a.m., and all ate breakfast together. The father went to work and the kids went to school. The mother didn't have a job, but she had a lot to do. My mother stayed there all day, cleaned the house, ran errands in the neighborhood, washed the dishes, made the beds, dusted, everything that a servant would do, and she stayed until after supper, cleaning up before she left, and getting home to me around eight p.m. On Saturdays, she went later and came home earlier because everyone in that family had something to do. On Sundays, she came home early, about two p.m., after serving and then cleaning up after a big meal. The best thing was on Sundays when she brought home a tremendous amount of good food to eat, everything that was left from the weekend. We really looked forward to Sunday afternoons.

Clothing. That was a serious item. No one had any money to buy clothing. Substantially everything that anyone in the Block wore was either a hand-me-down within the family, or something that a white

family had given them. Most of the children had no shoes. Any child that had shoes had only one pair, and they were saved for important occasions, or for when it was very cold outside. The greatest treasure was to have a coat. A coat stayed in the family for generations. There was no such thing as wearing out. Things were patched, repaired, altered, and finally ended up as rags.

Back to schools. Every morning when I got up, I could hear the ringing of a school bell, clang, clang, clang, at Lakeview School which was two blocks away. It was a beautiful school. Only white children went there, and they had a playground and the teacher who taught them to play games outside. There were tennis courts and a baseball field and swings and seesaws. It was beautiful just to look at, but no black person would set foot in the park, day or night. There were schools for blacks. They were generally eight to ten blocks away, a long walk. The buildings were not much better than our homes. There were forty or fifty children in a class. Many slept. A few were unruly. Many chose to leave early and wander around in the neighborhood. School was not very well organized, but the teachers tried. Most of them understood our plight. Most of them understood that we had very little knowledge. Actually, when I went to real school, starting at about eight or nine years of age, I loved it. I could listen to those teachers all day long. It opened up a fascinating new world for me. Most of all, I enjoyed learning new words and how to spell them and what different meanings they had, and then how to make a sentence, in real English. One of the happiest moments in my recollection is when the teachers gave us red paper and I cut out a heart for a valentine and wrote a message to my mother that said, "I love you. I am happy." She treasured that for many years. I think it was my first correspondence. I liked arithmetic, multiplication tables, addition, subtraction, long division. I don't believe many people even learned what long division is anymore, nor do they use it, because we are in a high tech age where such rudimentary things just don't matter anymore. But, it was not all rosy. The schools were either miserably hot or miserably cold. The lack of order was distracting. There was a lack of continuity, one teacher one day, and another the next, and then nobody on the next day.

We had no books. There was no playground. To go to school, you had to be old enough and wise enough to be able to find your way home, and sometimes most kids would find it not pleasing to go to school, and just did not go. When you got to be ten or twelve years old, you had some kind of a job, something to help out with at home, chores.

I told you about Woods Drug Store at the intersection of 10th Avenue and 26th Street. That was the southern-most point of my universe until I got a little older. It was what you would call today a strip mall. In the middle was that drugstore. There was an A&P grocery store, a beauty parlor, Mr. Hardwick's grocery store, the Birmingham News branch office, a Utopia Cleaners and some vacant spaces, sometimes occupied and sometimes not. The stores were in a semicircle, and right behind the stores was a large rocky field where trucks came to deliver. There was a black woman—her name was Hattie—and that's the only name that anyone knew, and she was in charge of that area. She cleaned all the stores, burned up the trash, and kept things as neat and clean as possible. She had been a slave and had moved to Birmingham from south Alabama to work for a white family as a domestic servant, and then she got this better job. She was mean as a snake. She didn't like anybody. She cursed everybody, black and white, who interfered with what she was trying to do. All of us were frightened of her. She had no teeth, and her hair was scraggly. There was one thing which she did, however, which everyone appreciated. Much of the stuff, in the nature of garbage, that came out the back doors, was preserved by her, and it was given out to people who came for food. Sometimes it was broken packages. Sometimes it was just stuff that had gotten too old or out of date—and I truly remember many occasions when I happened to be there and could take home something to my mother in the Block.

I told you that I would tell you about my parents. I loved both of them dearly. They were never married, but each of them put everything that they possibly could into my life. I was their only child although each of them had other children. My mother showed me all of the tender, loving care that any mother could. She nursed me when I was sick, fed me when I was hungry, clothed me when I was cold, and occasionally bought a

present or a gift, particularly at Christmastime. I always had a pair of skates. Black kids were permitted to skate in the streets, and also up in front of Woods Drugstore, but there were no hard surfaces in the Block. Mother worked hard. If she was not working for the white family that hired her, she was trying to keep our house clean and neat and take care of a bunch of children, some of hers, and some of her sister's. She looked for extra jobs. I don't ever remember her doing anything nice for herself, or having any time for herself. She was never alone, always someone underfoot, but I knew she loved me dearly. She never talked to me harshly, and she never showed any anger, but if I misbehaved, it was an event of discussion and explanation. She was a peaceful, serene woman, and everyone that knew her liked her. She had no education at all. She could barely read, barely write, only some basic essentials like numbers and names. She never wrote a letter and I don't believe she ever received a letter except from me. There were times when I was sick and should have stayed in bed, but with the permission of her employers, she would take me to work, in a basket, when I was very young. Later I could just sit in the corner where she worked. Whenever I went there, I had plenty to eat, and that improved whatever was ailing me in my health. There was a little all-purpose store across the street from the Block, and every now and then, she and I would walk over there with a few pennies in hand. There were glorious things that you could buy for a penny, and there were little wax figures that had some kind of a sweet juice inside, and you could drink the juice and chew the wax, like chewing gum. They were all-day suckers, as big as your hand. There was beautiful fruit, and there were cabinets of cookies and crackers. A trip to the store was like a mini-vacation, and we always came back with something for other people in our home. Mother told me about our finances. As I said, she only earned five dollars per week for long hours and hard work. She had to pay rent. We didn't have any utilities. She and her sister shared expenses, and everyone ate together. We shared clothes, but every now and then, some clothes would be brought into the family. Babies had diapers, but they were cloth squares that were washable and reuseable. Newspaper was a treasure. We never bought a newspaper, but my mother could bring one

home from where she worked, and it was used to cover cracks in the windows, start fires, and stuff into the bottom of shoes, if you had a hole in your shoe. I am told that in those days you could buy five pounds of potatoes for a nickel, a loaf of bread for a nickel, a quart of milk for a dime, but as the month went on, pretty soon, money ran out, and everyone worried about the last few days of a month and when rent would come due. It was tougher in the winter when she had to buy coal and kindling and arrange for us to have shoes and outer garments, but life was much cheaper in the summer. My mother's parents had been slaves. She was raised on a plantation, but her spirit was never in slavery. She loved freedom more than anything else.

My father was an altogether different type of person. He had a little education. He always had two or three jobs. He learned skills, first by working on share-cropper farms, and next by working in plants and factories, and then he learned how to plant and grow things and take care of yards. He knew how and when to trim hedges and cut limbs and prune back plants, when to fertilize and what to use, how to till the soil and plant and nurture grass, all from doing those things, not from going to school. I don't believe that he ever took me to his other home, but he came and got me often, at least once or twice a week. I remember a couple of times that he took me fishing on the Cahaba River, and a couple of times we just went out in the woods and spent time together and slept on the ground. Those were great occasions for me and I learned a lot. Most of all, I learned that I really wanted an education. I saw other people who were more successful in lives than my parents, and I saw how hard they worked not to get anywhere, and so I developed an ambition at an early age. My father talked to me and explained a lot of things to me and answered all of my questions. He had a lot of friends, and he had a very outgoing personality. He could talk to people that he had never met before.

It was actually at his initiative and totally to his credit that I began to learn about life outside of the Block, and this really begins the adventure of my life. My father gave up working for other people and had a little business of his own keeping yards and taking care of houses and cleaning

out basements and barns and cutting grass. Today he would be called a horticulturist. In those days, he was just a common laborer, but he knew what he was doing. Many times he would take me all day long and keep me wherever he was working. That's when I began to see the rest of the world, how other people lived, how different it was for white people.

In looking back on my many years, the most important years of my life and the most successful years occurred at and around the home of one of his favorite customers. That's a story unto itself. It's the first occasion in my life when I had any contact with white people, and I want to tell you about the glorious mansion in which they lived. It was near the top of Red Mountain where you could look down into the City of Birmingham and see the buildings and see the steel mills in operation. You could see from one end of Birmingham to the other on a clear day. It was a huge house, two stories tall with a large basement. This was a very wealthy family, and they had automobiles. There were several bedrooms and several bathrooms, and even a place to live in the basement. They had several radios in the house and telephones and electric lights. They had running water inside the house, in many different locations. It had a huge stove and a great big icebox. You would call them refrigerators, but they really were iceboxes. An icebox was about as big as half a car, and it stood much further and taller than I could reach. In the top there was a chamber and every day someone came to deliver a block of ice and put it in the top of that icebox. All of the food was put in the lower part, but the cold from the ice drifted down around the food and kept it cool. As the ice melted, there was a drain to catch the water in a pan below the icebox. I believe I must have emptied that pan a hundred times as I did other errands around the house. I didn't know anything about money, then, but every now and then, someone in that family would give me a nickel, or a few pennies, or when my dad got paid, he would give me a few pennies, and I began to have money of my own.

I need to tell you about that family. This family's name was Ragsdale. There had been several generations of this family before I came to know them. They were obviously very rich and very powerful for many years. As I grew older and knew the family better, I realized what an important

man the father was, and how valuable he was to the entire community. He served on many of the boards of directors, banks, insurance companies, some of the city and civic boards, and he was a very generous person. He probably recognized the inadequacy of the education for many of the local young citizens, and he pioneered a concept that years later became very popular all over the country. He endowed a school, which, incidentally, also sat near the top of Red Mountain, and it was known as the Ragsdale Magnet School. It was operated with several sources of funds, including public school tax, the Ragsdale family fortune, and many friends of the Ragsdales, and many other leading citizens who signed onto the idea. The teachers were superb. The building was fantastic. There was, however, an admission program. Admissions were with the approval of the Board of Directors of the School Foundation. Students fell into two categories. First, and more important, they were very talented and qualified and sincerely committed young people who truly wanted a better education. The second category was interesting. This category of students consisted of those who had not yet attained a reasonable beginning education, but who were thought, by their teachers, to have a special spirit and yearning to learn. It was in the second category that all of the conflicts arose because the student body began to obtain students from a variety of backgrounds, different economic status, broken families, minority groups. This was an embarrassment to the Jefferson County Board of Education and the Birmingham City School Board of Education because there was a racial mixture which was not permitted in the other schools. The conflict was resolved in an interesting fashion. Ragsdale offered to yield up any portion of any tax which was assessed against the people or the lands, and which was allocated to other schools. When that happened, the soul deciding party as to curriculum would be the Board of Directors of the school. The public school systems then feared that they would have no input and no influence and that this school would perhaps begin a flood of similar schools which would weaken and even perhaps destroy the public school system. The compromise was that the Board of Directors and the public authorities would jointly decide on the basic curricula that would be

required of everyone, but the Board of Directors of the school would have the exclusive authority about additional activities and courses. The school flourished. Its physical size could not possibly accommodate all who wanted to attend. Teachers vied for opportunities, as did administrators, to serve in that school. It was a very special location and a very special educational activity. It became apparent to me at an early age that education was the dominating drive in the Ragsdale family.

The family was very prominent. Many important community meetings took place in their home. Many great social events took place there. The family was a most cohesive unit. It was obvious that Mr. and Mrs. Ragsdale cared deeply for each other, and I never knew them to have a disagreement. It was likewise obvious that the children had a deep and abiding respect for their parents, and while they were not angels, they were respectful, and well mannered.

Those of us who worked there were treated in a handsome fashion. No one ever called me "boy," but Joe or Little Jim. The children in the family referred to my father as "Mister," which was unheard of and would have been an outrage in the general community, but they minded my father when he told them what to do, just as I did. In the household, there was a maid who took care of keeping the house in a clean and orderly fashion. There was a wash woman who took care of the clothes, washed, ironed, hung out to dry, folded, put away, and mended. There was a cook. She was really the center of all activity. She went to the stores and shopped for the food. She set the table, helped Mrs. Ragsdale plan menus, prepared the special silverware and crystal and dinnerware for parties and events. She was always prepared for an emergency with enough good food in the pantry or in the icebox so that with a very brief notice she could serve a luxurious meal.

On special occasions, my father was called upon to help serve the meals and to clean up after the parties, but he also had a uniform when he worked inside the house for such events. In addition, he parked the automobiles on the property or on adjacent streets. Many, many friends of the Ragsdale family had automobiles, and some even had chauffeurs. The Ragsdale manor was like heaven on earth. People would drive by and

point to it and tell stories about it and the family. Naturally, I was very proud and thrilled that I could work there on occasion. As a very little boy, I simply went with my father and I helped clean up around the yard. I had two special places that belonged to me. One was the basement of the house. It was huge, and it had all of the utilities and accommodations that existed upstairs. There was a bedroom, and if I was there late at night, I could sleep, perhaps overnight. There was a full service bathroom with a big bathtub and a wash basin and a flush toilet. There was hot water when you wanted it. Every day after working, my father and I went there to clean up. I am sure I never thought that my life would develop where I could live in quarters like that. The other place was more enchanting. The grounds were so large that there was a lot of maintenance to do. The greenhouse had a very spacious interior where plants could be grown and kept and maintained, with skylights, windows that could be opened with the pull of a cord and closed by releasing the cord. There were heaters to maintain a proper temperature against the weather, and fans that could circulate the air. The sunshine warmed this part of the service building and it smelled glorious. At one end of the building, there was a tool, machinery, and equipment storage space. I was never permitted to go there, unless my father was there, too, because he had charge of that space, and there was very valuable equipment there, and it was kept under lock and key.

At the other end, there was an equally sizeable sitting area, like a parlor. There were chairs and couches and a radio and electric lights, a small wash room, and a tiny library, with a few dozen books. That was my "home." I loved being there. Not only was it beautiful and comfortable, but it was enchanting. I would walk around and make speeches and talk to adults and recite rhymes, all out loud, but to myself, and I pretended to be an adult, and truly I felt important. It was from that very room that the future of my life began to develop. There were two paths to glory. One was to become educated and qualified, and the other was to share life with the love of my life. Her name was Cindy. She was beautiful, blond, blue-eyed, always well dressed, a nice smile, and an exciting personality. She was my age, and she was the youngest child in

the family. She launched me on these two paths, first by assisting in my education.

My learning was meager and spotty, but when I worked on the weekends, and special occasions, she and I always spent time together. She would come to the parlor in the greenhouse and teach me to read. While I was beginning to learn these things in school, she made them come alive to me. I learned the alphabet, a song to help remember the alphabet, reciting it backwards, sounding each letter with all of the nuances, and the combinations of the letters to make compound sounds. I learned arithmetic, memorized multiplication tables, practiced addition, subtraction, multiplication and division, including long division. These advanced portions of learning did not yet exist in the little school that I attended on a regular basis. My early experience with the nuns of St. Vincent's was mostly learning Bible stories and morals and behavior, and things like that, not so much basic three R's. I was getting a little bit of the three R's at school, but things were so disorganized that it was difficult to concentrate. In the same classroom, sometimes, there would be two or three teachers teaching different grades, and in the same grade, some students might be learning different courses and subjects. I could feel that my mind was growing and my interest was increasing when Cindy and I sat together with her as my teacher in this little parlor room.

In retrospect, I am quite certain and positive that she liked me, as a young friend, and I am equally positive that it did not bother her that I was black and she was white. She seemed to enjoy teaching me, and she took pleasure when I responded by learning and asking questions. She brought books, some of her classroom books, and read to me and explained to me. Sometimes, in her school, they were required to read books and make reports about them. She would bring those books and read some of them to me and discuss them and ask me what I thought. Never before had I had an opportunity to discuss things and ask questions and make comments because my life was so full of just surviving. What's worse, no one in the Block really gave any credit to anyone who had an education or was getting an education. That was superfluous. I was very careful not to overreach with my friends and

contemporaries, other children, in my home, or elsewhere in the Block because I would have been singled out. So, only my parents knew that I was learning on the side like this. Of course, her parents knew that, too, and approved of it. Sometimes she would bring me into the house, say, for example, where her mother was sitting or reading, and she would have me recite a poem that she taught me from those books. Sometimes, Mr. Ragsdale would stop and exchange comments with me. I remember that he asked me questions that I could not understand or answer, like why the clouds were moving by, or what happened to the sun when it got cloudy, or why the stars were always in different places. He never gave me answers, but he left me with a desire and intent to learn and to inquire. I felt very special when anyone in the family talked to me and when they asked me to do something, I was overjoyed. I frequently did special things in the house, and I sometimes ran errands, but I always loved to keep the area clean and neat and nice because I was proud of it, too. There was an atmosphere at the Ragsdale home that was like a fairy tale, different from anything that I had ever imagined. In my earlier years, when I went to work with my mother, I always stayed out of the way, and I was quiet, but observant. No one really ever spoke to me. In the Ragsdale home, it was different. I was almost like a member of the family, and of course, my dear, young "teacher" was the focal point of my life. I couldn't wait to share time with her, and best of all, it was obvious that she felt that way, too. For those earliest years, I was very careful that we never came too close to each other, never touched each other, not even to shake hands, because that would have been unacceptable, outrageous, deplorable, in the vast society where she and I lived. I was always courteous to her, but she was courteous to me, too. Sometimes we shared a meal in the parlor. She would bring it from the big house and we would sit together, enjoy each other's company, and then she would let me clean up. I don't believe that I was ever that happy in all of my early life, and, in all honesty, I cannot say that I have ever been happier since.

Let's go down the education road, first. Mr. Ragsdale decided that I, based upon my attitude and eagerness, was qualified to go to the Ragsdale School. My mother was most reluctant. I didn't have the clothes or any

financial capacity, and she was very much concerned about the mixing of people of different strata of life and different graces. Her fears were quite justified, and I want to divert, now, to tell you what we feared most, and the impact of the Ku Klux Klan on the black community, including me.

To read and study the history of the Ku Klux Klan would be a most enlightening experience for anyone, and it is a part of history which barely has vibrancy today, while in its beginning years it was one of the major controlling influences in society. When we speak of the Klan today, we see evil, meanness, wickedness, lawlessness, everything terrible. It was not conceived that way in the beginning. It was primarily a formation of like-minded white people who resented interference with the Southern way of life. They formed themselves into clubs, or neighborhood groups, to protest carpetbaggers, Northern influences, abolitionists, and they rallied to preserve the Southern way of life. There was a certain amount of nobility and respectability about being a member of the Klan, even though misbehavior was an early part of its creed, also. White people felt that they were represented by the Klan groups, and even though they did not agree with some of the misdeeds, they felt, overall, that it was valuable and necessary.

The Klan, generally, had three targets: Catholics, Blacks, and Jews. The most ostensible activities, however, were against blacks. The purpose and aim was to terrify black people into remaining slave-minded, subservient, and remote from society. As the years went by, there were a lot of atrocities. In my early years, it was quite frequent that we heard that a black man or a black boy was hung from a tree, by his neck, until dead, for some very minor infraction, like speaking unpleasantly to a white woman, or cursing some white dignitary. The most atrocious things that black people could do, which would result in punishment, was to have discourse or contact with white people, on an equal level. That was not going to be permitted. Just to keep us in our place, on a regular basis, white men in robes and on horses would ride through black neighborhoods, like the Block, just to remind everyone of their presence. If there was some particular person or family that needed a special warning, a cross was burned, and it truly terrified everyone. Sometimes, although I

was never a witness to it, the Klan would actually take a person away. Sometimes they would be whipped and beaten; sometimes just seriously threatened; but, also on occasion, they were never to appear again. There was no law enforcement—no law enforcement against these activities of the Klan.

Oddly enough, however, for several decades, the Klan had respectability in the general white population in spite of the nefarious and criminal activities. In fact, it was common knowledge that if you wanted to be elected to a public office, you needed the support of the Klan. I never went near the courthouse, but I was told, and I know, now, that all of the judges and other officials were members of the Klan, and proudly proclaimed the fact, although they probably did not have to get down in the gutter with the criminal aspect. In fact, your history will teach you that one of the most outstanding Justices of the Supreme Court of the United States was himself an active leader in the Klan in his early years. In his years on the Supreme Court, however, he was the most ardent protector of minority rights, but he never outgrew the image of having been a member of the Klan. His memory is honored, rightly so, in spite of that.

I never understood why the Klan felt antagonism toward the Catholic Church or Catholic people, but then, again, I did not know anybody who was Catholic, either, except the nuns from St. Vincent's, and they were always pleasant and wonderful people. The Catholics had subgroups, also, known as the Knights of Columbus, and they actually had a meeting hall for social and other activities not far from the Block, near Lakeview School. On one occasion, I believe, a group of Klansmen, in uniform, paraded around that building, just to show their presence. I don't know if the Catholic people were frightened or not.

I learned a lot, later, about how the Jewish people managed to have a truce with the Klan. Jewish people, for the most part, kept to themselves. They had stores or businesses and Klan members were customers and so there was a personal relationship, sometimes. Jewish people were kind to the black people who worked for them, but they never made an issue of that, or they never tried to elevate black people to a point where the Klan

would disapprove. There were many cases, however, in which the Klan was an active participant in the persecution of Jewish people, and the extrajudicial punishment of Jewish people, for a variety of causes, but it just didn't seem to happen where I lived. Jewish people were not warriors, anyway, like the members of the Klan had been in the Civil War and thereafter.

Well, the Klan dominated a portion of society in all of my early years, and they had an ever visible presence, and if they weren't present physically, there was an aura of fear. Apparently, as society matured, people became disenchanted with the illegal activities of the Klan and distanced themselves from the identification. The Klan lost its political force and its credibility began to wane. The death knell really came when a courageous district attorney in Jefferson County proposed and had enacted what was known as the Unmasking Bill, and the state legislature made it a crime to wear masks under certain circumstances. That included the hoods of the Klan. They actually prosecuted individuals for that and in my recollection and memory, the Klan really disappeared. It had a revival of interest when we had other hate groups like skinheads and neo-Nazis come onto the scene. I think the history of the Klan is a disgrace, but not all of the people who were members of the Klan were evil, and most did not sympathize with the brutality and the indignities that were committed. It is much easier to say this now, but if I or some friend or member of my family took a bold position, like this, in the Block, the inevitability of violence would arise. Well, I have talked too much about that, but I wanted you to know that the fabric of the life of a black person in Alabama, in those years contained a huge element of fear. I loved Cindy dearly, and I appreciated her very much, and I honored and respected everyone in her family, but at all times I knew my place. I was very careful about that because I wanted to be accepted. I want to be a special part of the Ragsdale family. I was so grateful for the time that Cindy spent with me, and I could tell on a weekly basis that I was gaining ground in my education. My language was better. My behavior improved. I began to have more respect, and I could see further down the road of my life.

I want to share a secret with you because so many years have passed that it doesn't matter anymore, and I am sure that if Cindy were sitting here, she wouldn't object. I am going to tell you an event that you have to evaluate based upon the times and the relationship of the parties. I knew from my very earliest years that I loved Cindy, but I am not sure what love was, based upon my background. I was raised more on a survival course than I was on establishing relationships. Yet, Cindy was a very important part of my life. In addition to the many times that she taught me and helped me and guided me, we talked about things. One day, out of the blue, she asked me to take my clothes off. I never questioned why she asked me to do anything. Even at that early age I think I would have given my life for her, so I did as she said. At that point I had already physically matured, and she looked at me and obviously observed me in a naked condition, and then told me to get dressed again. That was the first time in my life that I was ever undressed in the presence of a white person, man, woman, or child, but I was not embarrassed at all. However, I was curious, and I just stood there until she spoke, next. She said, "Joe, I didn't want to embarrass you. I've been raised in a very strict family environment, and I have never seen a grown man or even a young man without clothes, although I have seen little boys, brothers and cousins, and, obviously, I 've seen pictures." I told her that I didn't mind at all, and I assure you, now, that it made no difference to me and it was no matter of significance based on our relationship. In the Block children, as well as young adults, were frequently undressed and even before the teen years everyone knew and understood about sex, and it wasn't much of a big deal. In fact, a lot of times we simply took baths in a tub in broad daylight outside our homes. This does point out, quite poignantly, the difference in the backgrounds and the upbringings that she and I had. She knew only white people. I knew mostly black people, but of all different colors, coal black, dark black, black, dark brown, brown, tan, and even white. We understand mulatto—mixed breed, and we also learned about Indians and "half breeds." In the Indian nations it must not have been any different than it was in the Block. Children were frequently the results of unions of people of different races and colors.

White people were far more modest than we were. In retrospect, I also can tell you that they had a much higher sense of moral values. I don't say that all white people were honest, but I can truthfully say that almost no black people were completely honest, but you do have to define honesty. A hungry person steals, and not many whites were hungry. Most blacks were. Most white children were raised with considerable family discipline, and most black children were left to roam the streets most of the days. I thought the contrast would be interesting to you. Let me relate one more event. One day I was playing in the streets and on the sidewalk by Woods Drug Store, and there were several white boys and girls and several black boys and girls playing together. In front of the drugstore was a great, white, porcelain scale, taller than a person, and you could put in a penny and stand on the scale and find out how much you weighed. A little card would also come out, giving you a fortune prediction. Black children never wasted a penny, but several of the white children did, on occasion. I don't know what started the fight or the conflict, but a young black girl, about ten years old, a neighbor of mine, by the name of Liz, was arguing with a little white boy, about the same age, by the name of Bubba. One thing led to another and he cursed her by calling her an ugly black four-eyed bitch. She wore glasses. She retorted that he wasn't white, that the scale was white, and he wasn't the same color as the scale. That pretty much ended the exchange. The point, however, was that a black person and a white person had an argument about race, and there were no repercussions. It's the first time I remember any black person stepping over the line, or challenging a white person about anything, and there were no serious repercussions. I don't say that that gave me the courage to behave in a similar fashion, but it planted a seed in my mind that maybe, with confrontation or discussion, black people and white people might come to some common conclusions. It was many, many years after that that my thoughts came to fruition, and even at this late date, there are still considerable reservations about such a dialogue.

I guess that's enough for you. I would much rather that you ask me questions about things that you think would be of interest. I am going to be out of town for about two weeks, consulting in some litigation about

freedom of speech, the First Amendment. Contact me later and we'll have another session.

Early Maturity

PROFESSOR: Here we are together again, and I have fond memories, already, of our previous meetings. This time I want to be more brief, more concise, instead of rambling as I did before, and I want to talk to you about those years when I began to grow into some level of maturity. I think when we left off talking last time it was mostly about being very young and becoming a teenager. My teen years were particularly difficult.

My father began to lose his health, but he saw me regularly, at least once a week, and when I was about sixteen years old, he really became incapacitated and was unable to work anymore. My mother married a fellow who was much older than she, and who had several grown children. He apparently was financially comfortable and he moved into our modest little hovel. There just wasn't room for another man in the house, and all of the children, siblings, and cousins felt mistreated. I'm sure that's not what my mother wanted, and we were not mature enough to realize that she had the right to make a life of her own. On the one hand, he brought finances to our family so we didn't scrounge for food or clothing. On the other hand, he was a very dominating personality and he treated us with no respect. He really wasn't interested in me. He was very good to my mother. Frequently, they went away for days, and we were not supervised at all. Not that I needed any supervision, but I found myself with the responsibilities of other children, some almost my age. I wanted to run away from that. I had learned some of the important facts of life, and I knew that I could make it on my own, but I would be guilty if I left the others. I maintained my relationship with the Ragsdale family, and in fact, fully succeeded to my father's position. They bought a truck for me, and I was free to use it for my own personal affairs, as well as for the affairs of the family and in connection with the house. I actually had living quarters in the basement, my own personal private section,

and there was a door with a key that only I had, and that never existed in my life before. It gave me a sense of independence. It made me appreciate the Ragsdale family and everyone in it. I could retreat to be alone, to read, to listen to the radio. I never had a guest, but if I had wanted to have one, I certainly would have asked. I would not have brought a stranger into that household. Mrs. Ragsdale became ill. She was soon bedridden, and I was one of the few people permitted to care for her. She had full time nurses and they had their duties, but every day that I was at the Ragsdale home, I visited with her and spent some time with her until she began to lose her mentality. Mr. Ragsdale trusted me more and more, and by the time that I was finished with high school and ready for college, I was actually running the household with the exception of the food and groceries and social life that took place. I thought seriously about giving up college and making a career, but Mr. Ragsdale made it plain that the years would pass and the family would be no more, but the education would be forever. If ever there was a saint, he was one. He was very kind to me, very wonderful to his family, a great contributor in the community, and a leader that was respected by everyone. If I had been taught or learned to feel deep and abiding respect for a god, or religion, I would have prayed to him, for he was my god. Whenever I sensed that he wanted something or preferred something, it was a mandate to me.

But, going on, I had little or no social life. Most of my time was consumed with work, hard work, pleasant work, and when I was not working, I was reading and studying. I spent a lot of time in the public libraries. I went to every cultural event that was free—music, plays, athletics—trying to broaden myself and gain a perspective on life that would help me outgrow the Block.

College was a pleasant and unusual but trying experience. Working, studying, and worrying consumed all my time. I had very modest quarters that I shared with three other guys, pretty much in the same condition. However, academically, I prevailed, and soon was able, through my work and scholarships, to pay my own way. I tried to make an arrangement to repay Mr. Ragsdale, but he would have none of that. I regularly sent him my report cards, a summary of my activities, letters

of appreciation and evidence of awards that came my way. During law school summers, upon his recommendation, I became a clerk for Olive & Bates. I think I was the first black lawyer that most of them had seen. There was only one other black employee and she was practically a domestic servant. Sometimes I was sent on errands to the courthouse and I sensed that people were confused about who I was and what I was doing. They sometimes asked questions about my employment. I made friends with a lot of other law clerks, and for the first time in my life I began to have a social experience of going out with people. The law firm took us places and provided entertainment. Sometimes I didn't have the right clothing, but no one seemed to mind. We ate lunch together when there was a meeting in the law firm. When it came time to go out for lunch, I went alone. There weren't any places where black people could eat with white people. Several restaurants did have pick-up windows where you could get food and eat out, and I often ate out in a park or on the sidewalk, watching the world go by. I think I blossomed as a person, became real, during those summer sessions, and I was thrilled, exhilarated, when I was asked to come back on a permanent basis upon graduation. I was number two as a student in my law class. I really thought I was number one. Both of us had perfect grades, and I really don't think that the decision was based upon the fact that she was white and I was not. I also don't think that it was based on personality. Each of us had many credits and many awards, and I don't know what the deciding factor was. In my heart, I considered that as a student I was as good as she was. She was kind enough to tell me that she thought so, too.

There was a scholarship fund providing an opportunity for a summer experience immediately following graduation from law school, to the top student in the class. It was a trip to London and Paris, all expenses paid, about two weeks of exposure to the rest of the world. The awards this time were made equally to the two top students, number one and number two, and she went to Europe, and I was given the choice to go or to accept the cash equivalent, so I went to work with $1500 in my bank account. I don't believe that I ever knew anyone who was black who had $1500 in total assets, much less in cash.

But, on to the practice of law. I'm a little tired. Suppose we quit at this point and reschedule. When we start next time, let's do that with questions and answers, your questions.

Q and A

Q: Professor Smith, you wanted us to pose a series of questions for this discussion and we have gathered several for you, and I have written them out and I am going to leave a copy with you so that you can think them over between now and our next meeting and maybe add to them or maybe they will create some thoughts or remembrances that you want to record. First, are you still a member of the Bar Association?

A: Yes, in good standing.

Q: Next, why did you give up the practice of law?

A: Tom, I want you to hold that question. You will hear more about it later. For now, no comment.

Q: Have you been permitted to receive compensation for your services in addition to teaching at the law school?

A: Yes. It's been that way from the beginning. You know how much I care for the Constitution, and the constitutional law, and the many cases relating to the Constitution, so I have kept up a very avid interest in that, not only in the textbooks but in the court developments. I have written several articles, mostly in regard to the First Amendment because that is really my specialty. Most of the articles that I have written are for law journals or for textbooks, so there really is no income from that. Sometimes there is an honorarium and it goes to a charity. However, when I am asked by lawyers or law firms to meet with them and to help study and resolve and prepare for trials relating to the Constitution, it's on a fee basis. I don't have a fixed charge, and I never render a bill. If I am satisfied that it is an important question, then I love the adventure of it. When I am asked, and when I agree, and when the discussion of finances comes up, I say that I will simply leave that to the good judgment of those who hired me. For the most part, remuneration has been very handsome and generous. I have been a guest lecturer at other major law schools.

That's generally an honorarium that is tendered as a part of the invitation. I do this not for the money, because I am well paid here, and I am financially comfortable, but more for the opportunity to be involved.

Q: When you first began to practice law, did you find a lot of prejudice?

A: Certainly. A lot of it. Most of it was subtle, such as that other lawyers or court personnel just didn't care to deal with me, or turned away. Sometimes less subtle when judges or court personnel would ignore me or wait while they served other people first. There is a story, parallel to your inquiry, that I did not experience firsthand but which was told to me by a young white lawyer that practiced at the same time as I did as a beginner. He said that he had a very heavy docket on Monday mornings, a lot of small cases, in small claims court, and most of the lawyers knew that the judge would be very busy from the time the court opened, and for a couple of hours. Well, there was a very prominent black lawyer, who was not so prominent when I started practice, and he came to the courtroom with one small matter. The white lawyer invited him to come up to the bench and take care of his, but the judge refused and required him to wait behind the lawyers' area, in the spectators' area, until he finished with the white lawyer. Many years passed and that black lawyer became one of the most successful attorneys in the State of Alabama, mostly in the civil rights area. At the same time, the judge continued to advance, until he had a position on the Circuit Court. An organization which was then known as the National Conference of Christians and Jews had a custom to honor three or more citizens every year, at least one Catholic, one Jew, and one Protestant. Coincidentally, that judge and that black lawyer were honored the same evening, long after the civil rights struggles, and I saw a picture of them hand in hand at that ceremonial event. So, I guess you can say that I observed the transition, but it was painful. Black lawyers were not permitted to join the Bar Association. They could be licensed. They could be successful, but they couldn't join. When some of the brave liberal lawyers in the community wanted to change the tune, there were real animosities and angers that developed. Those in favor of changing policy were led by a

Jewish attorney, and the opposition, in favor of status quo, was led by a Catholic attorney who was very much a part of the white establishment, old Birmingham family. The liberals won. The leader of the opposition went on to become a renowned federal judge. Later, one of the young black attorneys who was first admitted became the president of that bar association. Again, notice the change in times and relationships. The black and white firms didn't mix. There was a black firm. There was a white firm, and there were sole practitioners, but never together. That changed a little bit when a civil rights lawyer came down from up East and joined a black firm. It was quite the source of gossip. In fact, courts, and many of the lawyers, treated that young white man just as they did the members of his firm. Then, a few years later, one of the large white law firms, in which many of the older lawyers were Jewish, decided that the proper time had come, and they brought in black lawyers, black secretaries, other black personnel, men and women. After that, it sort of became fashionable to be liberal, and in some cases fashionable to appear to be liberal. That was a long time ago. Things are much different now, and some of the things are still the same, but the black lawyer has to go the extra mile.

Q: That's really interesting. It's history to us, but it's your life. One could write a whole book about that, but it would have to be someone who not only read and studied about it, but lived through it. It's so commonplace these days that it's hardly noticeable with blacks and whites practicing law together, other minorities joining, judges of every color and religion, but I certainly do notice, even at this late date, voting patterns with most black people leaning toward the Democratic Party and most white people toward the Republican Party, at least here in the South. But, on to the next question.

Q: Surely you have accumulated during your lifetime some heroes, some special people that were meaningful to you other than the Ragsdale family, so tell us about some of those.

A: True. No one could ever measure up to the members of the Ragsdale family, certainly not to Mr. Ragsdale, certainly not to Cindy. But, let me see if I can think of a few that will entertain you. First, let me

tell you about a criminal trial lawyer by the name of Roderick Broadway. I met him in person, once, when he came to the law school to lecture on criminal defense, trial advocacy, and I remember how well, then, he emphasized constitutional rights. He was a medium-sized fellow, but with a powerful bulldog type of look, and a great mane of white hair. He was glorious to behold, and his voice was like an organ, deep and powerful. Because of that lecture, I got interested in some of his background. He came from a long family history of lawyers and doctors and other professionals. I think he came from Virginia, or somewhere up there, because he had a strange accent. He was said to have been the best criminal defense lawyer ever in the State of Alabama. He not only loved the law, but the clients who came with legal problems. Fortunately he was of some modest wealth, certainly, because compensation never entered into his program of legal representation. If someone walked in the door, they had a lawyer. That was applicable to Mr. Broadway, as well as other members of the firm. Skin color didn't matter. He was just as vigorous for a poor black coal miner as he was for a white bank president. Two things really stand out, and someone ought to write a biography of his life. The first is a humorous incident. He was called to the stand to testify on behalf of another lawyer as to the reasonableness of that lawyer's fees that he had charged to a client, and in due course he was sworn in, identified, and presented the court with a resume of his background and experience to qualify himself. Opposing counsel did not object to his qualification. He did testify that a very substantial fee was reasonable, not only because of the hard work in the case, but the results which were obtained. He was cross examined, vigorously, about cases that he had handled, how much he had charged, whether he was paid in advance, and things like that. He was then asked the question as to whether or not he considered himself a good lawyer, and he answered in the affirmative. He was next asked the question of whether or not he considered himself a very good lawyer, and he answered in the affirmative. The final question that counsel asked him was whether or not he truly thought that he was the best lawyer in the state of Alabama and he answered in the affirmative. There was murmur in the courtroom and a

few chuckles, too. When he came down from the stand, that same attorney who was not an enemy of Mr. Broadwater, and in fact knew him very well, personally, asked him if he thought he had stretched the truth a little bit, and Mr. Broadwater said that he certainly had not, that he had testified truthfully because he was under oath. However, that's not what was the most enchanting thing about my admiration of him. Way back in the 1930's, there were a series of cases in Scottsboro, Alabama, in fact known as the Scottsboro cases. The basic facts were that a train left the Chattanooga area, headed toward Birmingham, and at someplace along the way, several young black boys jumped on the train, for a ride, and they came into the company of two young white girls. Admittedly, there was some degree of socializing or togetherness, but at that point, the stories diverge. When the train stopped in Scottsboro, the girls complained that they had been raped by several of the boys. The boys vigorously denied that, but were immediately incarcerated. The oldest one was sixteen years old, and the youngest was eleven. In those days we didn't have scientific evidence, DNA, blood tests, various types of technology. Trials were immediately docketed and began. The jury selection was expedited. In those days there were no blacks or women on juries. They were tried in groups and the girls testified about every one, including the eleven-year-old boy, and all raped or assaulted them, according to their sworn testimony. Convictions followed immediately, with very little jury deliberation, and immediately thereafter, seven were sentenced to death, to the electric chair. There was an explosion of civil rights advocates, many from New York and Chicago, one being a former judge from New York, and I think his name was Lebow. There was quite a scandal about the treatment of the nonresident attorneys, but the judge became a hero, later. After much time passed, years, and the cases wandered through the courts, it became more and more obvious that they were not guilty, and portions of the testimony of the girls were recanted, and additional affidavits from new witnesses who were never called at the trial were offered on behalf of the defendants. All of this was to no avail until Mr. Broadwater appeared in the picture. He was cussed and discussed. He was hated by those who thought that black people

were not human beings. There were very few admirers. Even many lawyers who respected him questioned him severely about why he would undertake such a thing when it wasn't even in his backyard, and when there was no hope for payment. He never bothered to reply or defend his position, but proceeded over a period of time, one or two at a time, to get all of the Scottsboro boys freed. He became an international hero, but not necessarily in his hometown. That took a lot of bravery. He put a lot on the line at a time when he knew it would be unpopular. In the long run, years later, he, too, became a president of the bar association and an international president of one of the substantial brotherhood organizations, and he was in fact considered one of the very best lawyers ever to practice in Alabama. That's one of my heroes.

Then, as you might assume, among my heroes would be Martin Luther King. I never knew him, never met him, but, once again, I studied him and his history. More than any other individual, with the possible exception of Attorney General Robert Kennedy, he was responsible for the civil rights legislation and progress. He was discovered at a very early age as a great orator. All through his education, he was a debater and a speaker with a wonderful vocabulary and a brilliant delivery. He chose religion as his profession. He was soon recognized as a young pastor full of vitality and courage. At the end, you will remember, was his assassination, but the beginning was a profile in great courage. He knew he was putting his life on the line. He knew he was jeopardizing his family. He knew he was going to be unpopular. He probably didn't know that he would be accused of being a Communist, or a philanderer, but he dashed headlong into the fray, scrapped together a few people, and a few dollars, and the very first critical moment came about on Dexter Avenue in Montgomery, Alabama, when Rosa Parks decided that she was too tired to get up and give her seat to a white man. There is some absence of evidence as to whether or not she was truly tired, or if it was a setup, a provocation, but she was immediately physically mishandled, arrested, charged, and convicted, and on her way to the Supreme Court of the United States. Dr. King authored that scenario. He moved on to Birmingham and made many friends and some serious enemies. He fell

into the clutches of the police commissioner who was an outrageous and committed bigot and saw to it that King ended up in jail, the Birmingham Jail. There was a song about that. Dr. King wrote a letter while he was in jail, in effect a plea for reasonableness and peace and fairness. That letter rallied many to his cause. He was noticed by leaders all over the United States, and even all over the world, as a crusader for peace and equal rights. Not everything was peaceful in his demonstrations, however. He professed non-violence, but violence followed wherever he went, or wherever he sent his emissaries. A hotel where he once stayed in Birmingham, Alabama, was bombed and severely damaged. Many of his supporters, black leaders, were arrested, put in jail, and harassed with petty offenses like traffic violations or improper conduct in public, and things like that. Just as he was a crusader, he was crusaded against. He finally found some allies in the owners of the downtown department stores. Many of them were Jewish. Many of them were sympathetic to his cause. After demonstration upon demonstration upon public conflict and international embarrassment, the color line began to break when the department stores reclassified water fountains from white and colored to no designation, permitted black people to ride in the same elevators as white people, permitted joint use of restrooms, black and white, served black clientele at food counters, then even began to hire black personnel to work in the stores in capacities other than janitorial. There was quite a furor, but he persisted, sometimes not always in good faith. Upon occasion he made promises and commitments which proved unsound, and he reneged, backed away, or abandoned courses of action that he had assured others would take place. In effect, for the great cause that he supported, he was willing for his own integrity to be impugned. He cared not for his reputation, but he was careful along the way to see that he enjoyed the respect of many decent people, even if he was despised by ten times as many. The man gave his whole life to a single effort. He was successful, and the world is a better place today.

I want to embellish that little story a little bit by talking about Bobby Kennedy. He was the brilliant statesman and scholar of the Kennedy family. His father was a very wealthy rascal. His brother was a beautiful

showcase president, but Bobby was it. He's the one that made things happen, with the power of his office. He was constantly with Martin Luther King, personally, together, on the telephone, in communication, and he was very much an author of the pursuit of civil rights. He would have been a wonderful president. Unfortunately, assassination was his end, too. I can tell you one thing that he did that was remarkable. In the State of Alabama there had not been a charter issued for a national bank in the 20th century. Along came a group of blacks and whites, together, forming a bank and seeking a national charter. They were stymied in every direction they turned, opposed by other bankers, industrialists, Ku Klux Klans, white citizens council, arch-conservatives, almost every segment of society in Birmingham where they just were not going to stand for having a bank, a national bank, led by black people. The investment group was about to throw in the sponge. Robert Kennedy had a conversation with their lawyer and within forty-eight hours, the Deputy Comptroller of Currency, headquartered in Memphis, issued the charter and delivered it to Birmingham. My recollection is that the bank didn't do too well, but it surely made a statement.

Now let me tell you about one more such hero, from a different direction. When I started to practice law there were two female lawyers. One was a Mrs. Ross, and I don't remember the other lady's last name, but she was called "Nita." I never saw her and I never met her, but I watched her career. She was an extremely competent lawyer, a sole practitioner. She appeared in every court. She appeared in every tribunal. She appeared at every public meeting. She joined every woman's organization. She was much older than I, but her tracks were everywhere. She was on radio, later on television, in the newspapers. Everyone knew Ms. Nita. As far as I know, everyone loved her. She was kind and charitable, but most of all, she was the first real female advocate, a feminist. She fought in every direction for the rights of women to be equal. There were no women in law firms then. She fought for them to be active in politics. She encouraged women from all walks of life to be active in the political arena, and finally, at the urging of her friends, she decided to run for office. She sat on the City Council of the City of Birmingham. She

charted new courses, created new programs, and constantly dragged women into the arena, while at the same time, she was a very successful practitioner. She, too, took care of the poor and the downtrodden. I don't think she was ever wealthy, but no one, with a just cause, was denied legal services from her, just because they couldn't pay. That's a double statement, and that wonderful lady made a mark in life for the City of Birmingham and many of its inhabitants. That makes her a hero. She was not necessarily my hero, but she was a hero to a lot of people. Someone ought to write a book about her, too.

I have one final hero that I just want to tell you about briefly. In the law firm where I first began to work, there was a gentleman by the name of Bates. He was a senior in the firm. He was not even in the trial division where I was practicing. I ran into a very serious emergency, personally and professionally, in the trial of a lawsuit involving a fellow by the name of Drake. I was frantic. My supervisor, the head lawyer of the department, was unavailable, sick, and I needed strength and courage from someone else and I called upon Mr. Bates. He responded gloriously. He encouraged me to pursue a course of action which was risky. He encouraged me to rely upon myself and my own judgment. He only asked that I demean myself in a fashion that I thought would bring credit to the law firm and myself, regardless of enemies to be made or people to be damned. That was a threshold moment in my life, and I moved to a new and stronger plateau, and in fact the springboard that brought me to where I am today. I don't think I have ever adequately thanked him, but if you write something in this area, please let him know and let his family know what a pivotal personality he was in my life. That's enough about heroes. I am not much of a worshiper. I imagine that if I were a religious scholar I could pick some Biblical personalities, but that's not me. I will add this. In my teaching career, I hope that I have had a chance, an occasion, to inspire some person, or a few people, to love the law as I do, and to regard the Constitution of the United States as a very tender, meaningful and significant document, ranking with the Sermon on the Mount, the Ten Commandments, and with the speech, "I Have a Dream."

Q: What an amazing, almost unbelievable, series of events that have happened in your life! You have certainly been blessed with opportunities and dreams that became real. Is there anything else that you would like to add today?

A: No, I think that's enough. What constitutes my senior years is pretty evident, and easily known to you. I think I have fulfilled my commitment to you. You know me from my point of view. Leave it to others to add or subtract or correct. I do want to say how grateful I am to all of you for what you are doing. It's a real tribute, an undeserved honor, and I am humble in your presence.

More Q and A, The Next Years

PROFESSOR: I'm glad all of you are here, again. This is probably going to be our last conference meeting unless you have some special comments or questions that you want to pursue. I think I have revealed almost everything personal and business and professional from my years of life. I am greatly honored that you have chosen to do this. Of course, it's one of the most important and significant things that has ever happened in my life, but I also realize the importance of the history and the record, perhaps even that someone else might take inspiration not only from what you record, but the fact that you have undertaken the project. I believe we should pick up with further questions and answers.

TOM: Professor, once again I have been chosen as the spokesman. We know your time is limited and we certainly do not want to stress your energy level, but we have some gaps that we want to complete, please.

One thing we haven't covered at all is to mention some of the anecdotal experiences that you have had in the years when you were a lawyer and, perhaps some that you have had since you became a professor. Give us a couple of capsules or tidbits, please.

PROFESSOR: Okay, that's fair. I would like to tell you first a couple of anecdotes from the few years that I actually practiced law. This first one was probably the best lesson that I learned as a lawyer, and it had nothing to do with the law. I was representing a financial institution that sought

to recover certain personal property that it had financed for a resident of Bessemer, Alabama. The customer had defaulted, and we were seeking to retrieve the goods which had been pledged to secure the debt. The procedure was once called "replevin," then "detinue." In those days we had what you refer to as common law pleading, a rather archaic method of getting the case ready for the jury. It always consisted of a conference with the lawyers and the judge, haggling back and forth. All of that was simplified much later by statute, but that's what we were doing in the Bessemer Courthouse. The windows were open. It was hot outside, and the three of us, the judge, opposing counsel and I, were sitting at the judge's desk in his chambers. The question of law was whether or not this defendant was entitled to protection under the Soldiers and Sailors Civil Relief Act. That was the statute which had been enacted at the inception of World War II to protect soldiers and sailors who were called into the service. The purpose was to prevent foreclosures of homes, or the repossessing of automobiles which would be disasters for the wives and children left behind. The philosophy was that the family was suffering enough by having the breadwinner leave. It was a good idea. However, the statute by its very plain terms set out that the contracts and the rights protected preexisted the entry into the service, and that if a serviceman, or perhaps I should say a serviceperson these days, entered into a contract while on active duty, the protection didn't apply. The defendant's attorney, a gentleman by the name of Rock, who was very prominent in legal circles, and political circles as well, contended that a great hardship would fall upon the family if these properties were repossessed. The judge was relatively new to the bench, and well respected, a Mr. Goodlove. I said to the judge, approximately: "Your Honor, the Supreme Court of the United States has already decided this question and it has determined that there is no protection for one who enters into a contract while on active duty, and since that's what the Supreme Court of the United States has said, it's the law all over the land." His Honor responded to me, "Mr. Smith, that's not the law in Bessemer!" I adjourned the meeting, hired a Bessemer lawyer, and I never went back to Bessemer. That was known as home cooking. I think it's still true that

big city lawyers need local lawyers when they go into the hinterlands, and that's true all over the country.

The other was a very, very unusual experience. As a young lawyer I was very active in the courts and had a lot of business to do in the office of the sheriff. The sheriff then was a Mr. Harold McDonough, and he was probably the most powerful, political Democrat in the State of Alabama, with the possible exception of a federal referee in bankruptcy who also lived in Birmingham. The sheriff called me one day and told me that he had a friend who was moving from Phoenix City to Birmingham, and needed a little bit of legal help, and would I accommodate him, and I was anxious to assure the sheriff that I would, and I did. Now I have to tell you that Phoenix City preexisted Las Vegas or Reno, and it was known for gambling, prostitution, loan sharking, and all sorts of political conspiracies. It was both a hell-hole and fun place, but you were either an insider, or an outsider. Insiders controlled everything. Outsiders were guests and visitors who came to pleasure themselves. However, Phoenix City was becoming an eyesore and an embarrassment to the State of Alabama. Most of the good citizens of Alabama wanted to have it cleaned up. A seasoned lawyer by the name of Al Poythress decided to run for Attorney General with his basic political view to clean up Phoenix City. He won handily, and since there was no Republican opposition for that November, it became immediately apparent that he was going to be the next Attorney General. Just a few days after that, he was assassinated. There were several trials and a long series of newspaper articles and public clamor about the assassination until finally some of the infamous parties were acquitted, but one was found guilty and served time. With that background, this new client of mine had a lot of business actions. He was frequently in contact with me, but we never talked about Phoenix City or his relationship with our sheriff. Soon thereafter, the sheriff passed away and a new sheriff came onto the scene, Marvin Bully, an appropriate name. He became the successor as the predominant Democrat in the community. That aside. Just before I ended my practice of law, in fact even before the Drake case, this client confided in me that he, personally, was a part of the conspiracy that got rid of the new Attorney General elect

and in fact he had provided the impetus for the assassination. He didn't quite go so far as to say that he pulled the trigger, but he left me with that impression. He is long since dead. His family no longer lives in Birmingham, insofar as I know. If he were still living, according to Alabama law, he would be subject to prosecution, but I am sure there are no living witnesses who could testify against him. It was an interesting and enlightening experience. I hope those two vignettes satisfy your curiosity about that. Remember that I did not practice law for many years, and so things like these stand out in my memory with a lot of impact.

TOM: Would you care to tell us about how you became the professor of the Constitutional Chair?

PROFESSOR: No.

TOM: I guess that is a great curiosity because you were so young and had become successful as a lawyer and you gave up what was probably a handsome income or potential income, for a rather modest position, out of the limelight.

PROFESSOR: That's true. Next question.

TOM: Well, are there some important events that took place since you became a professor that might not be common knowledge?

PROFESSOR: Well, I guess I ought to take a chance at pulling up two of those to talk about with you. Back in those days the University of Alabama produced a winning football team almost every year and it was constantly among the top ten at the end of the year. Even during the Depression years, Alabama had a great football team and many All-Americans. There came along a coach who was undoubtedly one of the finest coaches ever in the history, and that's still true today. I'll leave you to pick which one. He was a great coach. Academically, he probably was average. I don't recall that he had any interests outside of Alabama football and his family. He had many friends who were prominent citizens in Tuscaloosa, who guided him financially and protected his good name and reputation. He died a very wealthy man, but that's apart from the point that I want to tell you about now. He reached such a successful point in his financial life that he felt independent of these counselors in Tuscaloosa, and he struck out on his own. He made a few

investments and joined some boards of directors, and he began to take prominent roles in the activities of the companies with which he was affiliated. I had been teaching about fifteen years, and I was participating in many of the community activities in Tuscaloosa, as well as in Birmingham. He called me late one night, around midnight, and begged me for an appointment for the next day, which was a Saturday, and he wanted to come to my house. I really thought he wanted me to help persuade a football player to come to the University, because I had never had any contact with him of any nature up to that point. I certainly wanted to accommodate him. Bright and early he came to my home, and I could tell that he was in severe distress. This is the story that he told, approximately:

Some of his business associates in one of the companies had engaged in a series of events that called for compliance with a Securities and Exchange Commission, and they published a prospectus for an offering. The offering was very successful in the raising of money, but the company did poorly thereafter, and a lot of good citizens and trusting souls lost their arses. A lawsuit was about to be filed for fraud and deception, predicated on fraud and violations of securities law and he knew that he would be the most prominent target, not only because of his name, but because of his financial worth.

He was afraid to discuss it with his own attorneys, and he wanted some guidance from me. We talked about things generally and I told him that was not my field of the law, but that I had some good impressions about that type of litigation because there were a lot of constitutional questions in class actions, which were not so well refined at that time. It turns out that the lead attorney who was about to file the lawsuit was a former student of mine, one of the finest students I ever had. I volunteered to talk to him. The coach was most humbly appreciative, and I could see that his nerves were frazzled and he was really coming apart because, while he might lose a lot of money in the litigation, he would lose his good standing and his good name. So, I contacted my former student and I offered to come and see him, but he insisted on coming to my house, and a few days later, he did. I was very straightforward and

forthcoming with him and told him exactly everything that the coach had told me, and we discussed a lot of the legal ramifications. I asked and urged him to make every possible effort to make a settlement, short of having to name the coach as a defendant in litigation. He assured me that he would. There were several other wealthy people who were probable defendants, and the company was not without assets. The truth is that the factual support for the legal theory was not powerful, and that it would be to the best interests of his client to make a settlement without the filing of a lawsuit, and without the instituting of a class action. That came about in rapid order. Several of the directors and officers of the company produced, from their individual resources, sufficient money to pay those who would be the named plaintiffs. They did not give the coach any assurance that others would not sue, but time passed and no one did. He escaped from the embarrassment and the loss. He was my friend for life. There was never an event that had to do with football that I was not invited to the finest seat, or placed on the podium, or in some fashion to be singled out as a statesman for the University of Alabama. When his retirement came, he had not forgotten me, and he invited me out to dinner at his country club. I would not ever be a member of a country club, certainly not in those days. However, I went with him and he offered me the deed to his magnificent home in Tuscaloosa, as a gift. I was stunned, because that house was worth a fortune. I declined and thanked him for the tender. The next thing I knew was that he had made a gift of that fine home to the University of Alabama, and the University of Alabama had conferred upon me the right to live it in, as long as I chose, and during my lifetime. So, that's why I lived in such obvious splendor. The truth is that I was somewhat embarrassed about the luxury of it because I have never been a thing person, nor have I chosen to be showy in my personal life, at least not since I have been a teacher.

PROFESSOR: What else can I do for you guys?

TOM: We've taken a lot of your time and you are right—the big picture is important. I do believe that your life and what we are doing is going to be an inspiration to others. You know writing about the Constitution of the United States is a pretty boring subject, and most

people don't care about it, but you have made the Constitution come alive for hundreds of lawyers, and through them, for thousands of clients. I think what we are doing really helps accomplish your goal because we are making the Constitution of the United States come alive, and I personalize it with Joseph Jasper Smith.

PROFESSOR: Thank you. Just keep me informed. If there are any details that you need for me to fill in, let me know. Needless to say, again, I'm grateful. I enjoy very much keeping personal relationships with you and your contemporaries who still seem like children to me, although most of you are parents and probably grandparents. Drop by for a visit when you can. Call me if you wish. My agenda has narrowed considerably.

Another Class Session:
The Joseph Jasper Smith Cases

P ROFESSOR: Good morning. I am sorry I am late, but I got caught up in traffic on the way. I owe you seventeen minutes which I will add to another class session so that you will get your full money's worth from this course.

Today, I am going to issue a challenge. We have spoken often and in detail about the Constitution of the United States, and the Constitution of this state, and the whole concept of constitutional rights. I sense that you are beginning to get the feel of appreciating the Constitution and recognizing it as a valuable tool, not only at law, but in life. I am going to tell you part of a story. My purpose, however, is not to tell you the entire story, but to challenge you to investigate.

A goodly portion of any litigation is careful and detailed preparation of the law and the facts. They are two separate skills. One could be the greatest scholar on earth and not be able to try a case. One could be an excellent performer before a jury, and not have the slightest conception of the use of the law. Either condition is fatal to the success of an attorney, and so you must groom yourself in both categories. Some of the large law firms have employees who are investigators and who go out and find the facts. Some hire independent contractors to do that for them, but most lawyers search for and find the facts for themselves. They may get help, but the gathering and evaluating and the patching together is the skill of

the lawyer, no matter how much help and guidance he gets from others. This is not a trial advocacy course.

This is not even something for which you are going to be graded and it will not affect the outcome of your scores at the end of the term. However, I am today establishing a book award and each of you, individually, or acting in concert with others chosen by you, are urged to make the investigation and the inquiry that I am going to describe and submit, in writing, by the end of the term what you have found. What I deem to be the most successful investigation and the clearest presentation will result in the award which may go to one person, or a group, and it will simply be the textbook of this course with a personal inscription from me and a personal footnote from the President of the University, and a final personal note from the Governor of the State. I have made those arrangements, and I can deliver them, and it is something, if you are successful, that you will want to keep and save and show to your grandchildren, not because of me, but because of the recognition of your excellence.

Here are the facts which I am permitted to give you. Notice, I say "permitted" because I have far more facts than I am going to tell you now. Many years ago a case was filed in the local Federal Court wherein the plaintiff was one Willie Drake, and the defendants were Northington General Services, International Solvents, and AAA Auto Services. The records will clearly show that I, along with an attorney by the name of Richard Olive, III, were plaintiff's co-counsel. You will quickly learn that the records in the case are sealed, that the case was in fact dismissed by virtue of a "settlement agreement." Soon thereafter there were a series of hearings and conferences charging me, personally, with certain acts which were alleged to be unprofessional conduct growing out of the Drake case. In that regard, there were personal interviews, conferences, hearings, and disbarment proceedings before the Supreme Court of the State. Shortly after those proceedings, I accepted the position which I now occupy in this law school. See what you can find out that I have not told you. Beyond what I have told you, I am not available to answer any of your questions or give you any directions or leads. However, I

admonish you that your behavior must be legal and ethical and appropri-ate in every respect. Treat this just as though you were investigating a case in the preparation for the defense of a client. Do all that you can that is within the bounds stated. Incidentally, I believe that the best presenta-tion will be one which includes citations and references describing and defining the sources of the information obtained, rather than simple, general conclusions. I have no objection to the fact that one or more of you may become embarrassed by the effort or rebuffed or even damned, because those things happen in the investigatory process. When the final document receives the award described, it will published to all of you, and you will have an opportunity to compare what you were able to do with those who were the most able. That's that.

Preliminary Meeting for
Willie Drake File: *Olive & Bates*

OLIVE: Would everyone please be seated. I am Richard Olive III and my claim to fame is being the grandson of the founder of this law firm. You have been put together as a team for the handling of the Willie Drake litigation. Some of you have attended trial and preparation of trial with me in the past, and some of you already know each other, but we need to form a very tight knit group of people who can work together for a long period in a very serious mode. You perhaps know that I am a senior trial lawyer and chairman of the trial division of the law firm. My special area in trial work has been plaintiff claims. I will tell you that this is the most exciting plaintiff's action that has ever come to my attention. Let's meet each other by self introduction, and I will tell you more about the case and your responsibilities.

JOE: I am Joe Jasper Smith and I am a senior associate of the firm, and I have had all of my law practice here, in trial work. I have been given the privilege of taking second seat in this case, and I will probably have most of the routine responsibilities in the preparation, so I earnestly solicit your maximum cooperation and sacrifice where necessary.

ERIC: I am Eric Zinder Adams. My friends call me E.Z. I am a junior associate in the trial department and this is the first time that I have been assigned to the trial of a case, most of my prior work being research, depositions, etc.

ETHEL: I am Ethel Christian. I have been with the law firm about twenty years, and I am a senior legal assistant assigned to complex trials.

I have worked with Mr. Olive on many cases in the past, and I will be the primary coordinator of the evidence, and our internal systems.

MARYON: I am Maryon Jones and I have been a legal assistant in the law firm for about seven years, and I have been working closely with Joe.

JACK: I am Jack Brothers. While I am new to the firm, only a couple of years, I have had considerable experience in the organizing of complicated cases. I am neither a lawyer nor a legal assistant, but I will be dealing with each of you in the process of accumulation and assembly and the planning of the strategy for trial. I am also the custodian of exhibits.

HENRIETTA: I am Henrietta Harrison. I am a secretary from the law firm staff pool. I will transcribe all of the dictation, all of the instructions, all of the memoranda, and distribute them to the parties as appropriate in this room, and I will send out all mail and distribution of material to people outside the firm, other law firms, and I will deal with the arrangements for expert witnesses and the examination of their files.

OLIVE: Well, I guess that tells us who we are. Now let me tell you about the case. Willie Drake is our plaintiff. This can be the most important case that this law firm ever handled. We are one of the few large law firms that do defense work as well as plaintiff work, and we find that in many worthy plaintiff cases, personally injuries, we have conflicts with other clients and we must bow out. This one, however, passes our conflicts check. The defendants are Northington General Services, a large conglomerate with headquarters in Seattle. They design, create, and develop new products in several different industries, foods, chemicals, mechanical contrivances, and others. They are a top Fortune 500 company, with an excellent reputation. They operate directly in every state of the United States and in thirteen foreign countries. They hold more patents either by creation or acquisition than any other single company in the United States. Obviously, under appropriate circumstances, they are a most desirable defendant.

The next defendant is International Solvents. It is a Japanese company that manufactures and distributes various solvents, cleaning fluids and materials, oils, powders, mostly for industrial use. Likewise, a worthy defendant.

Finally, AAA Auto Services is a small company registered in Delaware whose home office and major base of operations is in Decatur. They do all sorts of repairs and services on automobiles and they specialize in the installation and the repair and replacement of glass products like windows, headlights, and ornaments within the interior of a car. The services that they perform are in plants, manufacturing plants, and they have eleven operations in Alabama, Georgia, and the panhandle of Florida. They operate somewhat like a car wash in that automobiles are frequently driven into the plant, parked, serviced, and driven away by the owner, or if the job is complicated and protracted, the service is done overnight.

The product in question is called Everlast Seals. This is a solvent adhesive which was created and patented by the first defendant, manufactured and distributed by the second, utilized in the operations of the third. Willie was a longtime employee of a company affiliated in some fashion with AAA, perhaps a franchisee. He has been with the company eighteen years. He is thirty-eight years old, with a wife and three children, ages three, nine, and fourteen, all girls.

When the product was developed and marketed, it immediately became attractive to AAA. The product comes packaged in the same fashion as a dozen pencils in a box, and each one of these is about five inches long, round, and about the size of a pencil in diameter.

This is the process. When a new window or a windshield is installed in a car, or when one is replaced in a car, a small torch melts the end of the product as the product is moved slowly along the seam. This is very similar to welding. As it melts, it filters into the area where the glass is to be seated, and the product firmly adheres not only to the glass, but wood, metal, or any other firm surface. The real value is in the excellent seal that takes place. There is no discoloration. It is not visible, but water or other liquids cannot flow through it. You can imagine how many automobile windows leak, and windshields, as well. It's almost unheard of these days to have a window leak after this process.

Now comes the part that is most interesting to us. The welding process emits fumes that cannot be seen, but have a slight sweet odor, and this is wafted into the face of the employee as the torch and the adhesive

move along the area to be sealed. From that there is no escaping a conclusion that the employee inhales fumes.

Two or three years ago, Willie developed a bad cough and assumed it was a common ailment and did nothing about it for several months. Incidentally, he was not a smoker. His health began to decline. He never made the connection between the process and his medical problem, but a doctor team at the University of Alabama Medical School did determine the problem by a biopsy of his lungs. They found microscopic glass beads in the lung tissue which had created not only the cough, but the deteriorating of his lungs. Today he is a hopeless, helpless invalid, awake and alert, but unable to walk, great difficulty in talking, and constantly in use of oxygen. He could linger like this for quite some time because the situation is no longer progressing. We will clearly establish with expert testimony from chemists and medical authorities that the glass beads infused in his lungs are the same glass as the consistency of windows and windshields in automobiles, and have in fact tested the product and its utilization in a very detailed analytical report. I will explain to you later exactly what the tests were, but suffice it to say for the moment that they duplicated the sealing procedure with samples of the same product and drew the fumes into lung tissue and observed the development of the beads.

ERIC: Mr. Olive, I know that I have very little experience in the practice of law or in trial work, but isn't this a case which would be covered by workmen's compensation law?

OLIVE: Well, we will have to cross that bridge. The answer would be yes, if we sued the real employer. The real employer is a partnership of a father and son who own the franchise type operation where Willie worked, and he is their employee. There was a complicated ownership from AAA, somewhat like a franchise. We can go into this later because I am sure the issue is going to be briefed and argued vigorously before the trial judge. However, that's a good question. Good thinking.

Well, that's the summary of the case. I am going to be available to this group as needed, collectively, or on an individual basis. Joe will be the coordinator. I told you that this was a very important case, and it is for

Willie, but let me tell you what's lurking out there. We already have thirty-seven other clients who in varying degrees have suffered lung damage from the use of this product, in several different industries and activities. There are other lawyers and law firms who also have an interest because they have a few clients. All of them have agreed to assist and to observe in this test case, in anticipation of having a class action later. We are going to pool our efforts, and the costs of the trial, sharing all of the information among all the lawyers. This case, therefore, probably cannot be settled except for an enormous amount of money, nor can it be settled with any commitment that no actions will be brought by this law firm or other law firms in this consortium. This has a prospect of being a case as huge as the asbestosis cases, the implant cases, and other similar lawsuits. So, let me say this to you—you are in on the ground floor of something which could be momentous. Based on the time of all of us here and others that we might utilize and the actual costs, we could easily have millions of dollars invested in the preparation of the trial. It's your chance to ring a bell. I will offer you this additional incentive. While all of you will have other duties, when this case comes to trial, I will have all of you removed from all of your other responsibilities, perhaps two to three months before the actual trial date, and you will participate in nothing else but this through the final preparation and the trial of the case. If you have nothing to do and your responsibilities are fully met, then you may sit in with us on the hearings and motions and the actual trial.

Now, let me cover one last thing. We are probably eighteen months away from being in the courtroom. Alert your families that you may not be in control of your time and work ethic starting right now. You may tell them that you are in a major case and it has the highest priority, but please do not discuss this case with anyone other than this team or other parties in the consortium—and even be careful about that. If you have any reservations about whether you are in a position to discuss or reveal, then clear those through Joe or myself. I do want to ward off one concern before I close. You are chosen, all of you, because of your special skills and potential value in this case. We have a very clear chain of command and control. I will be the lead counsel and I will be present at every time there

is a hearing in court and during the course of the trial. Both of you attorneys will, likewise. The court and opposing counsel may be somewhat uneasy with the racial overtones because they probably have never seen or dealt with a black trial lawyer, but we have every confidence in Joe, and he has earned the right to get out in public and be up front. This will also have an impact on jury selection, and the impressions which you have need to be shared among us because I have never faced the selection of a jury under these circumstances. This law firm is different. Merit is the only test. So, let's get on with it. Joe, as soon as you develop the division of responsibilities and the assignments of the tasks, prepare a sheet and distribute it to everyone here. Your time entries will be under code number 1964-PTD0075. Be sure that all of your time and expenses are put into the system with that identification. In dictating your time, be very explicit and detailed because the consortium law firms are entitled to that. Have a good day.

FOR REFERENCE—

Index of Characters in Drake Suit:

Richard Olive III—grandson of founder of firm; senior trial lawyer and chairman of trial division of law firm.

Joe Jasper Smith—senior associate of law firm; taking second seat in Drake suit; will have most of the routine responsibilities in trial preparation.

Eric Zinder Adams—("E. Z.") —junior associate in trial department of firm; has never been assigned to trial of a case.

Ethel Christian—senior legal assistant assigned to complex trials; primary coordinator of evidence and computer preparation.

Maryon Jones—legal assistant in the firm; works closely with Joe.

Jack Brothers—does organizing and computerizing of complicated cases for firm; plans trial strategy.

Henrietta Harrison—secretary from law firm staff pool.

PARTIES:

Willie Drake – plaintiff; longtime employee of AAA, for 18 years; 38 years old; has wife and three girls, ages 3, 9 and 14.

Northington General Services—defendant; large conglomerate with headquarters in Seattle; designs, creates and develops new products; top Fortune 500 company; excellent reputation

International Solvents—Japanese company that manufactures and distributions various solvents and cleaning fluids mostly for industrial use.

AAA Auto Services—small company with home office in Decatur, Alabama; performs repairs and services on automobiles; specializes in the installation, repair and replacement of windows, windshields, headlights, etc.

Everlast Seals—product in question; a solvent adhesive which was created and patented by Northington, manufactured and distributed by International Solvents, and utilized in the operations of AAA.

Second Meeting of
Drake Case Team

JOE: Mr. Olive wanted us to get back together right away and begin to sketch out some of the preparatory work and divide up the assignments, and that's the purpose of this meeting. What I would like to do first is to create the format for maintaining our records and systemizing them and Ethel and Jack, you will please undertake this responsibility. You already have the client matter identification and we need to begin to create the subfiles. I want to mention some that we usually have, probably have in this case, and I want you to supplement this memo with your additional thoughts:

1. Client Identification and Fact Sheet—check his background and history, particularly if there has been any previous litigation.

2. Medical—we have several resources that fall into this category, the patient himself, first, all of the doctors that he has ever seen, at least for the last ten years, details of the medical need and care and treatment and results; then, the doctors and other staff members at UAB and we might as well include the chemists in this group.

3. A witness list, and I want to make this as broad as we reasonably can because I am sure we are going to have some unexpected events in a case of this nature, so we want to get as many names on our list, before filing, as we could possibly use in the case. When the time comes to prepare the list, let's reserve the right to add some more as needed. We need a fact sheet on every potential witness. When the defendants file their list, same procedure.

4. E.Z., I want you to plan the depositions, and I think we should get right into the meat of the case in the beginning with the executives of the various defendants, all the way to the top, and find out from these executives all the details of the creation of the product, the patent application, and get a copy, and the final patent, contracts between and among the defendants for distribution and sale, instruction manuals, and we really need to bear down and find what kind of research was done along that line.

5. I will take a shot at preparing the trial plan, the order of witnesses, and when we get closer to trial date, I want you, Jack and Ethel, to begin to schedule the convenience of the various witnesses that we will need.

That's my preliminary list, and I want you to add, now, any that come to your mind, and memo as to others.

ERIC: In the medical area, I think we ought to line up some local medical experts who are not physicians or others who have served the plaintiffs and maybe our law firm has some clients who could lead us in the right direction there.

JOE: Good idea. I think Mr. Olive can pursue that for us.

MARYON: Do you think this product would in any way come under the Food and Drug regulatory authorities?

JOE: I doubt it, at this point, but let's keep that in reserve. There is not any avenue that we cannot pursue in this case.

ETHEL: I think we ought to get financial background and histories and public registrations of the defendants, and let's see if we can determine the impact of this particular product on the total business activities.

JOE: Yes let's add that to the list, and in fact we can begin to gather that now. You, Henrietta, can draw down public statements from the SEC. While you are at it, let's find out if there has been any litigation for other products of these defendants and, specifically, but not hopefully, whether there have been any litigation or footnotes to public records which would indicate that this product had been contested.

JACK: Is there some way that we can present by pictures or diagrams, or something like that, for an impact with the jury, how these glass

products affect the lungs, perhaps a before and after? I remember that we did that years ago in the Pneumoconiosis, Black Lung cases, litigated in Jefferson County, Bessemer Division.

JOE: Yes, let's research that, and it occurs to me now that we ought to find out something more detailed and analytical about the glass and maybe that will give us an opportunity to add some additional defendants. It would be nice if we didn't have to rest this entire case on the fumes, but also the volatility of the glass products that were being sealed.

ERIC: Do we know who opposing counsel will be?

JOE: I am sure there will be a lot of attorneys and they will have a consortium similar to ours, and they probably will have a joint defense agreement, and we ought to try to explore that.

JOE: E.Z., how about checking this. When there are several law firms defending a case, and one lawyer passes to another lawyer confidential information from his client, does that information still remain confidential in the hands of the other attorney? Perhaps we could explore through all the attorneys to see what they have learned from others. I am sure there is a ton of paper stuff out there, and if we can find some potential witnesses who can testify without being covered by the attorney / client privilege, we could hit a home run. But, getting back to your first question, lead defense counsel will be Hank Longfellow of Gimble & Dollid, along with Simpson, Johnston and Baker, and Jamie Contreras has already surfaced and will probably be chief counsel.

ETHEL: Are you confident that we will be able to stay in the federal court?

JOE: Well, as sure as we can be. That's a great advantage in two ways. There are some statutory and case law limitations in the state courts that could weaken our claim substantially or limit the potential recovery. We clearly have diversity. We clearly have amount. Right now, unless there is some change, we have the finest legal mind in the State of Alabama as the assigned judge, and she has handled many complex litigation cases as well as those involving multiple jurisdictions. This will be a good forum in which to move into the class action, if we get that far.

E.Z.: How should we proceed with discovery?

JOE: No holds barred. I think we should initiate motions for production of written material as soon as possible. Let's see what we can find, or let's see what the soft spots are and where we get refusals to answer, and let's try to get our fact situation pretty much in hand before we begin the depositions. I would say that the motions ought to be prepared and filed within the next thirty days, and I will take the responsibility of preliminary drafting. I welcome any input from any of you. I want you, Henrietta, to put together the format so that I can present it to Mr. Olive in a couple of weeks. Any more questions? Any more comments? I remind you again to get your personal lives in condition for you to handle the time commitments. That's it. Let's adjourn.

Pretrial Conference

BAILIFF: The Court will come to order, please. All rise. The Honorable Henrietta Samuels, presiding.

JUDGE: Good morning, friends. This is the final pretrial hearing and conference, and I hope to conclude all of the formalities and schedule the trial date. The Court has already ruled that this is the proper jurisdiction and venue for the hearing of this cause. I have determined that counsel of record for all parties are duly qualified and entered on the rolls of this court.

JUDGE: I deny all motions to dismiss and I deny all motions to limit testimony. I have already ruled on the production of documents. The defendants have not fully responded to the production request, and I am providing an additional thirty days from this date for them to do so, or suffer sanctions.

JUDGE: There are too many expert witnesses scheduled, and I am going to limit each side to three—three for the plaintiff, one for each of the defendants, and you can coordinate among the defendants as to which ones you choose. In the absence of some special showing, by affidavit or otherwise, that's the limit, and from my examination of the depositions and the pleadings, it seems to me that the issues are very narrow and this will provide you with sufficient testimony opportunity. It seems to me a sufficient period of time to allow ten trial days, for this case. I would like each party to amend and update the witness lists and

the suggestion, as best you can, of the time on direct. Obviously I cannot at this time reduce the time on cross. We will just have to see how that plays out.

JUDGE: On Mr. Olive's motion for the protection of his client and the limitations on the plantiff's ability to testify, personally, I rule in favor of the plaintiff. I want to make this clear, however. Even though your client, Mr. Olive, may be able to speak very little, I want to keep the record clear and I will permit him to answer yes and no questions by the nod of his head, and each time, my bailiff will supplement the record by indicating 'the plaintiff says no', or 'the plaintiff says yes.' That will make the answers clear and if any one disagrees with the bailiff's determination of the answer of the plaintiff, object and I will review it with you. In addition, Mr. Olive, if the examination of the plaintiff is prolonged, I will give you rest periods. I do suggest that in your direct examination you frame your questions as best you can in order to get yes or no answers. I realize that the defendants will be objecting to leading questions. I will have to deal with each of those as they arise. I also want you to caution the plaintiff that he must do the best he can to speak when he is required to do so. I want him, as best he can, to avoid coughing or choking or gagging or losing his voice in the conversation. In other words, Mr. Olive, there will be sympathy enough without exaggerating his inability to speak clearly. Is that clear?

MR. OLIVE: Yes, Your Honor.

JUDGE: I have read your briefs on whether or not this is a case which could or should be restricted by virtue of the Alabama Workmen's Compensation statutes. Those are obviously not sustainable as to the defendants, in which there is no potential employment relationship. I reserve the ruling as to AAA. I will also decide during the course of the trial whether or not this is a matter of law, that the plaintiff is or is not a former employee of AAA, or whether or not he is and has been in fact an employee of the operator. I may submit that question to the jury. I am sure that for all of you, and for me, this is a question of first impression, since the agreement between the operator and AAA is most unusual, perhaps unique. Also, I am going to limit the witnesses to very brief

appearances on the question of employee, or not. I expressly overrule the objection to the introduction of the agreement between the operator and AAA. I want that in the record whether or not it is a question of law or for the jury.

JUDGE: I believe that covers everything that is before me at this time. Does anyone have any questions?

DEFENSE COUNSEL: Your Honor, from our client, the plaintiff has subpoenaed three executives, two of whom live in Seattle, and one in Hawaii. He has taken all of their depositions, exhaustively. I believe that to have all three appear and under his subpoena is excessive. We ask the Court for some relief.

JUDGE: Noted. I agree. Mr. Olive, choose two.

DEFENSE COUNSEL: Thank you, Your Honor.

MR. OLIVE: Your Honor, as this case has progressed, our client has weakened, and we would like, under the supervision of the Court, to do a video interview with the plaintiff as soon as possible. We would be severely handicapped at trial if the plaintiff could not appear in person, and we think it is a fair substitute to have his testimony taken in this fashion.

JUDGE: Any objection?

DEFENSE COUNSEL: Yes, Your Honor, this is a double burden for us to have to go through the examination and cross examination twice. This case has been docketed for a long time. I discussed it with Mr. Smith, Mr. Olive's associate, just last week, and I told him then that we would object.

JUDGE: Mr. Olive, how long do you think the direct examination of the plaintiff will require?

MR. OLIVE: I intend to examine him, myself, and I suggest not more than one hour.

JUDGE: I will grant the request subject to these conditions—not more than one hour of direct testimony, oral, only, no documents or exhibits, so you had better be prepared if you lose your client to get those things done through other channels. I will grant unlimited cross examination, but I want to caution defense counsel to be compassionate. I want the lawyers to get together and pick a time within the next ten days, day or

night, and if necessary, to do this at the plaintiff's home. However, Mr. Olive, your law firm will bear all costs and expenses for travel, and reasonable attorney's fee charges for attendance for up to three attorneys, and all the costs and charges will be billed directly to Olive & Bates by those attorneys who participate, fully itemized. If there is any dispute, bring it to my attention.

JUDGE: Anything else? Hearing nothing, this case is set for trial on September 6th, a Tuesday, Monday being Labor Day, and we will use all of that week, including Saturday, and I want you earnestly to try to finish testimony by Wednesday of the next week, arguments and motions on Thursday, jury charge Friday morning, beginning deliberations immediately. We will adjourn for an hour while you lawyers finish exchanging exhibits as ordered.

In the Men's Room

E.Z.: Joe, I noticed something very peculiar. All of Longfellow's files are within a single drawer and all of them are buff colored except a small one which is dark blue. I happened to be sitting there as he was juggling his files, and I saw some weird initials on the face of the file. He flipped it open once and shuffled some papers in there and closed it and moved it closer to him, as if I might be looking at it.

JOE: E.Z., I saw the same thing. Let me tell you what else. After you walked away and I was beginning to put my files back together, Mr. Longfellow went to every other lawyer and took a similar file from each one of them, perhaps five or six in all, put a rubber band around them and gave them to a runner. I saw him speaking firmly to the runner and pointing to the door, as if to say—get these out of here. Now there must have been something in those files, not only that was expected to be private and confidential, but that everybody else had, and they had to be gotten out of the way. I certainly would like to be able to discover the contents of that file, but we may be in for some surprises. Apparently they know some things that we don't.

E.Z.: Let's take a shot at it—maybe we can push Longfellow where he

might think we saw what was in the file. He might tip his hand.

JOE: How do you suggest that we do that?

E.Z.: I don't know, but let's think about it. Maybe I could say to him, in passing: "Oh, incidentally, did you pick up that little blue file that you had left on the table?", or something like that. At least that will let him worry about whether we know the contents or not.

JOE: Let's be careful. I smell a rat, but I'm not desperate yet. We certainly are not in a position to prove any malice or neglect or extreme carelessness, or anything like that, which means no punitive damages, and that won't ring the bell. It certainly won't be grounds to support a class action. You go on back to the courtroom, and I'll be there in a little while.

Office Conference—
Emergency

JOE: Mr. Bates, I was at the courthouse in respect to the Willie Drake litigation, and I was told to return to the office immediately to meet with you and others.

BATES: Yes, bring E.Z. with you. Everyone else on the Drake case is in Conference Room one. Let's go.

BATES: Joe, Mr. Olive just had a serious heart attack. He is right now in intensive care at University Hospital. The situation is desperate. His family and some of the members of the firm are there waiting. What are the chances of getting a postponement in the *Drake* case?

JOE: Mr. Bates, I really don't know. We had some real tension develop. There is a lot of anxiety in the case. All of our consortium counsel have come to town, and together with their staff there are probably fifteen of them. I don't think the judge is very happy with me because of some late motions that I filed and she has dressed me down pretty good. We are opening with some expert witnesses and they are standing by. I don't know what to say other than the fact that we are ready.

BATES: Are all the lines filled in on your trial plan or is there anything significant that is missing?

JOE: I think we are fully ready. Mr. Olive and I have gone over our opening statements. We have divided up the witnesses and we have actually rehearsed each other on the examination of the witnesses. We have not decided who would cross, but we thought we could determine

that as the defense witnesses were presented.

BATES: I'm sorry to have called all of you together, but this is one of the most significant cases in the law firm and we have our best team on it. I really don't know how our associated firms would feel about having second chair take charge. I have spoken to a few of them and they certainly agree that none of them would be qualified to conduct the examinations or to make the statements. Monday is Labor Day. I don't see any choice but to have this whole team and all of the other counsel who are involved in the anticipated class action sit down together and talk it out. The only question I have is whether we should alert the judge.

JOE: I think I can persuade everybody on our side to go forward, but I do think I need to call the judge and report the developments.

BATES: You take care of that right now, even if you have to call her at home. Have there been any discussions of settlement?

JOE: I will have to say practically none. There have been some suggestions about paying all medical bills to date. Mr. Olive wouldn't hear of that and rejected it out of hand, although we did report it to Willie. There has been no indication that any of the defendants might be willing to settle and get out, and we didn't think it was wise for us to initiate those conversations. If any defendant feels that he can buy his way out, then the move ought to come from him. It seems to me that the defense counsel are a pretty tight knit group. They don't seem to take positions contrary to each other at any time in my presence. I think we are facing a trial, but the judge might get us together early Tuesday morning.

BATES: Let's leave it at that. I will be available at home Labor Day and I will come to the office early Tuesday morning to see if there is anything to report. I'll stay in my office or in touch with my secretary throughout the trial if you need me. I think it is too late to introduce new personalities in the courtroom. However, if there are any offers, any settlement discussions, I want to be in the picture for that.

BATES: I would like for there to be very little conversation about Mr. Olive's condition until we know something more, other than for Joe to call the judge. Please stay constantly in touch with the office over the

weekend by letting us know where you are and where you can be reached in the event there are some developments. Joe, this can either be one of the worst or one of the best experiences you have had as a lawyer. Let's go get 'em.

(Shortly) Smith and Judge:

JOE: Your Honor, I am desperately sorry to contact you at home, and I apologize again for the intrusion, but I have to tell you that Mr. Olive has had a serious heart attack, and he is right now in intensive care and he is certainly unable to participate in the case.

JUDGE: I am certainly sorry to hear that. How's he doing?

JOE: We really don't know yet. The family and some of the members of the firm are there, but it's too early to tell and we have been asked not to discuss it until we know something more specific, but I can tell you that it sounds quite serious. It is certainly serious enough that he will not be available in court, and probably not available to counsel with us throughout the trial.

JUDGE: That's very distressing. Richard is one of my good friends. He was one of the first attorneys who jumped at the chance to have me appointed. I certainly hope he improves and quickly. As for you, young man, I don't envy what lies ahead of you. I hope you are not suggesting a continuance.

JOE: No, Your Honor, I am not. My firm is ready for me to go forward, and all of the attorneys who have been following the case with us are in town and they concur that we should go forward.

Bates Memo

M r. Bates, I am sorry to be getting to you at this late date because E.Z. and I have been scrambling to finish the preparation for the trial. Mr. Olive was not aware of this development, but I thought you ought to know. I know that I don't need to add this, but this needs the utmost and strictest confidence, as you will see.

From some items of information which E.Z. and I have picked up in the courtroom, in the hallways, and my one stroke of good fortune, we believe that there is a real sinister background to the Drake case. The depositions show that all of the principal parties and the expert witnesses contend that there were never any suspicions or reasons to believe that the product had been damaging or injurious, and certainly that there was no research done that would lead to the conclusion that it might have been such. We think we now have a written confirmation of the probability. Unfortunately, perhaps by my being impetuous, I did not fully evaluate these concerns and opportunities. Obviously, I have not been able to communicate to Mr. Olive.

I have filed some motions that met with the disapproval of the opposition and the Court, but I have under subpoena some attorneys who are from one of the defense firms, locally. I am confident that there will be personal attacks made on me, but I am up to that task. I am hopeful that it will not spread to the point where anything which I have done might bring discredit upon our law firm. There are no other copies of this memo.

— JJS

Response

Joe, thanks for the memo. I think I understand. Tread lightly. I am ready to back your judgment, but if you feel that you need me, I am available. I trust you to the extent that if you are doing the right thing and if you are serving your client, our law firm is going to be standing alongside you as you go through the struggle.

Olive is not doing particularly well. We are all very deeply concerned about him. If you hit a home run in the trial, it will unquestionably hasten his recovery. Good luck.

— *Bates*

Special Court Hearing

T he dark mahogany-walled courtroom was quiet, save for the ruffling of papers indicative of the final preparation for the case. The judge entered the room accompanied by the sound of a slight swish of robe. The lawyers for their respective sides watched with a little apprehension as the bailiff stood before them and spoke in a loud, deliberate voice.

BAILIFF: All rise. The Honorable Henrietta Samuels, presiding.

JUDGE: Please be seated. Let me say that I really regret having to be here, on a weekend, particularly Labor Day weekend, but I see no other opportunity to dispose of these two motions before trial, except now. Mr. Smith, these are your two motions, and I have read them. You are going to have to convince me that there is really merit, and that you are not playing games. So, we'll take up the first motion which is for special and unusual discovery. Please explain that to me, and let's get on with it.

JOE: Your Honor, I feel that it is necessary now to take some depositions of opposing counsel. I believe that we are entitled to discover and learn about facts, conversations, discussions, and other communications which have transpired among the various members of the defense firms. I know that Your Honor will initially take the position that all communications among defense firms are privileged because every communication must be between lawyer and client, but I think this is a

different situation. I readily concede that we cannot discover any communications between a defendant and that defendant's attorney. However, communications between a client and his attorney which are communicated by that attorney to others should no longer be protected by attorney/client privilege. For that purpose, I believe that we are entitled to see and examine the agreement among the defendants for joint defense. Part of this motion is not only to examine the lawyers, but to produce that agreement. We have reason to believe that there have been communications between and among parties who are not protected by the privilege. If we are correct, then any communications between the lawyers and each other, or investigators, or witnesses, should be discoverable, and we are entitled to learn whether or not witnesses and investigators who have gathered information for a particular lawyer, as that lawyer's work product, does, or does not carry over to the other lawyers who are defending their respective clients in this case.

JUDGE: Sorry, Mr. Smith. Unless you can show me something very specific, by affidavit, I am not going to give you additional discovery. The first grounds for the denial is that it comes too late, unless you have simply stumbled onto something in the last several days. Besides, I would expect you to show me extensive judicial decisions that would permit you to discover the defense agreement among the lawyers, or to pierce the attorney / client relationship from one defendant to the lawyer of another defendant. I take the position, second, that all matters from any clients or from any parties retained by the attorneys for the clients remain privileged as to all attorneys and all defendants. That motion is overruled.

JUDGE: The second motion is intriguing, particularly since I have overruled the first motion. You want to issue additional subpoenas, at this late date, for certain attorneys in the local law firm defending the local client. Clarify your position.

JOE: Your Honor, there are two grounds on which the subpoena should be issued and the interrogation should proceed. The first is that the law firm needs to be prohibited from proceeding in this case on account of a conflict, and the second is that as a result of or related to the

conflict, the Court may find that there is a conspiracy and a criminal event which would not only disqualify the law firm, but would discharge the attorney/client privilege.

JUDGE: Is that all you have to say on the issue?

JOE: Yes, at this time, Your Honor.

JUDGE: Mr. Smith, you realize that this is a very serious charge and insinuation.

JOE: I realize that, Your Honor, and I would not take that position lightly, or without what I consider just cause.

JUDGE: I don't take this lightly, either, first because it comes so late, second because defense counsel is highly regarded by this Court, and third, and most persuasively, you have said nothing concrete.

JOE: I realize that, Your Honor, but I have sufficient information that leads me to the conclusion that you will rule in my favor when I have an opportunity to present the witness or witnesses.

JUDGE: Mr. Smith, with considerable reluctance, I am not going to overrule your motion at this time, but I am going to reserve it for further consideration. If you want to proceed, right now, to disqualify the defense firm, I'll hear that this very minute. On the other hand, I am going to grant your subpoena and instruct the proposed witnesses to stand by, subject to the call of the court, and before I permit you to put a fellow attorney on the stand, you are going to have to produce something very specific. I want to warn you, most stringently, that I consider you may be stepping over the bounds of ethics and even decency. Be on your guard.

JUDGE: Bailiff, you may serve those subpoenas now, in my presence, on the defense counsel, and I will assume that the subpoenas will in turn be delivered to the parties who are named. Have a nice weekend. See all of you bright and early Tuesday morning. Be prepared for your opening statements.

Opening Statements

J oseph Jasper Smith looked down at his notes a final time before he arose and walked to the podium. He took a deep breath, barely perceptible. He glanced down at his hands and then scanned the faces of the jury as he began to speak.

JOE: Ladies and Gentlemen of the jury, I am pleased and honored to represent the plaintiff, Willie Drake. My law firm is Olive & Bates, a large general purpose firm in Birmingham, and we came to know Mr. Drake by virtue of the fact that he was a friend of one of the employees in our law firm. When we first met Mr. Drake in person, he was already an invalid, in a wheelchair, with some difficulty in communication. In the process of his appearance here in Court and on the stand, please understand that he will do the best he can to communicate. It will be difficult for you to understand some of his words, but we will try to help move that process along. He will not be on the stand very long, anyway.

In the course of his employment, beginning many years ago, Mr. Drake was a repair and service man. Among the things that he did, for many years, was to repair and replace the windows, windshields, and other glass items on automobiles. During the course of his employment, he came to use and be involved with a product known as "Everlast Seals." I hold here in my hand what looks like a pencil. When I introduce it into evidence, it will be passed among you so that you can see it and feel it and

touch it. It is a stable, inert composite of materials designed for a specific and limited purpose. We will prove to you how this product is used, and that in the process, by chemical action, fumes are created which in turn were inhaled by the plaintiff as a part of his job and work commitment, and that these fumes directly caused a lung condition which has damaged not only his lungs, but his ability to breathe and to speak. This came about as a result of his being exposed over several years, and in the course of the deterioration of his physical being, he had a lot of medical attention, some of which resulted in the conclusion that glass pellets of microscopic size are the culprit, and that these glass pellets arrived in his lungs as a result of the fumes which were produced by the burning of the product. We will have medical testimony which will elaborate.

Much of what I am about to say will be admitted by the defendants. We will prove to you that Northington General Services was a major corporation that ventured into the design and creation of new products, and in so doing acquired a multitude of patents. One of those patents was this product. We will show you that the product, once designed and created, was manufactured and distributed by International Solvents. In the process of distribution, these products came into the hands of AAA Auto Services which has its headquarters in Decatur, Alabama. While this part may be disputed, we will show you by testimony that AAA made this product available to the entity where these events took place that caused Mr. Drake to become ill.

You will be convinced by the preponderance of the testimony that these defendants have caused serious, major, permanent and damaging injuries to Mr. Drake from which he will never recover, and which have caused him to be ill, in pain, and limited in the enjoyment of life. Thank you very much for your attention.

LONGFELLOW: Ladies and Gentlemen, I am Henry W. Longfellow. I acquired that name at birth, and you will recognize it as a great poet of the not too distant past. While my name is also Longfellow, there is no kinship there. I am Counsel for Northington General Services which is headquartered in Seattle. My law firm is Gimble & Dollid. Our offices are here in your community. We have represented Northington General

Services for many, many years, and I am personally acquainted with the executives of that company and their operations. It is true, and we concede, that they created the product known as "Everlast Seals." We will prove to you that their chemicals department created this product with several different chemicals, not one of which could cause the injury to the plaintiff, and, taken all together, could not create fumes which would transport products in the fashion that the plaintiff claims. We are deeply sympathetic toward the plaintiff's conditions, but none of our laboratory tests show anything whatsoever to confirm his contentions. I think it is very important that nobody else has ever made such a complaint. Nobody else has ever filed such a lawsuit. We had no cause ever, and we have no cause now, to believe or accept the contention that this product was dangerous or damaging. We hope that you will understand our position, and accept that, and realize that we have no liability. You will hear from expert witnesses who confirm our views. In the proceedings in this case, we will also serve as local counsel for all defendants. Thank you very much.

JONO: My name is Isaka Jono. My family originated in Japan, but I was born here in the United States. My law firm is Thompson, Richardson and Harrellson. Associated with us is the outstanding law firm of Simpson, Johnston & Baker of your fair city. Our client is International Solvents. We are a worldwide organization with plants and factories and distribution centers in thirty-nine different countries. In the United States, we are headquartered in San Francisco, California. Our law firm represents International Solvents. We began our operations toward the end of the last century, manufacturing and distributing various solvent materials. Sometime ago, we learned that Northington General Services had a product known as Everlast Seals which had the capacity to seal together various types of goods, cloth, wood, glass, cement, and we felt that it was a product that was patented by one of the most famous and highly respected companies in the world, and that we could use it in our line of products for distribution. We were granted a license and we do in fact manufacturer Everlast Seals and sell it throughout the world. We have never had any reason to believe that the product was dangerous or

unsafe, in any way. We also did chemical analyses, finding no risk. We sincerely do not believe that the plaintiff in this case was injured by our product, but if he was, by any chance, it was purely happenstance and nothing which could have been foreseen before the events leading up to this trial. I think that our witnesses will satisfy you that we are totally innocent and that we have no responsibility to the plaintiff, although we deeply feel and understand his needs. We trust that you, pursuant to your oaths, will judge the facts fairly and honestly, as all juries are asked to do, and in so doing, you will find our company, our client, totally without blame.

I am grateful for the opportunity to appear before you and this Honorable Court. The judge has granted to me and other defense counsel, who are not residents of your great state, the privilege of practicing law for the purpose of this case.

HAY: Ladies and Gentlemen of the Jury, my name is Hay, Robert Hay, and I am a sole practitioner with my offices in Decatur, Alabama. AAA Auto Services is a franchising company. We set up small dealerships and assist them in planning their financial and business affairs and give them guidance and perform various services for them. Until the commencement of this litigation, we knew nothing about the product in question except that it was highly recommended and frequently used in automobile repair services. The sealing of glass and windows in automobiles is just a small part of what we teach our franchisees to do. We do not require the franchisees to purchase their products through us. In the initial setup of a franchise, we give them catalogs and samples of products and explanations of the use of the products, and manuals which teach employees how to utilize the products and perform the services. I do not believe that I can add anything to the opening statements in addition to what has already been said, except that opening statements are not facts or evidence, as the Court will instruct you, so please keep an open mind. When eye-witnesses testify, I believe that you will reach the fair conclusion that we have not in any way caused the injury to Mr. Drake. I am grateful for your attention.

Trial Day

JUDGE: All other opening arguments, presentations, having been waived, Mr. Smith, you may call your first witness.

JOE: Thank you, Your Honor. I call the plaintiff, Willie Drake.

BAILIFF: Mr. Drake, do you swear to tell the truth, the whole truth, and nothing but the truth, so help you God. . . . Plaintiff nods his head, yes.

JOE: Mr. Drake, are you thirty-eight years old, married, with three young daughters, ages four, ten, and fifteen?

BAILIFF: Plaintiff says yes.

JOE: Do you live with your wife and children, and are you retired and unable to work?

BAILIFF: He says yes.

JOE: In the process of your employment, did you utilize Everlast Seals, this product which I am holding here in my hand, as a part of your work and employment?

BAILIFF: Plaintiff says yes.

JOE: Will you try to explain to us, please, as best you can, how the process worked.

DRAKE: (In a raspy low voice) Yes—I'll try. I would line up the glass edge with the surface to which it was to be attached, and then light the torch and put it to the end of the tube, like you are holding, and move the two together along the place to be sealed, and the tube softened and

melted and dripped along just as in welding. It filled the space at the edge of the glass. It dried very fast, and almost before I was at the end of the glass, it had begun to set up hard. Then I went to the other side of the glass and did the same thing again, sealing both sides.

JOE: Did you wear any protection?

BAILIFF: He nods yes.

JOE: What?

BAILIFF: He points to his eyeglasses.

JOE: Did you wear protective goggles?

BAILIFF: He says yes.

JOE: Did you wear anything else?

BAILIFF: He says no.

JOE: Did anyone instruct you to wear a mask or filter?

BAILIFF: He says no.

JOE: Tell us as best you can how you began to use and how you learned to use this product.

DRAKE: (Same voice) Some of us went up to Decatur to AAA and they showed us how to do it and we practiced. They compared this way to do it with previous ways that we had done and everyone agreed this was the better way. It made a better seal and it locked up quicker. We actually made two trips up there, one for a full day, and one for half a day. There were three of us in all.

JOE: How did your company come to get the product into your place of business?

DRAKE: (Same voice) We showed it to our boss and showed him how it worked, and he called up and had some telephone talks with the people in Decatur and they shipped a case of tubes to us.

JOE: Did you smell anything—any odor—as you were doing this welding?

BAILIFF: He says yes.

JOE: Was it a sweet smell?

BAILIFF: He says yes.

JOE: Did it make you cough or choke or upset your stomach or anything like that?

BAILIFF: He says no.

Joe: About how long had you been using that process?

BAILIFF: He holds up four fingers, and then five fingers.

JOE: Are you saying four or five years?

BAILIFF: He says yes.

JOE: When did you first begin to notice any difficulty?

DRAKE: (Same voice) At first I began to cough, but I didn't think it had anything to do with my job, maybe an allergy, or something like that. So, I kept on working and my cough got a little worse, but I didn't pay a whole lot of attention to it. It wasn't bad enough to stay off work. Besides, I was pretty healthy and pretty strong.

JOE: When did you first see a doctor?

BAILIFF: He holds up two fingers.

JOE: About two years ago?

BAILIFF: He says yes.

JOE: What did the doctor tell you?

LONGFELLOW: Objection, Your Honor—hearsay.

JUDGE: Sustained.

JOE: What did the doctor do for you?

BAILIFF: He points to his mouth.

JOE: Did he give you some medicine?

BAILIFF: He nods yes.

JOE: Did he give you any instructions?

LONGFELLOW: Same objection.

JUDGE: Overruled—he can tell what he did—not what he said.

JOE: Well, Mr. Drake, tell us what you did with the doctor's instructions.

DRAKE: (Same voice) He gave me two medicines. One was like blue water and I gargled it three times a day. The other was a pill that I took before I went to sleep at night.

JOE: Did it improve your cough?

BAILIFF: He says no.

JOE: How long before you went back to the doctor?

BAILIFF: He says three.

JOE: Months?

BAILIFF: He nods yes.

JOE: What happened then?

DRAKE: (Same voice) He put some instrument down my throat. I was mostly asleep. After that, he put me into a machine to make pictures of my throat and chest. After that, a few days later, I had surgery.

JOE: Since you had the surgery, have you been back to work?

BAILIFF: He nods yes.

JOE: About how long before you went back to work?

BAILIFF: He holds up two fingers.

JOE: Two months?

BAILIFF: He nods yes.

JOE: How long did you work after that?

BAILIFF: He holds up four fingers.

JOE: Four months?

DRAKE: (Same voice) About four months—off and on.

JOE: Was your condition getting worse?

LONGFELLOW: Objection, Your Honor. He doesn't have any medical background.

JUDGE: Well, he knows what was happening to him and that doesn't require medical skills. Overruled.

DRAKE: (Same voice) Much—very much worse.

JOE: Is this your usual voice, now?

BAILIFF: He nods yes.

JOE: Tell us what other problems you have had.

LONGFELLOW: Objection, Your Honor, unless limited in some fashion and tied to Everlast Seals.

JUDGE: I overrule your objection, but I instruct the witness that in his replies, he must talk about or tell about conditions which were related to his employment and not other kinds of health problems.

JOE: Mr. Drake, the Judge says that you can tell about the difficulties that came about relating to your work.

DRAKE: I began to lose my balance and I became unable to walk. Then I used a walker, and after that a wheelchair, and now I can hardly

stand up. I can't take a deep breath. Sometimes when I cough, I gasp and choke, and that happens, now, every day, particularly in the morning when I get up. I can't dress myself without help. I can't take a shower without help. My system just doesn't work well anymore, particularly in the bathroom. I can't pick up anything that's heavier than a couple of pounds. I can still feed myself at the table, but I can't reach out to pick up anything. I can still read the newspaper and watch the television, but not for long, I get too tired.

JOE: Do you hurt anyplace?

DRAKE: (Same voice) My chest hurts all the time, and when I turn or bend or lean over, my throat hurts too. Lately in some coughing spells, I have been spitting up blood and other stuff. That hurts.

JOE: Are you on disability?

LONGFELLOW: Object, Your Honor. Not material.

JOE: Your Honor, we want to show that he has been evaluated and determined to be disabled and that he is getting social security benefits on account of that.

JUDGE: That's not material. If you want to show it, bring in the experts. The jury will disregard Mr. Smith's comments altogether. The question of compensation or remuneration of disability is not before the court or the jury. I caution you, Mr. Smith, to be more careful in your comments.

JOE: Sorry, Your Honor.

Joe: Are you receiving any financial benefits from your employer from any of the defendants?

LONGFELLOW: Your Honor, same thing, not material, and Mr. Smith is just trying to create an issue before the jury that is not justified.

JUDGE: Agreed. Sustained. Enough of that line of questioning, Mr. Smith.

JOE: Mr. Drake, when was the last time you were able to have sexual relations with your wife?

LONGFELLOW: Objection, Your Honor. That's not material, and again, he is playing to the jury.

JUDGE: I overrule that objection. The relationship has something to

do with the quality of life and his health condition. Proceed, Mr. Smith.

JOE: Please answer, Mr. Drake.

BAILIFF: He shows two or three.

JOE: Mr. Drake, do you mean two or three years?

BAILIFF: He nods no.

DRAKE: (Same voice) I meant to say a year or so, maybe more; I'm not sure.

JOE: Your Honor, I believe that is all with the plaintiff at this time.

JUDGE: Mr. Longfellow, cross?

LONGFELLOW: Yes, Your Honor.

LONGFELLOW: Mr. Drake, let me say that I am certainly sorry for the condition that has beset you. None of the defendants is without a real concern for your health and your future. I will try to make my cross examination brief so that you will not be under too much strain. Did you ever make a complaint to your employers about your condition?

DRAKE: (Same voice.) Not at first.

LONGFELLOW: Why?

DRAKE: (Same voice) I didn't know at first that my coughing was coming from using those tubes.

LONGFELLOW: When did you first question that or think that it might be related to Everlast?

DRAKE: (Same voice) When my doctors told me that I had glass particles in my lungs.

LONGFELLOW: Your Honor, we object and move to strike the answer. That's hearsay.

JUDGE: Overruled. Proceed.

LONGFELLOW: What measures have you taken to cure your health or to find out exactly what your problem was?

DRAKE: (Same voice) After they took those pictures and looked down in my throat, I had the surgery, and some of my lungs were removed and a part of my throat. They took those samples to study them. Then they told me—

LONGFELLOW: Object, Your Honor, he cannot say what someone else said.

JUDGE: That's right, Mr. Drake. It's called hearsay. You cannot tell what somebody else said unless the defendant was there when it was said. So, try to keep your remarks to what you know or what you learned without telling what someone else said.

DRAKE: They showed me some samples and I looked through a magnifying glass and I could see what they had taken out, and some small dots. They took those same samples to some doctors at the University of Alabama in Birmingham, and I went there and they examined me too. Some chemical people came in. I sat in a conference, my wife and I, while the doctors talked with the chemists.

LONGFELLOW: You cannot say what anyone said at that conference, but what happened after that?

DRAKE: They did some experiments. They pumped some liquids into my lungs, like you would flush a toilet, and I gagged and choked and coughed it back up, and they did that five or six times while I was in the hospital, and I could breathe better. That lasted for just a little while, and then I began to fall back.

LONGFELLOW: You have worked with other fellows at your place of business and at that place up in Decatur, and nobody else ever had such a complaint, did they?

DRAKE: I don't know—I've heard some others got sick, too.

LONGFELLOW: Your Honor, I move to strike the last part.

JUDGE: The jury will disregard what he heard, and his answer is that he doesn't know.

LONGFELLOW: Mr. Drake, I know this has been a hard period for you, not only your illness, but this trial and all of the things taken together, and I don't want to keep you any longer, but I have one final question. Do you have, of your own knowledge, any information that would prove that the product was defective or dangerous?

BAILIFF: He shakes his head, no.

LONGFELLOW: That's all, and thank you very much.

Expert Witnesses

The plaintiff produced Dr. Magellan, a surgeon of the University of Alabama at Birmingham, and a Dr. Fredrickson who was a pulmonologist. They described the conditions which they found in Mr. Drake at the time of his entry into the hospital. They noted that he was having considerable breathing problems and irritation in the lining of the throat, and that there was some atrophy both in his esophagus and bronchial tubes. Radiologists did studies and concluded that there was a massive involvement in the deterioration of the lungs and that exploratory surgery was urgent. The surgery took place, involving the removal of approximate forty percent of the lung tissue, a small portion of the esophagus and the trachea, noting, further, that there was complete involvement of the lungs in atrophy and discoloration. Gross tissue examination reflected foreign bodies that were not recognizable except to the extent they were microscopic and firm. The Southeastern Research Institute of Alabama provided chemists and chemical testing and analyses on the foreign product and concluded that the foreign substance was glass, perhaps, also, with sand. The pulmonologist concluded in his analysis that the path of the foreign substance seemed to enter the body through the nasal passages as well as the oral cavity, that the upper levels of the lung were more congested and involved than the lower levels, from which he concluded that the products came through inhalation. Very little was developed by way of cross examination except to the extent that these experts had never seen a similar situation before, nor any other situation

comparable. In the cross examination of the chemist, it was discovered that the Institute, in the process of testing, infused vapors from the process of sealing into the nostrils of mice in substantial quantities, and that, almost immediately, lung problems developed in the mice, similar to those which had infected Drake.

For the defense, the chemist concluded in a similar fashion as the chemist for the plaintiff that the foreign product entered through inhalation, but he also determined that the process of burning and sealing did not give off any amounts of detectable glass or sand products. He concluded, therefore, that inhalation must have been related to something other than this burning process. A renowned physician from Mayo Clinic agreed that the surgery was necessary and the findings were similar, but that none of the individual substances that went into the sealing material was toxic. He also believed that Mr. Drake could have had substantially more relief and comfort through a tracheotomy and expanders inserted into the air passages. A biologist from Tokyo testified for the defense in respect to his observations relating to the product and the burning process, that he knew of no studies or investigations which were done prior to this trial, and his testing of the product before international distribution satisfied him that there were no potential considerations of damage or injury, and that the entire product was inert. Upon further cross examination by Mr. Smith of all of the defense professionals, they each confirmed that none of them had any knowledge, nor did their companies have any knowledge or investigation which would lead to the conclusion that any danger might exist for Mr. Drake; that, further, they regularly investigate and test products, and have an excellent record of refusing products that have risk.

An executive at Northington General Services testified, from his own personal knowledge, in regard to the application and the patent, and confirmed that no testing had been done and that Northington had no reason to believe that any harm or damage could come from the use of Everlast Seals. When asked if he knew of any other potential cause for Mr. Drake's condition, he responded that perhaps there were other procedures in AAA Services where he was dealing with glass products and suggested that the possibility of cutting and shaping glass could have produced this unfavorable

result. On cross examination he admitted that it was a simple theory and he had no foundation for it.

An executive of International Solvents explained in considerable detail the internal operations, the purchase of the license under the patent, the preparation and manufacture of Everlast Seals in accordance with the patent and the international distribution of the product. He said that International had never had any cause or justification or feeling that the product could damage anyone, that they did not feel it necessary to put a warning on the product, and did not do so, and never had cause at any time since distribution began to believe that anyone could be injured or damaged by Everlast Seals.

An executive of AAA Auto Services testified along the same lines as to knowledge, but also indicated that International Solvents had given instruction pamphlets in regard to the use of Everlast Seals, and they in turn purchased the product from International Solvents, marked up the price, and sold to the various operators that utilized it, making a profit on those transactions. They also admitted that they taught and trained the individuals who used the product, that they had employees who did similar work and did the teaching and training. On cross examination, however, the AAA executive did admit that fumes came forth from the process, that there was a sweet odor to the fumes, that occasionally users coughed or sneezed during the process, that they had recommended the use of goggles to protect the eyes, and never recommended that anyone use a mask or a filter and that they did not consider that necessary. They denied any knowledge of any other person being afflicted in the same fashion as Drake.

In Chambers

J UDGE SAMUELS: Gentlemen, we have just about reached the end of this case. Any motions which are still pending, with the exception of the one to be discussed, are hereby overruled, and exceptions are noted for each of you as to any adverse rulings which I have just made.

SMITH: Your Honor—

JUDGE: Please don't interrupt, Mr. Smith.

SMITH: But Your Honor, we cannot continue these proceedings in this fashion.

JUDGE: And why not?

SMITH: Because the court reporter is not present.

JUDGE: This is a discussion and no evidence is being taken. I don't believe we have need of a court reporter at this time. Besides, I don't appreciate having the press on my back. They want into this conference, too.

SMITH: Your Honor, with all humility, I do, and I am not prepared to proceed further in this case, off the record, but I insist that other than the remarks that you have just made and the rulings which you have just given, this must be on the record, and I do believe the press is entitled to be here.

JUDGE: Why are you being so difficult!

SMITH: Please forgive me, Judge Samuels, because you have certainly

shown me every possible courtesy in this case, but we are coming to a point now where Your Honor might rule adverse to the interests of my client, and we might be entitled to an appeal, and I think that the statements and the discussions in this conference need to be on the record.

JUDGE: Well, I disagree, and I so rule. We are here to discuss a subpoena that you have issued and your desire to take the testimony of Mr. Dollid, or some other executive, of the defense firm of Gimble & Dollid, a most unusual posture, in any sense of the word.

SMITH: Your Honor, I realize that. We may be in uncharted waters, but if Mr. Dollid is here in response to the subpoena, I want to question him on the stand and before the jury, and I made that known to all parties a long time ago. Perhaps my refusal to proceed was premature. I have no objection to having discussions, but Mr. Dollid is here as a witness, and if the Court will excuse him during the discussions, so that I can preserve him as a witness, we can continue without a court reporter.

JUDGE: Agreed.

LONGFELLOW: Judge, this sounds like a lot of foolishness to me. I can't image anything which Mr. Dollid could testify about in this case. He has not been involved in the preparation of the litigation, and knows little or nothing about it. He is a senior partner in our law firm, one of the founding fathers, a highly revered and respected practitioner, and I will resist in every possible way permitting Mr. Smith to embarrass him.

JUDGE: Mr. Smith, it's your turn, maybe the only turn you will get, but I am giving you the floor for you to tell me what possible use in this case you can make of Mr. Dollid from his own personal knowledge, and before you explain, let me make it very clear that I will fully protect attorney/client privilege for Mr. Dollid, and everyone in his law firm.

SMITH: Your Honor, that's fair enough.

Mr. Dollid is removed from the conference in chambers.

SMITH: I, too, have a great respect and admiration for Mr. Dollid. While I have never had a transaction with him, he is peerless at our Bar.

However, I am convinced, reasonably convinced, that Mr. Dollid and other members of his law firm have information which this court ought to hear about this very case. I want to interrogate him because he is the head of the law firm, and because he has been there a long time, as to some practices which may be both unethical and illegal.

LONGFELLOW: That's ridiculous.

JUDGE: Proceed, Mr. Smith.

MR. SMITH: Information has come to Mr. Adams and myself that could first disqualify every law firm appearing for the defendants; next, pierce the veil of privilege between attorneys and clients, and perhaps reflect criminality on the part of the attorneys in conjunction with their respective clients. I know that I need not cite to Your Honor the many cases and decisions where the attorney/client privilege does not apply when the attorney and the client are engaged in inappropriate or illegal activities, jointly.

JUDGE: That's a broad, brazen, and wild statement, but having said that, I am going to give you your opportunity, but we're going to have Mr. Dollid examined here in chambers, with your court reporter. Unless you can show something very substantial to support those generalities, I am not going to require that he take the stand.

LONGFELLOW: Your Honor, he has not said one specific thing. He continues with generalities. How are we supposed to prepare or deal with claims which have not been made a part of the record?

JUDGE: That's a good point, and at some point in the examination of Mr. Dollid, I may extend time or in fact rule out all or some portions of the testimony. At this point in time, I do not believe that Mr. Dollid is going to appear before the jury, but Mr. Smith is entitled to his chance. Please call Mr. Dollid and have him sit here, next to my desk.

Mr. Dollid returns and takes a seat next to the judge, and the court reporter assumes the position in front of Mr. Dollid, facing him, and administers the oath.

COURT REPORTER: Mr. Dollid, do you swear to tell the truth, the

whole truth, and nothing but the truth, so help you God?

DOLLID: Certainly, yes.

JUDGE: Mr. Smith, proceed, with caution.

SMITH: Mr. Dollid, I want to state and acknowledge for the record that you are one of the most outstanding attorneys ever to practice law in this jurisdiction, that you are highly regarded by the Bench and Bar alike, that you have led the great law firm of Gimble & Dollid for more years than I have been practicing law, and I appear before you humbly, and respectfully.

DOLLID: Thank you.

SMITH: Have you seen and examined the joint defense agreement entered into by all of the parties defended in this litigation and all of their lawyers.

LONGFELLOW: Your Honor, we object. We debated that point in chambers once before.

JUDGE: Yes, Mr. Longfellow, you are correct, but I have not ruled against it; yet, at this moment, I am not going to rule for it, either. Proceed, Mr. Smith.

SMITH: Mr. Dollid, my question was whether or not there is such an agreement, and if so, have you seen it?

DOLLID: There is such an agreement. Mr. Longfellow asked me to review it in a general way and I have read it.

SMITH: Did all of the lawyers appearing in this case sign it?

DOLLID: Yes.

SMITH: Did all of the defendants sign through a duly authorized representative or officer or director?

DOLLID: Yes.

SMITH: Does that agreement deal with facts and information related to the product known as Everlast Seals?

LONGFELLOW: Objection, Your Honor—he's going into the contents of the document.

SMITH: No, Your Honor, I have not asked for specifics, but only the general subject matter so that it can be related to this case.

JUDGE: Overruled; proceed.

SMITH: The Judge says you may answer the question.

DOLLID: Yes.

SMITH: Does the document deal with the components, the chemistry, of Everlast?

LONGFELLOW: Objection, Your Honor—the agreement is also a part of the privilege between attorney and client, and whatever that document says, it is privileged.

SMITH: Your Honor, generally, what Mr. Longfellow says is true, but before I proceed with another part of this interrogation, I want to show that all of the defendants and all of the lawyers acted in concert and dealt with this very sensitive part of the case, the risk features of Everlast.

JUDGE: Sorry, Mr. Smith, but you have not produced any testimony that would permit this court to rule that the defense agreement is not privileged.

SMITH: Your Honor, at least at the moment, will the Court indulge me by withholding the ruling as to whether or not the defense agreement is available as testimony before the jury, but since this is not within the hearing of the jury, the Court ought to know the contents to see if the contents are such that they should be presented to the jury.

JUDGE: Mr. Smith, I am just not going to give you any comfort about that, but I will agree, as you move onto another subject, to withhold any ruling of a final nature that says that the document is not, in and of itself, admissible.

SMITH: Thank you, Your Honor.

SMITH: Mr. Dollid, are you familiar with the custom in your law firm for an activity which is identified by the acronym—CONCLIFI?

LONGFELLOW: Your Honor, we object. This is a fishing expedition. He's not entitled to know the inner workings of our law firm.

JUDGE: Objection overruled—proceed, Mr. Smith.

SMITH: Mr. Dollid, the Judge says you can answer that.

DOLLID: I am.

SMITH: Were you familiar with that identification before you were invited to look into this lawsuit?

DOLLID: Yes.

SMITH: Will you explain to the Court what that acronym means, and what it signifies.

DOLLID: May I confer briefly with Mr. Longfellow?

JUDGE: Yes, we will have a ten minute recess.

Ten minute recess.

JUDGE: The last question posed to you by Mr. Smith, Mr. Dollid, was to identify and explain that acronym, and even before you object further, Mr. Longfellow, I overruled your objection at this point. That does not mean that I am going to admit as testimony, but I think this exploration is in order.

DOLLID: Those initials stand for "Confidential Client File."

SMITH: And Mr. Dollid, when does that apply or what effect does it have?

JUDGE: Yes, Mr. Longfellow—same ruling as before—proceed, Mr. Dollid.

DOLLID: We have a big law firm and some of the matters that we handle are extremely sensitive and we do not want them generally circulated throughout the law firm where other lawyers, or other personnel, might happen upon them, and thereby breach the confidence of attorney/client privilege.

SMITH: Where is the confidential client file related to the Drake case?

LONGFELLOW: We object, Your Honor.

JUDGE: Objection overruled.

DOLLID: I don't know.

SMITH: When did you last see it?

DOLLID: A week or ten days ago, after this trial started.

SMITH: Mr. Longfellow, do you have the file?

LONGFELLOW: Objection, Your Honor. I am not the witness.

JUDGE: Nevertheless, Mr. Longfellow, you are an officer of the court and you must answer that question.

LONGFELLOW: Yes, I have it, locked in my desk in my office.

SMITH: We would like for that file brought to Your Honor's desk.

JUDGE: Mr. Longfellow, send for the file, or go and get it. My ruling in this regard does not make it admissible, nor does it make any portion of it available to anyone in this room without your approval, at this time.

SMITH: Mr. Dollid, was that file at one time in this courtroom in connection with this trial?

DOLLID: I believe so.

SMITH: Do you know why it was removed?

LONGFELLOW: Again, an objection, Your Honor.

JUDGE: Overruled. Proceed.

DOLLID: Yes.

SMITH: Will you please tell the Court why the file was at one time here in the courtroom and has been removed?

DOLLID: When I read the file myself, several days ago, I felt that it was unsafe to leave such confidential information in the courtroom where someone might take it, improperly, or accidentally, and thereby breach the attorney/client relationship and privilege.

SMITH: Were you alarmed by what you saw in the file?

LONGFELLOW: Your Honor, we object to that—what is an alarm—he's asking for an emotional reaction.

JUDGE: Agreed. Sustained as to that question.

SMITH: Mr. Dollid, were you surprised or disappointed by anything you saw in that file?

LONGFELLOW: Same objection.

JUDGE: Same ruling.

SMITH: Mr. Dollid, obviously I do not need to remind you that this is testimony, under oath, and I know you respect the oath and this Court, but will you tell the Court if you found anything in that file that was illegal or unethical?

LONGFELLOW: Same objection.

JUDGE: Mr. Smith, divide that question.

SMITH: Yes, Your Honor. Mr. Dollid, did you find anything in that file that was unethical?

DOLLID: I'm not sure about that. I have not read the file with that question in mind, nor have I done any research.

SMITH: Well, Mr. Dollid, I think that is somewhat evasive, and I will come back to it, but I will now proceed to the second half of the question—did you find anything in there that was illegal?

LONGFELLOW: Your Honor, we object to that, and we ask for a brief adjournment.

JUDGE: No, proceed—Mr. Dollid, answer that question.

LONGFELLOW: Your Honor, may we have a brief recess?

JUDGE: Ten minutes.

Ten minute recess.

LONGFELLOW: I am not sure where this interrogation is leading, but it is embarrassing, and I would like to confer with my co-counsel, some members of my firm, and I also would like an opportunity to have further discussions with Mr. Smith about settlement.

JUDGE: Mr. Smith, what's your pleasure?

SMITH: Your Honor, it's getting late in the day. Mr. Adams and I will be available for settlement discussions beginning now, at any time between now and midnight, and if those prove not to be fruitful, I would appreciate adjourning until early tomorrow morning, before the jury is due to be here. I think they may attribute all this delay to me, and become impatient with me, when it is not at all my fault.

JUDGE: We are adjourned until seven a.m. tomorrow. I will inform the jury that they need not report until ten a.m. If you reach a settlement, inform me as soon as possible, including all hours of tonight. If you don't, and if midnight passes, we will proceed with this interrogation in my office and I will at that time make a ruling. For your benefit, Mr. Longfellow, I realize the serious consequences of the questions which have been asked, and I realize the embarrassment, and perhaps the disappointment that this matter is coming to light in this fashion, so please govern yourself accordingly during your negotiations. You, Mr. Smith, will remain, and I want you to explain to me, as best you can, how you reached this point and this conclusion. That conversation will be off the record.

Is that satisfactory with you, Mr. Longfellow, and all of the other defense attorneys?

ALL: Satisfactory, Your Honor.

JUDGE: Then we are adjourned until tomorrow morning, as indicated.

Judge and Lawyer

JUDGE: Joe, you put on quite a show. I hope you are not embarrassing yourself.

SMITH: No, Judge, I am quite comfortable in what I am doing, and this conference and this testimony have only added fuel to my concerns that my generalizations have a considerable amount of merit, and, now, I believe things may be more serious than I suspected in the first instance.

JUDGE: Would you care to tell me how you got onto the track of this?

SMITH: Judge, first let me say that I have a very high regard for you, and if I have misbehaved or if I have been overbearing, I deeply apologize. It's a tough case for me. Mr. Olive may have handled it differently. He doesn't even know about this aspect of the case, but I have reported it to Mr. Bates, and he has given me the green light to do as I see fit. I appreciate his confidence, but more than that, I appreciate the way you have treated me. I don't mind being reprimanded when I am out of line. I object to some of your rulings, but I chose not to debate those because I knew when I got to the real meat of this problem, the Court would begin to sense impropriety. Now, you have asked me how I got started on this line, and let me say that I would rather not reply at this time.

JUDGE: Why not?

SMITH: I'm young. I'm black. No black lawyer has higher standing in this community than I do, even though I am not a partner. I have come

a long way and I never have wanted to stumble, nor have I been satisfied simply to be equal to others. Yet, I am not a fool. I know that every word I say and everything I do are held up to the shining light of the sun and scrutinzed. Let me give you an example. In that last ten minute adjournment, I went to the men's room, and I heard Mr. Longfellow say to one of his associates—"I'll get that black son of a bitch." I know that I am confronted not only with vigorous and competent resistance on the other side, but I am also aware that they are looking over my shoulder all the time. The details of what you have asked me are known only to Adams and myself. In an abundance of caution, I have said to E.Z. that I consider him my lawyer, that he is representing me, if necessary, and that he will represent me if necessary, and that we will make financial arrangements later. I guess that creates an attorney / client privilege, although some of the information was known to him separate and apart from what he has learned by discussions with me. So, I have no doubt whatsoever about Your Honor's integrity, but I could be prejudiced if some conflict arose and you were called upon to testify about the substance of this discussion.

JUDGE: Well, that's a pretty smart idea and I agree with you. I was just trying to be helpful. I don't know what you stirred up, but I imagine you are going to be getting some substantial offers. You need to be very sure, all along the way, that your primary concern is for Mr. Drake. He's a sick man. He's not long for this world. He's leaving a wife and three children. Every dollar could be very, very important to him.

SMITH: Judge, don't think for a minute that that is not my greatest concern. There were many times during the trial when, visible or not, I was terrified. I realize that some of my expert witnesses did not stand up as well as I had hoped, and I probably could have done a better job of cross examining theirs. Mr. Olive certainly would have. I don't know what would happen to my career, but I know what would happen to me as a person if I walked away from this case drawing a blank, leaving Mr. Drake and his family with nothing. On the other hand, the only offers they have made so far was to pay all of his medical expenses to date and pay half again of that as legal fees. I turned that down, cold, flat. In trying

to evaluate this case for Mr. Olive and others, in our trial conference, we all agreed that this case could not go for less than a million dollars. That was before I had all the weapons which I think I have today.

JUDGE: Don't get too ambitious. A million dollars is a lot of money.

SMITH: I certainly realize that. My total net worth today is not even $50,000, so I can imagine what one could do with $1,000,000. On the other hand, I know that the hospitals and doctors are going to be coming after their money by asserting lien claims, so after legal fees, it will come off the top, and I am sure that what's left will not be enough for him to live in minimum comfort, or to take care of his children or to educate them.

JUDGE: Joe, I am very much aware of the fact that there is hovering in the background more cases like this and class actions, probably. There may be a tendency on your part to try to hit a home run in this case so that the defendants will be more willing to settle and deal with a class action, but that's not something that you can afford to weigh in representing Mr. Drake.

JOE: You are exactly correct there. In fact, we discussed that at length in the office and with other attorneys who have cases, and are withholding other claims pending the outcome of our case. Everyone knows that Mr. Olive and I are free agents in this case and to this client, and it is a heavy burden. If we blow it on some technical ground, or some lack of preparation, we may have destroyed the rights of others. In other words, we are aware and we are cautious, but the Court can be assured that Drake is our only concern. We are going to win, lose or settle, for him.

JUDGE: One other matter. You are a good young attorney. You have seasoned well. You could be a role model for other black lawyers coming along. That's also a heavy burden, and I am sorry that you have been offended in the past, or that you were offended by what Mr. Longfellow had to say. I'm surprised at him, too. You have a good career ahead of you and I am sure that partnership is on the horizon.

JOE: Yes, I'm pretty certain of that, but I want to share something with you, very privately so you will understand me a little better. I love the practice of law. I love trial work, but I don't feel fulfilled at what I'm

doing. So much of what a young lawyer has to do coming up is aimed at producing hours and money. I didn't realize that when I decided to be lawyer. I thought it was more of an adventure, like Sir Lancelot, that I would be out there doing great things for people. I have also had a lot of experience with people in trouble, not just criminals, but financial trouble and family trouble, and things like that. I think I could be helpful there. I have a friend who is doing that, and she feels very rewarded and successful. I might even like to teach.

JUDGE: Young man, I know that you are going to be successful and good at whatever you undertake to do. If ever you are going to make a career change, do it sooner, rather than later, because when you have a family and a home and things like that, you begin to lose your flexibility and your mobility because of the commitments which you take on for yourself. Good luck, tonight. I'll see you in the morning. At least you can sleep from twelve to six, and I'll see you at seven.

Cindy's Turn

DOLLID: Cindy, Mr. Longfellow and I need to talk to you in a very serious vein. We are right now asking for your resignation, and we want you to pack your things, your belongings, and leave the office today.

CINDY: Goodness, what have I done?

LONGFELLOW: You have breached our confidentiality and you have embarrassed the law firm.

CINDY: I don't understand. Please tell me what you think I have done that is wrong.

DOLLID: We are in the course of a serious trial in which it is clear to us that you have made available to other people confidential material from our client.

CINDY: I've done no such thing. I don't know what you are talking about. If I have slipped up and made a mistake in some fashion, I want to know what it is.

LONGFELLOW: Don't you have the slightest inkling of why you are here and why you are going to be gone?

CINDY: No, I don't. Please tell me.

DOLLID: What is your relationship with Joe Smith, the attorney with Olive & Bates?

CINDY: Gosh, I don't know how that's involved, but I've known Joe since both of us were children. He worked for my father at our home.

LONGFELLOW: Of course, but you know he's an attorney.

CINDY: Yes, I do.

LONGFELLOW: You know that he's with Olive & Bates.

CINDY: Yes, I do.

LONGFELLOW: Are you aware of the Drake case?

CINDY: No, what's that?

DOLLID: Please don't play games with us, Cindy. This is more serious than you might think at the moment.

CINDY: Look, I'm confused. You are threatening me. You are accusing me. I don't have the slightest idea what you are talking about. Joe Smith is a good friend of mine and has been for many years. My father helped him get his education. My father recommended him to Olive & Bates because that was the law firm that performed services for my family. What else can I tell you?

DOLLID: You have probably told us enough, but you are not forthcoming, not very truthful. We are very much aware of the fact that Mr. Smith has access to our very confidential files, and that he could not have gotten those without your assistance.

CINDY: Mr. Dollid, I truly don't know what you are talking about. Joe and I very rarely discuss each other's business. He's in a different kind of law. He does nothing but trial work. I do nothing but domestic relations. Tell me, please, specifically, what it is that I am accused of doing.

LONGFELLOW: In the pending case of Drake versus Northington General Services and other defendants, in which we are involved, Mr. Smith has produced information which can only come from you having to do with our confidential file in that case, and the fact that we have such confidential files.

CINDY: Well, I don't want to be impertinent, but none of that makes any sense to me. I didn't know Joe was trying a case. I don't know what the case is all about. I have given him nothing and told him nothing. I haven't even seen him for a few weeks, and the last time we just had lunch together when we ran into each other at the courthouse.

DOLLID: Well, frankly, we just don't believe you. There's not another

way he could have gotten that information except through someone internally here in our office. There are very few people who know about the defense of this case, and you would be his only contact. Nothing you can say is going to alter these facts or our conclusions.

CINDY: Did Joe tell you this?

LONGFELLOW: No, it's just obvious.

CINDY: Naturally I am very uncomfortable, first of all, even being in the presence of two of the most senior members of this law firm. I have never had any professional dealings with either one of you. I have a good record with this law firm. I have regularly received good reports from my supervising attorneys, and I have been told that I am properly on track for partnership.

DOLLID: I don't know what has happened in the past. We have not reviewed your file because all of that doesn't matter.

CINDY: Mr. Dollid, aren't you concerned at all about me? You are putting my whole career on the line for something that I didn't do and about which I know nothing.

LONGFELLOW: Like Mr. Dollid said, it doesn't matter. He wants you to pack up and get out and we are calling for your resignation.

CINDY: In all humility, I am not going to resign. That suggests that I want to leave and I don't. It infers that I might have done something wrong, and I haven't. Fire me, if you insist, but don't ask me to take responsibility or suffer guilt when I have no guilt. I just cannot imagine being discharged under these circumstances, but I certainly recognize that I don't have a contract. But, if you are going to fire me for an unjustified cause, I don't propose to suffer any negative consequences from that. Whatever I have to do, I'll do. Again, I don't want to be impertinent. I love my job. I love this law firm. I have been thrilled with the practice of law, but I don't need to work for a living. My family is pretty comfortable. My earnings are pretty good. I can get a job elsewhere, and when I apply, I will expect this law firm to give me a favorable recommendation, and if you don't, you will hear from me again.

This is a disgrace and you are being unfair. Nevertheless, when your

dismissal letter hits my desk, I'll begin clearing out. Shame on both of you.

LONGFELLOW: Your attitude is pretty much like your friend, Joe. Both of you are arrogant and we feel like we are able to run this law firm and we will be able to continue to manage it successfully without you. You'll get your letter.

Cindy and Joe—Dismissal

CINDY: Joe, I'm sorry to bother you at your home, but I am really upset.

JOE: What is it, honey?

CINDY: I've just been fired.

JOE: For what?

CINDY: I don't know.

JOE: Tell me about it.

CINDY: I really don't know. Mr. Dollid and Mr. Longfellow called me into a conference and insisted that I resign and they wouldn't give me any details.

JOE: Tell me what they said.

CINDY: It was something about you and a lawsuit involving someone named Drake.

JOE: Now I know. Don't do anything rash. In the next few days, you and I will sit down and talk about the whole situation, but believe in me and trust me.

CINDY: But they've accused me of dishonesty, unethical behavior, and things like that.

JOE: You are not guilty of a damn thing. They're just pushing you to try to get to me, and I promise you, I swear to God, those two guys are going to be punished for even discussing this matter with you.

CINDY: Joe, are you in trouble?

JOE: I really don't think so. We are about to settle a case, and I cannot talk to you about any details until after that.

CINDY: What shall I do?

JOE: Nothing. Unless they fire you, just go to work as usual. If they try to do anything to you or embarrass you, pick up your pocketbook and walk out. Please don't sign anything until you and I get a chance to talk about it.

CINDY: It's going to be miserable around here.

JOE: But not for long. Please believe me. I could be wrong, but I think I'm about to teach Mr. Longfellow a lesson or two, and I already know that he hates my guts, but I assure you that he is not in a position to take it out on you or punish you for anything which he thinks I've done. Stand pat.

CINDY: Okay, Joe, but I'm scared.

JOE: Don't be. I've never let you down. You have always been the most important person in my life. I would go to hell for you. I am not going to let anything unpleasant happen to you.

CINDY: Should I talk to my dad?

JOE: Not yet, please. Just be patient for a few days and I will call you as soon as I am free.

CINDY: But I don't want anything to happen to you, either.

JOE: We'll talk about that, too. You know I love you.

CINDY: Me, too. Call me.

Seven A.M. Conference

JUDGE: I appreciated your call last night and I am thrilled that you have reached a mutually satisfactory conclusion. I would like to hear from all of you and I would like to know what your recommenda tions and instructions are in regard to the jury.

JOE: Your Honor, I will outline, in a preliminary fashion, the basic terms of the settlement. I have some notes that we made last night, but I have not reduced them to writing, and I am confident that Mr. Longfellow will want us to have an exhaustive and detailed agreement in regard to many things. Here's the deal:

First, the defendants will decide among themselves the question of contributions and participations, and in consultation with their insurance companies.

Second, they will immediately reimburse the plaintiff for all expenditures of any nature related to his illness, which he had to pay, and, also, they will pay all bills, charges, and costs that have been assessed but not paid, including hospitals, doctors, and insurance companies who have made payments to providers.

Third, in like fashion, they will, upon signing the agreement, pay the sum of $1,000,000 to the plaintiff, for pain, injury, suffering, etc., in a fashion that it will not be taxable income.

Fourth, they will purchase an annuity from an insurance company with the highest possible rating, and subject to our approval, which will

pay $10,000 a month to the plaintiff as long as he lives, the same $10,000 per month to his wife, as long as she lives, or until the youngest child has completed up to four years of college, and after the arrival of that event, $7,500 per month to his wife, as long thereafter as she shall live. All of this will be characterized as payments for his pain and suffering, on an installment basis, with the agreement that I will be permitted to draft the language to protect the family against tax consequences, as best I can.

Fifth, the defendants will in like fashion pay all costs and expenses incurred in these proceedings including the actual costs of court, depositions, expert witnesses, travel, reproduction, just everything. We are to supply an itemized list of those advances, and they will reimburse our law firm.

Sixth: They will pay our law firm attorney's fees in the amount of $3,000,000.

Finally, Mr. Longfellow's firm will, from whatever resources it chooses, endow a professorship at the University of Alabama Law School in the amount of $5,000,000, which they may handle as they see fit, and as a contribution, if they chose to do so, and the endowment will designate that the selection of the professor, from time to time, will be initiated by the University Administration with the approval of the then serving dean, and the senior member of my law firm. As long as the chair is vacant, all of the income may be used for salaries and expenses of professors and instructors in the law school, and to the extent that the chair does not require the use of all of the income in any calendar year, it may likewise be used for other salaries and compensations within the law school. I believe that's the essence of the agreement.

JUDGE: Mr. Longfellow.

LONGFELLOW: Yes, Your Honor, that is the basic substance of the agreement from a financial standpoint. There are other aspects which are of equal importance to the defendants and the parties. I likewise made notes of those aspects which deal with things other than money. All the parties expect to accomplish in a detailed writing the following:

1. A written settlement agreement to be approved and executed by

the plaintiff's law firm, Mr. Smith, the plaintiff, his wife, all of the law firms involved in the defense, and all of the defendants. This will be a confidential memorandum that will not be filed in court. The substance of the agreement may not be made available under any circumstances to anyone, without severe penalties against the guilty party.

2. No other lawsuits will be filed or participated in or referred by Mr. Smith, his law firm, or any member of his law firm, whether for individuals or classes.

3. Upon execution of the document, the appropriate parties will have thirty days in which to make all of the payments except the first million dollars to the plaintiff and the reimbursement of the plaintiff's out of pocket medical costs. Within the thirty days, all of the rest of the monetary commitments will be accomplished, including obtaining the annuity.

4. The jury will be dismissed with a statement from the Court, as the Court may choose, that the parties have gotten together and have settled and compromised, and that all parties are, of course, grateful to the jury for their service and for helping to bring about this disposition

5. Finally, we would like to ask the Court to use its utmost abilities and talents to secure the confidentiality of this disposition. That's all.

JUDGE: As to the last item, you can be assured of my good faith, and I certainly understand the sensitivity of various aspects, and I will do everything within my power to protect the settlement from disclosure, without, any guarantees, of course, and obviously, if any of the parties to the confidentiality agreement are put under subpoena or are required to be witnesses, including myself, then the party seeking to avoid those consequences will have an ample opportunity to resist and protect, whatever and however that might come about.

JOE: Your Honor, this is about where we got up hung up last night. True, we have resolved financial aspects. Let me respond to Mr. Longfellow, and I am about to make some concessions which he will hear for the first time. As to the document, generally, I agree, obviously subject to the right of myself and my law firm to review. I certainly join

the request to the Court in respect to the termination of the jury. The thirty day delay is satisfactory. The general concept of confidentiality, subject to those comments which the court made, will be satisfactory. I will not commit my law firm against representing other plaintiffs similarly situated, or participating, or even leading in class actions in respect to Everlast Seals. We are just not going to agree to that and, not only that, I believe it would be unethical and certainly inappropriate for there to be such an agreement or a requirement. It probably would be against public policy. As for myself, however, and this is a major concession, I will agree for the rest of my career to avoid my personal involvement in any litigation regarding this product. Further than that, I will not go.

LONGFELLOW: Your Honor, that's just not satisfactory with us. We're paying a tremendous amount of money here and we don't want that or anything in this case to encourage other people to initiate litigation, and our insurance carriers have urged this provision.

JOE: I would hate for this settlement to rise or fall on that issue, but we stand pat. We will not agree to that. In a further effort, however, I want to outline a thought process, and I have not given much consideration to it, but at least it's on the table for discussion.

I know that you are very much concerned about the confidentiality of the law firm's file, and I am assuming that your law firm, all the defense counsel, and all of the parties, either have the same file or similar files. If that assumption is correct, then there may be no need for the utilization of your special confidential file in other cases. We will then expect that your law firm, Mr. Longfellow, having been the focal point of this particular issue, will not defend any of these defendants in any other actions for injury or damages relating to the product. Our law firm cannot avoid sharing the existence of that file with other attorneys who have been observing our progress in this case and who undoubtedly intend to pursue litigation on the same basic facts. It naturally follows, then, that whoever defends these defendants in future cases will have witnesses who will testify truthfully, or who will be fully informed about what has transpired in respect to the product. In effect, you simply lose

the position which was illegal and improper in the beginning. That file only protected the secrecy of something which never should have been a secret at all, at least not in depositions and trial testimony.

LONGFELLOW: Well, that approach is going to need some further discussion.

JUDGE: Fine. We have over an hour before we need to concern ourselves about the jury, but I want everyone to stay together until this is resolved. Let's start with a ten-minute break, and defense counsel may use my private office, and we will remain here in this conference room. Adjourned.

Ten minutes later.

LONGFELLOW: Your Honor, we have agreed to this final modification, with one exception. We want an affidavit from Mr. Smith and his law firm that they do not have any copies, records or memos, relating to our confidential file.

SMITH: That's fine. We don't have that, and I have no objection to making that affidavit.

LONGFELLOW: Then tell me how you came to know the contents of the file, or even the existence of it.

SMITH: I won't answer that.

LONGFELLOW: You are just a stubborn ass.

SMITH: True. Having said that, however, and in view of the special animosity that Mr. Longfellow seeks to visit on me, I am going to add another condition, that in the settlement agreement, all of the parties defendant, and all of their counsel, will give a very general and broad form release to me and to Mr. Adams covering any cause, thought, suggestion or possibility of a claim against either of us.

LONGFELLOW: Why should we do that when you are not willing to respond to our inquiry about how you got into our file in the first place.

SMITH: It doesn't matter. I am not going to discuss your file with you. I have said I will make an affidavit. This case will not be settled without the release which I have just required.

LONGFELLOW: Well, we are prepared to do it, and we will draft it and try to have it available to you by tomorrow, but just remember that the world keeps turning, and your time will come, too.

JUDGE: Let's have none of that. We have an agreement. I understand it. If necessary, I will participate in the drafting of the approving. I will dismiss the jury as you have requested. I want you to know, however, that I am going to take a very serious and dim view if this agreement is not reduced to a mutually satisfactory writing by sunset tomorrow. Now I have a technical problem to deal with, and my priority is first.

There is at least some kind of remote possibility that something will come up or that you will change your minds, or that you will fail to consummate this agreement. I will be left without a jury. So, I am going to present to you a joint declaration for all defense counsel to sign, agreeing to waive the trial by jury and permit the Court to serve as jury, finder of facts, and the ability to render a judgment. I am not going to let the financial aspect of this settlement get away from us. I will award the same financial aspects to which you have already given your consent. I will not be able to create a settlement or confidentiality document for you. Is that agreeable to everyone?

Hearing no objection, if you will wait about fifteen minutes, I will doctor up my usual form of jury waiver and have it available for your signature. I want someone here from every law firm to sign on. Good luck, gentlemen.

Joe and E.Z.

JOE: I'm sure the dust has not completely settled, yet, but I have gotten a lot of telephone calls of congratulations and a multitude of inquiries.

E.Z.: So have I, and in fact, a lot of the people who work in this law firm are curious and want more information. I have simply said that we have a confidentiality agreement and when they say that a confidentiality agreement does not mean that it's confidential within the law firm, I tell them to talk to you, Joe.

JOE: Yes, I've had a lot of that, too. I know that the storm clouds are gathering and we haven't heard the end of this, but at least we delivered a magnificent result to our client. His family is thrilled. They are financially secure. He won't live long, but he will live in peace and with the comfort that he need not worry about the financial future of his family. In fact, he told me when I gave him his first check that he hoped his wife would see fit to marry again, if the right guy comes along. I think that's a pretty brave statement for a fellow who knows he's dying.

E.Z.: Have you heard from the Bar Association?

JOE: Yes, but informally. An attorney called me and asked for an appointment to discuss a recent complaint, and I told her to call me after the first of the month. She didn't seem impatient.

E.Z.: What do you think the complaint is, and who do you think filed it?

JOE: I don't have any doubt who filed it—either Longfellow, or his client, or someone at his instructions. I know that he has been terribly embarrassed by the exposure, and he assumes that it is his total responsibility, even though his law firm is equally at fault. He hates my guts, so he's the natural culprit, but I have no idea what the charges might be. But, I want to remind you that you are my friend, and you have been my attorney and I want to continue to consider you my attorney so that everything that you and I know, to the maximum extent possible, can continue to be privileged. I will want you to go to the hearings with me, but I'm working out my own game plan, and I'm probably going to speak for myself.

E.Z.: You know what they say about a lawyer who represents himself.

JOE: Yes, and it's probably true, but I just don't want to infect anyone else with the problem, and I certainly don't want our law firm to appear to be a part of the problem.

E.Z.: Well, let me know when something develops and you can be sure I'll be with you. I think you did a marvelous job under most difficult circumstances, and I wish that the files were not sealed and that we didn't have a confidentiality agreement because I would like to brag about the results that you got.

JOE.: That time might come. Let's get back over to the office and see if we can get a chance to visit Mr. Olive.

The Book Award:
First Student Meeting

Present: Tom Brown, Harry Blackmun, Jr., Douglas Chancellor, Esther Halevi, and A. J. Kay.

TOM: Thank you for coming. For myself I have decided on a course of action and inquiry to try to win the book award in Professor Smith's class. I have a general idea that I want to share with you. All of us were together that wonderful evening, at the beginning, and had some personal moments with the Professor and his lady friend. I think we would make a good team. We have many different backgrounds, colors, religions, and so we would be quite representative of the whole class. More than that, though, I have felt that we have sort of grown together since that experience, and maybe we could be the best team in the class. So, if you want to sign on, I am anxious for you to do so. I don't mind serving as the coordinator. If any of you want to join me, this is an invitation. If you don't, honestly, I'll understand, but I will tell you that I think it ought to be a lot of fun.

HARRY: Count me in.

DOUGLAS: Me, too.

ESTHER: I will do what I can, and I really do appreciate being invited. At the beginning, I decided to skip the challenge because I have a lot of personal problems, including economics, but I would love to be a part of you guys; so, I'm on board.

A.J.: I think this is a great idea. Whether we win or not, we can have a lot of fun, and I look on this as an occasion when we can become permanent friends, not only because we have been classmates, but because we did a project together. Over my lifetime I have been able to join in some very important personal relationships and I still have friends from my grammar school days. I like to stay in touch. When our law school years are over, we will probably go in many different directions, but I think it would be great if we stayed in touch. Besides, having lived in Tuscaloosa and having my family here gives me a leg up on some other people who might not have the same contacts.

TOM: Since you didn't know exactly what this was all about, I want to tell you some thoughts that I have had and then you can add to them and then we can divide up the responsibilities. My first question was why he made this challenge at this time. Obviously he is aging and may be nearing retirement and he wanted to try something new, or, I suspect there is some information out there that he does not want to tell, or cannot, that he would still like to have made public. Remember how strongly he emphasized that he had given us all that he would give us, so I assume that there is a lot more, but the lot more may be something that he could not tell us. He's just using this as a tool to improve us as lawyers, making us competent investigators, but I truly believe he has another motive.

A.J.: I agree with that, and I know that I will enjoy it. In fact, I was talking to my father a few weeks ago and commenting favorably about Smith as a professor and a person, and my father was curious to see how he got such a powerful position in the law school at such a young age. My father knew that he had been a successful young lawyer, but never made partner in his law firm. My father is a substantial contributor to the University, and to the law school. Maybe that's why I was accepted. I am just suggesting that I might have some contacts here that would be valuable in doing the research.

HARRY: You know I smell a race issue involved here. There was quite a battle before any black people were admitted to the University, and likewise as to the law school. Here we have someone of a not very mature

age or experience suddenly becoming a professor, being black notwith-standing. I'd like to pursue that angle.

ESTHER: Well, I haven't thought about it, but Harry's thought gives me an idea. My background has kept me involved with Jewish agencies, some of whom were engaged in civil rights matters, and I've heard a lot of interesting stories about the civil rights days and how black people were treated. I might make some inquires in those directions.

TOM: Good idea, both of you.

DOUGLAS: Well, I'm still the loner, an outsider, perhaps a renegade, so you guys are going to have to put up with me. I know I'm a complicated personality, but I promise you that it is part of my defense mechanism. This is a great pleasure to me because I don't ever remember anyone inviting me in to participate on an equal basis, like this. Maybe in our investigation there has to be some head knocking and butt kicking, and I'm probably the one for that job because I really don't care a whole lot about what most people think about me. I haven't had many friends in my life, so this is going to be a new experience, and I will learn from you about life and togetherness, while I am trying to help our cause. If I were to win the book, with you, I think it would be one of the greatest accomplishments of my life.

TOM: Well, enough said for the moment. I suggest that we each do a little bit of thinking and planning and discover avenues of investigation and inquiry and then come back together and talk more in detail. I don't want time to get away from us so how about next Saturday afternoon.

ESTHER: I'm sorry, but I have to work.

A.J.: There is a football game.

TOM: How about Sunday?—No objections?—Okay, let's meet back here next Sunday at two p.m., and this time let's all bring our legal pads and begin to put our thoughts down on paper.

Second Student Meeting

Sunday, two p.m.

TOM: Thanks for your calls and your notes and your comments because I think we have created a huge agenda that we will never be able to accomplish while going to school and trying to live our private lives. I have come to the conclusion that we need to pick and choose those most salient directions and pursue them and then get back together someplace down the line and see what we have and where there might be some gaps. Please permit me, as your chairman, to make these assignments and if I ask you to do one that you don't want, say so and we will pass along. Those that remain will be mine to look at and try to deal with or even make other assignments. Incidentally, I want to do this within this close-knit group. It's our project. There are others who are competing and I certainly don't want to exchange any information that we have. I hope you agree.

The first issue has to do with the courts. Obviously there was a case, and some kind of hearings, and some kind of records that ought to be public or located. Doug, how about you running in that direction.

DOUGLAS: Fine.

TOM: Esther, I know that you are busy, but maybe you can make some calls or write some letters and let's find out if some of the defense organizations got involved in it because of the race question.

ESTHER: I can do that. I am on the junior district board of the ACLU, and I am also doing some work for the antidefamation league and the American Jewish Committee. I guess I have fallen into the personal commitment of fighting for minority rights. While my first emphasis was, of course, on behalf of Jews, I have come to learn that blacks, and others, have suffered equally, or worse. Incidentally, there were Jewish civil rights being litigated and fought for long before anyone took on the plight of blacks. Yes, I can handle that.

TOM: Harry, how about you starting with some individuals, Cindy, first, perhaps members of her family, maybe even some of her friends from her law firm where she used to work, and see if can head up something with the NAACP.

HARRY: Great, that's me.

TOM: A.J., you are ideal for this. Let's see what we can find out about the University and the job. Maybe you or your dad can find someone inside who can get us the employment contract, something like that. I thought of a more direct way if you cannot turn up something valuable, and that is for all of us as a committee to try to get a conference with the President of the University and tell him exactly what we are trying to do and solicit his assistance. That may be a little bit on the arrogant side, and I doubt that anyone else in the class would even think of approaching him, but, it's a way to go. Incidentally, I am sure that all of you are as aware as I am that we are about to be confronted with some final examinations, and, after all, that's what we are here about. I don't think we are going to have a whole lot of time in the next couple of weeks. If someone stumbles onto something really big, let's call a meeting, but if not, let's each try to fit in some time during the next couple of weeks just to make a start. I am willing to bet that when we get together next time, the experiences which we will have had and the information which we exchange will begin to multiply.

My wife and I are going to a spaghetti dinner at our church tonight, and it's an open gathering where we can have guests. If any of you can come, I would like to invite you now. It's a free meal, and a pretty good one, but I am sure there will be a charity plate somewhere if anyone is so

inclined. It is certainly not required. The reason I think you would be interested is because the pastor has begun a series on interfaith and interracial issues and the impact on our church. Food is served at six p.m. It's the big church over on 15th Street. Come one, come all. We'll be able to get a table together. Good afternoon, and, again, thanks.

Harry and Cindy

ARRY: Mrs. Ragsdale, thank you so very much for agreeing to see me. I know how busy you are and I can see that there are people waiting outside to hire you. I would have been glad to meet you in the evening or come to your home or any place or any time, but since you have granted me a midday appointment, here I am.

CINDY: Yes, I'm intrigued about why you are here. I think you said you wanted to talk about Joe. He is almost everything in my life, and if there is any problem about him or around him, I want to be a part of the solution.

HARRY: No, not that way. It's not a problem, at all. He gave us an assignment and challenged us to do some investigations and I have been assigned to inquire into some matters by visiting with you.

CINDY: He very rarely tells me anything about what goes on in the classroom. I do get to meet a few, like you, in the social environment at our home, or occasionally we will run into someone on the street from his classes, but for the most part, he lives in his world and I live in my world until the two worlds become one. But, go on.

HARRY: Let me make it plain that the Professor neither instructed me to visit with you nor indicated that I should not, but he doesn't know that I am here.

CINDY: Well, then, don't tell me anything or ask me anything that

you wouldn't want me to pass along back to him.

HARRY: I don't mind that. He issued a challenge to our class, and five of us classmates have joined together to meet the challenge. Naturally everyone who comes to his classes has had the same curiosity as to how he became such an eminent professor and such a well-renowned scholar, having started here at a very young age, and having been the first black professor ever on the Alabama Law School staff. The challenge that he gave us was to investigate, to research and see what we could find out about how he ended up in this position.

CINDY: That part is easy. He always wanted to be a teacher. He always wanted to help people, and I think he loves the Constitution as much as he cares for me, so he was a natural Constitutional Law professor.

HARRY: That's not what I mean—what got him out of the practice of law and into the classroom?

CINDY: I'm going to be honest with you. There's a lot about that that I don't know. I've never pursued him for the information. We were already dear friends. He had something that upset him and he had some arguments with some attorneys and conflicts with the bar association, and he decided that he would be happier as a teacher.

HARRY: Are you familiar with what he calls the Drake case?

CINDY: I certainly am. That part I know, firsthand, not because Joe told me. The trial was in progress and settlement discussions were apparently in progress, and the head of our law firm, Mr. Dollid, and the lawyer trying the case, Mr. Longfellow, called me at the close of business and fired me. They didn't tell me any reason. They did ask some questions about Joe and my relationship with him. They suggested that I had been dishonest or unethical. They first asked me to resign, and I wouldn't, so they simply terminated me. I called Joe, late at night, and he was at his office preparing settlement negotiations, but I interrupted him. He listened to my story and he was very sympathetic, and he assured me that nothing was going to happen to me, and that I was not guilty of anything, and I should simply refuse to resign or to sign anything, and that matters would clear up and go away. After the case was settled, and there was apparently a lot of animosity in connection with that, I asked

Joe, again, what it was all about. He told me that he was under a confidentiality agreement, and he wanted to abide by that, but that he had clarified anything that would have reflected unfavorably on me. That's the end of what I know.

HARRY: What happened with the Bar Association?

CINDY: I don't know a lot about that, either, because those discussions and conferences and hearings and reviews and appeals all were confidential and excluded from the public because, apparently, there were some rules about such actions in the bar association. I received a call from a young lady, and I didn't remember her name, and I don't, now, but she wanted to interview me in connection with those proceedings involving Joe, and I refused. I'm sure that's what Joe wanted me to do. I'm also sure that if he wanted me to be helpful, and if I could be helpful, he would not have hesitated to call me into the picture.

HARRY: How long after the Drake case did the bar proceedings begin?

CINDY: I'm not sure—a few weeks—perhaps a month or so.

HARRY: How long did the bar proceedings last?

CINDY: I don't remember that, either, but I know there were some appeals that finally ended up in the Supreme Court, but Joe was completely exonerated.

HARRY: How do you know that?

CINDY: I shouldn't say that I know that, but I am very confident that Joe was exonerated. Sometime later, a member of the Board of Bar Commissioners was introduced to me at a function where Joe was present, too, and the Commissioner and I ended up talking to each other, away from other people, and he told me what a great lawyer and a great gentleman Joe was, and that he could have been one of the greatest trial lawyers in the state. I'm sure he would not have said that to me if he had some reservations about Joe's character or behavior.

HARRY: How long after the Bar proceedings did Joe practice law?

CINDY: He really didn't. Because of the bar proceedings he had substantially curtailed his practice and was phasing out most of his cases, although he continued to have offices at Olive & Bates. It was shortly, immediately, after the termination of the Bar proceedings that he was

invited to apply for the position to be a tenured professor of Constitutional Law at the University of Alabama Law School. He did, and he was accepted. He took a three month period to clear up all of us personal and financial affairs, and he started teaching at the beginning of the next semester. He's been there ever since, and I really am proud of him and all that he has accomplished. What else can I tell you?

HARRY: What was the first time that he taught?

CINDY: I'm really not sure. It's been a real long time—long enough for him to retire with a full pension.

HARRY: Maybe this is too personal, but what were his finances when he began to teach?

CINDY: At the end of the Drake case, he just had walking around money. He had made a decent living for several years, lived as a bachelor in a very conservative way, but I am sure he just didn't have a whole lot. I know he got a very substantial terminating bonus from the law firm, and I think that was primarily because of the Drake case.

HARRY: What are his financial situations now, if you don't mind telling me?

CINDY: I assume he's extremely wealthy. He has a handsome income. We don't file joint tax returns, as you know. He does a lot of free lance work. He is very generous, giving money and property away regularly, and he's not a fool, so I am sure he can afford to do those things that he does. He does not require a high standard of living, and he's very comfortable without luxuries. In fact, he really doesn't like for me to give him a present. He says he has two of everything that he needs, and he doesn't much care for things, anyway. He did tell me some time ago that I would never have any financial worries because he was going to provide for me to my utmost content. At that time, I was already pretty well to do myself, and there were inheritances within my family.

HARRY: You've been wonderful. Tell me anything else that you think I ought to know about the professor or that might help us win the award for the best investigation.

CINDY: This might help. There are several organizations that assist impoverished students to enter college and graduate school, students

who really cannot afford it, but have the qualifications. Joe puts up the money in many cases. He has taken several young people as they enter undergraduate school and carried them all the way through. I think he leans on the University administration to help, but he writes a lot of checks himself. He feels that he is the guardian of those whose education he has encouraged, and he frequently brings one or two to the house for dinner, unannounced, and if I am prepared, we have something; if not, we simply take his guest out. He loves writing, and he writes beautifully. In addition to textbooks, he writes about social problems and intellectual opportunities and very often about the United States Constitution. He is a very, very special person, and I know of no one in my whole life whom I have respected as much, perhaps, maybe, my father.

HARRY: You've been very, very kind. I appreciate it very, very much. When we finish our investigation, we are going to share it with you. Is there anything that you have said that you would not like for us to put into our report and publish?

CINDY: No, not at all. Have at it, but if there is anything in there negative about Joe, you are going to have to deal with me later.

Memo from Esther

H i, guys. I had to make a quick trip to New York, but in the process, I have run down some of the leads that we have talked about and I think I have some excellent information. It is true that the Anti-Defamation League of B'nai B'rith, the American Civil Liberties Union, and the National Association for the Advancement of Colored People, all, were interested in the Professor's case. They were very much aware of the fact that he was the first black lawyer ever to be disciplined, or presented for consideration, by the local Bar, and apparently never before had any black lawyer had an action that went to the Supreme Court. The ACLU still had an active file, and I can get access to it and have it reproduced, if you desire. Unfortunately, I was not able to find the individual lawyer in any one of the organizations who actually appeared in the cause, but this is what the file shows in chronological order:

A. A personal interview by a member of the local Bar.

B. Consideration for local committee.

C. Presentation before the Board of Bar Commissioners.

D. Hearing before the Supreme Court of the State of Alabama.

E. Lawyers from the respective defense organizations were permitted at every level as observers, with the approval of Joseph Jasper Smith. Apparently the rules permitted any attorneys chosen or approved by the party under consideration to attend. It does show, however that E.Z. Adams was noted as counsel of record, only.

F. The hearing at the local level and the hearing before the Board of Bar Commissioners were adverse to Joe. The rule, at that time, was that the records were sealed, and no one, including the accused, would have access to them. (That's not the end of that issue).

G. The hearing before the Supreme Court was before all nine judges, which was unusual, apparently. The hearing lasted over a period of three days and was terminated about thirty days later with an order of dismissal.

H. Fortunately, the Supreme Court's proceedings are preserved in the Supreme Court, and whether they still exist or not, at this time, I do not know.

I. This is the most interesting part. Immediately, a matter of days, after the Supreme Court took the matter under advisement, the Alabama Bar Association changed its rules in very material ways. The changes include open hearings if the accused desires, subpoena powers, including the right to require the complaining party to appear, and a further right for production of documents by the complainant or the accused. Finally, at the request of the accused, all proceedings can be made public, although in the absence of the approval of the accused, they remain confidential and private, except to the extent that the punishment involves publication.

I think I have a permanent job, but I will be back for about a month, and I will try to run down these other areas, unless you want to go on in my absence. I've loved it.

Harry Calls A.J.

HARRY: A.J., this is Harry. I think I've run into something. I interviewed Cindy. She seemed to tie together very closely some bar association proceedings involving the Professor with his immediate commencement as a professor at the University of Alabama Law School. Maybe you can connect those.

A.J.: That's a good idea. I haven't gotten started, yet, and you are really jumping off to first base. I'll see what I can find. If you run into anything else, call me.

HARRY: Go back to your books, boy.

Harry Calls Doug

HARRY: Doug—this is Harry. I need a few moments to talk about the award.

DOUGLAS: Man, I'm busy as hell. I'm not the student that you are, and I'm cramming for exams.

HARRY: I don't mean right this minute, but I have a good lead on your investigation in the courts about the Professor, and I just want to say a few words and then I'll let you go.

DOUGLAS: Go.

HARRY: Something apparently happened during the course of the settlements of the Drake case because in some fashion, Cindy was dragged into it, and if my guess is correct about the timing, whatever happened caused Joe to be ready to give up the practice of law, or at least change his direction and then he was successful in his conflict with the bar association. So, something must have happened for which he was charged as to his character or his behavior. That ought to be a good lead.

DOUGLAS: So noted, buddy; see you soon.

Harry Blackmun Report

D ear Tom—I'm knocking this out on my computer as quickly as I can to get it into your hands for our next meeting. I'll be there, but right now, I'm out of town on an interview. You know that my mother had some excellent connections with civil rights organizations and defense groups. She read Esther's report and she called someone who reviewed the report and the information with her and added some more insight.

Apparently, this is what happened. There was an adverse ruling against the Professor by the local bar and the Board of Bar Commissioners, and then it ended up in the Supreme Court for action on the recommendation of discipline. The Board apparently recommended a six month suspension with publication, and that was the form in which it was presented to the Supreme Court.

Joe's position, initially, was that it was necessary for him to respond to the notification, but that he was unable to get any information and he simply took the position that he was not guilty. The charges, in descriptive form, accused him of going into the files of another law firm during court proceedings and taking away information, abusive language to opposing counsel, impertinence and disrespect to the Court, and concealing information that he should have brought to the attention of the Court. As I said, all of those were denied. At the original Bar Association hearing, and the hearing before the Board of Bar Commissioners, Joe raised constitutional questions.

Once again, he pleaded that he was not guilty, but he then challenged the right of practicing lawyers to exercise judgment over his behavior and to mete out punishment to him because all of them were in competition with him, as a lawyer. His response stated that all of the members of the Board of Bar Commissioners and all of the members of the bar committee were active, practicing lawyers, just as he was, and it would be unfair, while they competed for business in the same arena, to be judged by them; and that therefore his rights were being deprived without due process.

Then, before the Supreme Court, he filed a formal pleading in which he raised those same questions, took the same positions, but then was more explicit. He first challenged the Supreme Court's right to hear his matter because all of them, all members of the court, had received political contributions from one or more of the members of the bar association where the complaint was filed, and from the members of the Board of Bar Commissioners. He did not contend that the Supreme Court was corrupt. He said that they were ethically barred and like all other courts and judges, they should not participate in an activity which gives the appearance of wrongdoing. And, finally—this is a shocker—he said that the charter of the bar association and its rules and regulations are totally unconstitutional because they do not grant due process. Specifically, he had not been able to examine complaining parties, nor get records, nor be confronted by his accusers, and that his right to practice law is a valuable right which was threatened by this process. Apparently that's what set the fire, not the question of whether Joe was guilty or not guilty, or whether he should be punished or not punished, but whether or not his actions would bring down the whole bar association.

There were some notes, also, that representatives of the Supreme Court, the president of the state bar association, and the governor, appeared for a series of conferences, discussions, long distance telephone calls, etc. I can only conclude from that that some kind of a settlement or agreement was made which resulted in Joe terminating his practice and becoming a teacher.

It looks like we've gotten a long way past the Drake case, because that was just the catapult that started the bar proceedings. There is one other very interesting fact. There was never any proof, from any source, that Joe took the file, went into the file, copied the file, or ever had access to it. We may never

get the answer to that. I know that the professor said that he had told us all that he could, but if we confront him with all that we have found, he may answer that question. See you soon. —Harry.

Recorded Telephone Conversation from A.J.

.J.: Tom, this telephone call is a great and exciting moment for me.

TOM: What's up, A.J.?

A.J.: I first want to tell you how I got what I got. I struck out trying in the usual and normal courses and avenues to get a copy of the Professor's contract with the University. My father and I wiggled in every direction, with no result. The standard answer is that all contracts are private. We also struck out with the Legislature. Apparently all salaries in the law school are grouped together in one line item, and even though I managed to see the budget request, it didn't shed any light. Then, lightening struck. The state senator from Tuscaloosa, who is also a good friend of my father, suggested that we try to discover it through the Freedom of Information Act because federal funds are also fed to the University. When I inquired, through usual channels, I learned that it sometimes takes three or four months to get an answer, but dad called his Senator and he turned on the spigot.

TOM: And—well?

A.J.: I'm sitting here right now, looking at the contract. There are a lot of things that are blacked out, but the substance of everything that is important to us is here. The contract was signed twenty days after the Supreme Court dismissed disciplinary hearings. I got that date from Esther's memo. Putting two and two together, hoping to come up with four, it looks to me like the employment agreement probably was a part

of the disposition of the disciplinary proceedings, which means there was some kind of a settlement. Then, Dad contacted the law school and got some information, a lot of written material, that describes the Chair of Constitutional Law. Lo and behold, the initial funding and the creation of that was also contemporaneously related to the dismissal of the Drake suit. Do you think it's possible that as part of the settlement of the Drake suit, one of the requirements was the establishment by the law firm of Gimble & Dollid of a substantial chair contribution, with the possibility that the Professor would get that chair? I'm not sure that makes a lot of sense because he was just a young lawyer, not even a partner of Olive & Bates. Or, on the other hand, do you think that the settlement included the establishment of the chair because of the horse trading with a claim or a potential claim against Gimble & Dollid? Or, better than that, a more probable scenario is that the chair was established as a result of the settlement of the Drake suit and Joe Smith had some pressure on Gimble & Dollid, and, later, when the Professor was about to win the disciplinary action before the Supreme Court, that thought was revived that the end of Joe's law practice would be the beginning of his professorship. What do you think?

TOM: All of that sounds plausible and exciting as hell. I'm anxious to see the contract. Can you send me a copy?

A.J.: I'm going to get it hand delivered to you right away. I just want to mention one important feature. The contract for employment for Joseph Jasper Smith is for life, except that the law school can terminate his teaching, but continue his compensation. Someone put some high level pressure on the law school and the University, and I would bet a coconut that the pressure came from the Supreme Court, maybe with some help from the Legislature. This whole project turned out to be more exciting than going to law school. I'm beginning to wonder whether or not our end product should be published, even if we win.

TOM: We can deliberate that point, later. I think we are going to have a meeting in the next few days and the reports that haven't come in in writing, in one fashion or another, can be presented orally. We do have to bring this to a conclusion pretty quickly. Thanks—great job.

Recap Conference

Present: All five students.

TOM: We've come a long way, but we are running out of time. I've made some notes of our previous discussions and the memos that you have sent to me or called in to me, and I think I can put together a skeleton that needs some more fleshing out. Everything seems to be tied to a timetable of events, and here are the ones that you have produced:

1. In the Drake case, Mr. Olive became ill with a heart attack and couldn't participate and the mantle of leadership fell on Lawyer Smith, our professor.

2. The case, from the court reporter's notes, did not seem to be particularly dramatic at any point, and while the injuries to Drake were significant and extensive, apparently no one knew in advance that such could happen, probably no testing done.

3. Mr. Dollid was subpoenaed. Whether he appeared or not is not clear. Some representative of the local press and media demanded access to a private conference in the judge's office and that was refused. Just a comment, here, it probably would not be refused today under the law, and probably would not have been successfully excluded under the law of that time, but it wasn't pursued.

4. That night, Cindy was fired from her law firm by two top attorneys, one of them Mr. Longfellow, the trial lawyer in the Drake case, and her friend, Joe, assured her that she had no guilt or responsibility.

5. The settlement terms have not yet been learned by us, but the class action settlement is public record, and was very substantial, so we must conclude that the Drake case was the pivot on which the rest of the cases rotated.

6. Cindy leaves the firm and goes into private practice.

7. The Professor decides to discontinue the practice of law, at the same time disciplinary proceedings were commenced by the bar association. His friend, E.Z. Adams, appeared to represent him in the disciplinary proceedings.

8. Apparently there was a substantial bonus paid to Joe at or soon after his departure from his law firm.

9. There was an interview attempted unsuccessfully by the bar association, a young lady who was on the ethics committee who tried to visit with Joe and Cindy.

10. There was a preliminary hearing by the Board of Bar Commissioners of the State of Alabama. We don't know the ruling.

11. There was a hearing before the entire Supreme Court of the State of Alabama. There are records of the proceeding in the Supreme Court, but we have not been able to locate them yet. We do know that the professor is still a qualified member of the bar, in good standing, so we might guess that those proceedings were not adverse to his interests.

12. Almost immediately, Joe becomes a law professor at the University of Alabama Law School. We know a few of the terms of that. We don't know, yet, how certain the position was, or if he merely earned it by his performance. For us to go further, we need at least to infer that something happened through the bar proceedings that led to his becoming a professor, and we need to try to tie that together.

13. The ACLU and Anti-Defamation League of B'nai B'rith and others observed the disciplinary proceedings. The names of their attorneys appear on the Supreme Court entry records. We don't have anything definite from them, yet.

That's about it. Does anyone else want to add anything or insert anything in the time schedule?

DOUGLAS: I have a lead, but I'd like to keep it under my hat for right now. Through a personal contact, I have learned where the closed files of both law firms, Olive & Bates, and Gimble & Dollid, are stored. I'm trying to think through or find a way to get to those files that does not violate the instructions about pursuing this investigation in a legal manner.

ESTHER: It's not completely true that we don't have any information from ADL and ACLU. I've had some conversations which lead me to believe that the attorneys for those organizations consulted with Joe and helped draft some agreements.

A.J.: I'm onto a pretty good lead. I've tried to get the full contract between Joe and the University as to how he became a professor, and a tenured professor. I've been blocked at the University level, but I've got two other directions to go. First, some of the funding from the University of Alabama comes from the State of Alabama, tax funds, and they come about as based upon applications and requests from the University. I may have a lead there. In addition, the University receives federal funds from various sources, in various divisions, and there may be some reporting requirements. I do know this, to add, now. The Professor came in on a permanent basis, different from any other law school teacher, probably. In the archives of the Tuscaloosa Times, at that time, there was an article at the beginning of the school year with several items of notice, such as a new football coach, and the approval for the construction of a new indoor tennis and track facility, etc., and it mentioned the retaining of Joseph Jasper Smith, a young attorney, as a tenured professor on Constitutional Law. Now, why is that important, or how would that come about? My dad tells me that it is very unusual for someone to establish a permanent or a semi-permanent position at the beginning of a career, so there might have been, or must have been, some outside influences or forces, and based upon your time and schedule, Tom, it was quickly after whatever happened in the Supreme Court. I'm going to follow that lead. Doug, I would like for you to join me in that effort since

you originally accepted the responsibility of investigation of courts.

TOM: I think we are all reaching the same conclusion, but remember that part of it is to document, and I would hate to submit a conclusion which is very logical and very acceptable to us and have it turn out to be foolishness because we failed to pin down our facts and support our conclusions. We agreed at the beginning that we wouldn't share our information with anyone, and, obviously, no one wants to share any information with us. I have learned that there is a three man group who got an interview with Mr. Bates, even though he's retired, now, and with the managing partner of Gimble & Dollid. The presiding judge of the Tenth Judicial Circuit, headquartered in Birmingham, was a member of that firm before he went on the bench, and one of the three fellows working together is his son. I don't think we ought to pass that along to anyone else because it's easy for everyone to find out, now, the name of that chief judge, and his namesake, son, who is in our class. There may be that there are a lot of other smart people out there who have exercised some energies in different or even better directions than we have. So, let's go as quickly as we can toward closing. Get all of the additional information that you can to me by next weekend, and what we don't have, we just don't have, and what we do have, I will put into a draft, and we will just hack it out together. Incidentally, to me this has really been an exhilarating experience, and I am grateful to each one of you, and I'm sure that we have learned about each other, and that may be the best part of the whole effort.

Chancellor Memorandum

I felt this should be in writing because I think it is significant, and raises some interesting questions and problems. I visited with Maryon Jones at the Olive & Bates law firm. I chatted with her generally, discussed what the project was, and asked if she could be of some assistance or guidance. I really wanted her to tell me as much as she knew, but she said that she knew very little about the disposition of the case except that she did know that there was a very strong confidentiality settlement agreement, and everyone in the law firm was admonished against discussing any of the contents and subject matters of the files and anything to do with the Drake case or the settlement. I asked her who in the firm might be able to tell me about the old files in the case, and she volunteered what she did know. She said that their firm had a pretty much standard policy, like most of the other large firms, of maintaining current files on site, and then transferring old files to a warehouse. The warehouse files were divided into two segments, upon the original delivery of a group of files that were kept and considered current but inactive. As to those files, when they occasionally needed one, they could send to the warehouse and get it. The files were maintained by the years as well as the alphabetical index. When a file had been in storage and had not been activated for a period of ten years, it was destroyed, and the warehouse company did the destruction. She said that she had on many occasions sent files to Harrison Storage and Disposition Company, in Birmingham, and upon a few occasions had to send and retrieve a file. In her experience, there never had been a file that was more

than ten years old that she needed. She also volunteered that most of the large law firms had the same policy and used the same company. Since it was more than ten years since that file would have gone into storage, I didn't have much hope of finding anything, but I thought I would give it a try, nothing to lose. I also realized that even in making the inquiry, I might be violating the Professor's instructions about doing things in a proper fashion, so I decided to tape record whatever conversations I had, and I did that. Before I tell you the conclusion, I want to give you a transcription of the tape. I went to the warehouse and introduced myself.

DOUGLAS: Hi, I'm Doug Chancellor. I've been asked to come and see if I could locate an old and inactive file among the files of Gimble & Dollid.

CLERK: Do you have your letter of authorization?

DOUGLAS: I didn't know I would need one to get into the old files that may be destroyed or in the process of being destroyed.

CLERK: Well, I don't know about that. I'm not even sure the old files of that law firm are left that haven't been destroyed, so I don't mind you taking a look at that. Those files would be in the basement, under the law firm's name, with a red tag on the gate. The red tag means that those files are ready for shredding. Look at whatever you want, but you cannot take anything away because we have to destroy the files. You may get lucky because we don't always destroy them immediately after the ten year holding period. We wait until it's convenient and destroy a lot of files at once from several different law firms. Good luck.

I then went down into the basement where there was another clerk. I told him I was looking for the destruction area of the Gimble & Dollid law firm to determine if certain files had in fact been destroyed. He took me to the gate. I entered, and he left me. I guess I got lucky, because it had been a long time since any of those files had been destroyed, and some of them were fifteen or twenty years old. I looked into other areas with other law firms' names on them, and some of them were full and some of them were empty, so I guess whenever they got around to it, they just cleaned out a whole section. Anyway,

as you might guess, from the way I am making this presentation, I found the file. I spent two hours crawling over piles of files and cabinets until I got back to the year of Drake case. When I got into that year, the files were in alphabetical order. I readily found it. It was huge. It was filled with pleadings, exhibits, charts, affidavits, correspondence, everything that you would think would be in a big case. Then, at the end, there was one portion of the file that was in a different colored folder, and it had a tab on it that said "CLICONFI." It wasn't very thick, but I found a gold mine. Unfortunately, the settlement agreement was not in there, but there was a lot of correspondence back and forth among law firms who were defending the case together. The primary concern was what kind of investigation and information was available to the defendants about testing a product called Everlast Seals. I just want to give you a couple of highlights at this time in this memo before I conclude what else happened.

Apparently the company that held the patent did not do any testing of the product to determine if it might be harmful on humans, but they did do some testing on mice. They found that burning the product in an enclosed area with mice caused lung problems. That's as far as they got, except that in granting a license to a company called International Solvents, Northington General Services warned about potential harm and required an indemnity. The indemnity wasn't there, but that was covered in the letter. The letter was attached to something else, which I assume, from the content of the letter, was the license. There is correspondence from International Solvents to Northington General, several months later, where they said they had done some further testing in Japan. They had some chemical analyses that showed that the fumes from the burning created glass particles in the lungs of other animals, and that they were concerned about the impact on human beings. The letter went on to say that they would not continue to distribute or to manufacture the product if Northington General required an indemnity. Attached to that is a brief one page amendment to the contract which waived the indemnity. Then there is correspondence from the International Sales Manager of International Solvents to AAA Auto Services in Decatur, Alabama. It's a form letter and it has a stamped signature, but it says, in essence, that they make no representations or warranties in respect to the use of the product, its

potential harm or damage to other products or people. It goes on to say that tests have indicated that such harm could come about from protracted use.

I knew I was onto something then because that's the product that was involved in the pleadings. There is a huge bunch of depositions. I didn't have a chance to go through those. The transcripts from the court trials were not there, but I want to make an educated guess that during the course of the trial the defendants contended that they had no knowledge, or had done no testing. This special file contained confirmation that those were false positions to take. There was also a letter of transmittal from Gimble & Dollid to defense counsel of the other defendants sending that material. Nothing was attached, but the references in the letter indicated that they were attaching correspondence as well as some chemical investigation reports. I sat and thought for awhile and I decided that simply taking that and concealing it would probably be a violation of the instructions that the Professor made, but it also might be illegal, although it occurred to me that the law firm claimed no further property rights or interests in the files because they were set for destruction. I decided to play it safe and I went back to the clerk's desk with the file. There was a different clerk there, and I once again introduced myself and here's what happened:

DOUGLAS: I've gotten the portion of the file that I came for and the clerk who was here before you told me that we couldn't take anything away, back to the law firm or anything, and I guess that included stuff that was ready for shredding. I'd like to ask a favor, please. Give me about fifteen minutes to run down to the corner where there is a quick copy place and let me make copies of a couple of items in this file and I promise to be back here right away and put it back where I got it.

CLERK: Sure, that's fine. We don't really care anyway, because anything in that basement area is dead stuff. It doesn't matter to anyone, but we do have a rule.

DOUGLAS: Thanks. I'll be right back.

As you might have gathered, I have photostat copies of several items in that file. I didn't have enough time to do it all, and I returned the file to the very

place where I got it. I guess in my own defense I want to tell you to look carefully at what I have said in the conversations because I never represented that I came from that law firm. I never represented who asked me to get the file. I did not end up keeping the file. I hope that's an adequate position, but I guess we need to discuss it.

The Last Class

ROFESSOR: I am pleased to report that I have received all of your final examinations, and they have been put in numerical order, and they are comfortably sitting in my desk drawer, locked. We have made many references in the past, in other class meetings, to the Clinton cases. We have discussed many constitutional aspects of those cases. In the remainder of this class session, which will be brief, I propose to do two things. The first is to give you an opportunity to improve whatever grade you get from the examination, and the second is to award the book for the best investigatory process by students.

We now must evaluate briefly the history of some of the facts and the times in which the Clinton cases occurred. As you know, there were several of them, some civil, some criminal, some investigatory. History will ultimately decide what happened, and that will not be based upon court or other decisions, but rather how the future will remember the past. To illustrate that point, I want to give you two examples.

The first was President Franklin D. Roosevelt. He was elected in 1932, took office in 1933, closed all of the banks immediately. Commerce came to a standstill. The Democrats were disappointed and the Republicans were angry. Here was a man who had every material thing that life could offer, including great personal stature and family fame. Yet, the first act he took seemed to be a strike against the very people who put him in office. Soon thereafter he began to show his strength and

created artificial programs within the federal government for feeding and clothing and sheltering the poor and the downtrodden. There was the WPA, the CCC, and a host of other acronyms, and then the pumps were primed and flooded the economy. People who lost great fortunes in Wall Street were still jumping out of buildings because they could not make the adjustment. People who had hardly made a living in the early 1930's were beginning to eat and get jobs. As things progressed generally throughout the United States, and improved, he became a saint, a savior. He was the only President ever to be elected for four terms. He never came near to losing an election, although his opposition, primarily Wendel Willkie, was the most deserving individual and probably would have made a good president. Alf Landon could have been an adequate replacement. As we moved into World War II, Roosevelt became a military hero, and the most dominant personality in the world, probably in two thousand years. He was a hero to everyone and then he died. Suddenly the emphasis changed. He was a communist, a conspirator, paid off his cronies, turned back refugees from our shores, and cast a long dark shadow. With the many years that have passed since 1945, the year of his death and the year of victory in World War II, he has once again become a most illustrious past president. The second example immediately followed him, Harry S. Truman, a country boy, a clothing merchant, a third-rate politician, who happened to be standing in the right place at the right time. He had been picked as a vice president because he was inoffensive and constituted no threat to anyone. He was just a country bumpkin. Not only the United States, but all the nations of the world were in dismay. How was this modest character going to cope with Joe Stalin and Winston Churchill, among the rulers of the world. Then, the climate began to change. He integrated the military services. He, as President, made us the first nation to recognize the State of Israel; he cursed in the same fashion that the rest of us did, bitched and complained when someone spoke ill of his daughter, and generally acted like one of the common masses. He suddenly became everyone's friend, a good old boy. As the years went by, his masterful technique proved to be correct. He, and he alone, caused the first atom bomb to wreak destruction on the

human race. He was reelected in a time when no one thought he had a chance and he defeated Thomas Dewey who would have been a very powerful and perhaps great president. This is the triumph of the little man, and the truth is that almost all of us are always little people. With that background, what of Bill Clinton, a country boy from a small town in Arkansas, a politically ambitious individual who suddenly found himself embroiled in a multitude of conflicts and controversies, many of which were of his own doing. He was in and out of court, flying around the world, solving problems, creating problems. We may yet be too close, even though your lifetimes did not overlap his presidential service. I am now going to recite to you some constitutional questions which grew out of or were discussed during the Clinton years. If any of you choose to do so, I would suggest that you pick one of these constitutional questions, do some legal research, and file a brief with me as though I were the Supreme Court of the United States. You will lose nothing by declining. If you choose to write such a brief, and write a good one, it may have the result of improving your grade in this course. I will read any briefs that are sent to me and I will study them in detail and I will evaluate them, just as I will the final exams. Whatever your grade is, if you have done a worthy job, it will be increased. If you already have a straight "A", then for the first time in my professional career, then I am going to give an "A+". If you are going to do a half-assed job, just don't do anything. If you are going to do a great job, it will be a good experience for you, and I may even contact you and discuss some ideas that you have presented, and perhaps some which you have not. In any event, here are the constitutional questions:

1. Is the President of the United States, while serving in office, subject to a grand jury subpoena, a petty jury subpoena, a civil subpoena, a subpoena from Congress, or any administration body?

2. For the purposes of impeachment, what are "high crimes and misdemeanors?" Before you rush into this aspect, which sounds somewhat simple, read very carefully every word in Article II, Section 4 of the Constitution, dealing with impeachment. I think you will find that "treason" is a very clearly understood word, and that "bribery" is a very

clearly understood word, particularly if there is a "conviction." There are not many different views as to what constitutes an act of treason or a bribe. The emphasis, however, should be on what constitutes "high crimes and misdemeanors." The Constitution does not define that.

3. You have read and often heard the expression "separation of powers," which in a general way means that each of the three branches of government shall be autonomous, and neither shall control the other. You probably once heard of a president who, upon learning of an adverse decision from the Supreme Court, said something along the line that the justices had decided it and now they were free to enforce it. The residual meaning of the comment was that the Supreme Court decided what the law was, but they did not have the power of government, of armies, navies, militias, with which to carry out the court's edict. In recognition of that, the impeachment of a president was to be determined by the Congress. If the Congress impeached the president, the president is in office until he is removed. Who gives the order to use force to remove the president? Those are illustrations of the question of how a president is "removed," if he refuses to leave. As a related part of this question, begin with the premise that the Office of the Attorney General is a part of the President's Cabinet, and is in the Administration, not Legislative, not Judicial. By what right, if any, can the Congress bring the Attorney General before the bar of the legislative body and explore into files that are within the Executive part of the government, and in the Attorney General's Office. Can an Attorney General in fact be impeached for exercising and insisting upon the separation of the powers?

4. Let me next call to your attention some particular portions of the Constitution in an area which we did not cover during this course. Among the powers of the President, Section 2, it says—"He shall have power, by and with the advice and consent of the Senate, to make treaties." In Section 8, the powers of Congress, they are granted the right to regulate commerce with foreign nations and among the several states and with the Indian tribes. Suppose that the President of the United States, with his advisors and other executives, enters into a commercial agreement with a foreign nation, say China, to exchange technical,

military, and commercial information to facilitate the trade and transactions between the two nations and between businesses of each nation. At
what point under such state of facts does the Senate have the right to
approve or disapprove? Suppose that the agreement is not called a treaty,
but rather a contract. Is there a difference between a treaty and contract?
To shed some light, history teaches you that Japan attacked the United
States military forces in the Pacific on December 7, 1941. Soon thereafter, the President of the United States, Franklin D. Roosevelt, appeared
before the Congress of the United States, in joint sessions, and obtained
a declaration of war. He then entered into certain agreements or com-
pacts with Britain and France, later Russia, and other nations, for mutual
defense. Were those agreements treaties? You will not find these answers
in the Constitution, but you will see the rights and the powers that are
created there.

And now, my final act of teaching before this great class is to award the
honor of the first autographed book, by me, a textbook for you, to that
individual or group who presented the best documented and most
eloquent analysis of the Drake cases and the Joseph Jasper Smith cases.
Many of you did extremely well. I warned you, and it came to pass, that
many of you followed the footsteps of others, and probably aggravated
people who were being contacted from so many directions by so many
interested neophyte lawyers. I have received some repercussions from
that, as though I had turned loose a pride of lions upon an individual, or
a court, or a law firm. Some of you discovered facts that I never knew.
Substantially all of the investigating that you did fell within the ambit of
propriety, although there were some instances, very close to the line,
maybe even over the line. I'm not certain about that. Before I tell you
who the winners are, I want to fulfill, partially, a commitment that I
made to you in the beginning. I told you that I would share with all of you
the report of the successful individual or the group, and I propose to do
just that. The Law School has agreed to undergo the expense of reproduc-
ing the winning report. I have taken the privilege, however, of excising a
portion having to do with a confidential file of a law firm, the contents
of which I have never seen. I should not have given you the impression

that I would present the successful report to all of you, unabbreviated, but in the distribution that you receive, you will find a reference to the file, but not to the contents.

The winners are Tom Brown, Harry Blackmun, Jr., Douglas Chancellor, Esther Halevi, and A.J. Kay. I know that there has been a great comradeship among many members of this class, and particularly among those five winners. It was a heroic and magnificent effort with an astounding result. They are to be congratulated. If they practice law with this type of investigation, they will unquestionably succeed. I am going to single out a few of you who also did most worthy service and study because I am proud of the results, across the board. I now have the five books, autographed, with a personal and individual note to each of the recipients, and I ask that the five of you, please, come forward and receive your book. I am sure the rest of the class will applaud your results.

Since we won't meet again this term as teacher and student, I want to say that I hope that you have enjoyed these sessions, but mostly I hope that you have learned to begin to think like lawyers. Most of you, I believe, will be in my class again next semester, so I want to give you a preview. We are going to take on a massive project in the law school, with your class as the impetus, to create something for the whole world of lawyers and judges. We are going to take the Constitution as it is presently written and amend it, and we are going to start all over and recreate it in a special fashion. We are no longer going to deal with amendments. There is going to be one document, and it will be the Constitution. Every line and every paragraph and ever thought must be updated with language as to what the law is today. That will require research of every portion of the Constitution as to the cases which have been decided by the Supreme Court under each section. For example, if we are talking about a portion of what we now refer to as the First Amendment, perhaps dealing with religion, you are going to have to create and massage language from hundreds of cases which have been decided so that instead of simply referring to freedom of religion, you will have a lengthy analysis as though the Constitution had been rewritten to include those decisions which are equivalent law. It's such a

massive undertaking that I doubt that it will be completed during your tenure here in law school, but I want to start it as soon as possible. You might do some thinking about that during your forthcoming period of relaxation. You might even test yourself by selecting a section and see what research you can do to make it state the law today. So much for that.

There is an area of the law developing under the Constitution that is working its way through the courts and I just want to touch on it with you a little bit. I doubt that we will have any cases to supplement our textbook as yet, and probably not even during the next term. This is the situation. There are some religions which are considered "on the fringe," not that they fail to be identified as religions, but they are not accepted generally, publicly, and they are scoffed at or ridiculed. We went through that issue in a tiny way when the Rastifarians chose to have marijuana as a part of their religious services, but the issue has been greatly magnified. There are now people called "Witches Faith." This is the old New England concept of witches and covens, and a very secret religion, but they want that religion illuminated and presented in the public school system as a comparative religion in the same fashion that other religions are taught, still safeguarding the freedom of and the freedom from religion in the school system. There are atheists and agnostics who have created philosophies which they call religion and which teach the absence of God, a nontheistic concept, and, they, likewise, want a presence in the school system. There is now a segment of the Latter Day Saints who have disowned the precept of single marriage and who profess a religious right to multiple wives. That fringe group has been ousted from the main church, but they have put forth the idea that their religion expects and commands a man to have many wives, as was done in the Old Testament. They want to teach that in the public school system. Thus, we are having another great wave of dealing with the freedom of religion and what is acceptable in the school system, and who shall judge what is acceptable in the school system, and at what level. I am considering an assignment of this area of the law for the next book award, because it will not be the interpretation of a Supreme Court decision, but of the Constitution and litigation on the way to the Supreme Court. As you can see, this will give

you an opportunity to research as a trial lawyer as though you were the representative of one of these litigants whose religious ideas are totally rejected by the vast majority of our citizenry. The lawyers who actually litigate for those causes will be damned, criticized, ostracized, by the standard religions of those which do meet acceptability standards. Therefore, don't relax and think that you can coast through next year. It's going to be challenging and exciting.

Book Award Review

Dinner at the home of Tom and Mary Lou Brown, with the Professor, Harry, Douglas, Esther, and A.J.

TOM: Professor, Joseph Jasper Smith, this is probably the last time that the seven of us will have a chance to meet together, in private, although each of us hopes to share a lot of things down the road of life with you. We are grateful for the award. It was truly a challenging and interesting experience for all of us. We think we solved most of the problems, and apparently you thought so, too. There are, however, some gaps. Even though you had said that you had given us all of the information that you intended to give, and since we have exposed a lot of the things that you would have kept secret, we are hopeful that you will shed some further light so that our project can be complete, in this form or another.

PROFESSOR: Well, I don't know about that. It's nice to be here with you, again. I'm always sad when a very good class comes to the end of a semester. Yours has been one of the best and I predict great futures for all of you and all of your friends in the class. At least, now, you will understand me more as a person than a professor. That was the purpose of the first social meeting at my home. It's been fulfilling. Have a shot at some questions, and I'll just decide on each one whether I have anything to add.

HARRY: The Bar Association proceedings involved several different levels. You should have received a visit from a selected member of the local committee in the process of investigation. No where is there a recorded substance of that meeting, or at least we have been unable to find it. What can you tell us?

PROFESSOR: Well, that's sort of an easy one. I don't want to start off in a negative position. The young lady called me for an appointment at my law firm and asked for the opportunity to come over to my office, and she did. At that point she had not talked to anyone else, and certainly not Cindy. She wanted to know my view of the charges and what my responses would be. I asked who filed the charges and she couldn't tell me. It wasn't that she wouldn't, but she just didn't have that information, either. I asked her if she would get the information so that I could make some direct inquiries or at least interpret the background of the charges, and she said she couldn't do that, either. I said that if I didn't have any information other than what was already said to me, I just didn't see the need to be interviewed or to take a position since I was not clear about the charges or the reasons for them. She warned me that the failure to cooperate in an investigation was itself a chargeable offense, and I guess I taunted her, or upset her, anyway, but I told her that I wanted to exercise all my constitutional rights as long as I could. She didn't like that, and she asked me if I was taking the Fifth Amendment, and I told her that I was exercising all of my constitutional rights, including the right to be left alone, and I asked her to leave. That was ungentlemanly of me, but I felt that she was a representative of an antagonistic body. I guess I filled in that blank.

A.J.: What did you and Mr. Adams learn or suspect about the blue file or its contents?

PROFESSOR: I can answer part of that. I have never seen the contents. E.Z. and I had an encounter in which there seemed to be a great secrecy or an urgency about those files, and then when it appeared that every one of the defense counsel teams had a file exactly like it, then we made some guesses. First we guessed that in that file was the confidential joint defense agreement that we wanted to see; then we wondered if there was

something in there that was so secret that it could be embarrassing, and if it was that secret, and so embarrassing, what could it be? We took a major risk and decided to make a run as though we knew a lot more. Obviously, a lot more is known, now, but we were just playing our hunches.

A.J.: Do you have any objection to our exploring further into the contents and maybe making some publication of them?

PROFESSOR: No, I really don't want to do that. You already know that there was a settlement that was extremely confidential in the Supreme Court, and I put my honor on the line to maintain confidentiality.

A.J.: But the statute of limitations has barred that, long ago.

PROFESSOR: There is no statute of limitations on my honor, and I personally would not care to see the file, examine its contents, or have it published. What you do, you are free to do on your own, but not necessarily with my encouragement or blessing. Now, I have a question. I would like to know the route that was taken to get that file, or what you would have to do to get it again.

DOUGLAS: Well, I guess that burden is on me to answer that. I discovered that all of the major law firms stored their files in a certain warehouse, and, after a period of storage time and inactivity, those files were shredded. It just occurred to me that the files from your old law firm and the Gimble & Dollid firm might be there. I did not represent myself to come from either law firm. I merely said that I had been sent there. You know that I don't have a lot of charm, so it was a very matter of fact conversation, and the nice lady pointed me in the right direction. In fact, there was a whole room full of your law firm's files, and I didn't expect to find a blue file there. I went to the cage of Gimble & Dollid, and there were tons of recently active files in cabinets, numerical and alphabetized, etc., but there was a side room in which many of those files had been moved aside for shredding. Incidentally, they were not necessarily in the same order as the numerical files which I concluded to mean that some of the files got old and were pulled out and some of the files had had some activity and remained. In any event, I managed to find the file and I managed to copy a portion of it, and then I restored the whole file. At this

time it is probably still there because there seems to be no rapid transfer from the inactive files to the shredder. The shredding, apparently, was done whenever it was convenient, and they cleaned out whole bins at a time, and not necessarily in any particular order. I'd be surprised if the file wasn't still there.

PROFESSOR: That's pretty skinny. Do you think you could be charged with breaking and entering?

DOUGLAS: No, I had permission from the lady at the desk.

PROFESSOR: Do you think you could be charged with some kind of fraud and deceit?

DOUGLAS: I don't know about that. We never really studied it.

PROFESSOR: What would you do, now, if you released the contents of the documents and you were charged with fraud and deception and the theft of the contents of a file that belonged to someone else.

DOUGLAS: Well, first I would check the Constitution. Then I would check the law of the state to see if there was such a crime. I think I would take the position that it was abandoned property and nobody claimed or wanted any interest in it. But, most important, I think I would go to see a lawyer by the name of Joe Smith and ask him to represent me.

ESTHER: I'm glad to be back for a few days. My life has taken quite a turn. I did my area of the investigation, but I wasn't on the ground like most of you guys. I also have a question. What in the world ever caused the Gimble & Dollid firm to make such a huge contribution to the Law School, and how did it come about that you were the first professor to occupy the chair, and at such a young age?

PROFESSOR: Esther, that's two questions. As to the first, no comment. As to the second, I attribute it solely to the superior wisdom of the Dean of the Law School and the Chancellor of the University. Please don't take any inference from that comment.

MARY LOU: Well, I wasn't on the team and I didn't do any investigation, but I have a half interest in the award book because half of everything that belongs to Tom belongs to me, half or more. Since that makes me more than a bystander, maybe I'm entitled to a conjecture. What about this scenario—The Supreme Court is upset because the

entire existence of the Alabama Bar Association is under attack which includes an attack on the Supreme Court, and, leaning toward the possibility that the court would have to rule adversely to the Bar, the Court sought a solution. The solution first of all needed to be dismissal of the charges or Joe Smith would never have agreed. Joe Smith had long ago indicated a yearning or a desire to be a professor. What you refer to as the blue file contained incriminating evidence against a defense law firm, and probably their clients, and Joe Smith wanted revenge because they probably instituted the disciplinary proceedings in the first place. He thought he would make it palatable by requiring them to make a deductible contribution to his law school; by requiring that and establishing the financial aspect of the chair, he would have a job for life. How about that!

PROFESSOR: That could be pure baloney! Do you think that it would have been within my conscience to blackmail anybody for the purpose of getting a job. I came here at the invitation of the Chancellor of the University and the Dean of the Law School. What might have gone on among others is not in the record, nor is it known to me, nor do I care to know it.

DOUGLAS: Professor, suppose I told you that I knew that the Governor of the State of Alabama got involved in it.

PROFESSOR: I wouldn't know it and I wouldn't believe it, and I wouldn't comment about it.

DOUGLAS: Well, what do you think of the fact that the Bar Association suddenly changed directions and created more protections and constitutional rights for those lawyers who were being challenged, and it fell right after your case was dismissed.

PROFESSOR: I think what I think, and you can think what you think. Other than that, no comment.

ESTHER: Did you negotiate your employment contract with the University?

PROFESSOR: Sort of.

TOM: That's an evasive answer.

PROFESSOR: Yes, evasive.

A.J.: Were you given a terminating bonus when you left Olive & Bates?

PROFESSOR: Yes, $1,000,000, before taxes.

A.J.: Had you already resigned from the law firm?

PROFESSOR: I don't think you would call it a resignation. I had been invited to be a partner, and I truly wanted to be a partner, but I felt that the disciplinary proceedings would bring discredit on me and the law firm, and I didn't want that to happen. I asked to be excused from any further responsibilities and to have an indefinite delay in the question of partnership. The law firm continued to provide me with office space, all the extras, secretarial help, and the services of E.Z., and others, throughout the disciplinary hearings. They gave me a going away party.

TOM: At the time you had the going away party, did you already have the job with the University?

PROFESSOR: No comment. This inquisition is over. You guys need to feed me and take me home, but I have loved every minute of it. While I am generally not too sentimental, I want you to know that I treasure every moment that we have spent together, and I will remember the rest of my days the things that you and I shared together. Mary Lou, thanks for the hospitality of your home and for your support of Tom.

DOUGLAS: Professor, I know that we are at the end of the road in respect to the investigation, but among the matters which we have in our portfolio, including those items which came from the confidential client file, there was one memorandum that I really wanted you to have. It will make you feel better, and it will prove that your hunch was correct about the contents of the file. Of course, we never had the original, except momentarily, but here is a clear photocopy of the Contreras Declaration.

PROFESSOR: Thank you—I'll take a look at it later.

Later That Evening— Tom and Mary Lou

TOM: Hasn't this been a great experience, with the Professor? MARY LOU: Yes, certainly, and I have enjoyed even the little role that I have played in it. He is a most remarkable gentleman, and his character is outstanding, and I can already see the impact that he has on students, particularly you.

TOM: Compare our lives—you and I have had everything that life has to offer, good background, good education, good upbringing, the material things, this chance to become lawyers, and I can hardly think of anything else that we could say is missing from our life; yet, compare that to his. He began with nothing and things got worse. He had no organized family. There was a probability of no education, no material things, and a constant struggle just to survive and get along in life. Then, when you and I decided to get married and spend the rest of our lives together, it was a glorious moment for us and our families. We have a future that can hardly be less than perfect. When he reached that age in life, he had almost no hope, and his future was like a roll of the dice. If Mr. Ragsdale had not come into his life, he would just have been another black man struggling to make a living and probably being very angry at the world.

MARY LOU: Worse than that, if he hadn't been given a golden opportunity, out of the blue, he probably would have been a fighter against society, maybe even a troublemaker, because he did have a fighting spirit. So, he ends up on the good side instead of the bad side. But, I wonder if you really can compare our lives to what he has had. He

was a very lonely person. He had no friends, and he really was not accepted by his peers. When he went to law school, he was more of an object than a student, a curiosity, a black boy with no family and no record except his academics. So, if you look at us, starting law school, and him, at the same time, it is as different as black and white, and that's not a pun.

TOM: In spite of all of the adversity and the odds being against him, he is without a doubt the most prominent black person in the State of Alabama today. His contacts reach far beyond the state. He has already become a legend. I think he is a very humble and sincere person, even though he paints himself as a tyrant in class. There is a sweetness about him, particularly when he talks about Cindy or talks to Cindy. They both sort of passed over the time when they shifted from a distant but personal relationship to a very personal relationship. I do remember his brief reference to the first time he kissed her. I cannot imagine how in those days such a personal relationship could develop.

MARY LOU: I can't, either, but I have to confess that I have been wondering about their private life together. Their backgrounds were so much different, and the cultures and the divisions between blacks and whites would have been an insurmountable object. Frankly, I don't remember the first time that you and I began to mess around, or how we advanced from stage to stage, but they must have had the same type of experience and probably even before they moved in together. I bet it was a very difficult time when they were already very close and members of their families were still living. I guess there was a lot of running away and hiding and pretending, but mostly I guess it's really none of our business.

TOM: Well, it may be some of our business. I don't care about any sordid details or intimacies, but the romance is probably the most important part of his life history. They were happy children together, with a barrier between them. There was at least a moment of intimacy, or curiosity, when she wanted to see what a grown boy looked like naked. But, even then, for years there was a wholesome relationship but not apparently intimate. I don't know how many more years they have together, but it cannot be many. Someone really ought to write a book

about them and the diversity of their backgrounds and how they lived through racial change and how they survived conflicts. It would be interesting reading, but it would also be a historical reference. If it isn't done while they are both living, there will be some things omitted which would be critical while they are still able to remember.

MARY LOU: You know, it's strange, that the only identification he seems to have with law relates to the Constitution, but he has also taught courses in evidence and federal procedure, and he still does some seminars in those areas. To me, if there are any classes where I have an option to take a course from him, I am going to do it.

TOM: You know law school has been easy for us so far, really interesting, and we have had the opportunity to discuss things together and study together and help each other, but we have a long way to go. Next year we are going to have to decide a specific direction because when we clerk for law firms, we ought to have an idea of the areas that we want to get exposed to. We both need to get busy and prepare some resumes. I imagine that's a mad scramble, particularly when you and I would like to try to be in the same community and I guess a lot of others would like to travel away, long distances, to big cities, and things like that. I think in my resume I am going to put in a preference to do trial work.

MARY LOU: I really just don't have an impression yet of what I would like to do. The trial part seems to be glorious and exciting, but it's probably also full of pressure, and I would probably opt for something that doesn't have as much controversy and is more academically oriented. Look at the Professor and Cindy. They had a similar situation, going through law school, and he went for trial work and she went for domestic matters. He had a constant battle and she seems to be excited about helping people. Anyway, I think it's too early to try to decide a direction.

TOM: I have a direction—back to the bedroom. We didn't talk about Joe and Cindy and having children, or avoiding having children, but it's not too early for us to get serious about our plans, so it's time for a little practice.

Man of the Century Award

CHAIRMAN: Good evening, Ladies and Gentlemen. You are about to share in a most enjoyable evening. This is the first of what will be annual meetings of the Joseph Jasper Smith Chair of Constitutional Law, University of Alabama Law School, and the Joseph Jasper Smith Philanthropic Foundation. It is my good fortune to preside, tonight, as a result of becoming the President of the senior and graduating class. This is going to be the format for the years to come. Within the recent past, a philanthropic foundation was established by the initiative of what is known as the "Great Class of '48," some students who were most favorably impressed by the presentation of Professor Smith. Long after their graduation, they chose to honor him in this fashion. Similarly, the law firm for Gimble & Dollid created an endowed chair for Constitutional Law at the University of Alabama School of Law , and the first professor who served in that chair was the same Joseph Jasper Smith. These two organizations have coordinated their efforts through the years, not only to honor the Professor, but to enable many students to gain an education, to attend the law school, and to get started in the practice of law in the State of Alabama. Thus far, the joint efforts of these organizations have awarded 293 scholarships. Of those, 123 are presently, actively, practicing their profession in the State of Alabama. With us, tonight, are also all of the seniors in the law school in this just graduating class. The people just mentioned are the invited guests of the

institutions. The rest of you, good friends of the University and of the Law School, have had to scramble for tickets to this event, and your success was based upon the luck of the draw. The attendance was vastly over-subscribed and we have a full house.

To begin the program, we have invited Bishop Toolong Sage, the Bishop of the Diocese headquartered in Birmingham, Alabama, for an invocation. Following that we will all rise and sing together the Star Spangled Banner.

BISHOP SAGE: Let us all, tonight, pray together for the righteousness of mankind, for the doing of good things, and the respecting of others, so that our society will become caring and concerned about our brethren. May we all be inspired to worship and to believe, each in his own fashion. May we also, this very night, honor the memory of a great professor who was not only an accomplished teacher, but a great role model. May we ever be grateful for those who by their charity and generosity established these organizations and created these noble purposes. May the Great Provider give forth his many blessings to those who are justly deserving, and guide all of us in the ways of the righteous. Amen.

CHAIRMAN: Please be assured that the right to offer a prayer, in this forum, in this fashion, is in total compliance with the Constitution of the United States, and now please rise for the Star Spangled Banner.

After the meal was over, the Chairman stood up to resume the evening's festivities.

CHAIRMAN: At this time, and for the purpose of awarding the honor for the evening, I am pleased to introduce to you the Dean of the University of Alabama School of Law, The Honorable Jefferson Polk.

POLK: Thank you very much. It is indeed an honor to participate in this first annual meeting of these wonderful philanthropic groups. I had the great pleasure of knowing Joe Smith, for several years, but in his declining years. I have recently had an occasion to read a biography of his life, and many salient portions are a part of my own memory. The picture that was painted was a beautiful tapestry of a century of hard work,

personal sacrifice, and great character. He and his life brought great credit to our Law School and to the State of Alabama. As a very young man, he rose from abject poverty to impress many people favorably along the walk of his life, and to gain a very handsome education, to practice, very successfully, as a trial lawyer in a major law firm in Birmingham, Alabama. Some members of that law firm are here with us this evening. Above all of his other virtues was his commitment to the Constitution of the United States. He is nationally renowned and he has left footprints that will probably never be filled by others who walk the same road.

Tonight, however, in his honor and in his memory, a very select committee has chosen to honor one of our own living lawyers and a graduate of our Law School, and a student from that great class of '48. The criteria for the selection of the person to be honored required that he or she will have been, at some time, a resident of the State of Alabama, that in some manner he or she shall have been involved in the legal profession, lawyer, judge, teacher, writer, or other similar capacity; that he or she shall have exhibited good character and shall have benefitted our State and its general population in some manner. We will label those chosen as the "Men of the Century." Tonight we honor such a man— Harold Halfacker. He is with us tonight, and he will make some remarks.

As a young man, he grew up in northern Alabama, in a small community where his family was very highly regarded, but people of modest, financial circumstances. He was educated in the local schools and graduated with honors from Birmingham Southern College in Birmingham, and after military service, he entered the Law School. He won all of the honors that were available. He was an outstanding student and a great leader, and upon his graduation, he returned to his home community to practice law. He was extremely successful, highly regarded, much admired, and very active in the Bar Association. He had friends and clients throughout the State of Alabama. The time came when many leaders of the bench and bar conscripted him to hold out for the Office of Chief Justice of the Supreme Court of the State of Alabama. He was successful and served admirably for several years, remodeling the judicial system, creating integrity throughout the courts, obtaining the

appropriate financing for the operation of the judicial system and for the retirement of the judges. He was much appreciated for that service, and he next became a United States Senator where he served several terms. He was extremely successful in representing the State of Alabama, and he was regarded throughout the Federal Congress as the most knowledgeable and incisive scholar of the Constitution of the United States. He served as Chairman of the Judiciary Committee. He was constantly in demand as a lecturer and a public speaker. He rose high in the seniority of the Senate, and he retired several years ago to return to his home community and enjoy a quiet, family life. He has truly been a role model as an attorney, a judge, and a senator, a leading philanthropist and community citizen, and a man of great capacity to love and care for others. I am pleased to present to you the first honoree, Harold Halfacker.

HALFACKER: Thank you so much, Dean, for those kind and wonderful remarks, and I am grateful even for the exaggeration. There are not many in the audience tonight who are still able, at my age, to participate in such an event, and to enjoy the many blessings that have come my way. In fact, tonight, I realize that I have been chosen and anointed, but the opportunity which you have given me, for which I am duly grateful, is to extol the praises of my Constitutional Law Professor, Joseph Jasper Smith. Throughout the State of Alabama, lawyers, judges, all of the court system, and most of the litigants, his name is majestic. He was a young man when I first met him, the youngest professor at the University of Alabama Law School. He had the ability to inspire, to challenge, to get the best out of each student, and to make each student feel that their professor had a vital, personal interest in the students, individually, and collectively. His entire life was one of sacrifice. From very humble beginnings, he bootstrapped himself into becoming an excellent trial lawyer. His tenure in that capacity was limited. He sacrificed his career for the ultimate good of all of the lawyers of the State of Alabama, and the Bar Association, as well.

We know, from history and some sparse records, that his last major litigation was on behalf of a man by the name of Drake who had suffered grievous injury from a faulty product. Whatever occurred in those

chambers or courtrooms is not full well known, but growing out of that litigation, there was controversy, and the integrity of Mr. Smith was challenged. He laid down his whole career and sacrificed his undoubtedly successful future to uphold the Constitution of the United States. His actions resulted in making the Bar a more successful, more honored, and more appreciated institution. He pointed out, in his own good fashion, some of the defects or problems which were inherent in the processes of the Bar Association in its disciplinary activities. He protected, for all who came after him, through the future, the rights of a challenged party. At the end of that career, he was chosen to become a law professor, which was probably his lifelong ambition, and one which he considered to be the greatest reward which could come to him for all of his sacrifices. He was a great professor. He was a great teacher. He was a great friend. His vast accumulation of wealth was never reflected in his behavior, or his presence, except through his generosity of giving. He lived modestly and quietly. He had no children, but a lovely companion who shared life with him for all of the rest of her days. That man was truly a role model, and perhaps those words are used too often, too frequently, too lavishly, but I believe that every student who came into his classroom had a secret hope that he could equal that Professor in character and competence. So, while I thank you most appreciatively for the honor which you have bestowed upon me, I pay homage to one of the greatest citizens who has ever lived in the State of Alabama. Thank you for this wonderful evening.

Epilogue

1
The Joseph Jasper Smith Philanthropic Foundation was estab
lished, flourished, acquired capital and contribution in excess of
$36,000,000. A multitude of students have had, before this
publication, financial support and scholarship assistance to attend the University of Alabama, and the University of Alabama Law
School. The mandate to the Board of Governors has been fully effective.
Substantially all of the recipients were financially disabled or limited,
approximately seventy-five percent are minorities, twenty-one females,
twenty-seven of the black race, male and female, nine from Asian
countries, one blind white male, seven different religions, two with no
religious commitment, and two mixed race students. The name of
Joseph Jasper Smith prominently appears in all scholarships and in all
publications. The Estate of Joseph Jasper Smith, after certain specific
bequests, has bequeathed approximately $4,000,000 to the Foundation
for its general purposes.

2. Joseph Jasper Smith passed away after seeing the Foundation fully
functioning, and after the publication of the story of his life. He lived to
see the book in circulation, signed and autographed many copies, had
many television and radio interviews, and a documentary series on public
television. There exists in the atrium of the Law School of the University
of Alabama a bronze life-size bust, with his name, years of service as
Constitutional Law Professor, and a hermetically sealed copy of the book

251

of his life alongside a replica of the Constitution of the United States.

3. Just before the commencement of his tenure as Professor at the University of Alabama Law School, there was established a charitable fund, for the Law School, beginning as "Chair of Constitutional Studies." Joseph Jasper Smith was the first designated scholar. Those funds which now exceed $10,000,000 are available for the use of the University of Alabama Law School and for support, compensation, and benefits of its professors and staff.

4. Contributions are regularly received in memory of Joseph Jasper Smith, both to the Foundation and to the Law School. The total available funds to honor his memory exceed $50,000,000, at this writing.

5. Tom Brown and Mary Lou Brown, husband and wife, were two of the initial members of the Board of Governors of the Foundation, with Tom Brown serving as its Chairman. Tom Brown has recently tendered his resignation upon his appointment by the Governor of the State of Alabama to serve as Chief Justice of the Supreme Court of the State of Alabama. Mary Lou Brown practiced law briefly in Tuscaloosa, Alabama, before accepting a position as Executive Director of the Volunteer Legal Aid Society of the State of Alabama, headquartered in Birmingham, Alabama. She continues in that capacity. Mr. and Mrs. Brown have five children, four grandchildren, all of whom at this writing reside in the State of Alabama.

6. Douglas Chancellor and Esther Halevi were married in a very private ceremony in the Law School at the time of their graduation. Mr. Chancellor converted to the Jewish religion. They have one daughter. Mrs. Chancellor is the Executive Vice President of the American Civil Liberties Union and oversees litigation. Mr. Chancellor is General Counsel to the Public Health Authority for the State of New York, a full time position, in which he has the responsibility for the oversight of the welfare of children, eighteen years of age, or younger, who are wards or are in the custody of the State of New York. He has published a book, "Child Care Without Parents", which has received great acclaim.

7. Harry Blackmun, Jr., upon graduation, accepted a position as

associate with Olive & Bates, the same law firm where Joseph Jasper Smith was an associate in his early years. Mr. Blackmun, unfortunately, was murdered in a drive-by shooting in the parking lot of the building where he was employed. His mother, Mrs. Harry Blackmun, Sr., passed away shortly thereafter.

8. A.J. Kay became Dean of the University of Alabama Law School and served nine years.

9. The confidential file of Gimble & Dollid was never published or released, officially. General contents, however, became known through an investigation by students of Professor Joseph Jasper Smith. All of them have chosen to continue the confidentiality as was originally intended in the Drake case.

10. Several individual class actions were filed, and one class action was filed in the Southern Division of the Northern District of the State of Alabama, alleging the same premises and cause of action as in the Drake case. The negotiations resulted in a settlement that involved the termination of the manufacture and distribution of Everlast Seals, and the cancellation of the patent. The defendants paid all costs of the litigation, including attorney's fees in the amount of $30,000,000, and a common fund of $180,000,000, after fees and costs, for distribution to the members of the class consisting of ninety-two individuals in varying degrees of illness, to be allocated by a committee established by the Court. The non-class claimants reached individual settlements which were not disclosed. There was no provision made for individuals whose claims might develop in the future. The defendants contended that those claims would be barred by the statute of limitations.

11. Eric Zinder Adams became a partner in his law firm, and at this writing he is a senior partner presiding over the Trial Division. He maintained his close, personal relationship with Joseph Jasper Smith until Mr. Smith's death.

12. Maryon Jones was discharged as a legal assistant in the Olive & Bates law firm upon the contention that she had a conference and a discussion with a student by the name of Douglas Chancellor.

13. Cindy Ragsdale predeceased Joseph Jasper Smith. She left a very

substantial estate, a portion of which was inheritance from her family. Approximately one-half of her estate was left to family and friends, and the remainder was put into a charitable remainder trust for the benefit of Joseph Jasper Smith, provided that he could designate charities, or 501(C)(3) organizations to receive the income or the principal from the charitable trust during his lifetime, and the remainder would then go to the general fund of the Greater Birmingham Foundation.

14. This book is in its third publication, with a continuing demand. At its initial publication, it was on the New York Times Non-Fiction Best Seller's List for thirteen weeks, at one time being #2.

15. Among the personal effects and records and documents of Joseph Jasper Smith, there was found one memorandum from the confidential file of defense counsel in the Drake case, as follows:

From: Contreras
To: Longfellow
Re: Drake

Henry, I'm sorry that this needs to be in writing, but I want to tell you the decision which I have reached and which is fully supported by my law firm in respect to the defense of the Drake case.

1. This is in furtherance of the last face to face that you and I had on these issues which deeply concern us. I have again reviewed all of the contents of our separate confidential files that relate to our united defense, and these are my conclusions:

A. Our law firm should withdraw from the litigation completely, but we are willing to stand still, to the extent that we don't withdraw on the record, but we do not participate, and I will not attend the trials.

B. The standstill is to avoid any potential impact on a jury that we are running from a fight. In addition to that, I do not believe that another attorney, at this late date, could get up to speed to participate affirmatively.

C. The proposed expert witnesses will be telling the truth,

the whole truth as they know it, but they have not been informed of the testing that has been done, at length and in depth, by Northington and International. If those tests had been made available to our expert, or to the opposition, they would have a devastating effect, create a clear path of guilt and perhaps wantonness.

D. If we were to put the witnesses on the stand, as their depositions presently are postured, I believe we would be giving to the jury and to the Court facts which are misleading.

E. If that be the case, then we may have a very serious ethical violation for which all of us could be exposed to disciplinary action. We have also notified our malpractice insuror.

F. Finally, and perhaps most important of all, the various letters which have been exchanged among the defendants, and among them and their attorneys, and among the attorneys, through the mail, and over the telephone, could well be the foundation for criminal prosecutions, mail fraud, wire fraud, etc.

2. We have already communicated our position to our client, in confidence, of course, and they are quite comfortable, or as comfortable as they can be, with your leadership of the defense team. They will share in the expenses according to the Joint Defense Agreement. We are refunding the fees which have been paid to our firm. Our clients are prepared to go forward with the defense as presently cast. If you choose to put the parties that we have represented onto the stand for examination, you will probably find them continuing to be very supportive of the defense posture to date and willing to remain committed to that. We aren't.

3. Please don't misunderstand this memo. We have nothing but the highest regard for you, your law firm, and other defense counsel. If it is your determination to continue, as presently cast, I suggest that you and the others apply the most strict security and protection for your files, and particularly the confidential file which I am returning herewith to you.

Printed in the United States
64147LVS00006B/323